BEAST

Books by Elizabeth Reyes

Desert Heat

Defining Love

Moreno Brothers Series

Forever Mine

Sweet Sofie

Forever Yours

When You Were Mine

Always Been Mine

Romero

Making You Mine

Tangled—A Moreno Brothers novella

5th Street Series

Noah

Gio

Hector

Abel

Felix

Fate Series

Fate

Breaking Brandon

Suspicious Minds

Again

Rage

His to Guard

Uninvited

Boyle Heights Series

Lila

Beast

BEAST

(Boyle Heights #2)

Elizabeth Reyes

Beast

Elizabeth Reyes

All Rights Reserved. This book may not be reproduced, scanned, or distributed in any printed or electronic form without permission from the author. Please do not participate in or encourage piracy of copyrighted materials in violation of the author's rights. All characters and storylines are the property of the author and your support and respect is appreciated.

This book is a work of fiction. The characters and events portrayed in this book are fictitious. Any similarity to real persons, living or dead, is coincidental and not intended by the author.

Copyright © 2017 Elizabeth Reyes

Edited by Theresa Wegand

Cover Design by Amanda Simpson of Pixel Mischief Design

PROLOGUE

Los Algodones
Baja California, Mexico
Age: Twelve

Leonardo

"Auxilio!"

The backhand across Leo's mother's face landed with such force she was instantly knocked out.

"Drag her ass into the bedroom," Rogelio hissed. "I'll take care of her when I'm done with this."

Leo felt his eyes nearly bulge out of his head when Rogelio pulled out the glowing red end of the branding rod he'd stuck in his mother's wood-burning stove. "No!" he cried out, trying in vain to come loose from the tight grip of the man's goons.

"Hold him still!" Rogelio barked; then that evil smile spread across his face again. The man holding Leo's left arm with both hands lifted his arm higher for Rogelio. "Yeah, right there," Rogelio said with a chuckle. "I want this right in the front of your arm so there's no way you'll be able to hide it. That oughtta teach that *puta* mother of yours to fuck with me."

Squirming in a desperate attempt to pull away from the iron rod coming toward his arm, Leo pleaded, "No, *please!*"

Leo's cries were once again in vain, just like when the man and his goons beat him mercilessly earlier for attempting to defend his mother. Without warning, the searing pain had him screaming again until he was coughing and nearly choking. Rogelio laughed as he held it there to Leo's arm for what felt like an eternity. Leo had never experienced such excruciating pain. The pain he'd felt earlier all over his beaten body was suddenly drowned out. He felt none of it now, only the piercing burn of his arm he thought might fall off.

Finally, the animal pulled it away, but the pain remained. In fact, it seemed to worsen with every breath Leo gasped. The two men at either side of him dropped him and left him writhing and gasping for air between sobs on the floor.

"Keep an eye on him while I take care of one more thing," the evil man said to the other two men as he undid his belt buckle and reached for the bedroom door.

Any strength Leo ever possessed, had been sucked out of him earlier when he'd tried first to defend his mother then himself. They'd beaten him until he could barely move, all while he listened to his mother's tortured cries. She'd been forced to watch the beating, since the man had insisted it was all happening because of her *fucking disobedience*.

Leo was going in and out of consciousness now, and he wondered if he might be dying. Somewhere in the distance, he could hear his mother's cries again. Instinct had him trying to get to his feet again, despite the blistering pain that seemed to cover every inch of his body. Just as fast, the other men were on him.

Hearing his mother's cries again in the bedroom gave him a fight he had no idea he could possibly still have in him. But the men were too big—too strong—for him, even if he hadn't been in so much pain. Still, even though he could barely see—his eyes were nearly swollen shut—he fought with every ounce of strength he could muster. The ringing in his ears was a blessing now. Between that and his own screaming for the bastards to let him go, it made his mother's anguished cries less deafening—at least to his ears. His heart broke with every one of her screams.

But he could still hear her, and it only made him cry out, even more tormented, for them to spare his mother. Still wrestling with the men and trying in vain to come lose, he continued to fight. "Beat me, assholes! Burn me! But leave her alone!"

One moment he was hysterically fighting for his life and his mother's, and the next, Leo was sure his heart stopped because everything went black.

ONE

EIGHTEEN YEARS LATER

East Los Angeles

Allison

Eyeballing the assortment of pastries near the coffee pot in the employee break room at 5th Street, Allison Rico chided herself for skipping breakfast. She'd been running late, but she knew better. It always resulted in her giving into temptation. Rule number one was never leave home hungry.

"No," she whispered under her breath. "You'll just wait until you're done here and then go grab a healthy snack at the juice bar that'll hold you over until lunchtime."

She had plenty of tofu chorizo at home leftover from yesterday. Lord knew her sister Lila never touched the stuff. That morning, Allison had been too excited and had changed twice before heading down to 5th Street, the gym Lila worked at, for this interview. She'd hit Lila up weeks ago to ask her boss for this interview on the work-release program they were starting, and finally it was her chance.

"Sorry about the wait," Gio said, yanking her out of her thoughts as he walked into the break room. He took a seat across from her at the table where she sat. "Had a few things I needed to get squared away, but I'm all yours now."

Pushing her glasses up, she glanced down at her notebook. "That's quite alright," she said, attempting to sound as professional as possible.

Lila had warned her about the man's amazing green eyes. Still, she hadn't quite prepared for them. Clearing her throat, she glanced up at him again. "Thank you for doing this for me by the way. I'm not sure if my sister explained, but, since I'm a freshman in my college journalism class, my stories either usually don't make the final cut or get buried in the back pages of the paper. I'm hoping this will garner enough attention to make a bigger headline."

"I think it will," he said with a smile. "There's been quite a buzz about this, and as you can imagine, many do have concerns and questions about the security issues and such. So, I'm actually glad for this."

"Exactly," Allison said with a nod. "And as I told my sister when she expressed her concern about it as well, while I can understand there'd be some apprehension about this, I'm a strong believer that everyone deserves a second chance. I think this is a very positive thing. I'm assuming these are non-violent offenders you're allowing on this work-release program, right?"

"Right," Gio said immediately as Allison made notes. "The criteria for the county to even be considered for work release is already stringent enough. They're basically giving these inmates, who would otherwise be finishing up their time behind bars, the chance to finish it on the outside, living at home while they work at certain establishments willing to take them on. We volunteered to be added to that list. But to us, this is our home. Our families are here often. My wife is here almost every day as is Abel's and Felix's. We're not about to take any chances here, so we reserve the right to add our set of criteria on top of those set by the county."

"For example?" Allison asked without looking up.

"Well, for starters, the county makes exceptions for violent offenders, if they won't be working within a certain distance of their victims. We make zero exceptions. If they're doing time for a violent offense or have *ever* been convicted of a violent crime, then they're not eligible for our program. We conduct our own private and extensive background check."

Good to know.

He followed up to explain that they had very specific criteria for whom they were taking on. "It's not as selfless as it may seem." He sat back in his chair. "Sure, we're all for helping community and those who deserve a second chance and all. But we also have our own special interests in mind as well. They'll be working here, doing maintenance, cleaning, doing the laundry, even helping out in the juice bar, keeping the back end up to health-code standards. You know, mopping and washing out equipment and stuff. But we're only accepting those who are interested in training to box."

Allison glanced up, intrigued. "So, they have to be willing to fight for you?"

"No, just train." Gio sat up and leaned his elbows on the table. "The prisons and jails have their own recreational programs, and most include boxing. We've staked out a few and made note of those we'd be interested in if they were ever eligible. If we see potential and we can train them to sign on as amateur fighters who might eventually turn professional and they're willing to, then it's a win-win. They *are* looking for a new start, and this could be it."

"Interesting." Allison made more notes, glad for the two girls who walked into the break room and asked Gio something about their schedules.

It'd give her time to catch up, since her shorthand sucked still. She prided herself on being a professional through and through, and a real journalist had to know shorthand.

One of the girls winced when Allison finally looked up. "I'm sorry. I didn't know you were in the middle—"

"That's fine, Frankie." Gio smiled. "But Nellie would be the one to ask about the schedule this week." He motioned to the pastries. "It's Friday. You know what that means, right?"

"Oh, yeah." The two girls smiled big, walking toward the pastries. "Donuts and, oh my God, La Favorita *pan dulce*. My favorite!"

Gio's frown wasn't missed as he watched the girls help themselves to the pastries.

Allison's eyes were instantly back on her notes. Don't look at the donuts. Don't think of the donuts. Don't smell the donuts. Remember how tight your jeans are!

Frankie just *had* to make a comment about the donuts among the pile of pastries before she could make up her mind about which she was taking, damn it. And, of course, she had to decide out loud between the lemon or raspberry-filled jelly donuts. Only Allison's favorite! *Go away!*

Finally alone with Gio again, Allison got back to the subject of the work-release program. He told her more about how they'd be keeping tabs on them. How they used the buddy system and, basically, were given the responsibility of staying with their buddy the whole time they were on the premises. "At any given time, if I ask any of them where their buddy is, they need to know exactly. It gives them each accountability and a sense that they're trusted to look out for each other. At the same time, it keeps us from having to babysit them every second."

"So, they do get free time? As in just time for them to work out on their own?"

"Yeah." Gio nodded. "Even during their training, we train them as we would all the other trainees. We show them what to do, supervise a bit just to make sure they've got it, and then let them finish training on their own. These are men and women who are really trying to get rehabilitated. It all started back in jail. They first had to work hard to prove themselves. Getting here is a great feat and a privilege they know they're lucky to have. They're not gonna ruin what they know is a good thing. So, me and the other owners are more than confident that this will work out fine."

He explained more about their compensation and a few of the other stringent rules. He also said most were good guys. "Some may not look it." He chuckled. "They've had tough lives, and it's evident on their hardened exteriors, but so far, I've met every single one, and I've been pleasantly surprised by how respectful and humble they all are."

More people walked into the break room, distracting Gio momentarily. Again, Allison took advantage of the distraction to work on her notes. One of the guys approached the table and smiled at Allison with a nod.

"Sorry to interrupt, G. But when you get a moment, can you come to the big training room? Felix is here, and we're trying to have a quick meeting about what we were talking about the other day."

"Yeah, I should be done in a few," Gio said, as the guy grabbed a *pan dulce* then walked out.

"Actually," Allison said as she finished up her notes, "I think I have everything I need except . . ." She glanced up at him, meeting his eyes again. "You think it'd be possible for me to interview a few of the guys in the program? I know you said they're hopeful about turning their lives around. But I think it'd be nice to get an account from them firsthand as to how they feel about the program and what else they plan on doing to rehabilitate themselves, stuff like that."

"Absolutely. I don't think I could right now, but—"

"No, I didn't mean now," she clarified. "I have to get going anyway. But if we could set it up for later, that'd be great."

"Sure, just let me know when's good for you, and I'll set it up."

"I will. Oh, and Lila said I could get my membership renewed with you?"

She'd leave out how long ago it'd expired, since one look at her ever-expanding behind was probably clue enough that she hadn't stepped into the gym in months.

"Just go up to the front desk and let them know you're her sister. They can renew it for you."

Allison thanked him then started packing up her backpack. Gio excused himself, but then he just *had* to add, "And help yourself to some of these." He shook his head. "Every payday it's the same thing. Someone decides we need to celebrate and take a break from the healthy lifestyle, even if for only one morning." He grumbled something else as he picked up a maple bar on his way out.

Smiling, Allison nodded as her eyes zoomed onto the jelly donut calling her name. Gio left her alone, and even before she finished zipping up her backpack, she could already feel herself giving into the temptation. The stronger willed side of her reminded herself of her hypothyroidism. It was bad enough she had to be on meds to help speed up her thyroid so it wouldn't totally kill her metabolism; adding things like jelly donuts to her diet wouldn't help.

But then her weaker side argued right back. She *was* going to make a real effort to get her ass back in the gym. One little donut wouldn't kill her, and she could start working out sooner than she'd planned, now that she'd be renewing her membership.

Exhaling loudly, she gave into temptation and, taking a napkin, reached for the glorious donut. Her mouth was already watering before her lips were even on it. She walked out of the break room, licking the excess jelly from the little hole on the side of the donut. Allison had to refrain from groaning as she bit into it.

Jesus. Why did it have to be so damn good? Maybe because she hadn't allowed herself to have one of these in forever. She figured deprivation would do that to you. Just like when she gave into that Big Mac after not having one in over a year. It was the *best* burger she'd ever had.

She slowed down when the jelly dripped out the side of her donut and nearly onto her blouse. She managed to catch it with her tongue then licked the rest off. Feeling like a sloppy, donut-eating pig, she glanced around, hoping no one noticed her orgasmic reaction to the pastry. For a second, she thought no one had; then she saw *him.*

She could only imagine he was part of the work-release program. He was what Gio described as rough-looking. Though tough would be more accurate in this guy's case. Dangerous even. He was very tall, bald, with tattoos and bulging muscles as far as the eye could see, only his hardened expression was *anything* but respectful and humble. His eyes slowly lifted from her body to her lips until they made eye contact and then there it was—that look of utter disgust. She was still licking her lips clean, and his eyes dropped down to them again for a moment before he shook his head and turned away.

The mortification slapped her like a bucket of ice water in the face. Trying desperately not to let the asshole get to her, she lifted her chin and tried to shake it off. So many times in her life during moments where she found herself trying to be strong—brave—needing to overcome an uncomfortable situation, she asked herself the very question running through her mind now. *What would Lila do?*

Her older sister was the epitome of strength and self-assuredness. Of course, she had every right to be. She'd soon be a superstar boxer. Yet she was beautiful enough to be a fitness model as well, for crying out loud. Still, over the years, her sister's strong will and ability to shake off any kind of insecurity had begun to rub off on Allison. She may not have the looks and athletic abilities her sister possessed, but she was not about to get down on herself over one nasty sneer.

Fuck him! was exactly what Lila would say. Allison had heard stories of strangers fat-shaming heavy people they saw enjoying a large meal at a restaurant or something sinful like her donut. Even online where fat-shaming was rampant, she'd always thought it incredibly rude and intrusive. No matter how fat anyone was, *no one* had a right to take it upon himself to shame them. And while Allison was aware she could stand to lose some weight, her sister and best friend Jen were forever insisting she wasn't fat. She'd never actually said she was, but she *could* do without some of the extra junk in her trunk. Regardless, no one, and especially not some jerk she didn't even know, had any right to make her feel bad about it.

With a quick spin of her heels, she went the opposite way because she refused to walk by the guy. Just because he was clearly in the shape of his life and *still* working out didn't make him any better than she was. He was probably what her sister so often referred to as an idiot meathead who thought being in shape gave him the right to be a dick with anyone who wasn't.

Despite the little rant going on in her head, her face still felt flushed. She tossed the rest of the calorie-bursting donut in the trash and made her way to the front desk. That was it. She was renewing her membership, and she'd set a workout schedule as soon as she could.

Getting her membership renewed took a little longer than she expected. Apparently, they'd made changes, and she now had choices on the type of membership she wanted. By the time she was done, she'd almost forgotten about the idiot from earlier. She was almost out of there when, in her haste, she rushed away from the front desk absentmindedly and collided right into what felt like a human wall, a very muscular and tall and *blurry* wall she reached out to hold onto. It happened so fast she didn't even realize her glasses had fallen. The blur in front of her put her glasses back on gently. As if running into someone hadn't been mortifying enough, it was *him*.

The guy who'd been so disgusted with her earlier was peering at her now in the strangest way. Taking her hand off his unbelievably hard arm, she felt her heart thudding and her eyes going even wider. For a moment, they were both rendered speechless as his eyes went from hers down to her lips. They remained on her lips a little longer until, to her utter surprise, he brought a finger up and touched the corner of them.

"You missed some."

They both glanced at his finger with the smidge of raspberry jelly still on it, and for a moment, she thought she might die. The expression he wore suddenly was such an odd one Allison braced herself for him to either wipe the jelly off on her shirt, disgusted, or lick it clean. But he did neither.

Being that close to such a huge and daunting presence, along with the even deeper mortification now, she was still so thunderstruck she had no words. Otherwise, she might've said something in response to what felt like continued distaste in his near glare. It bore deep into her with a purpose, searching her eyes almost as if he might say something, but he didn't.

Before she could gather her wits, he muttered what sounded like curse words under his breath followed by a near growl. Allison couldn't make it out, but given the tone, she was sure it wasn't very favorable. Then just like that, he and the guy with him walked around her without so much as another word.

Just like back in high school, it wasn't even until she was out the door and at her car that the zingers she *should've* shot back in response to his nasty glare and rudeness started coming to her. "Oh, I'm sorry. Didn't mean to run into you and your fuck buddy there." She brought her hand to her mouth, feigning exaggerated embarrassment as she tossed her backpack onto the passenger seat. "Sorry, I meant *jailbird* buddy." She plopped into the driver's side with a huff. "Sorry I wasn't born with enough middle fingers to let you know how I feel about what you think of me!"

She started up the car then worked on plugging her ear piece to her phone. She absolutely refused to give any more thought to how infuriatingly hot the guy was—therefore likely full of himself.

"God, I should've said something to him!" she said, banging her steering wheel as she pulled out of the parking space. "I should've slapped his hand away from my face."

Not stand there in a complete trance.

Thankfully, before she could start reciting anymore lame comebacks she knew full well she'd never have the nerve to say anyway, her phone rang. She hit the answer button, pushing the earpiece farther in as she drove through the parking lot.

"Oh, my God, you're not gonna believe what just happened to me." Jen groaned; though Allison could tell it was a playful groan. "This is why I don't date white country boys or rather why they don't date me." She laughed so much it snapped Allison right out of her irritable mood. "OMG, I'm an idiot. I still can't get used to his southern accent, so I *keep* messing up. I had a missed call from Jaxson, so I called him back, and he answers but says, 'Hold on. I have a piece of ass in my mouth.' Then the phone gets all muffled, and I'm like *what the fuck*? So, the second he comes back on the line, I start going off on him. 'Don't let me interrupt you and your piece of ass.' Halfway through my rant, he interrupts me to emphasize it was a piece of *ass,* which only riles me more"— she squealed with another giggle— "until I realize he's saying *ice*. I felt so stupid I hung up and called you. What do I do?"

Allison was laughing so hard she was glad she was at a red light.

"Shit, that's him calling again," Jen said, sounding panicked.

"Just answer it and tell him what you told me—that you're an idiot," Allison said, still laughing. "I'm sure he's laughing too."

Grudgingly, her friend agreed, and they were off the phone. Allison thought about *her* own embarrassing incident today again after hanging up with Jen. Despite the fact just thinking about it gave her the chills, she decided her bestie's was way worse than hers. She wouldn't give it another thought.

TWO

Not since Allison had mentioned the look she'd gotten from the work-release meathead to her sister had she thought about it again. By then, she'd been so over the mortification she'd been able to see the humor in it. She admitted to and teased her sister that she thought the tattooed bad boy was kind of sexy. Of course, she left the part out about him being such an asshole he just had to point out she was still drooling the donut jelly. She hadn't even mentioned the second run-in. Even so, Lila still didn't think the incident was funny.

Not at all.

As usual, her sister had been instantly annoyed by what little Allison *had* told her about the guy putting his hand on her face to further humiliate her. When Allison tried to explain to her that she'd been practically making love to the jelly donut while this guy with a perfectly sculpted body was working out, Lila wasn't having it. She'd immediately jumped all over Allison for her constant self-depreciation, so Allison was done talking about it—at least to her sister.

In addition to Lila's annoyance with the guy's rudeness, she'd been adamant that Allison not get any funny ideas when it came to doing more than just interviewing these *dangerous* men. Even now, weeks after the embarrassing incident, as Allison stared at her new and improved self in the mirror, she had to scoff at Lila's unnecessary worry. Regardless of how little respect her sister seemed to have for meatheads, fact was they clearly took staying fit very seriously. The discipline alone had to count for something. It also meant no one with that kind of mentality, when it came to keeping his body in tip-top shape, would be impressed by a little makeup and a new hairdo when her out-of-shape body was still seriously lacking.

Though Allison had to admit finally stripping away those god-awful bottle-cap glasses was a huge improvement to her overall appearance. That alone would've been gift enough, but her sister had not only gotten her a newish car last week for her birthday, she'd also surprised her with an entire makeover—including those contacts she'd been promising her for years.

Turning sideways, Allison examined her outfit in the full-length mirror. She was grateful that at least her belly was flat enough. It wasn't nearly as tight as Lila's six pack, but at least it was one part of her body she had under control. If she were taller, she might appreciate the near D cups she thought made her look heavier. But unless she had a breast reduction, she couldn't do anything about that. Turning around to look at her bubble butt again, she frowned. *That* she could do something about, and she had every intention to.

"Holy shit!"

The gasped exclamation had Allison jerking her eyes away from the mirror and at Drew, who'd just walked into the ladies' room at the gym. Drew brought her hand to her mouth, her eyes practically bulging out as she took Allison in from top to bottom.

"Charlee told me about the makeover, but . . . whoa." She shook her head, smiling big. "I didn't expect all this."

Allison felt her face warm, but she smiled. Drew was Charlee's best friend. Charlee's husband was Hector, the youngest co-owner of 5th Street. Allison had met Drew a handful of times and had since decided she really liked Drew. Unlike the other wives who were a lot older than Allison, Charlee wasn't *that* much older. Hector was the youngest owner, and his wife and Drew were his age. So, it was much easier to relate to her than the other women.

"It's just a little makeup and new hairdo."

"Are you kidding? You look amazing! *So* much older too." Drew took her in from top to bottom as she circled around Allison. "You went from this meek little girl with such a baby face anyone would mistake you for a high-school kid to sexy and sophisticated." She shrugged. "You could probably still pass for a high-school student if you wanted. That baby face is still under the new makeup and sexy arched brows, only I'd hardly refer to you as meek now."

Allison knew *meek* was Drew's nice way of saying mousy. Allison knew exactly how she came across with those glasses so thick she could fry a grasshopper with them. But Drew was right. The new look had given her a little pep in her step she'd never had before. Even that pompous editor in her journalism class had been nicer to her lately.

Drew wasn't heavy but often complained about being out of shape. Ever since she'd had a baby a few years ago then fell into a deep depression when her baby daddy admitted he was in love with another *man*, she let herself go. But she was in a new relationship now with a guy she said was perfect, and she was determined to get back into shape. So, their diet woes had bonded the two girls.

Needing to hurry to her CrossFit training, Drew promised to give Allison a call and tell her about it since it was her first day. Allison walked out into the gym and to the area where Gio said he'd be meeting her. His earlier text letting her know he'd have two guys for her to interview had inevitably reminded her of the guy who'd made no qualms of showing his distaste for her weeks ago. Gio had wanted to know if she needed more than two guys to interview.

God no. She'd said two was fine. Just thinking about it made her heart speed up, but she was glad she hadn't seen *him* anywhere in the gym when she'd first walked in today. And she'd made it a point to look out for him. As big and daunting as he was, she didn't think she could miss him. At least he hadn't been in the same area where he'd been working out the last time.

She walked over and stood just outside one of the training rooms. Drew was in there doing her CrossFit, and it *did not* look like fun. But Allison was determined to at least try and get into better shape. She glanced around as Gio walked around the corner and out of sight, not sure what to do with herself.

Fortunately, her awkward alone time was fleeting because, within moments, both Lila and her major-league-baseball-star boyfriend, *Sonny Sabian,* arrived from different directions. Allison smiled as Sonny pecked her sister. The man was truly a heartthrob the way all the articles referred to him online and on TV. Allison was just glad Lila had gotten past her initial apprehension that, as big a celebrity as Sonny was, he could genuinely be interested in her.

"You look different," Sonny said, taking her in just as Drew had—completely astounded by the change.

Lila told him more about who had done the makeover. She was a friend of Bianca, Gio's wife, named Toni and was the same lady who had given Lila a makeover just weeks ago. Though of course, unlike Allison, her sister didn't really need one. She'd just gotten done up for some ritzy charity event she'd attended with Sonny.

Sonny commented on how womanly Allison seemed now with the new look, while Lila gushed about how she seemed to be glowing. Then she made the other comment

Allison hadn't been expecting: about having seen heads turn when Allison had walked in. That had Allison laughing nervously and waving off the nonsense. But she did admit to being beyond glad to be rid of the glasses finally.

"Best damn birthday gift ever, but . . ." She eyed Lila suspiciously because it suddenly dawned on her why her sister would be there when her shift as a youth coordinator was over. "I know why you're here, and you need to be gone. I don't want you anywhere around, threatening these guys I'm interviewing with your evil eye. I'm already nervous enough as it is."

She clarified that she was *nervous* not scared the way she knew her sister thought she *should* be of the big bad work-release guys. But Allison made it clear she was only nervous about botching the interview and how she needed to get it right. She'd leave out what else had her insides roiling now, the more she thought of it.

Lila assured Allison she had this and then had the nerve to say her days of snapping were long behind her. Neither Allison nor Sonny, who knew Lila too well, even *attempted* to keep a straight face.

Just then Gio got there. He, too, did a double take when he saw Allison. "Wow, you look different." Allison had to giggle now as she glanced at Lila, who smiled proudly. "Bianca said the makeover had made a big difference, but I didn't think she meant this much."

"It's the bottle-cap lenses being gone that make the biggest difference," Allison said, knowing her sister was probably already annoyed at her response. "It's what feels most different to me anyway." She smirked before adding, "My head feels lighter."

"They weren't that bad. I thought you looked cute in them," Lila shot back quickly.

"Yeah, if you're into nerdy little bookworms with glasses so thick they could see into the future."

Again, her sister was quick to give her a disapproving look but then turned her attention to Gio, who began explaining about the guys Allison would be interviewing. "As I explained to Allison when she interviewed me, it might be hard to get past the hardened exteriors of some of these guys, but trust me. I wouldn't allow them around my friends and family if I couldn't vouch for them being respectable guys just trying to change their lives."

Allison's insides were just beginning to knot up when she heard the cheery voice behind her. "Ready when you are, chief."

The cheery voice gave her hope. Somehow, she just couldn't imagine Mr. Disgusted sounding this friendly. Gio and Allison turned around to face what Lila and Sonny were already looking at, the two guys she'd be interviewing. She'd been right. It wasn't the guy from that day who did the talking. But to her horror, Mr. Disgusted stood next to him. Allison had to refrain from gasping, especially because, up close, he was *incredible*. Sure, she'd give Lila he was intimidating looking as all hell, but the softer expression he wore now gave him a much less menacing appearance than that first day. Then again, he wasn't looking at Allison this time. Of course he didn't appear disgusted. His eyes were on her gorgeous sister instead. He hadn't even noticed Allison.

"Hey," Gio said, smiling. "Right on time. Here she is."

He motioned to Allison, only before he could do any introductions, Noah, one of the other owners of the gym, rushed by on his phone, distracting Gio. "Give me a sec, guys. I gotta tell him something before he leaves."

Gio rushed off after Noah, leaving them all standing there as both guys peered at Allison curiously. Then it happened. She saw the corner of his lip twitch, and he sized her up from top to bottom, stopping at her lips for a moment before their eyes locked.

"Jelly?"

The obvious emotion Allison *should've* felt over this was embarrassment. Except she wasn't even sure if what hearing that deep resonant voice addressing her again did to her *was* an emotion. But what his eyes did to her as they bore into her *had* to be. She breathed in so deep her sister was already reacting to it.

Just as fast as she'd begun to quiver emotionally, her brain switched back to reality. As the heat of utter mortification rose from the back of her spine to her neck, Allison did her best to not react. She knew too well her hotheaded sister was probably already feeling a heat of a different kind scorch through *her* veins. As expected, Lila was first to break the uncomfortable silence. "*Excuse me?*"

"Yeah, it is *Jelly,*" the guy said, ignoring Lila yet continuing to peer at Allison.

She wasn't sure what to make of the odd expression. It was too hard to be playful yet nowhere near the revolted one she'd been treated two weeks ago.

Allison could almost feel the heat radiate off her sister's body. "She has a name, and it's not Jelly, asshole."

"Whoa!" The guy with him, who'd been just as stunned as the rest of them, laughed nervously, turning to the *asshole.* "Dude, what are you doing?"

Like a ray of light shining through the cloud of mortification that hovered over Allison, it suddenly came to her and she touched her sister's arm. "Lila, no—"

"No, bullshit!" Lila said, taking a step forward, but thankfully Sonny held her back. "That's fucking rude. Who are you to—?"

"Lila, I don't think he means what you're thinking," Allison said, almost certain what the guy was referring to. It was still embarrassing but not nearly as bad as what she knew her sister was thinking.

"What *are* you thinking?" the guy asked with that sudden look of distaste, the same one Allison had tried in vain to forget about.

Again, thankfully, Sonny was there to intervene and took a step in front of Lila.

"That Jelly's an offensive way to refer to someone you don't even know." Sonny's words, while firm, were far calmer than her sister's, but he made a point to stare the guy down, since he was just as big as him.

"But I *do* know her," the guy retorted to Allison's surprise.

"And you call her Jelly?" Lila asked, trying to get around Sonny, only he stood staunchly in place, not letting her. "That's still fucking rude."

"I don't know what you think it means, but—"

"I know what you meant," Allison interrupted the guy, her heart thudding when he turned and those intense eyes locked in on hers again.

I know her?

Eyeing Gio, who was on his way back, she turned to Lila with a purpose. "It's not *at all* what you're thinking. I'll explain later."

Allison lowered her voice, praying her still too riled up sister would just let it go. "Please go now. I can handle it from here on."

"*Why* and how does he know you?" Lila asked through her teeth.

"From the last time I was here," Allison said quickly, nudging both Lila and Sonny away.

"So, did you all get acquainted?" Gio asked as he reached them.

"Sort of," Allison said then turned to Lila. "I'll call you as soon as I'm done." Her pleading expression willed her sister to just believe she'd be fine and go. Then she mouthed the words, "I promise."

Shooing her sister and Sonny, who finally complied and walked away, she turned back to Gio and the two guys. Unlike earlier, it now appeared that he was avoiding making any eye contact with her. When Gio asked if they'd exchanged names and Allison informed him that they hadn't, the guy even looked away when Gio began the introductions.

"Allison Rico, this is Rodney Henson," Gio said, pointing at the other guy, then motioned to *him*, who was still glancing around indifferently, so unlike when he first laid eyes on her minutes ago. "And this is Leonardo Ledesma."

Leonardo met Allison's eyes for just a moment. The slightest nod followed without so much as a hint of that near smirk he'd worn earlier as he glanced away again. Aside from his name, she didn't know a thing about him. Yet already it was clear that his reaction to her today was uncharacteristic for him. His barely there acknowledgment, which now felt obligatory for Gio's sake, was more like him.

"From my own experience with interviews, I know there's a lot of stuff discussed off the record," Gio explained as much to Allison as she did to the two men. "So, for privacy reasons, Allison will be interviewing you in the boardroom separately."

Good Lord, she'd be all alone with Leonardo now. Somehow, Allison had expected the informal interview to take place in the break room again, with people walking in and out around them. Maybe somewhere even more public like one of the tables by the juice bar. To her utter relief, Rodney volunteered to go first. She thought she'd prepared enough, but this changed everything. Both men were tatted and as hard-looking as Gio had described, but for whatever reason, Leonardo unnerved her to no end. She needed a moment to get herself together.

"Oh, wait. I have that call with my PO," Rodney said with a grimace, making Allison's heart thud, and she instantly panicked.

PO? Call? What?

"That's right," Gio said as they all walked together toward the boardroom. "That's cool. This works out." He turned to Allison as he opened a door to a darkened room then flicked the lights on just inside the doorway. "You can interview Leonardo first."

Allison walked into the room, gulping so thunderously she was sure they'd all heard. Adding to her already altered nerves, Gio didn't even walk in with them. She turned just as she reached the long boardroom table. Gio was standing at the door still, and Leonardo pulled out the chair directly across from where she stood.

"There's water bottles in the fridge over in the corner if you need one," Gio said with a big smile as Allison nodded, walking over to the fridge. "I'll close the door so you can have some privacy. Just send Leonardo out to fetch Rodney when you're done with him."

Allison thanked him then turned to Leonardo when the door closed behind Gio. "You wanna a water?"

"I'm good."

She walked back toward the table, taking subtle but deep breaths as she pulled out the seat directly in front of Leonardo and sat down. This time Allison avoided looking up from her notebook, focusing instead on keeping her hands from shaking. When she finally had to glance up, he was eyeing her, not in that appalled way he had the first time. Only it still held an air of displeasure—irritation even.

Focusing on her breathing so he wouldn't pick up on just how intimidated she was by him, Allison looked him straight in those intense eyes. *What would Lila do?* Clearly, her sister had already proven, no matter how big and daunting this guy was, she *was not* intimidated by him. That's when Allison's first question for him came to her.

Swallowing hard, she lifted her chin and tried desperately to muster some of her sister's strength. "You know me?"

The panicked flash in his eyes was so fast Allison would've missed it, had her own eyes not been inescapably glued to his. But like with everything else when it came to this man, she had no idea what to make of it because, just as fast, his brows furrowed and the expression of utter displeasure he'd worn earlier went even more severe.

THREE

BEAST

"I was volunteered for this." Leo sat back in his seat, crossing his arms in front of him. "I didn't know anything about it until I got here today."

He wanted that last statement perfectly clear. If he hadn't been fucking annoyed with Rodney already for volunteering him to do this, he was beyond annoyed now.

Allison appeared as confused by his response to her question as he expected her to be. He took in the lift of her brows, making sure he didn't show any more of the effect she had on him as he'd already let slip.

"*Okay* . . ." she said, obviously not satisfied with his answer to her inquiry. "But you said you knew me."

"You know how I know you, *Jelly*. Explaining it would've taken too long, and I wanted to be done with that before Bravo got back."

"Bravo?"

"Gio." He sat up, feeling even more exasperated about all this. "One of the owners of this place and someone who can get me sent back to the pen if I screw this up. I couldn't have your crazy-ass sister going off—"

"First of all," she said, sitting up as well, and Leo forced himself to keep his eyes on her face and away from that voluptuous rack bulging underneath her snug shirt. "My sister is not crazy, and I won't have you referring to her as that. Understood?"

She paused as if to wait for him to agree or apologize. It shouldn't have surprised him that the sister of such a spit fire would have some spunk. But it did. Not only did it surprise him, the hardened expression on such an otherwise sweet face amused him. Despite the inexplicable temptation to give in and offer an apology—it wasn't happening. With each moment they stood staring at each other in a silent stalemate, Leo felt himself searching deeper into those big dark eyes of hers. It was insane. He wasn't even sure what he was searching for, but he couldn't look away. When it was clear he wouldn't be offering so much as a nod in response to her question, she went on.

"You *don't* know me and my sister's aware of that. So, you referring to me as Jelly *understandably* set her off." Watching her lift a stubborn little chin had Leo swallowing hard again, but like with her previous statement, he managed to refrain from further reaction. "I was thinking the same thing she was obviously, until I remembered my first encounter with you—"

"The jelly donut," Leo said, resting his arms on the table. "I remember."

How could he forget? He'd even dreamed of the day he'd been envious of a fucking donut. The way she'd licked and sucked that thing had him feeling shit no grown-ass man should feel over something so petty. Wiping the jelly off her face had been bad enough, but at least he hadn't given into the thought he'd had the moment he saw it still there on the corner of her mouth—to lick it off.

"But you *don't* know me," she reiterated.

"No, I don't."

This time he'd concede at least to that, but he'd be damned if he'd admit to her or *anyone* else just how much she'd pestered his thoughts since that day. Especially *why*.

"You just caught me off guard today," he continued, annoyed that he was having to explain any of this to her. "When I realized you were the same *kid* I'd seen that day. . ."

Those widening eyes had Leo momentarily pausing, but he refused to allow them to continue to trip him up. "You just look a lot different is all."

She cleared her throat then mercifully dropped the eye contact when she glanced down at her notebook.

"Your glasses," he said, once again going against his better judgment, but he was curious. "You don't really need them?"

Though she continued to focus on her notebook, she had glanced up for a moment in response to the question. Watching her face tinge with color was something else. He'd seen his share of seemingly embarrassed or shy girls. Most of those times while he'd said something far more scandalous, he often questioned how genuine *their* reactions really were. Girls like Allison were rare in Leo's life. Already he could tell there'd be so many other things he could say to her that would turn her beet red, but she was blushing over his questioning her *glasses*.

"I do." She cleared her throat, pulling a strand of hair behind her ear, then made eye contact with him again. "Just not when I'm wearing my contacts."

There was no question about it. Allison was as genuine as they came. No way could she be faking the flush of her cheeks. Leo should swallow back everything else he wanted to ask her. Get on with the damn interview and be done with this. Instead, his lips were once again moving, and the curious inquiry flew out without further consideration.

"You look so much younger with them on. How old are you?"

"Nineteen," she said without breaking the eye contact, despite her face still glowing with deepened color. "Just had a birthday a few weeks ago. This . . ." She motioned a hand up and down in front of her. "The whole makeover thing was a birthday gift from my sister."

She paused as she opened her water bottle and brought it to her lips. Leo blinked slowly, taking in a very deep breath as her plump lips caressed the bottle's opening and she drank from it.

"Don't women get makeovers to look younger, not the opposite?" Again, the words were out before he could put anymore thought to them, damn it. What was worse was her off-put expression had him scrambling to backpedal. "I mean, in your case, older isn't *old* like in a bad way. I'm just saying it's ironic that the outcome of yours was the opposite of what it's normally supposed to be."

Her instantly furrowed brows had him cursing himself for having opened his mouth about this in the first place. Having talked himself into a fucking corner, he had no choice but to admit it. "Not that you don't look *amazing—*" *Good would've been enough, you idiot.* "I just mean you're *nineteen,* and I saw what you looked like before. I don't think you needed a makeover."

Her expression softened instantly, even as the glow of her cheeks deepened again. Twisting the cap back onto the bottle, Allison shrugged, indulging him with a small but sweet smile. "The glasses being gone is probably what makes the biggest difference and why you think I look so much older. Thank you for saying I didn't need a makeover, but I really did. I hadn't aged since I was eleven. The hands of time needed a little nudge."

Leo stared at her, silently, aware that every moment he sat there it became increasingly harder to not take in every detail of her delicate features. That only reminded him that he needed to get out of there, especially now that he'd confirmed she was very young. Maybe she wasn't as young as he'd initially thought but still. "Just so you know . . ." He straightened up, determined to get back to what they were supposed to be talking about. "You're supposed to be interviewing me," he said, attempting to get back to his harder demeanor. "About what? Because I didn't know anything about this."

The pinch of her brows coming together had him looking away like a coward. Never in his life had he been so tempted to apologize when he'd done nothing wrong. Only speaking to her without the utmost respect and delicacy felt wrong. Just like visually groping her had felt the first time he'd laid eyes on her, remembering what her soft warm body pressed against his felt like had been too damn distracting for days after.

"It's, uh . . ." She cleared her voice again. "It's for a story I'm doing on the work-release program here at 5th Street. I thought it was an interesting and unique concept. Lila was able to work out an interview for me with one of her bosses; then I requested to speak with some of the workers directly." She glanced down at her notebook again, pausing for a second before going on. "But I'm sorry you were volunteered for this against your wishes. You're right. If you didn't sign up for this, then you shouldn't have to be here. You're free to go. I'll just interview Rodney."

Torn between getting the hell out of there or staying put, Leo sat up even straighter but didn't get up. *What the fuck was he doing?* She'd given him his walking papers. He should stand up and get out. Be done with this. The fact that he was still sitting there even *considering* sticking around longer, was further proof that his first instincts about this girl were spot on. She'd be nothing but trouble if he so much as got *any* funny ideas about her.

"What's a PO?" She glanced up at him, and he was quickly caught up in those overly expressive eyes again.

"Probation officer." Leo's own curiosity had him sitting back in his seat already. "You don't ever want miss a call from them. It could cost you big time."

"So, you're on probation even though you're on work release?"

Apparently, she'd taken his answering her first question as an invitation to continue with the interview. Leo continued wrestling with the conflicting arguments going on in his head.

*You should get up and walk out **now**. What harm can come from sticking around and answering a few questions?*

It *was* a bad idea and Leo knew it, especially given how his dumb ass had already reacted to seeing her again. How easily he'd lost control of his curiosity. Leo could tell himself all he wanted that this was nothing more than having been drawn to her curves that first day. That, just like any of the other girls who'd turned his head at the gym, she was just another piece of ass he should steer far away from. The rules were clear enough, and the only thing he should focus on while on work release was this job and the training he agreed to do.

But this *was* part of his job, right? Gio had asked Rodney to do this, and while Leo hadn't been there to pass on it the way he would've respectfully done so, especially had he known who was doing the interviewing, he *was* doing Gio a favor. Bad idea or not, this would be complimentary to his character, not a risk. Besides what harm could one interview with a *college* student possibly be? No matter how young she'd appeared to be, he now knew she was legal.

"Your probation starts the moment you're sentenced," he said, hoping with all hope he wouldn't live to regret not ending this when he'd had the chance. "It's usually longer than the time you do in jail. Work-release means I get to finish my time on the outside as long as I comply with the restrictions of the program."

"And those are?" She glanced down at her notebook as she began taking notes.

Clearly, her offer to let him walk was off the table now that he'd obviously—and possibly very stupidly—passed on it. Breathing a little easier because this didn't seem *too* bad after all, Leo began listing some of his restrictions. He was allowed to be at the gym while he was working or training for boxing. He'd be subject to random drug testing and in-home visits. "I can't leave the county, unless I have special permission. I have to attend the required therapy—"

"What kind of therapy?" She glanced up at him, curiously.

Leo pressed his lips together tightly, breathing in deeply again. It was beginning to feel like a habit he'd have as long as he was around her. "Anger management." He shrugged, attempting to make light of it, and moved on to something else. "It's just one of the standard requirements. Like the random urine tests for drugs, even though I'm not in for anything drug-related."

"What *are* you in for?"

Christ, those eyes. For as too young as his head kept harping she was, there was something so incredibly sultry about the way she gazed at him sometimes that said she was *all woman*. Maybe this *was* a bad idea after all. Clearing his throat again, he decided to share only as much as she needed to know for Gio's sake. The guy and the rest of his business partners had done so much for Leo. So that's how he'd look at this. This was a favor for Gio—for 5th Street. But he didn't need to tell her everything.

"I've had my run-ins with the law in the past. What I was charged with this time wouldn't have been such a big deal had it not been for my priors." Inevitably, he shook his head in frustration, just thinking about it, but he went on. "In the past, I'd been pinched for fighting in an illegal underground fight club. I hadn't been back there in years. The day I was arrested again I just happened to be there looking for someone when the place got raided. But I wasn't fighting this time. Except the probation board wasn't having it."

Shaking his head again, he decided that was as much as he was sharing with her about that. To his surprise, unlike earlier, she wasn't busy writing this time when he glanced up at her. She was staring at him with this look of disbelief or . . . *awe?*

"You were an underground fighter?"

Leo followed her eyes as they proceeded to roam his face, neck, and forehead. He was sure she *thought* she was making the connection about the scars. If she'd ever been witness to him in the ring, she'd know that was *far* from the case. His opponents were the ones who walked away with such scars.

Never Leo.

The scars he'd carried for most of his life had nothing to do with his time in the fight club. "I was," he said but didn't offer more.

"Can you tell me about that?"

She set her pen down, and Leo wondered now if this was what Gio had meant by her asking things off the record. When he glanced up at her again, she nodded as if to answer his unspoken question. "This is completely off the record. I'm only asking to satisfy my own curiosity. Only time I've ever heard of a fight club was the movie. But even that I never watched. Just heard about and saw some of the clips since it's often mentioned online and such. I didn't think they actually existed."

Once again, she had him wrestling with his thoughts. She'd said several things after the one thought he'd been stuck on the moment the words left her mouth.

Satisfy her.

Straightening up again, he didn't even care if she noticed how much he'd been fidgeting from the moment he sat down. He'd yet to sit still for more than five minutes. The reasons were insane and he knew it. Nineteen or not, she was still just a kid, an *innocent* kid he had no business having these thoughts about.

Glancing around, he wondered if he should take her up on her offer now. Get out of there while he still had the chance to do so with his conscience intact.

"Leonardo—"

"Call me Beast," he said too quickly—frantically. But hearing her say his name was already doing to him what he'd had a feeling from day one would happen if he ever saw her again. "It's what most people call me."

Her brows came together again, and she tilted her head. "*Why?*"

Those eyes. Jesus Christ, those fucking eyes were going to be the end of him. Glancing away for the sake of his own sanity, he stared down at his fisting hands on the table but shrugged, attempting to seem less tense. "Fight-club thing."

That was half the truth anyway, but no way was he telling her everything. Already his telling her *anything* at all about it was for one reason only: the pleasure of satisfying her—even if only her curiosity—for now.

Fisting his hands tightly as his insides heated with the annoyance that his mind would even go there, he focused on finishing his answer. "I picked up the name then, and even though I haven't been involved in that shit in years, the name stuck."

"Was it because you were a *Beast* in the ring?"

Leonardo stared at her playful eyes now. Refusing to lighten up and welcome any more playfulness, his response was nothing more than a nod.

Her eyes widened a bit in reaction to his hardening glare. "Were you just that good or was it all an act like those wrestlers on TV?"

Unable to keep from glancing down at those sweet lips—lips he thought of more than he cared to admit all because of her love affair with that fucking donut—Leonardo shook his head. She had no idea, and for the sake of making sure the questioning about this ended *now*, he'd give her a taste. "I'm not into theatrics, Ms. Allison, and I'm not proud of the name."

He paused, surprised about adding that last part. What the hell was he doing now? For years, he'd been *very* proud. So, he wasn't now. Why did he feel the need to make that clear?

Glancing away and feeling more than exasperated with himself, he added the next part because he *needed* to. She looked too damned intrigued—too full of curiosity. Leo was anything but intriguing. He was everything a sweet girl like her should detest—dread.

"I was unpredictable. Dangerous. I got the name after one particularly gruesome fight, and the reason for it is why it stuck."

"What's the reason?"

And there it was. Stripped of the playfulness she'd used earlier, her tone now oozed of dread. She was afraid to know, but just as he imagined, she had to.

"It's not like the boxing your sister does." He stared her straight in those enrapt eyes, knowing what he'd say next would have her looking at him differently—the way she *should* be looking at him. "These fights aren't regulated. Anything goes. I'd heard the guy I was fighting was as dirty as they came."

He thought about it for a moment before he told her the rest. Maybe he should make his reasons for doing what he did clearer—explain himself—but then he thought better of it. It was in *his* best interest to make sure the inquisitive little reporter would think twice about asking anything more. Only he couldn't take looking into those eyes anymore, so he glanced down at his fist when he said it. "I let the attempts to gouge my eyes go, but when he tried to knee me in the groin, I ripped his jaw off."

He waited for a response to that, but there was none. He should've been happy about that, glad he'd stunned her silent. Instead, he had to quiet the alarm in him that she may be packing her shit and wanting to end this interview now. It's what she *should've* been doing.

Once again, he was forced to deal with the frustration of giving into glancing back up at her. Instead of dread, he saw that same intrigue he'd seen earlier. Her eyes were glued to him as if waiting for him to share more. Only she didn't look stunned or afraid. She tilted her head as she'd done earlier in question. "But you don't do that anymore," she stated it as if it were fact not a question. "And you're not proud of it. Yet you prefer being called Beast to Leonardo?"

Hearing her say his full name again, not just Leo, had him squeezing his fists even tighter. His utter weakness when it came to this surprised him as much as it annoyed him. He contemplated walking out again before she might notice what she so easily did to him without doing *anything*.

"Leonar—"

"Yes," he said before he was forced to hear it again. "I prefer Beast. Listen . . ." He looked around, feeling the panic multiply. "Are we almost done here?"

She picked up her pen, appearing a little panicked herself. "I'm sorry. I got off the subject of the work-release program and didn't get a whole lot of questions in about that. Is it okay if I ask a few more quick ones?"

Leo nodded, hoping the questions *were* quick, but once again was irritated at his inability to just say no to her. It was already happening, the unrelenting desire to want to satisfy this girl he knew nothing about. It'd won over the common sense of doing the smarter thing—getting the fuck out of there.

Thankfully, her follow-up questions were few and, as promised, quick ones. The interview was finally over, and he was almost out of there—on his feet even—when she hit him with one last question.

"Is it okay if I interview you again?" Leo turned to her, surprised to see the excitement in her eyes. "My editor might have some follow-up questions. For once, I think he'll finally be impressed with one of my stories."

Say no. Say you'd rather not. Say you can't. Damn it. It's partly true.

"I don't think it's up to me."

"I'm sure Gio would be fine with it, but if you'd rather not do the whole formal interview thing with us setting an appointment to meet, I can just text you any follow up questions I might have."

Before Leo could even consider his rebuttal—his *absolute* refusal to the insane idea of exchanging numbers with her—she was tapping away at her phone's screen.

"It might not even happen," she said, still looking down at her phone. "I think I have enough, but I usually think of something I'm slapping my forehead with the next day. So just in case, what's your number?"

It might not even happen.

When he didn't respond immediately, she lowered her phone. "Or not," she said, sounding slightly embarrassed. "I'll start working out here at the gym soon. If I have any other questions, maybe I'll just track you down and—"

"Area code three-two-three . . ."

He finished rattling off his number before she could finish her thought about *tracking him down*. The last thing he needed was the anticipation of her walking up to him at any moment. He chose the lesser of two evils. If she ever texted him, he'd keep it straight and to the point. It also meant not having to deal with looking into those eyes. The entire time with her had felt like a challenge—like one of the sparring matches he had in the ring. He'd been bobbing and weaving, trying to avoid getting hit with another one of those paralyzing moments.

Just when he thought this round was over and he'd made it out unscathed, she hit him with another jab. "And, Beast?" He'd been wrong. Hearing her address him directly by his nickname was just as unnerving. Their eyes met, and once again, he was caught in them. "Ms. Allison is way too formal." She smiled, only this time it wasn't playful—it was sweet—it was *beautiful*. "You can call me Ali. It's what most people call me."

Leo nodded, turning quickly to get the hell out as soon as he could. Trudging out of there and toward the training area, Leo fisted his hand tightly, beyond frustrated about how poorly he'd handled the entire interview. The only thing he could hope for now was that he'd never have to address her at all. After today's experience, he knew now, without doubt, that avoiding her was something he'd be doing at all costs.

FOUR

Allison

Allison had already explained to her sister about the Jelly misunderstanding with Leonardo earlier that day. Even over the phone, it was clear her easily annoyed and worrywart sister hadn't been too convinced that it was nothing more than just that—an innocent misunderstanding. Despite the odd vibe Allison thought she'd picked up from him during the interview and the compliment that'd left her breathless, she knew better. She'd chalk up his reaction to her as just how he explained it. Like everyone else, he'd simply been caught off guard by how different she looked. And the compliment? Well, that was something she'd be keeping for herself, but she refused to make anything more of it than him trying to explain himself out of a comment that had initially come out all wrong.

She could now admit her new look did make a big difference. She smiled, remembering how even Carson, the pompous editor of her school paper, had done a double take the first day she'd gone into class after her makeover. Normally, the only time he focused that much on her was when they disagreed about something—which was often—though he called it healthy debating.

It'd made her nervous at first. Allison had never been one to enjoy the spotlight, and ever since the makeover, it was exactly where she'd been—at school, her job, and now at the gym. But regardless of her sister's misgivings about Leonardo, his reaction to her, even if, at first, it'd had her heart thundering because he remembered her, was perfectly in line with everyone else's.

But maybe the fact that he'd remembered her enough to even have a reaction *was* a little inappropriately exciting. When Allison had called Lila earlier to explain the misunderstanding to her, she'd stupidly been too giddy about it. Lila had instantly called her on it. If Allison had thought for even a minute that the man could possibly ever look at her in any other way than he had that time, she never would've admitted to her sister she thought he was sexy. She managed to backpedal today when Lila questioned why his remembering her excited Allison so.

Breathing in a little too deeply, she realized she'd really have to play this down around Lila. As close as she was to her sister, this *would not* be a subject they could giggle about the way they often did about other things. Lila had so much on her plate lately. Her career as both a boxer and fitness model was taking off, and she had the upcoming fight for *the* title she was training so hard for. Allison refused to give her more to worry about. And she knew this would worry her sister to no end, even if it was *nothing*. So, she'd save any silly thoughts of Leonardo for Jen or even Drew.

As she'd predicted, Carson had been impressed with the story. She felt even better now about not chickening out when she'd had the presence of mind to ask Leonardo for his number. Carson did have more questions. Questions Allison felt stupid about not having thought to ask, but then the conversation had veered off into a far more interesting one. As interested as she'd been to hear more about Leonardo's work-release experience at the gym, she'd been strangely fascinated hearing about his underground fighting. Just another thing she'd have to tone down when she told Lila about it.

Leonardo had been frustratingly hard to read. One moment he indulged her with a smile; then the next he was glaring. Her heart fluttered, remembering how at times that same glare seemed to wane, and there was something almost vulnerable about the way his panicked eyes had taken her in then quickly glanced away. She had no idea what to make of it, but it was why she'd rewritten the text she'd sent him earlier half a dozen times. She wanted to get the tone just right. Professional but not too stuffy. Friendly but not overly playful. Despite his questioning her about her age and the comments that followed, he just didn't seem the type to be open and social. As broodingly skittish as he'd seemed half the time, she didn't want to spook him into not responding. His *kid* remark had been duly noted.

That coupled with his remark about it not being up to him when she asked if she could interview him again, not to mention his comment about not having signed up for *this shit* in the first place, confirmed what she'd begun to think. Given all his restrictions, he really was walking on thin ice. And just like his reason for stretching the fact that he knew her, he wasn't looking to piss anyone off or break any rules. So, while she'd finally decided on just the amount of *friendliness,* she worried now maybe it'd been too long. Glancing down at her phone, she read the unanswered wordy text she'd sent.

Hello, Leonardo, Ali here. Thank you again for the opportunity to interview you. I spoke with my editor, and just like me, he's highly intrigued by your story. But he also had more questions. So do I. Not just about the work-release program either. Let me know how you'd prefer to do this. Via text, over a phone call, or we could set up another in-person interview. Your choice. Looking forward to hearing back from you! =D

Allison frowned, hitting speed dial as she walked over to the fridge. Maybe she shouldn't have used the word intrigued. It was too telling of how she was really feeling about him. But who wouldn't be? Allison hadn't shared with Carson what she'd spoken to Leonardo about off the record. All she told Carson about Leonardo's charges was that he'd violated his probation due to some prior fighting conviction. She'd left out the illegal fighting ring he'd done it in. Even without knowing that, Carson really was interested in hearing about Leonardo's plans for becoming a boxer.

"Hey, how'd it go?" Jen answered, sounding as enthused as Allison knew she'd be.

"It was very . . . interesting."

Allison had told Jen all about her only other encounter with Mr. Disgusted. By the time she done so, she'd been over feeling so humiliated about the incident, and they'd been able to laugh about it. Unlike Lila, Jen had appreciated Allison's hot description of the bad boy. She told her about both interviews, beginning with the near disastrous start.

"He remembered you!" Jen gasped as excited as Allison had to admit she'd been for a minute there.

Jen's excitement made Allison's insides do a little fluttering, but she made sure to go back and forth about each guy's interview and not just focus on Leonardo's. Unlike with Carson, Allison told Jen everything, including about Leonardo's underground fighting club. She knew without a doubt she could trust Jen to keep it to herself. He hadn't said it was a secret anyway. But sharing something so personal about him with Carson versus her trusted friend just felt wrong.

She did however share what she'd been *dying* to share with *someone* because she could hardly stand it anymore. "Leonardo is so freakin hot!" she blurted out after calmly letting Jen in on the other more professional stuff that went on during her interviews. "I mean like nerve-wrackingly so. The whole time I was talking to him I had to remind myself to breathe."

"The cage fighter?"

"Not cage fighter." Allison laughed. "Underground fighter. *EX* underground fighter," she clarified further. "Pay attention, will you?"

Jen laughed now too. "*Whatever.* Like I'd know the difference. I'm still trying to get straight what's considered country and what's redneck. You don't even wanna know how many times I've insulted Jaxson. But forget him. Right now, I wanna know about *your* man."

"*My* man?" Allison laughed nervously, feeling her face heat as she leaned against the kitchen counter. "All I said was that he's hot, and I'll add deliciously intimidating because he is. He's a mountain of muscles, tattoos, and mystery. But don't get any crazy ideas."

"Why not? You said he remembered you. Not just you but a pretty significant detail."

"About me inhaling that donut." Allison huffed as she poured herself some juice. "He was probably just *that* disgusted," she added, ignoring her still-sputtering heart and for some reason keeping to herself that he'd said she looked amazing *and* that he didn't think she needed a makeover.

With her heart speeding up again, she did share with Jen something she would not be sharing with her sister: that, unlike Leonardo who'd been the far more reserved of the two, Rodney had been quite the obnoxious flirt. Thankfully, before Allison could put even another thought into what Jen had previously tried to imply about there being more to Leo remembering her, Jen suddenly remembered something about the other story they were working on together. She began filling Allison in on it. Allison tried to concentrate on what her friend was saying but couldn't help being distracted with thoughts of Leonardo. She reminded herself that even her excitement over his remembering her, the profound way he'd looked at her at that moment, and his saying she looked amazing were just all new to her. She'd never gotten much attention from guys—especially ones as daunting as Leonardo. She refused to even entertain the ridiculous notion.

Jen got back to the subject of Allison's more exciting assignment—the hot ex-cons. Allison took it in stride as their normal boy-crazy girl talk. It was nothing more than harmless intrigue. Her journalist's mind was hungry to know more about his situation. The underground fighting. Was that where he'd gotten all the scars she'd noticed? She could interview the guy for *hours* if he let her.

There was a beep in her ear, and Allison gasped when she pulled the phone away to see what it was. "Oh my God." The words escaped her before she could compose herself.

"What?"

"Uh . . ." She tried to click over to read the text response from Leonardo, but her phone wouldn't allow it. "I, uh . . . I just got a text from . . . Carson. I forgot to turn something in," she added quickly to explain her knee-jerk reaction to seeing the text. "Let me call you back."

As soon as she was off the call with Jen, she clicked over to read the text. "This should not excite you so much, *Allison.*" She mimicked her sister's admonishing tone, even if she was smiling from ear to ear as she began to read Leonardo's response.

Text me whatever you need to know and I'll try to get back to you as soon as I can.

There was hardly a trace of affability. Nothing cutesy about it at all. Yet, Allison couldn't wipe the ridiculous smile off her face. She knew her text had been too assuming. She hadn't asked if he'd be okay with more questions, simply asked how he'd like to go about it. She was being trained to do that as a journalist. If she wanted the story—the facts—she *had* to be unrelenting. Go after it, without the slightest hesitation. It was why, in spite of how nervous he'd made her, she'd forced the courage to ask him for his number today. Part of her had wondered if, even after he'd given her his number knowing full well it was what she'd be texting him for, maybe he'd still turn down the request. *That's* what had her smiling so big now. She was in.

Regardless of how doubtful she'd been that he'd agree to more questions or even bother to respond, Allison was always prepared. She already had a list ready to go. But then who was she kidding? Off the top of her head, she could think of a million things she'd like to ask him. The list wasn't necessary.

Without bothering to look for said list, she decided to *try* and keep this response shorter.

Leonardo.

She changed her mind about starting it that way and tried to hit delete, but she hit send instead. "*Ugh!* Damn it."

As quickly as she could, she put together another one, then reread it.

Thank you, Leonardo. I appreciate this. I'll have the questions for you in the next day or so. You can respond at your earliest convenience. There's no rush.

She hit send, smiling a little too big. The high of any new exciting story always got her giddy. She knew this was all this was, especially because, from her conversation with Carson, it appeared this story might have a better chance of making the bigger headlines.

As much as she'd like to even entertain more silly thoughts of the intriguing Leonardo, *for the fun of it*, she worried it might affect the way she handled this story. She may not be as professional if she had any diversions while she was supposed to be focusing on just the story. Like now for instance. She shook her head almost laughing at the irony.

"Stop thinking about it," she muttered to herself as she pranced back to the table with her juice.

The sound of the apartment door opening had her turning without thought before taking a seat. It wasn't until she'd made eye contact with Lila's disapproving scowl that she realized *how* big she was still smiling.

"Okay," Lila said, dropping her purse down on the sofa. "What else did this man say to you that still has you all smiles?"

Shit.

FIVE

Even realizing she'd blown it *yet again,* Allison was still incapable of completely wiping the smile off her face, so she decided to just go with it. Though she did attempt to save a little face. "Nothing. And who says I'm still smiling about that?"

"So, you admit you *were* smiling about that earlier?"

Damn it. She decided to just concede and be honest. "Look." Ali said, sitting down in front of her open laptop. "I know for you it's the norm to be noticed by hot guys—"

"Now he's *hot*?"

Allison cocked an eyebrow. "Are you really gonna argue that he's not? I mean, yes, he's riddled with tattoos, but that body . . . Come on? And you have to admit, despite what you may think of him, he *is* good-looking."

God, was he ever. The more Allison thought about it, the more her insides fluttered. She went on to argue that she could admit her annoying editor was pretty hot too. It didn't mean anything.

"I sincerely hope you're not even considering doing anything with this guy—"

Allison scoffed before her sister could even finish. Leave it to Lila to take the edge off any of this by saying something so utterly laughable. It really had Allison giggling now. She explained that all she'd done was interview the guy and had kept it as professional as possible. Then she added, "You have to understand this is completely new for me. Unlike you, I'm not used to guys noticing and remembering me, much less guys like him."

Instantly, Lila was rolling her eyes. "Ex-cons, you mean? So, what *did* they do time for?"

Explaining about Rodney's boring ole grand-theft-auto charges, Allison smiled inwardly because she knew what Lila would think of her finding Leonardo's charges far more intriguing. But feeling wicked because she did like to tease her sister, she decided to use Leonardo's nickname of choice instead of his real name. "Get this. *Beast* did time for being part of an underground fighting ring."

She explained how he hadn't been fighting when he was arrested but was hauled in with all the others anyway. But she decided to tone it down because, once again, Allison's fascination about this was all too apparent. So, she left out the part about him already being on probation to begin with.

"Underground fighting?" Lila sounded as appalled as Allison expected. "And his name is *Beast*?"

Allison explained that, despite the name he'd been given because of his days in the fight club, he was now using the boxing ring as therapy. She did a little comparing of her sister to *Beast* before going into a rant about the unfairness of underground fighting being illegal. "If two grown-ass people wanna fight for the sake of entertainment and have other *adults* bet on them, then so be it. These laws are all about the government wetting its beak."

The rant went on a little longer, and maybe she was going a little overboard defending the illegal not to mention grisly sport, given what Leonardo had shared about it. Of course, Lila made sure to ask if she was done with her interviewing him and confirmed what Allison already knew: that Lila didn't want her keeping in touch with him if she didn't have to.

Allison attempted to be playful rather than deceitful, but she knew Lila wouldn't be happy about the fact that she wasn't done with him. "Perhaps," she said, lifting a brow but continuing to type on her laptop.

"No perhaps, Ali. I'm serious. If you've got everything you need for your story, then I don't want you staying in touch with this *man*."

And there you had it. Lila was not about to sugarcoat her feelings about Leonardo: a *man* eleven years Ali's senior. Allison hadn't even decided if it was worth arguing about when thankfully Lila changed the subject to talk of them possibly having to find a new place soon.

"Really?" Allison asked, genuinely surprised as she glanced up at her sister.

With Lila on her way to fighting professionally and being so damn good at it, she'd since landed a lucrative endorsement deal. Not that she'd need it if things worked out and Lila ended up with her loaded boyfriend forever. But Allison knew her sister. It'd be a cold day in hell when Lila would allow herself to be dependent on anyone else.

But like the car Lila had bought for Allison, she figured their continuing to live in a low-income apartment building was going to change too. Allison was just surprised Lila was bringing it up this soon.

Lila told her more about Sonny's offer to move them both in with him. Of course, Allison wouldn't balk at the idea of moving into Sonny's big mansion. She just wished her sister didn't seem so apprehensive about it. The girl over thought *everything*.

Lila assured her she was trying to think positive. That it was just a huge decision. "I just wanted to run it past you to see if it's even something you'd be okay with."

Hearing her phone buzz had Allison's heart speeding up. Thankfully, Lila walked back into the kitchen just as Allison's eye read who the text was from. *Leonardo.* Unable to wait until she was somewhere alone, she tapped on her phone screen and read it, confused at first.

Yes, JELLY?

Still confused by the odd text, Allison clicked back to her text because she didn't remember asking him a yes or no question. It's when she noticed the second text she'd written after her goof of sending the one with just his name was still sitting there unsent. Then she remembered how twice he'd asked her not to call him Leonardo—one of the times he'd been oddly adamant about it. It had her giggling suddenly.

Scrolling up to the first one she sent him, she realized she'd used his name in that one too. Was he being facetious about her continued use of Leonardo? Or was he really annoyed by it and, judging by Lila's reaction to his referring to Allison as Jelly, he thought she might be offended by this still? That only made her giggle more.

"What are you giggling about?"

Allison's smile went flat as she glanced up. Just by the way Lila was peering at her, Allison could tell her sister already knew *who* had her smiling so giddily—again.

Attempting to make less of it, she shrugged, hitting send on the text she never sent, then sent a follow-up text that explained the one with just his name was a goof and that she'd thought she sent the second one. "He texted me earlier. I thought I'd responded—"

"He who?" Lila asked, a bit sharply.

"Beast," Ali said simply because she refused to start keeping things from her sister, especially some harmless texts.

"*He's* who you're texting with?"

Ali glanced up at Lila. Okay, maybe she would have to at least be more careful about toning down her inexplicable excitement over some silly texts. But she still wouldn't go the untruthful route. She was doing nothing wrong, and the bottom line was, as much as this might bother Lila, Allison was an adult now.

Still, she'd do her best to put Lila at ease about this. "It's not really texting. I could swear I'd responded to his earlier text with the info he sent me, but I guess I never hit send. So, he was asking if I got the text."

"What else did he say that has you giggling, *Allison*?"

Allison smiled big because it just couldn't be helped. Her heart was still pounding a mile a minute. "He's still referring to me as Jelly. And I already told you it has nothing to do with my butt spread. It just made me giggle to see it written out."

Seeing another text from Leonardo pop up on her phone screen had Allison standing up quickly. She could only keep up the nonchalant act for so long.

"I have to get this story written, at least the first draft, so I can run it past my editor tomorrow," she said, closing her laptop and gathering her things, explaining she'd be doing so in her room.

Unable to help herself, she glanced down at the text preview on her screen.

That's three times now, Ms. Allison or . . .

With her heart at her throat now, Allison felt guilty lying, but there was no way she could share her excitement of what sounded like another facetious text from someone *so* not the type. Mindful that, when she was not being completely forthright, she tended to have diarrhea of the mouth, Allison held up her phone as she started out the room and attempted not to spew.

"See that's all he wanted: to confirm I got his text. I'm not *texting* with the guy, so don't worry. Aside from his *jelly* remark, he was actually very professional. Used some big words too. In fact, he came across as pretty smart. He's not as loathsome as I know you're thinking, Li. But again, you have nothing to worry about. This is probably the last I'll hear from him."

Shut up. Shut up. Shut up!

Talk about *violent* diarrhea of the mouth. Lila appeared to be ready to respond to Allison's spewing words, but fortunately, the tea kettle went off, interrupting the moment. Allison hurried to her bedroom door, stopping just before going in.

She turned to her sister with a big smile before Lila could get back to the subject. "Let me know when we move into that mansion." She winked at Lila then added, "Stop over thinking everything, Sissy. I think you and Sonny are perfect for each other."

After a few more encouraging words from Ali assuring her she truly believed Sonny's feelings for her were genuine, Lila finally smiled and took a deep breath with a shrug. "I'll give it a few days before I decide. But I'll let you know as soon as I do."

With the subject changed successfully, Allison said goodnight and made a quick exit. The moment she was behind the closed door of her bedroom, she was smiling big again as she read the whole text from Leonardo.

> That's three times now Ms. Allison or is it Jelly? As long as I'm Leonardo to you, you'll be one of the two to me. Personally, I prefer Ms. Allison for our professional relationship, but I'll leave it up to you.

This was what she hated about texts. You could never just assume someone was playing around or serious. Being playful in *any* way was *so* unlike the broody man she'd interviewed today. She was more inclined to believe he was serious, possibly even annoyed by her continued defiance of his one request from her.

He *was* doing her a favor. Allison didn't want to ruin this by being unprofessional. Since he'd pointed out that this was what their relationship was, she'd keep it that way. She tapped away at her screen as she always did, as quickly as possible. When she read the text back carefully, she frowned at the number of typos and *incorrect* autocorrects her phone had taken the liberty of making. She fixed the mistakes then read it back again.

My bad, Beast. Personally, I prefer Leonardo. But I'll try to be mindful from here on about what you prefer to be called since I prefer Ali or Allison over the other two options.

She added one more sentence just to say she was putting the questions for him together and should have them to him by the next day. Setting her phone down, she smiled as she placed her hand on her chest. Her silly heart was still thundering away.

It made her think of the only other time she could remember her heart ever doing that. In the beginning of her first semester of her journalism class when she'd met Carson, both her and Jen's jaws had dropped when the professor introduced the editor of the school's paper to the class.

He looked like something straight out of a soap opera. He was tall and well-built with light brown hair that had these natural golden highlights. His eyes were a light sexy gray, and his teeth were so straight and white she first thought him *too* perfect.

For a better part of those first few weeks, her heart had thundered incessantly every time he addressed her or she had to run something by him. That was until he turned into a pompous *jerk*.

Apparently, he didn't like being corrected and didn't take constructive criticism well, even if she had done so in the most polite and well-meaning way possible.

The buzzing of her phone on her dresser pulled her out of her Carson thoughts. Seeing the name on the screen instantly had her heart hammering again. She'd been certain she'd heard the last of *Beast* for tonight. Already chewing the corner of her lip with anxious anticipation, she picked it up and read the text.

Her mouth fell open as she read it. Once again, she had no idea what to make of his puzzling hot-and-cold personality. But then this being a text, she also had no idea how to interpret it.

SIX

BEAST

Downing what was left of the water in his glass, Leo peered at his roommate's too smug expression. "What did you do?"

"I took care of it," Orlando said, laying Leo's phone down on the kitchen counter.

Leo walked over to where his roommate put it down, almost afraid to look at what this asshole did. "I swear to God, O, I will beat your fuck—"

He stopped when he read the words on the text already sent to Allison.

> Why tomorrow? I'm free to chat tonight. Get the questions together and give me a ring. I look forward to it.

Just as Orlando started to chuckle, Leo slammed his glass into the sink. His roommate's stupid smile went flat as chards of glass splattered everywhere.

"What the fuck?"

"What the fuck's right!" Leo barked back, holding out his phone to Orlando. "Fix this shit. I don't want her calling me!"

"What's your problem? You said you wanted to be done with this."

"She's a kid—"

"So what? She wants to interview you, not fuck you. And I thought you said she was a college student. Last I checked, most college students are adults. What's the big deal?"

"I didn't wanna do the interview in the first place, O." Leo huffed as he trudged past Orlando and out the back door because he had a sudden desperate need for air. As expected, Orlando followed close behind. "Now she thinks I'm looking forward to chatting with her because of your dumb ass."

"My dumb ass did you a favor then," Orlando shot back, sounding smug again, but before Leo could retort, he added something even more infuriating. "Wait. What is it about this chick that has you so twisted? When you first told me about the interview, you were weird about it. Then she texted you, and you got all tense and moody as fuck. Look at you now."

Leo froze in place when he realized he was pacing a little too anxiously. He started up again a little slower, trying to be less obvious.

"She's a kid," Orlando said under his breath, more to himself than Leo.

"She's a kid?" Orlando said louder as his and Leo's eyes met and Orlando's went wide. "Is it because—?"

"No," Leo snapped as he stalked back inside the house.

"Is that why—?"

"It's not," Leo said, his insides turning when he glanced at his phone still on the counter and saw he had a text from Allison.

Orlando must've noticed Leo staring at his phone because he dropped his previous questions for a new one. "Did she respond?"

Leo grabbed the phone before his friend could even think about trying to get it. "Doesn't matter. I'm done responding to her. and I'm done talking about this."

He stalked into his bedroom and closed the door behind him. Tossing the phone on the bed without bothering to read it, he did some more infuriated pacing. "Fuck," he muttered under his breath then shook his head.

He'd ignore her. That's all there was too it. If she called or even texted again, he'd ignore her until she got the hint. Answering a few more of her questions via text he could've handled. But now his idiot friend had ruined even that. Leo had to end this now.

As if mocking him, his phone rang before he'd even finished his thought. Leo turned to the bed, refusing to move. Then he remembered it might be his probation officer. Muttering under his breath, he walked over to his bed and picked his phone up. As much as he hated to do it, he dropped it unanswered when he saw the name on the screen.

"God damn it, O," he muttered as he walked to the door.

Locking the bedroom door so Orlando wouldn't get any stupid ideas about answering his phone if it rang again, Leo stalked into his bathroom. He slammed the door shut because the phone was still ringing and the temptation to answer it was already festering.

"You're not doing it," he growled at the infuriated guy in the mirror.

With a nod, he started the shower then pulled off his shirt and stripped out of his shorts and briefs. This shouldn't be so hard—

He froze when he glanced down at the irony of the wording of his thoughts. He'd been so angry and worked up he hadn't realized even frustrated thoughts of her had gotten his cock worked up as well. Truth was, for as much as he kept telling himself she was a kid, after getting an upfront and personal look at her and speaking to her, he knew he was dealing with a much more mature woman than he first thought. She'd handled herself in a professional way, even when she practically snapped at him over the comment about her sister. Those womanly curves any hot-blooded man could appreciate were Leo's weakness. His attempts to chastise himself about having such thoughts for a girl so much younger than he was were quickly squashed when he met up with Rodney after the interview. The guy had wanted to compare notes but not just about the interview. "Did you get a load of the rack under that blouse and the fuck-me-up-against-a-wall ass? Hell yeah, I'd fuck that ass in a heartbeat."

The shameless pervert had even rubbed his dick down over his shorts, evidence that Leo wasn't the only grown-ass man who could visualize such offensive things about this girl. It'd been as eye-opening as it'd been infuriating.

Taking a deep breath, Leo ignored the unwarranted annoyance. This shouldn't be so difficult. Orlando was right about one thing. Allison was a reminder of a time in his life he'd tried desperately to forget for years. But it was more than that and Leo knew it. He had to steer clear of her. There were no two ways about it. Just as he'd been saying for years about all women, he was even more certain about Allison now. She had the very poison it'd take to reawaken the Beast that Leo had managed to sedate for so long.

Seven days. A whole fucking week since he'd stopped responding to her and Allison was *still* texting Leo. She stopped calling after the second time he didn't bother to call or even text her back. He hadn't responded to the call or any of her other texts. But one thing that was becoming very clear about this chick was she was persistent. Orlando was still insisting Leo call her and just be done with it.

"She's a journalist," Orlando reiterated as Leo muttered under his breath when he saw the latest text pop onto his screen. "That's one notch above the bloodthirsty paparazzi. She won't stop until she gets her story. Just call her already. I don't see what the big deal is. Unless..."

"I'm not calling her," Leo said before Orlando could continue. He opened the door to Orlando's truck. "Thanks for the ride. This should be the last time I need you to get me here. Bones said my bike should be ready by tonight. Rodney's dropping me off at his place to pick it up after work."

"No worries. You're on my way to the shop anyway. I can keep dropping you off as long as you need me to."

With a grateful nod, Leo walked away. Truth was there'd been two days in the past week when he'd begun to think maybe Allison had given up because he'd gone the whole day without a single text. Leo would never admit it, but he knew his irritable mood had been because of that. Then the following day she'd sent another, and he'd been beyond relieved. It was the stupidest thing. He had no intention of returning her texts, but something about knowing she was that determined to speak to him added to his already out-of-place intrigue.

He couldn't return her texts. This was what he'd been afraid of from day one. He could not let himself get sucked in. No matter what.

"Hey, stranger."

The voice. The unexpected vision before him. In a snug workout outfit that hugged every curve of her body no less. But more than anything those eyes. If Leo didn't know any better, they were challenging him but to what? It was all so breathtaking Leo hadn't even realized it until it was too late.

He was smiling.

Their eyes locked, and he tried backpedaling his once again baffling reaction to her by wiping the fucking smile off his face. He'd been irritated by her text just a few minutes ago, and now he was smiling like an idiot?

"I take it you've been busy?"

The question didn't carry the same enthusiasm her greeting had. Leo knew it had everything to do with his changing mood and what she was trying to suggest over the more likely reality: why he really hadn't responded to any of her texts and calls—because he'd been ignoring her.

Good. It was better than her knowing the truth. "Yeah, I have actually."

Why?

Why was he incapable of just cutting the cord? Why couldn't he be the dick he normally would be and tell her he hadn't been busy. He just hadn't felt the slightest inclination to return her calls. He was no longer interested in continuing the interview. He was no longer interested in satisfying her in any way.

Because those last three statements were absolute bullshit and he knew it. He started walking toward the area where he'd be doing his training as Allison walked alongside him. "I figured as much. I'm not trying to be pushy, but since you did say you were looking forward to chatting that night—"

"Texting," Leo said before she could finish the thought. "It's better if we do this over texting. That night I did actually get busy, but I think texting is still the best way to go about this."

"Oh." She sounded a little deflated, but Leo refused to continue looking in those eyes.

He stared straight ahead. "I'll start responding to some of the questions you've sent me tonight."

Really? Just like that? He'd gone from being adamant about ever communicating with her again to agreeing to respond to her texts so easily? Fucking hell, it was happening again. Maybe he should just get this over with already the way Orlando kept insisting. Leo still had forty-five minutes before he had to report to his training. He always made sure he got here this early just to be on the safe side.

"Okay, well—"

"Actually." He turned to her and instantly regretted it because, God damn it, he was certain of it now. Every time he got another good look at her this close, it became clearer and clearer that he needed to stay away from her. Or rather he needed to make sure she stayed away from him. She was staring at him now, waiting for him to finish revealing why he'd interrupted her.

Leo glanced around. There were plenty of empty tables at the juice bar, so he turned back to Allison, determined to end this today. "I have a few minutes before I have to start my training. If you want, we can do this now." He motioned over to the tables.

"Oh," she said, lifting her small duffle and unzipping it. "That'd be great. I just . . ." She smiled so sweetly Leo had to look away. "I really don't mean to be so aggressive. It's just that my editor's really been on me about finishing this and well . . ." She paused as they reached a table and took seats across from each other. She pulled her notebook out of her bag. "It's been a challenge so far to impress him with anything, so now that I actually have a chance to, I'm determined not to blow this."

Leo stared at her, taking in what she'd just explained as he was once again caught in her engaging eyes. But he didn't comment. He just nodded, and in the next moment, their eyes locked. Just as he'd suspected and she'd confirmed during that first interview, behind those innocent and sweet eyes there was so much more to this young woman. Leo wasn't just being paranoid or overly cautious about this. This could be disastrous. He'd fought the temptation of answering her calls or responding to any of her texts tooth and nail, and now here he was, not a minute into this conversation already sucked in. As much as he wanted to glare at her—silently send a warning that he was not the kind of guy she wanted to use said determination on—he couldn't.

Eyes like hers weren't meant to be glared at. Not by Leo or anyone else who'd dare to do so in his presence. Oh yeah. He'd been here before. Doing anything else but getting sucked into her eyes was an impossibility he'd never understand. Not then. Not now.

"Okay," she finally said after the long silent moment, shaking her head in what Leo imagined was her attempt to snap out of the insane trance.

Clearing her throat, she brought a hand to her chest then cleared it again.

"You need something to drink? Water?" Leo asked, standing up because he needed to.

She brought her fist to her mouth, still clearing her throat. "Maybe."

"I'm getting a Red Bull." Leo took off the weight-lifting gloves he'd put on in the truck and dropped them on the table. "You want one too or just a water?"

"Red Bull sounds good." She reached in her backpack and pulled out what looked like a coin purse. "Here—"

Already shaking his head, Leo turned toward the counter. "I got it."

Once he reached the counter, Leo took a long deep breath as he waited for the attendant. Thankfully, she asked him to give her a minute while she finished unpacking some energy bars from a box. Leo nodded, needing the minute—maybe more—before he went back to sitting across from Allison. Glancing around, he did a double take when from his peripheral vision he saw Allison had company at the table now. A guy he'd seen around the gym plenty of times sat across from her. Possibly a trainer. He was smiling big—too big.

"Thanks for waiting." The girl behind the counter pulled Leo's attention away from Allison.

Focusing on the girl's eyes, he did what up until just recently he usually had to force. Now was no different. He smiled. "I'll take two Red Bulls." The girl smiled back, but despite what might be considered an attractive shade of hazel eyes, they had nothing on what Allison's eyes did to him. It was maddening, so he kept his eyes on the juice girl even as she walked away, focusing on her ass. She was youthful-looking enough. Early to mid-twenties at least. Still, she didn't look nearly as off-puttingly young as Allison *should* to Leo.

"We're out of Red Bull at the moment." The girl walked back from the fridge, holding two cans of something else. "Our delivery today is late. But we have these. They're pretty good."

Leo glanced down at the cans she set down on the counter then at her nametag and made note of it. Paulina. "Are they flavored?"

"Not really. But they don't taste much different from Red Bull. Biggest difference . . ."

The giggling behind him distracted Leo momentarily. Then the guy chuckled, and instantly Leo was focusing on what the guy was saying and not a word of what Paulina said.

". . . I'm serious," the guy said. "I literally have to wrestle it off him to wash it now. It's like his security blanket. You have to get me another."

"I can do that," Allison chirped.

Leo's eyes went from the cans on the counter to Paulina, who was looking at him as if she'd just asked him something. "I'm sorry, say again?"

"Do you still want them?"

"Yeah." He nodded, feeling stupid as he pulled out his wallet and opened it.

He paid then took another deep breath before turning around. Seeing how comfy the guy had made himself in front of Allison was more annoying than it should have been, and Leo knew this. Rolling his neck, he reminded himself he had no business feeling anything when it came to someone getting chummy with this girl. Never mind that Leo's duffle bag was sitting in the chair next to the guy and his gloves were right under the guy's nose. A clear sign that Allison wasn't sitting alone.

He arrived at the table just as the guy reached across the table and touched the charm hanging on her necklace. Leo placed the energy drink in front of Allison and opened it for her.

"You're in my seat," he said, opening his own drink.

The guy's head jerked up, took one look at Leo, and was on his feet immediately. "I'm sorry. I didn't realize—"

"No, that's okay," Allison said too quickly. "I'm just doing a quick interview before my workout."

The guy nodded, offering a friendly smile to Leo. The most Leo could do was refrain from glaring, but a smile wasn't happening. It'd been one thing for the guy to take his seat and chat away with her. But it was a whole fucking other thing to be putting his hands anywhere near someone who may or may not be his girl. Instead of smiling back, Leo was barely able to muster a nod before taking his seat across from Allison.

"I'll see you in a few," Allison said.

The guy didn't smile quite as big as he had earlier. Glancing at Leo one last time then at Allison again, he nodded, smiling nervously now with a weak wave. "Yeah, I'll see you later."

"He's my trainer," Allison explained, glancing down at her energy drink, "for my CrossFit training." She glanced back up at Leo curiously. "They didn't have Red Bull?"

Leo shook his head. "They're out, but she said it's pretty much the same thing."

Allison studied the can a little more before looking up at him again. "Energy drinks tend to make me jittery, and Red Bull is the only one I've ever had, but I guess if it's the same thing . . ."

She shrugged, taking a sip of it. Leo took a sip of his own, glancing away to avoid being witness to any possible lip licking.

"The first day really kicked my butt," she said as Leo turned back and was instantly drawn back into those eyes. "Nestor worked me out so hard I was aching for days. But as much as I hate it during, I love how I feel after."

Again, Leo stared at her without comment, just as he had when she explained about her determination to impress her editor. "I haven't decided if I'll be doing this long term," he said.

Allison's brows pinched in confusion from his comment, and it nearly had Leo smiling again. "It was one of the questions you texted me. I only have a half hour now, so I thought I'd move it along."

"Oh." She sat up straighter, taking another sip of her drink, then cleared her throat again. "Yeah, sorry."

"I don't have much family either," he said, remembering one of her other questions. "So, there's no one really to approve or disapprove of my being a boxer."

"No wife or kids," she asked then cleared her throat—again—before glancing down at her notebook to write something down and added, "No girlfriend?"

"No wife. No kids. No fucking way."

The last comment had her looking up. Her expression was a strange one. The brow lifted, but to his surprise, there was a twinkle in her eyes. "Are you aware you do that?"

"Do what?" he asked, confused.

"I noticed it the first time I interviewed you, and you've been doing it today again. It's like a subconscious habit." Her eyes brightened, and that alone had his heart rate accelerating. "You start to smile but then almost instantly. . ." She snapped her fingers. "It morphs into an almost angry glare."

He shook his head, scrambling to decide whether he should smile or glare. She'd just called him on it. Clearly, just as he had with her, she'd been paying close attention to all his expressions, even the ones he kept letting slip. "Hadn't noticed," he said, settling on a deadpan expression.

With a tilt of her head, she smiled again, making it impossible to hide the twitch at the corner of his own lips. Especially now that he knew she was watching so closely.

"Is it a jail thing?" Her expressive eyes went even wider. "I've heard you're not supposed to look people directly in the eyes and keep your emotions to yourself?"

Never in his life had he avoided looking someone straight in the eyes out of fear. At least not until very recently. Only he knew that wasn't the kind of fear she was talking about. Before he could retort, she added something else that had him reeling.

"Because I know you do smile." She indulged him with a playful smirk. "I've seen you do it, and it's a very nice one. You should do it more often."

Allowing the smile to spread across his face this time, had the voice in his head going ape shit. "I've never noticed, but it could be," he lied just to move this along again ASAP. "Is this part of your interview, because I hate to have to remind you again." He glanced at his watch. "Tick tock."

Her smile flattened, and she straightened out again, clearing her throat yet again then chasing whatever was stuck in that sweet throat with another long swig of her drink. He'd been doing it again. With every question she posed, every expression he'd been indulged with, he took in each of her delicate features: her perfectly groomed fingernails and slender fingers, the swell of her bottom lip, and the dramatic way her lashes draped over her big dark eyes each time she blinked, especially when she seemed rattled.

"Okay, so, where were we?"

She glanced down at her notebook; then there it was when she looked up and their eyes met again: that cute tilt of her head and the ever-curious twinkle in her eyes. His head was once again screaming the reminders at him as his heart thumped in his chest.

"No fucking way?"

With no other recourse because they were back to this, Leo nodded but said nothing, regretting now that he'd elaborated on that.

"And you're referring to a girlfriend?" she added.

He was going back to his curt answers. No more elaborating on anything. So, he simply nodded.

"Why's that?"

"Because I don't do girlfriends." Before she could think otherwise, he added, "I haven't had a relationship with one in years that is, and I won't ever again."

Alright, that's enough. What the fuck happened to not elaborating? Oh, that's right. His stupid ass just had to make sure she didn't think he'd meant he did boyfriends. Like it mattered. Fucking idiot! That only added to her already too curious eyes.

"May I ask why?"

Once again, the voice in his head was cursing at him to say no—begging him to just shake his head and leave it at that. But as usual, instead of listening to those voices, before he could think it through further, the words—the scornful thoughts so full of contempt that were supposed to stay in his head—spewed out. "Because women are poison."

SEVEN

Allison

There were a couple of things about Leonardo that Allison had begun to pick up on. Aside from the subconscious habit she'd asked him about, there was something else she couldn't quite put her finger on, but she'd seen it in his eyes more than once now. Not just today but that first day she interviewed him.

Something made him nervous. Almost panicked him. Each time it'd been fleeting because it was obvious he did his best to hide it, but there'd been no missing it the few times Allison had caught it. Like now for instance. He'd made that last declaration with such conviction as if it were fact. Then just as quick, the panic flashed in his eyes as if he might take it back.

Only he didn't.

There was no way Allison *wasn't* biting now. "Women are poison?" She tried not to sound derisive since he was clearly serious.

"They are," he said with finality and without any trace of humor. "But again, I don't think we have time to get into that, and I *know* it's not anything you wanna hear about or need for your story."

"No, it wouldn't be in the story," she agreed, clearing her throat then taking another big sip of her drink as she glanced down at her notebook. "But I wouldn't mind hearing you explain why you think that." She cleared her stubborn-ass throat again then downed another sip before adding. "Not sure if I should be insulted or not."

"Do *you* realize you do that?" His question had her looking up, and to her surprise, his expression had gone soft again. "Is clearing your throat so much then taking a big swig of your drink *your* subconscious habit?" Just like earlier when he'd smiled the first time, her heart pitter-pattered seeing him do it again. "You do that a lot."

She nodded, needing a moment to catch her breath. That smile didn't happen often, but having admitted to him that it was a nice one was a gross understatement. Good *Lord,* when it did happen, it was all-consuming. Just like earlier. Just seeing him walk into the gym had had her heart pounding erratically. All week she'd chickened out about approaching him. Obviously, he'd been ignoring her calls and texts, but she really was desperate to nail this story. So, she'd sucked it up today and just done it. Then they were caught in that . . . She wasn't even sure what to call it, but she'd felt the air completely sucked out of her. Now the smile was doing the same thing to her all over again.

Unlike when he was being all broody and it was difficult to make out, *believe* that something *she'd* done or said would spawn the puzzling hardened tone, there was no doubt about this. His smile was genuine. It was tender, and it was absolutely because of her. But had his amusement with her stupid dry throat really caused this complete change so suddenly?

Just like the panic that had flashed in his eyes more times than Allison could keep track, now there was also something vulnerable about the way he—dare she even think it? *Gazed* at her now. Once again it was fleeting. His gaze didn't morph into a hardened glare this time, but he did seem to catch himself, toning it down significantly.

Letting out a slow subtle breath, Allison lifted her chin, and to her surprise, the amused gleam she'd seen in his eyes before made an appearance again.

"I, uh . . ." She touched her hand to her throat as she annoyingly had to clear it again. "I get dry mouth sometimes, and it spreads to my throat."

Not sometimes. Only when she was incredibly unnerved, but she'd keep that part to herself. Now his smile flattened as his eyes lowered.

"Are you okay?"

Allison glanced down at her hand that was midway to her mouth, holding the can of energy drink, and felt embarrassed when she saw it. Her hand was shaking so visibly there was no way she could deny it. She set the can down a little too hard and it hit the table loudly.

"I'm fine." She touched her clammy forehead because she was suddenly feeling lightheaded, and her thumping heart could no longer be ignored. She'd chalked it up earlier to Leo being the reason it was racing so fast, but there was more to it now.

"You sure?" The concern in his eyes warmed her as much as it mortified her. "You're sweating—a lot."

Allison grabbed a napkin from the dispenser on the table and dabbed her forehead then her neck. Jesus, was she really going to do this? Pass out on the guy? From her rapidly speeding heartbeat, she could tell something *was* wrong.

"How much caffeine did that thing have in it?" Allison motioned to the can in front of her.

Leonardo's eyes were immediately on the can; then he picked his up. "I don't know, but the girl said it was just like Red—" He stopped when the girl walked by, clearing up the table next to them. "Paulina? You said this was just like Red Bull, right?"

The girl turned to him then to Allison, who was still wiping her profusely sweating forehead with what she knew was a shaky-as-shit hand. The girl's eyes widened a bit. "I said it tasted almost the same, but the biggest difference was it had the highest amount of caffeine of any energy drink on the market. I warned you—"

"Oh God." Allison stood up in a hurry. "I'm gonna be sick."

As if she wasn't mortified enough, she rushed to the nearby trashcan because there was no way she was making it to the ladies' room. Barely able to make it to the can, she proceeded to hurl into it loudly. The moment she felt a break in the nausea, at least long enough for her to make it to the ladies' room, she made a mad dash there.

Oh God! Oh God! Oh God! That didn't just happen!

Before she could give it another thought, she was on her knees inside one of the stalls, puking her brains out. When it felt safe to finally just sit her ass down on the cold floor, she did and grabbed toilet paper from the dispenser to wipe off her mouth.

"Are you gonna be okay?" Allison glanced up at *Paulina* from the juice bar, whom she hadn't even noticed standing at the door of her stall. "Your boyfriend is really worried. He wants me to call someone to come in here."

"No, no, no!" Allison said, straightening out and attempting to get up but felt lightheaded again.

Paulina grabbed her by the arm. "Are you sure?" Paulina asked again. "I could get Nellie or Ella for you. They're both here right now."

"No." Allison shook her head adamantly, regretting it instantly when it only made her dizzier, so she stopped. "I'm fine. Really. Between my meds and a protein drink I took before I got here that already had added energy inducers to help with my work out, drinking that energy drink was obviously not a good idea."

She'd leave out that not only had she drunk it, she'd guzzled it each time she'd needed to calm her nerves. The last thing she wanted was for any of this to get back to her worrywart sister, so getting two of the gym's owner's wives involved in this was out of the question.

"I just need to wash my face, and I'll be fine. This isn't the first time this has happened."

Technically true. She'd felt lightheadedness and jitters before from too much caffeine but never anything like today. God, how could she be so stupid? Even a Red Bull, she drank slowly and *never* finished. Anything with caffeine, she drank sparingly. She just figured today a little pep might help with her altered nerves.

"And he's not my boyfriend by the way," Allison explained as she glanced up from the sink, slightly flattered that anyone would even think it. "I was actually interviewing him for my college paper. I'm good now," she added, aware she was still talking a mile a minute. "Can you just please tell him I'm fine and he can go to his training. I'd hate to make him late on my account."

"Okay," Paulina said, not looking the least bit convinced, but Allison *was* feeling a little better.

She smiled at Paulina, trying to reassure her, then looked down at her hand the moment she was alone. Her stupid hand was still shaking, and she took a deep breath. When she looked up into the mirror, she groaned. In her haste to bathe her face in the heavenly cold water, she didn't even think of her makeup. She wasn't wearing a whole lot to begin with. Lila was always very vocal about her annoyance with the girls that got all done up to work out. Clearly, they weren't anticipating working up a sweat as much as they were anticipating trying to pick up guys.

Allison had every intention of getting good and sweaty. She wasn't exaggerating when she'd mentioned Nester working her out good. But she had wanted to look decent in case she finally got the nerve to approach Leonardo again. So, she'd applied a little eyeliner and blended in lip liner. Now any trace of makeup was washed completely clean.

Oh well. She supposed it didn't matter. Leonardo had likely already left to report to his training. He had seemed adamant about not having too much more time. Rinsing her mouth out a few times then wiping the few traces of smeared makeup from the corner of her eyes, she finally walked away and out of the ladies' room.

To her utter surprise, Leonardo was standing just outside the ladies' room, holding her duffle bag. She'd been privy to many of his expressions, but the one on his face at that moment was a new one. Once again, the flash in his eyes was too noticeable. He seemed troubled at first glance, but as he took her in a little more, something changed, and as usual, she had no idea what to make of the odd way he stared at her.

"I'm so sorry."

"About *what*?" she asked at a loss.

"Paulina. She said she warned me more than once that for some people that shit can be way too strong." He shook his head, looking almost wretched. "I don't know how I missed that. I could've warned you."

"It's not your fault," Allison said, attempting to reassure him because he really did look sorry. "I should've known better. I never drink an entire Red Bull much less down it the way I did this drink. It just snuck up on me, I guess, but I'm fine now."

His eyes followed her hand as she attempted to run her fingers through her hair. Then to her surprise, he reached out and helped pull a strand of hair behind her ear. His hand lingered there for a moment until he moved it away, grazing her cheek and making her shiver in the process.

"No, you're not." His concerned eyes went from where he'd just touched her, to her hand, then back to her eyes. "Your hands are still shaking. Maybe you should skip that Cross-Fit thing. Just for today."

Allison had to breathe in deeply to get over what something as simple as his touch did to her. Focusing on what he'd just said, she considered arguing that she was fine enough, but truth was she wasn't feeling it. "Maybe I'll just wait a little. Start the class a little late today."

"I don't think you should." The urgency in his tone surprised her. "I mean . . ." This time *he* did the throat-clearing thing. "You were sick, Ms. Allison. Scared the shit outta me. I mean—"

"Ms. Allison?" She lifted her brow though she couldn't help but smirk. "Really, *Leonardo*? I thought we were past this."

"Hey, Ali!"

They both turned to Nester's voice. He stuck his head out of the training room where she normally did her training. "We're just waiting on you. You ready?"

Allison and Leonardo exchanged a glance before she turned back to Nester. "I think I'm gonna pass today."

"*What?*" Nester asked, as surprised as she'd expected him to be. "It hasn't even been a week." He pushed the door open further then walked all the way out of the training room and toward them. "I know it's hard at first, but I promise you it gets easier."

"I'm just not feeling too well suddenly."

Nester looked her over a bit guardedly, and she suspected Leonardo standing there with her had everything to do with it. "You look fine to me." He smiled a bit suspiciously. "You sure you're not just trying to get out of—?"

"She's not feeling well," Leonardo reiterated for her in a tone so hard it had Allison's head jerking in his direction. "I can vouch for her if there's any doubt, but she's not doing the class today."

There was a quick awkward silence, but Allison killed it before it got too uncomfortable. "I was sick to my stomach just now." She motioned her still shaky thumb to the ladies' room. "And I'm just not feeling up to working out anymore."

Nester's expression changed from stunned by Leonardo's lethal declaration, to concerned. "Are you sick?" He reached out and touched her shoulder. "You okay to drive home?"

"I'm fine. I can drive. I just don't feel up to a major workout."

"Understandable," Nester said immediately then turned to Leonardo. "Didn't mean to imply she was faking it." He laughed nervously then glanced back at Allison. "But you've seen for yourself what the dropout rate has been so far, and it's only the first week."

Allison shook her head with a smile. "Remember I'm a stubborn one. I'm determined to finish this even if it kills me. I'll be here tomorrow, ready to go."

"Good." Nester started to walk away still looking at her. "Not to scare you or anything, but you'll be making up for today."

With a wink, he turned around and rushed back to the training room. Allison turned back to Leonardo, who eyed Nester then turned to her. "Shouldn't you be at your training?" she asked, suddenly concerned. "I don't wanna get you in trouble."

Leonardo shook his head. The softer concern in his eyes from earlier was gone now, replaced with his usual hardened expression. "I'm good. Trainers never get there on time anyway. We usually have a good fifteen to twenty minutes to warm up before they show up."

"Still." Allison shook her head. "I'm okay now, and with my luck, today will be the first time they're there on time. I don't want to cause you any problems. Thank you for waiting to see if I was okay. I really am."

"And you're sure you're okay to drive?"

"Absolutely." She took a deep breath, grateful that she really was feeling better. "But lesson learned. I'm done with energy drinks. Never again." She saw him wince, but before he could start apologizing again, she remembered something else. "Listen. My sister worries, like too much about *everything* when it comes to me. Can you, uh . . . not mention what happened today to anyone? You know like Gio or anyone that might mention it to her?"

"I'm not much for talking." His expression softened. "I don't usually do too much chatting with anyone about anything other than what's necessary."

Allison smiled as he nodded a silent goodbye and began walking away. *Good to know.* Not just because she didn't want today's mortifying incident to get back to Lila but *all* of this. This was way too close to Lila's big fight, so Allison didn't want any of it getting back to her: their texting, her continued interaction with this man, every bit of it, which reminded her . . .

"Leonardo," she called out, going after him.

He slowed and turned to her. His expression wasn't exactly an inviting one now. Then she remembered another thing and smiled big. "Uh . . . I mean Beast." She caught up to him where he stood peering at her with a vacant expression. "Will you be here early again tomorrow? Or would you rather we finish the interview via text?"

Assuming.

She was doing it again, using the skills she'd been taught by her journalism professor and teachers since high school. You never confirmed whether you had the go-ahead to interview or further question a source. You only confirmed when and how would be best to move forward with it. Was it pushy? Yes, but it came with the territory. If she wanted to be successful in this business, compete with the multitude of other journalists out there trying to get the story first, she had to perfect the art of subtle aggression.

Bracing herself, Allison waited for a response because Leonardo didn't say anything for a moment.

"This next week isn't good for me. It's why I was hoping we could knock this out today."

"When *is* good for you? I'll wait until I have to."

His eyes swept up and down her slowly; then oddly he closed them for a second and took a deep breath. "I'll respond to the questions you sent me when I can get to them."

"But I have more," she said before he could dismiss her because it felt like he was about to do just that.

It wasn't the first time she'd seen him work his jaw, but just like the other times she'd seen him do it, it did something to her. She should feel bad. Clearly, it was a sign that he was agitated. Instead, it excited her because, despite the agitation and her initial fear that he was dismissing her, he still hadn't.

This was another thing she'd begun to pick up on about him. He wasn't nearly as hard as the first impression she'd had of him, not nearly as hard as it appeared he may want her to think he was, which only made his strange behavior all the more curious to her. His sticking around to make sure she was okay and seeing the genuine remorse about her reaction to the energy drink debacle had given way to a hint of a softer side he hid well. Though not well enough.

His body language screamed he was done with the interview, done with any more questions, and done with *her.* But if she was right about his softer side, he wouldn't be dismissing her just yet.

"Send them over," he said gruffly. "I'll get to them when I can."

Like when he let a smile escape then quickly snuffed it, Allison did the same with the huge smile that spread across her face as soon as she caught it. She wasn't sure what his reason was for doing so, but in her case, she didn't want him to know she was on to him.

"Thank you." She bit her lower lip to hide how smug she felt.

Her journalism professor would be proud. Most would shy away from being so persistent with such a daunting and seemingly unapproachable *source*. Yet Allison had managed to get him to agree to answer all her questions more than once now.

Despite the mortifying incident that interrupted their interview, Allison walked away feeling triumphant.

EIGHT

BEAST

"Why hadn't you told me?" Kit demanded as she eyed Leo while climbing into the passenger side of his truck. "You're Beast? You're La Fiera?
 Well, shit.
 "Not sure what you're talking about."
 "Cut the BS! I knew you'd try to deny it or play dumb. I did my research, mister! This is huge and you kept it from me."
 "For good reason," he said, squeezing the steering wheel and gulping hard as he stared straight ahead.
 "But why?" Her uncharacteristically hard demeanor waned to a near whine that almost had him smiling. "I thought we were friends. I wanna go see you—"
 "No." He turned to her with a purpose, and any chance of smiling was long gone. "That'll never happen."

The window behind Kit shattered loudly, and she screamed—

With a sharp flinch, Leo jerked awake. It took a minute to figure it out as he lay there, breathing hard and feeling his heart thud against his chest. But when he did, he nearly growled. It was happening again and he knew exactly why.

He hadn't agonized about this, much less dreamed about it in a very long time. Not until . . .

Something had to give. This was fucking ridiculous. Why couldn't he just say no to her? Why couldn't he put his foot down the way he normally would? What the hell was his problem?

Tapping his phone screen on his nightstand, he yawned with a frown when he saw it was only two a.m. The bottle of Nyquil next to the phone was a reminder of how shitty he'd been feeling when he hit the hay, and he wasn't feeling much better now.

He rolled onto his side, tucking his pillow tightly against him and instantly feeling the heavy slumber sink in fast. *Good.* Closing his eyes, he did his best to think of work. His training. *Anything* else but *her* and that damn dream that woke him.

Despite his body being so ready to just give in, it took him a while to finally succumb to the exhaustion.

"I hear you're into virgin pussy now?" Orlando asked as Leo walked into the shop. "What's the matter? Threesomes with your groupies ain't cutting it for you anymore?"

Unwilling to fuel his inane comments, Leo ignored them and asked about what he was there for. "Did we get the delivery?"

"Yeah, in the safe." Orlando leaned back into the engine of the Mustang he was working on. "Seriously, man, Bones said he saw that same girl getting in your truck again. Is that who you've been with all night? Why you're late?"

"Nope. Just gave her a ride."

It was all he'd give him. What Leo did on his down time was his own damn business. He started to work the safe open.
"Yeah, but it's not the first time, right? And—"
"She's a kid, O," Leo said, trying not to sound as annoyed as this line of questioning was beginning to make him feel. "I've had plenty of virgin pussy, but I don't do kids."
"C'mon. I don't care how young she is. Any girl who goes by Clit is just asking to get laid."
"It's Kit, you idiot." Leo swung the safe door open and pulled out the package of cocaine. "Did you inspect this?" he asked because he was done talking about Kit.
Orlando was quiet for a second then cracked up. "Bones is an asshole. He swore up and down it was Clit. He even said she—"
Leo didn't bother looking up or giving him the satisfaction of appearing the least bit interested in what he didn't finish saying. Instead, he started to inspect the bag of drugs.
"You lost, sweetheart?"
Leo pushed the stash back into the safe at the sound of Orlando's question. They got street whores in there all the time, looking to suck dick for a hit. Leo couldn't—
"Beast?"
His head jerked around at the sound of Kit's voice because she **should not** be there. But his breath caught when his eyes met Allison's eyes instead. "I just wanted to talk to you."
His head was spinning now. It was Allison standing at the door of the shop, but it was Kit's voice he was hearing. He glanced around to make sure Kit really wasn't there and he wasn't just confusing things. He had taken a hit earlier. That had to be it. He wasn't losing his mind.
"I just wanted to talk to you." The tears began trailing down her face.

"*What do you mean?*" His heart started to pound with an unreasonable ache, but he was frozen to the spot because there was no doubt about it now.

It was Kit's voice she was speaking in. Only then did he realize she was clutching her chest and there was blood spreading around the fabric under her hand. "*I just wanted to talk to you.*"

Leo shook his head, still not understanding. "She said she just wanted to talk to you, man," Orlando explained.

"*No.*" The sound of his voice was barely audible because he understood now and something was squeezing his windpipe.

"She said to tell you—"

"*No!*" Surprised that his voice was working loud and clear again, he said it again even louder. "*No!*"

"She wanted me to tell you—"

"*Shut the fuck up!*"

The door was shoved open just seconds after Leo's eyes shot open. He still wasn't even fully awake when the glare of his bedroom light hit his eyes, making him squint in reaction.

"What the fuck?" Orlando asked, holding a bat over his head.

Nine, his other roommate, was right behind him, holding a wrench. The moment it hit Leo that he'd just woken from a nightmare screaming like a little bitch, he was frowning in annoyance, despite his still pounding heart.

"I think I took too many meds." Leo sat up on the side of the bed.

From the screen of his phone that lit up the moment he touched it, he could see it was almost six now. He was done trying to sleep.

"*What?*" Nine asked, as exasperated as this was beginning to make Leo feel. "You were fucking dreaming?"

"I guess." Leo shrugged. "I don't know." He stood up, trying desperately to squelch the ache in his heart.

"What the hell were you dreaming about?" Nine asked.

"I don't remember."

One glance in Orlando's direction, and Leo knew his best friend knew the truth. "Almost time to get up anyway," Orlando said.

"Bullshit, it's still dark," Nine said, walking back out the door. "I'm going back to bed. Try and keep your shit down," he added loudly.

Orlando stopped at the door. "You okay?" Leo nodded, feeling stupid but didn't say more. "Need to talk about anything?"

"Nope."

His friend knew him too well to keep pushing, so he didn't. "I'm making breakfast, you want some?" he asked as he walked out the door.

"Yeah." Leo walked toward his bathroom, still feeling shook up as fuck, not to mention even more congested than he had last night. It was a wonder he'd slept at all. "I'll be out after I shower."

He stopped before walking in and went back to his phone. Sure enough, there it was when he checked: a text from Allison. Without even reading it, he hit delete. If he'd suspected it before, the morning's rude awakening was just further proof. For whatever reason, this *random* girl was beginning to fuck with his head—making him see and feel things he'd vowed to let go. If everything he'd started to feel already just from being around her a few times hadn't done it, the dreams had. He was done dealing with the little reporter. For good this time.

NINE

Allison

Apparently, she'd jumped the gun. Smug had never been Allison's thing, and now she felt stupid for feeling even the least bit the day Leonardo agreed to stay in touch, even though he'd ignored all her previous texts and calls. It'd been almost two weeks since she'd had any contact with him again. At first, she thought maybe he was just avoiding her since he was obviously back to not returning her texts or calls.

After several days of not seeing him at the gym, she'd finally broken down and asked Gio as casually about Leonardo as she could. He'd at least confirmed that Allison had been wrong about what she'd begun to suspect: that Leonardo was ducking behind punching bags or diving under boxing rings to avoid being seen by her because she hadn't seen him at all in days. He'd been sick. Bronchitis to be exact. Bad enough that the doctor had signed off on him taking the week off.

But after coming in this past Monday just to see him and he still wasn't back, she'd given up on him. At least for now. She had too much going on this week with work, a paper with a looming due date, and Leonardo's wasn't the only story she was working on. On top of it all, she'd also had her hands full in the last couple of weeks getting settled into her new home. Lila had finally agreed to just take the plunge and move in with Sonny, but only after Allison had been accosted by the paparazzi outside their apartment building more than once. They'd do anything to get the story on her increasingly famous boxing sensation sister and her superstar baseball-player boyfriend.

So, Allison had gone from living in the projects in a rundown neighborhood to a mansion in Los Feliz, surrounded by other mansions owned by equally rich and even famous homeowners. Despite everything else going on in her life, Leonardo had constantly plagued her mind.

But she'd just have to set trying to get that interview with him aside until she could catch up on all her other assignments. It was Thursday now, and since she didn't have Leonardo's story ready, she'd have to push up the other one she'd been neglecting.

"How we doing with that connection of yours?" Allison asked as she sat down next to Jen in the computer lab.

"I'm waiting on a call. But get this. I mentioned you interviewing the work-release guys over at the gym to Marcelo, and he said that was a good place to start for this story."

Allison peered at her, not quite understanding. Marcelo was Jen's older brother. He'd been in and out of trouble for years until he finally did what Jen had thought was the smartest thing he could do and enlisted in the Army. He'd since completed his tour and hadn't reenlisted. Now it seemed he was reconnecting with the wrong crowd again. It was why they'd asked him about the drug dealing on campus, a story Allison and Jen had been chasing for weeks.

Remembering Gio's speech about the strict criteria they had for the work-release contenders, hearing what Marcelo had suggested was a little disappointing. "He thinks Leonardo or Rodney are involved in this?"

Jen smiled, shaking her head. She explained how Marcelo thought guys like Rodney and Leo, who've done time, might know more about the top guys running the show on the outside, since, on the inside, guys with heavy sentences feel like they have nothing to lose and do a lot of talking. "You think you can get another interview with them and slip in the questions—off the record?"

Allison frowned, remembering her failing efforts to get in touch with Leonardo again. "I might with Rodney. But I'd have to go down there and find him. I don't have his phone number like I do Leonardo's. That guy hasn't returned any of my calls or texts in over a week, and before you ask, yes, I've been persistent."

"Well, you did say he was the more reserved of the two. Oh!" Jen's eyes went wide with excitement. "You said Rodney flirted obnoxiously, right?" Jen fluttered her lashes with a smirk. "Remember, if it takes a little flirting to get your story, so be it. Maybe Leonardo will give Rodney your contact info so he'll call you if Leonardo thinks it'll stop you hounding him."

"Hmm." Allison thought about that then pulled her phone out of her backpack. "Maybe."

After all the other texts Leonardo had ignored, she refused to put too much thought into this one. He'd likely be ignoring it too. But Jen had a point. He just might respond if he thought it'd get her off his back. Tapping away at her screen, she put a quick text together then read it back silently.

Hi, Leonardo. Can you please give Rodney my number and ask him to call or text me? I never got his number. Thanks!

She hit send without giving it another thought. In spite of her heartbeat speeding up because this was the first text she'd allowed herself to send him in days, she wouldn't be holding her breath or getting her hopes up. She felt ridiculous now for thinking, even for a second, that she'd begun to read more into the way he looked at her.

The very thought had a flush of heat shooting up her neck and onto her face. That such a complicated, mysterious man like Leonardo would have the time or inclination to even look at her with anything else but professional interest was so absurd it embarrassed her.

Pretending to dig in her back pack and glad Jen was busy typing something on her computer keyboard, Allison took her time, willing the flush to pass. Last thing she wanted was for Jen to notice her reddened face.

Jen caught her up on some more of what Marcelo had told her, which wasn't a whole lot. Allison logged onto the computer and typed up some of the notes she'd taken in her notebook.

An hour later she still hadn't heard back from Leonardo when she saw Carson enter the lab.

"Shit," she muttered.

"What?" Jen glanced up.

"Hunker down," Allison said, doing just that, and Jen followed suit.

"Why?"

"It's Carson. I was hoping to avoid him until I had to see him in class in a few days. He's gonna ask about the story again, and I still don't have anything new to add."

"Leo didn't respond?" Jen asked.

"No," Allison said, shaking her head with a frown.

Then she had an idea. This was around the time Drew worked out at the gym. She pulled out her phone and tapped away again, asking her if she was there. Drew's response was immediate. Yes.

This time Allison put a little more thought into her text. Lila was close with most of the wives of the 5th Street owners—her bosses. But Charlee, Drew's best friend, was one she spoke least of since she wasn't at the gym most days like some of the other wives. Still, Allison wasn't sure just how close Charlee was to the other women. She had to be close to Nellie since they were sisters-in-law. She wasn't ready to ask Drew just yet to keep this from getting back to Lila. For all she knew, she'd never get another moment alone with Leonardo. So, calling attention to her interest in speaking to him—secretly—would probably raise more brows than not.

Can you tell me if the guys I interviewed are there today? The ones I pointed out to you before?

Allison continued to hunker, hoping not to be seen by Carson. He'd since sat down on the other side of the room, seemingly oblivious of her presence. She waited a few minutes this time for Drew's response. It made her wonder if Drew wasn't walking around looking for them or, worse, asking someone about them and telling them why.

Only good thing was Lila wasn't at the gym today. So at least Allison was sure Drew wouldn't ask her. Finally, Drew responded again, and Allison read it quickly.

Yep, they just walked in a few minutes ago and ROWR! The one you said was hot is looking fine as wine.

Of course, that had Allison's insides stirring, but it also made her frown in disappointment. She'd assumed maybe he was in training when she'd sent the text over an hour ago. That it was why he hadn't responded. Now she knew that wasn't the case. As obnoxiously flirty as Rodney had been, she thought he would've called or texted her as soon as Leonardo gave him her number. Again, assuming Leonardo had bothered to even read her text.

Another text popped up on her screen, making Allison's heart thud. But she was back to frowning when she saw it was just Drew again.

Well, shit. Now I'm craving a glass of wine, but I can't unless I skip dinner for that ONE glass since that'll tap me out on my calorie allowance for today. THANK YOU, ALLISON! >.<

Giggling, Allison responded to apologize with a sad face but was glad the focus was off what she'd initially asked about. They went back and forth a couple more times with Allison letting Drew know she might stop by the gym in a bit and Drew saying she'd look out for her.

The second she finished sending her last text, Allison began wrapping things up.

"I'm gonna make a break for it." Allison glanced over the computer screen to see if Carson was still there. "Drew just confirmed Rodney is at the gym right now, so I'm going for it."

"Cool." Jen glanced over her screen as well. "I think he left. I don't see him, do you?"

"No," Allison said, relieved about not having to get too sneaky.

Zipping up her backpack, she stood up and swung it over her shoulder. "I'll call or text you and let you know what I got."

Jen held up a hand for Allison to high five. "Do work, partner. And remember to flutter those lashes if you have to."

"All over it," Allison said, high-fiving her before walking away.

She'd made it all the way out of the lab and into the main hallway of the building when she heard Carson. "Ali!"

"Damn it," she muttered under her breath as she slowed then turned to see him speed up toward her.

"I'm glad I saw you," he said as he approached her.

"I still haven't finished with the story. But it's where I'm headed now. To interview—"

"That's fine, Ali." He shook his head as he reached her. "It's not what I was gonna ask about. Take your time with that. There's no rush."

Allison nodded, relieved and a bit curious now. Aside from anything related to the class, they'd never really discussed anything else.

"You look cute by the way." He smiled awkwardly as he glanced up and down at her outfit. Before Allison could thank him about the uncharacteristic compliment, he went on. "The lecture tonight, Dr. Rosenbaum's lecture on investigative journalism . . . You're going to that, right?"

"Oh yeah." Allison glanced down at her watch. "I've been looking forward to it actually. And . . . thank you." She felt weird about adding that when the moment had passed, but she touched her skirt so he'd know what she was talking about.

"You're welcome." He smiled a bit awkwardly again, glancing away. "I'm going tonight too. A few of us are, and then we were planning on grabbing a bite to eat after and discussing the lecture. Nothing fancy, just a burger or something. Feel like joining us? I'm always up for a good debate."

He winked, smiling bigger this time, lessening the awkwardness. Allison smiled, despite still feeling stunned. At least he'd mentioned a few of them, meaning this was not his way of asking her out. Or was it? "I, uh . . . suppose," she said because he caught her so off guard she didn't have time to give it much thought. "I mean, do you know where yet? I could just meet you guys there."

"No, we usually just wing it. But if you meet up with us, we'll watch the lecture together then just decide when it's over where to head to."

"Okay."

"Great," he said before she could say more. "I'll text you when I get there tonight so we can meet up."

A few classes nearby let out, and Carson was quickly approached by two of the other students from their journalism class. Glad for the interruption, Allison said she had to get going and walked away.

The whole way to her car, Allison couldn't shake how befuddling Carson's unexpected invitation, coupled with the compliment, felt. She wasn't sure what she was more surprised about: the fact that Carson had gone out of his way to invite her to do something outside of school or that she wasn't as thrilled as she would've imagined being just a few months ago.

Once behind the wheel of her car, she turned it on, feeling her insides do a little summersault in the process. Only she knew it had nothing to do with Carson's invitation. Turning her car on had just reminded her where she was headed and who'd she be seeing soon. She knew Rodney had nothing to do with her jittery insides either.

⁕

Halfway to the gym, Allison was second-guessing her decision to not go home and change before heading to 5th Street. Ever since the makeover, she'd been trying to get up on the latest fashion. She'd never been one to care much about that stuff, but she figured it was a good time to make a little effort. Now that she lived in uber-trendy Los Feliz, she got to see a lot of the absolute latest in fashion just by walking around the shopping district with all the fancy boutiques.

Though she refused to pay the astronomical prices those expensive boutiques charged. Jen's very talented seamstress mom could recreate some of the trendy outfits they'd seen. The plaid tennis skirt she had on now was something she'd seen in the window of those boutiques and around school. She thought the look was cute, but at her request, the skirt was not as short as the ones she'd seen on some of the girls at school. Still, it was shorter than she was used to wearing. And while she'd seen other girls wearing the skirts with long-sleeved spandex crop tops, Allison hated how much attention it brought to her boobs. But both Jen and even Lila had assured her that the whole outfit along with the thigh-high socks and short boots was cute and the in thing for girls her age. She knew Lila wouldn't hold back if she thought the look was slutty. But it still felt odd walking into the gym, wearing a skirt versus her usual workout outfit.

Determined to get this over with and stop obsessing about why Leonardo had chosen to just ignore her, she walked into the gym, holding her chin up. The first thing she was accosted with when she turned the corner toward the area she knew they trained was Rodney's wolfish grin as he took her in.

She expected nothing less, no matter what she'd been wearing, but she couldn't help feeling visually assaulted anyway. She responded with an equally big smile because she'd be doing exactly what Jen had suggested: using her womanly charm to get what she needed. Though of course she'd only go so far. She wasn't about to give him a reason to disrespect her. But she didn't see the harm in smiling sweetly.

Leonardo saying something to him instantly distracted her. Allison felt her face heat when it was clear by the way the other guy with them turned to look at her that they were talking about her. Maybe Leonardo was just now telling Rodney about her text? What else could they possibly be saying?

She knew it wouldn't be unheard of for guys to be exchanging smartass or even lewd comments as they watched a girl on her way to interact with them. But unlike Rodney, who continued to smile widely at her when he turned to her again, Leo was doing anything but. In fact, much like the very first time she'd noticed him, she might even say he looked disgusted.

Thank God she'd texted him about Rodney earlier. At least he should have a pretty good idea of why she was there. It wasn't to see him in case that was the reason for the irritated expression.

Taking a deep breath just before she reached them, she smiled big. "Hey, guys."

"Well hello, Allison," Rodney said, his eyes taking a full sweep of her from top to bottom. "Don't you look incredibly sweet today."

"Thank you." Willing her cheeks not to turn bright red, she turned to Leo. "Did you get my text?"

Allison had seen many of this broody man's glares. But the one she was treated to now as he removed his lifting gloves was without question the worst she'd seen so far. Then she remembered his lack of response and that glare might be his way of saying, *Which one? You've sent so many.*

"The one I sent earlier," Allison clarified as he dropped the gloves in a tote and started toward her, "the one about—"

"It's lunch time," Leo said, interrupting her. "How 'bout you and I grab something to eat."

He'd ignored her texts all this time, and now he wanted to do lunch and expected her to just drop everything? "No thanks," she said, lifting her chin. "I'm not hungry."

His indifferent shrug was almost insulting until he added, "We can finally finish that interview."

She peered at him for a moment, still confused by his sudden change of heart, then remembered. "Oh, that reminds me. I actually need to talk to—"

His suddenly towering over her with such a lethal glare had the words catching in her throat. "You're not talking to him, Jelly." He turned to the other two guys, who seemed as surprised by this as Allison was. "It's about that time, right? I'll see you guys back here in an hour."

When he turned his attention back to her, she did her best to match the glare; though her jittery insides didn't make it easy.

"Just walk outside. I'll explain out there."

It felt more like an order than a request, but her curiosity had piqued too much to argue. "*Fine*." She huffed, trudging alongside him, beyond curious now and a little excited about finding out what the heck this was about.

TEN

BEAST

Thankfully, all it took was a couple of other girls in tight spandex outfits to walk by for Lenny and Squiggy to start gnawing at their fists. It was a big enough distraction to give Leo enough time to walk Allison away from them without them asking questions.

"Explain what?" Allison asked as soon as they stepped outside the gym.

"Trust me. You do not want that guy to have your number."

Just like that, the animated little brows and those eyes were at it again. "What do you mean? I just wanted to ask a few more questions for my story."

"It really is my lunchtime." He glanced around the parking lot. "I'd offer to drive you somewhere, but I'm on my bike and only have the one helmet. We can walk across the street and get some tacos. I can explain about Rodney while we eat."

Allison nodded, understandably still looking a little perplexed. Taking a deep breath as they silently walked through the parking lot, Leo decided he'd just have to suck it up and do this. He'd begun to consider doing this the moment he walked into the gym today and overheard Rodney—once again—talking about how much he needed to get laid. For a moment today, despite Leo's irrational annoyance over reading Allison's text, he thought maybe this would get rid of her for good. As much as the very thought nearly sickened him, he knew he could pawn her off on Rodney, who'd be more than happy to oblige. But the more the horny bastard went on so obnoxiously about what he'd do to every girl who walked by, the longer Leo put off mentioning Allison's text to him.

Rodney's comments about what seeing Allison did to his cock the moment she walked into sight today had sealed it. No fucking way was Leo giving him her number, not without giving her fair warning first. If she still wanted the douche calling after she'd been warned, then that was on her. Though she'd have to give him her number herself because Leo sure as fuck wouldn't be doing it, *regardless*.

"Is he dangerous?" Allison asked as they reached the stop light. "Because Gio said they do an extensive background check on all the workers."

"Not in the sense that I think he'd be out to *hurt* you." Leo stepped off the curb when the light turned green. "He's just a perverted prick with only one thing on his mind at *all* times. It's all he thinks and talks about, so I thought I'd warn you first. If you heard half the shit that comes out of that guy's mouth, I'm pretty sure you'd rethink giving him your number."

"About me?" she asked wide-eyed as they reached the taco place.

"About every girl he's ever around." Leo held the door open for her.

She walked into the small but busy restaurant, and Leo walked in behind her. *What I'd give to bend her over in that school-girl outfit and fuck her with it on.* Rodney's exact comment as she'd walked toward them today had Leo grinding his teeth again. As much as Leo hated to admit it, the outfit did have that look exactly. She wasn't the only girl he'd seen wearing something similar lately, so he knew it was a trend. The thought that there was a miniscule chance that she'd worn the outfit for Rodney, had Leo grinding his teeth even harder.

They ordered their food at the counter. Leo motioned for her to go first. Clearing her throat, she glanced up at the menu then began ordering. "I'll have one *asada* taco, one *buche* taco, and a diet soda."

"They're the little ones," Leo informed her, knowing two of these little tacos would be an appetizer for him.

"I know." She smiled. "That's all I want."

Leo stared at her for a moment until she glanced away. Then he turned to the girl behind the counter. "I'll take three *al Pastor,* a*sada,* and *carnitas* tacos. Three of each.*"*

Allison tried handing him a ten-dollar bill, to which Leo shook his head, handing the girl his debit card. "You already paid for my energy drink last time."

Leo squeezed his eyes shut. "Yeah, please don't remind me about that."

"It wasn't your fault," she said with a chuckle.

"It was."

It really was. If he hadn't been so busy trying to listen in on Allison and the trainer's conversation, he might've heard *Paulina's* warning.

"No, it wasn't." Allison insisted as they took their drinks and walked to a booth together. "It was mine for gulping that drink down the way I did. Something I *never* do with energy drinks."

That piqued his curiosity. "So, why'd you do it that day?"

They slid into a booth across from each other, and he took in her sweet timid smile. "I was nervous. It was why I kept clearing my throat so much. Remember you called me on it just before I had to make a mad dash to the trash can?"

Just like all the times it'd happened before, Leo didn't even realize he was smiling. Before he could hastily wipe it off his face, because he remembered her calling *him* on that, he toned it down instead.

"What were you nervous about?"

He was a grown-ass man. Despite establishing that she was far more womanly than he'd first pegged her out to be, she was still young. He knew what a young impressionable girl like Allison might still be nervous about. The tinge in her cheeks confirmed what he already knew—he shouldn't be asking her things of this nature. It shouldn't matter. But it did, and though he was fairly certain of the answer, and what a risk this was to even go there, he wanted to hear her say it.

She lifted and dropped a delicate shoulder, but as she always had, regardless of how timid she seemed sometimes, she looked him straight in the eyes. "Talking to you makes me nervous."

Leo gulped as he was easily caught in the beautiful eyes once again. He'd expected her to be vague, maybe blame this interviewing stuff being a bit new to her and *that* was the reason for her rattled nerves. Not be *this* honest about it.

He could only hope now she meant he made her nervous for the right reasons. "Because I'm a felon? That's understandable—"

"No." She shook her head adamantly. "That's not it at all. Gio assured me you're all good guys who can be trusted. He said you guys may've made some mistakes in the past but are looking to rectify them, and I believe him."

There was so much conviction not just in her words but her eyes as well. Any trace of a smile he might've still worn really did go flat, and he swallowed hard.

"Why do you do that?"

The question pulled him out of the trance he'd begun to fall into. Trying not to be too obvious about what those eyes had the power to do to him, he glanced away.

"Do what?"

"The first day I saw you," she said, and the moment he glanced back at her, her eyes seemed to search his. "The day I was eating that *jelly* donut you seemed utterly disgusted. Can't say I blame you really. I'm aware I need to lose some weight. Still—"

"*What?*" Leo asked, feeling almost pissed.

"Yeah, I get it." She smiled at the guy who dropped off the tray of food at their table. "Fat-shaming people isn't cool, but I could see how me being in a gym, inhaling a donut, when most there are trying to lose weight or stay in shape, would be a little off putting—"

"I didn't have a problem with you eating a donut," he said, floored that she'd even think that.

Of course, he wouldn't be admitting he'd enjoyed it and that the visual was still clear as day in his head. Even worse, disgust was the *furthest* emotion he felt whenever he revisited the visual. He couldn't believe this was what she'd been thinking all this time.

She rolled her eyes, lifting a taco from her plate. "Okay, whatever," she said, taking a bite.

Leo was momentarily distracted by the orgasmic flutter of her lashes as she chewed then licked her lips and wiped them with a napkin. Like a kitten following a bouncing light against a wall, his eyes followed her every move as she finished chewing, licked her finger clean, then took a swig of her soda. She finished by wiping her mouth before addressing him again.

"I saw how you looked at me that day. Disgust doesn't even begin to cover it, and like I said, I guess I get it, but today . . ." She wiped her mouth again and Leo refrained from retorting to her unfounded accusation the way he wanted to because he was caught on that last comment. "You did it again today when I walked into the gym. Rodney smiled at me, but you . . . you had that same look of utter disgust—"

"Of course Rodney would smile at you," Leo said, motioning to her. "Look at you. You're fucking adorable. And Rodney's a pig who can't even appreciate that. All he thinks of is perverted shit. Hearing his comments was what had me looking so disgusted. But that first day had nothing to do with that donut. It was the furthest thing from my mind."

Allison closed her mouth since it'd fallen slightly open as he'd spoken. Just like the last time he'd been around her, the words had unleashed without permission. He'd admitted he thought her adorable and there was no taking it back, but he was adamant she not think he was disgusted with her in any way—for any reason—especially the one she was so sure of.

After a few silent moments with her taking in what he'd just laid on her and him trying to recover by taking a few bites of his tacos, she finally spoke again. "So why *did* you look at me that way? Then again that same day when I almost ran into you as I was leaving? You certainly didn't look like you were *appreciating* anything."

Leo took advantage of the moments it took him to finish chewing his food to think his next words through this time. He took a drink of his soda and wiped his mouth slowly.

"I was disgusted with *myself*," he admitted, hoping this wouldn't cost him, but he couldn't think of a lie fast enough. "You may have a baby face, but the rest of you is . . ." He glanced around nervously. "I shouldn't have been looking at you *at all* but didn't realize it until my eyes made it up to your face and you looked so damn young . . ."

He stopped to shrug as he picked up another taco because he couldn't tell her the whole truth. His nearly going hard for what he'd been certain the moment he'd met her eyes was a *kid*, was beyond disgusting.

Her laughing had him glancing up at her again, and he stopped short before taking a bite of the taco. "*What?*"

"Oh, wow. And here all this time I was thinking you were disgusted with my fat ass." She laughed again. "That's not the funny part. I was pissed, you know. It's just ironic how wrong I was."

Leo stared at the twinkle in her beautiful eyes for a moment before taking another bite of his food. Again, he took his time, *needing* to keep his mouth shut for a while. Already, he'd said way more to this girl than he ever intended to.

"So, were you really going to finish that interview or was that just something you said to get us out of there?"

Since he'd already admitted to having been looking at her that first day, and in a way he shouldn't have, hence his disgust, Leo didn't bother hiding the smirk this time. He kept chewing slowly without immediately responding as she continued to stare at him, with a raised brow.

"I was gonna get back to you eventually."

Her mouth fell open, but she closed it quickly, and once again, his eyes followed her every move. "No, you weren't." Before he could think of a proper come back to that, she added. "Can I just ask you *why*? Were my questions really that intrusive? Am I too pushy?"

Leo peered at her as he took a drink of his soda. "I got sick and then just got busy." He managed to keep a straight face because at least it was half true.

"Look. You don't have to own up to it, but I think I know when I'm getting blown off." She cocked a playful brow then shrugged. "I'm a first-year college journalism student. I'm trying to learn from my mistakes, so I was just curious why you blew me off."

Though Leo caught the effort to keep the playfulness to a minimum in the smile that spread across her face, there was no hiding it. It had his heart speeding up for two reasons.

One: she could say all she wanted that she was only asking for the sake of strengthening her journalism skills, but Leo knew better.

Two: as much as he was trying to fight any conversation with this girl getting too cutesy, it was exactly the direction this seemed to be going. Worse yet, he was enjoying it a little too much.

Despite his misgivings about this, Leo couldn't help smirking. *Never* in his life had a smile been so contagious to him, and he felt hopeless to try to fight it anymore. "You really expect me to believe anyone's ever blown *you* off?"

She started to smile then stopped to ponder that for a moment. "Hmm, I guess not. But I know when—"

"Nope." Leo shook his head, feeling too pleased with his make-believe triumph. "I think you owe me an apology."

"Apology for *what?*"

"What do you mean for what?" He feigned shock—another first for him.

Since when did he become this cheesy guy? But the insanity went on along with the nonsense he continued to vomit. "First, you accuse me of doing something you obviously know nothing about, and second, you accuse me of not *owning* up to it." He brought his hand to his chest, remembering a time when he had been this playful. A time that felt like a lifetime ago. "I'm appalled."

Seeing her laugh made his whole ridiculous rant worth it. Even as he bit into his taco, he couldn't take his eyes off that breathtaking smile.

"Okay, I apologize," she conceded, albeit with a roll of those big beautiful eyes. "So, are you really gonna let me finish interviewing you?"

"You don't have paper or pen." He smiled smugly, shoving what was left of one of his tacos into his mouth.

"Don't need them. I have an excellent memory," she shot right back, moving her empty plate aside.

"Are you sure you don't want anything else?" Leo asked, looking down at her plate. "Two tacos ain't shit."

"No, I'm good." The smile waned ever so slightly, but then she seemed to remember something, and her eyes went big again. "Oh, before I forget and this was why I asked you to give Rodney my number, since I figured it was pointless to ask you. This has nothing to do with my story on the work-release program, so it's off the record. I have another story I'm working on. Well . . ." She frowned, taking a swig of her soda.

It was only then that Leo noticed she wasn't doing nearly as much throat-clearing as she had in the previous interview. Clearly, his far more lighthearted demeanor today had made her more comfortable. He could only hope his *saving* her from Rodney's inevitable advances and admitting more than he'd planned on, along with his teasing, didn't have her thinking they'd be *friendly* after today.

"It's more like research for my investigative journalism you'd be helping me with, not an actual story, since I don't have enough for a story yet. And it's not that I think you'd know every criminal in the Los Angeles area or anything. It's just that . . ."

Now she cleared her throat then paused to take another sip of her soda.

"Easy with that soda," Leo warned with a smirk. "There's caffeine in that too."

As expected, the color in her face deepened a bit. *I fucking love it!* The words nearly slipped out. He managed to avoid having them spew out as they had so much with her already. But the big smile couldn't be helped.

"Don't be nervous, Ali."

Their eyes met and there it was: another moment like they'd had the last time he'd been around her. It was a simple comment, but Leo knew better. The tone, the playfulness, the irrepressible smile along with the fact that he felt incapable of looking away from those somewhat stunned eyes . . . It was too damn obvious what was happening. He wasn't just being lighthearted. He was flirting with her, making it clear just how drawn he was beginning to feel to her when it was the last fucking thing he should be admitting even in an unspoken way.

She blinked, mercifully releasing him from what'd begun to feel like a hold she had on him.

"I'm not," she said softly. "I just don't want you to think I'm making assumptions about you. You said yourself that you'd been in some trouble in the past, and with you having been in jail, I thought maybe you'd know or had heard something about the key players in the drug-dealing world in this area."

"I might," he admitted without a flinch before she could beat herself up too much about asking.

Truth was he did know a lot of the scum of the area. Too many of them. Hell, not too long ago, he'd been a big part of that scum. More than anything, he needed to derail the direction this interview had taken and move this along. They'd been sitting there for over a half hour, and this was the first question that had anything to do with her journalism that she'd asked him.

"So, it's been rumored that there's been some drug-trafficking *on* campus. Even worse, we've heard some of the faculty might be involved." The innocent surprise in her eyes almost had Leo smiling again. As if that would be so unheard of. "Professors even, but we haven't been able to get any leads."

Leo peered at her for a second. "How's that investigative journalism? Sounds like something the cops should be looking into, not a first-year journalism student."

"Well, I'm pretty sure they are. But I mentioned how hard it's been to impress my editor, right? So, my friend Jen, who's also in the class, and I thought maybe if we could break the case and get the exclusive on it, we'd definitely have a chance at the front-page headline."

Leo listened, ignoring what hearing how anxious she was to impress this editor did to him—again. She told him about Marcelo, her friend's brother, trying to get them some info.

"What we know so far is that one of the guys dealing goes by the street name Scar, but according to Marcelo, he's just a small-time pusher, not someone who'd be involved in something this big."

Leo listened intently because he *had* heard of a Scar. He wondered if he might know Marcelo too but didn't ask more about the guy because his thought process was sidetracked when she told him the next part.

"We thought we witnessed an on-campus exchange," she said this with that same air of innocent excitement. "Even took a picture of it, which mind you, we were caught doing and were even chased."

"They chased you?"

"Yes! One of the guys, that is, the one doing the exchange—Scar." Her tone was that of someone completely unaware of the real fire she could be playing with. "It was how Marcelo was able to identify him from the photo we showed him. We managed to lose Scar the first time he chased us on campus but then saw him again a few days later when we were standing at the bus stop. He drove by, made a skidding U-turn when he saw us, and we ran."

"The fuck? And you're still *investigating* him?"

"He didn't catch us again, and that was weeks ago," she said this as nonchalantly as she'd told him everything else. "Only other time he scared us again was last week when he very creepily said good morning to us, addressing us by our full names. '*Morning, Allison Rico and Jennifer Navarro,*'" she said in what might've been a cute attempt to sound like a dude, only Leo was too caught up in her alarming account. "Other than that, he hasn't been around a whole lot, so we haven't had any more incidents. But he's not even who we're interested in anymore. We want the big fish behind all this."

Leo stared at her as the visuals of the dreams he was still having assaulted him.

"I can think of a few possibilities, but I'm *not* telling you. You have any idea how dangerous this is? This guy went out of his way to point out he knows exactly who you two are."

The infuriatingly adorable disappointed look on her face should've done him in. But he'd be damned if he'd give in. If she thought he'd have any part of her getting herself into further danger, she was dead wrong. And Leo had been an idiot for allowing himself to get so fucking chummy with her today when he knew better—knew from the very start she'd be nothing but poison.

Glancing down at his watch, he wiped his mouth. "Less than half an hour left. You might wanna get started on the questions about the work-release program."

For an instant, it appeared she might protest; then she did it again. Just like when she'd admitted to noticing a lot about his expressions and calling him out on it before, he'd noticed hers throughout every conversation they'd had since. It was as if, in such a short amount of time, she'd become this intuitive to his ever-changing moods—especially when it came to her—but she didn't push.

Leo wasn't sure which was more alarming: the entire conversation today or that she let this go just like that, lifting an understanding brow as she went on with her interview without further argument. Leo could sense things when it came to her now too. Even if they did get through this interview finally, one thing was very clear. Just like he knew it'd be even more impossible to dig her out from under his skin after today, determined little Ali wasn't done tormenting him.

He'd concentrate on getting through the rest of today for now and worry about that when the time came. But one thing was for sure. After today, there was no way Leo would be able to stomach even one more of Rodney's perverted comments about Allison. Further proof of how easily Allison would be trouble for him. Unless Leo wanted to risk blowing this and being sent right back to a jail cell to finish out his time, there was no doubt in his mind about this now. He needed to get this perfectly straight with that asshole first thing.

ELEVEN

Allison

It'd been several weeks since Allison had lunch with Leonardo that first time. But she accepted that it'd likely be months if *ever* that she'd stop experiencing what she did every time she walked into the gym now. The accelerated heartbeat. Her insides spinning faster and more out of control with every step she took into the gym. She thought it might calm with time, but each time it only got worse.

Fortunately, with Lila being so incredibly busy promoting her upcoming fight, she was gone too often to question or worry about Allison's social life. Not that Allison had much of one. But she'd worked out a perfectly synchronized gym schedule that often led to her *running* into Leo. For starters, she made sure her time there was only when Lila wouldn't be, which was a lot lately. She also tried to mingle with other gym members and trainers, both female and male alike. She hoped it'd make it less obvious who was hands down the *only* one responsible for her motivation to be there as often as she was now. If it ever got back to Lila that she'd been seen chatting with the work-release guys, Allison would be able to retort how many others she often chatted with as well.

Her sister knew Allison was far more social than she'd ever been. So, if it should ever get back to her, it shouldn't surprise her. Allison was ready with all her "I'm an adult" and "Everyone deserves a second chance to prove themselves" rebuttals to anything Lila might throw at her about her continued *connection* with Leonardo. But so far, none had been necessary. Poor Lila was just too consumed with everything going on in her own busy life. Allison was determined not to give her more to deal with. But she just couldn't bring herself to stop feeding that temptation to see him again as often as she could.

It didn't happen every day because that'd be too obvious. But at least twice a week now she and Leonardo just so happened to *run* into each other around his lunch time. They'd grabbed a few more tacos and burgers from the other place across the street a few times now, each time getting to know each other a little better. He was still so hot and cold, but as nerve-wracking as it still was *every single time* they spent any time together, it did feel as if they'd begun to build an unlikely camaraderie of sorts.

Allison wasn't even sure what she was hoping for. She wasn't sure yet if even considering anything with a man who said women were poison was wise. All she knew was she couldn't get enough of what he did to her now, especially when he looked at her as he often did. After several weeks, she was convinced now she wasn't just imagining it anymore. She did something to him too.

As hard and as cold as he could go, it was happening less and less. She was seeing more of the lighthearted side of Leonardo each time they chatted.

"Look." She smiled big as she walked up to Leonardo, instantly losing herself in his intense eyes. She handed him her phone so he could read the main headline of the latest edition of her school's online paper. "I finally made the front page, and it was the story on the work-release program that got me there. So, I wanted to thank you."

As he'd been doing more and more lately, Leonardo gazed in her eyes for a long moment without saying anything, before taking the phone with a smile. Allison breathed in deeply, trying to calm her racing heart, but it was becoming increasingly harder to do so. Each time she was near him now, it became clearer that whatever rules, restrictions, or walls he'd initially put up when it came to her were slowly coming down.

Allison assumed he was reading more than just the headline since he was quiet for a few long moments. "Thank me?" He finally looked up from his phone. "You wrote the story. Stuck to your guns until you finally had all the answers you needed. You earned this, Ali, and it's well deserved. Congrats. You should celebrate."

She smiled, taking the phone when he handed it back. "Thank you," she said as she walked alongside him.

"This is gonna sound like a weird question." The comment had Allison looking up at him curiously. "You don't have drug paraphernalia or weapons in your car, do you?"

Allison peered at him, puzzled by the question but even more surprised to see the man laugh for the first time *ever*.

He shook his head. "You're too much, Ali."

Apparently, her expression was as befuddled as she'd felt. Allison laughed now too, warmed by the sweetness in his eyes, despite the odd turn their conversation had taken. "Why would you ask me that?"

"I've been hearing good things about that new seafood place on Lorena," he explained, still smiling big as they walked out the front door. "Haven't tried it but just now had a thought. Maybe we could go check it out for lunch to celebrate your story making the front page. Only I can't have you on my bike without a helmet. Can't chance getting pulled over. It's not far from here but not close enough to walk there and back in under an hour. So, I was thinking, if you want, we can go in your car. You just can't have anything in your car that violates my probation. So, no mace or bongs?"

"No." Allison laughed nervously, even as her insides went a little nuts.

Silly as it sounded, despite them having lunch together on several occasions now, driving to a sit-down kind of restaurant where they wouldn't be ordering at a window made it feel more formal—almost like a date—since he did say they'd be celebrating. Clearing her throat, she nodded, gesturing toward where her car was parked.

"I have nothing illegal in my car or even legal like pepper spray. Even though I do own a bottle, I just don't have it on me today."

"Bongs are legal in California now," he said with a smirk. "*I* just can't be around that shit, not while I'm on probation anyway. You're free to smoke away though, just not around me."

"Are you kidding? My sister would kill me."

"Why? It's just like alcohol now," he said as they reached her car. "As long as you use it responsibly, you're good."

They got in her car, and it was almost comical how big he looked in it. The only other person usually in her car with her these days was Jen, and she was tiny compared to him.

Allison hated to remind him because she got the feeling their age difference was a big deal to him. But she figured he'd known how old she was almost from day one and a number didn't define your maturity. Rodney was a perfect example of that. He was now Leo's *former* work-release partner. Leo had since requested to be switched because as he'd explained, he just couldn't deal with the guy's immature ass.

"It may be legal, but I can't even drink alcohol legally yet, so weed is out of the question for me as well. You got a taste of what my sister's like." She grinned, feeling evil, but even he smirked at the comment. "She'd literally kick my ass if she ever found out I was doing anything illegal."

"Is that right?" He turned to her curiously, just another one of the many expressions she'd been privy to now from this otherwise reserved and once utterly mysterious man. "I've been meaning to ask you. I know she didn't like me—at all—that first day. She know we're . . .?"

He glanced out the window, pausing for a moment, but that last word nearly stopped Allison's heart. *We're* what? Before her mind could even finish the thought, he finished his comment. "She know we're still in touch?"

Gulping, Allison put on her sunglasses. This time she did the stalling before responding. Over the years because of her sister's unpredictable reactions to so many things, Allison had gotten good at stalling for a few moments to think over her answers to some of Lila's questions. In this case, she feigned having to concentrate extra hard on backing out of the parking stall.

"Ali?"

"Hmm?"

Rubbernecking all the way around now to make a good show of her need to focus, Allison's mind raced for an appropriate way to respond.

"She doesn't know, does she?"

Glad for the dark sunglasses, Allison turned to face him as she finished pulling out of the parking space. "She hasn't been home much these past few weeks," Allison said very matter-of-factly, as she brought her eyes back to her driving, and lifted her chin. "And when she has been, our conversations have been mainly about her upcoming fight and her modeling shoots. Her life has changed so drastically in the past few months. So, yeah, I don't think I've mentioned it."

She refused to turn to him, and for once since she'd started talking to him, she couldn't quite make out what felt like a sudden change in mood. His overwhelming presence was such a large part of that car now Allison could literally feel him tense. At least it was what his sitting up a little straighter felt like to her. Only thing she was sure of was he likely didn't buy her not *thinking* she'd mentioned it. He knew damn well—as well as she did anyway—that she knew she hadn't. Was he mad? Insulted? *Hurt*?

His chuckling surprised her. They reached a stop, and she turned to him, but he was looking out his window. "What?" He shook his head, still glancing out the window but didn't say anything. "*What?*"

He turned to her with one of those big beautiful smiles that made her heart flip. "Nothing."

Allison felt her brow arch a bit defensively. Was that a sarcastic chuckle aimed at Lila? So what if she'd kept it from her sister. He had no idea *why* she wouldn't want to add to her sister's worry.

"Something's amusing?" she asked as she pulled into the parking lot of the restaurant.

"I just think it's cute that you'd be afraid to tell her."

"I'm not *afraid*." Allison was aware she sounded a little too defensive, but it was the truth. "I just know she'd worry. I told you she worries about *everything* when it comes to me."

Allison had already told him about being orphaned at a young age. That it'd been just her and Lila for years. Though they hadn't gotten too deep into it, he did know how close she and her sister were. So, he had to understand this.

"She'd be right to worry about this."

Allison turned to him, confused. "About what?"

"Running with the wrong people—wrong crowd—is one of the top reasons people end up in trouble."

His expression was a strange one. It was relaxed enough, and he didn't seem upset or anything, but there was something strained about it, despite the slight smirk he still wore.

"Look it up," he added as if she might not believe him. "It's well documented."

"Having an occasional lunch with you isn't *running* with you," she said, feeling that familiar flutter in her belly. "And I don't think of you as the wrong people or crowd. You said you've learned from your mistakes, and you're obviously trying to better yourself. It's the first thing I'd point out if Lila ever had an issue with my . . . staying in touch with you."

Talking about this made her insanely nervous. It was like they were actually addressing what was happening when, so far, they'd both been pretending what they were doing was meaningless. Something that just happened on a whim. Not something either of them looked forward to and thought of constantly given the continued *moments* that kept happening.

"I'm just saying," he said as he opened his door. "I'd be more surprised if she *didn't* have an issue with it."

They got out of the car and walked around it to the restaurant's entrance. The reminder that it was more of a sit-down restaurant than a fast food place like the others they'd frequented so far had the flutters in her belly going again. Seeing a few of the regulars from the gym made her a little nervous. This would be more than just grabbing a bite to eat if she ever had to explain it to Lila. But just as quickly, her belly was doing the fluttering again.

Simple things like hearing the waiter say, "Table for two," and then their eyes meeting as they sat down across from each other were *way* more exciting than Allison knew they should be. The waiter gave them menus then took their drink orders and left to fetch them. Someone else dropped off water and chips and salsa.

"Let me see that article again."

Leo held out his hand. Allison cued it up on her phone screen and handed him her phone. As usual, it made her nervous to watch someone read anything she wrote, so she focused on the menu instead. She heard him chuckle.

"Intimidating but gentle giant?"

Surprised that he was already at that part, she glanced over her menu with a smile, even as her cheeks heated.

"You're already there? You read fast."

"When you're locked up, it's the one thing you do most."

He went back to reading, and she went back to her menu, reaching out for a chip and dipping it in the salsa every now and again. She was trying to decide between the garlic shrimp or the chipotle crab cakes.

"What did your sister say about the front-page article?"

"Haven't told her."

The moment the words were out, she wished she could take them back. Allison had since mentioned on more than one occasion how *huge* it would be to get a front-page story. How much she'd been wanting this and how Lila was her biggest cheerleader assuring her it'd happen. She may not have gotten too intimate in their conversations yet, but if he knew anything about her, it was how close she and Lila were. She glanced over her menu, and sure enough, he was peering at her.

"You haven't told her?"

Of course, he'd be surprised she told him first. "She won't be home until later." She glanced back down at her menu. "I don't wanna tell her. I wanna *show* her."

That was partially true; though Allison knew she'd put off calling Lila in her haste to tell Leo about it. She knew full well she could easily show her by including a link to the story in a text.

She took a quick sip of the water the waiter had since dropped off. "I just wish the timing had been different," she said, trying to steer the conversation in another direction.

"You mean that this hadn't happened when everything is happening for her?"

"No." She shook her head, surprised by his interpretation of this. "Not even close. It's just that everyone knows about the ongoing head butting Carson and I do, have been doing since—"

"Who's Carson?"

"My editor," she explained, grabbing another chip. "I told you, on top of the fact that he's been so hard to impress, he and I get into it a lot. The whole class has been witness to many of our *debates*. Then he and I—"

She caught herself before saying it, nearly choking on her chip in the process. Taking a sip of her water again, she coughed then cleared her throat, pointing at her neck, explaining the obvious. "Went down the wrong way."

Glancing back at her menu, she tried to reason that his asking so immediately who Carson was didn't mean anything. He just needed clarification before she went on with her story. That was perfectly reasonable. She was being ridiculous to think he'd care either way about what she'd almost said without thinking. "The chipotle crab cakes look good."

"You didn't finish," he said, and she glanced over her menu, stupidly pretending not to understand. "You and Carson what?"

As innocuous as his tone was, there was something just slightly demanding about his inquiry.

"Oh." She shook her head. "I'm just being paranoid because it's my first front-page story."

"Paranoid about what?"

Taking a breath, she decided to just say it. What was the big deal? She really was being ridiculous in assuming he'd be even the slightest bit annoyed with hearing about her night out with Carson. A few days prior when she arrived at the gym, she'd been witness to him chatting with one of the female trainers notorious for flirting. For once, Allison was glad for his broodiness because he didn't appear to *appreciate* being bothered while he was trying to train. But then it happened. The girl said something then giggled loudly about it. While it wasn't nearly as beautiful as some of the smiles Allison had been treated to, he cracked a smile, shook his head, and then said something to the girl that had her twirling her hair with her finger and smiling a little too big. Never in her life had Allison experienced what scathing jealousy felt like.

It was *ugly*.

So, it was only for that reason that she'd prefer to spare anyone feeling even remotely what she had. But again, she reasoned it was very unlikely that he was feeling anything close to the silly butterflies she felt around him. Swallowing hard, she put her menu down, watching as he tried to fish a piece of avocado out of the salsa with his chip. "We had dinner just a few weeks ago for the first time ever, and then next thing you know I get a front-page story."

The movement of his chip in the salsa bowl slowed almost to a standstill. She glanced up at his face, but he was still staring at the chip. "A romantic dinner?"

He finally gave up on the avocado and bit into the chip with just the salsa. His eyes were on hers now, vacant of any emotion; though the intensity was ever present. Allison's mind raced. While the dinner hadn't been a romantic one, her relationship with Carson had definitely changed since then. Her concern over the timeline of that happening and her story making the front page was a valid one.

Allison knew what she'd be up against should she ever get her hopes up about anything happening between her and Leo. Already his continuing to allow even a friendship between them was a surprise. Being completely honest about this now would only pile on more reasons for him to steer clear of anything more than even this unlikely friendship between them. She risked having him cut her off altogether. Only Allison's heart yearned for even a *sign* of what she'd begun to suspect: that he too was beginning to feel for her the insanity she'd begun feeling for him weeks ago.

Did she dare be completely honest and see how he reacted? Or should she be vague, tone it down considerably, and not risk his possibly going back to ignoring her again?

Chewing the corner of her lip, she took a deep breath, feeling her heart thud against her chest as her head continued to debate.

TWELVE

BEAST

"No," Allison said, shaking her head, then bit into a chip.

The single word relieved some of the irrational tension he'd begun to feel. Though he did his best to hide it. This was further proof of what Allison was already capable of doing to him. It'd been just weeks since he'd met her and unwisely began to let her in. Already, there'd been too many times when he'd had to calm his unreasonable sense of entitlement.

It was one thing to feel like the horny assholes down at the gym, who'd seen him around Allison enough times now, should at least question whether she was off limits. So, his annoyance with them openly sizing her up the way they did when she wasn't looking—but Leo caught it—was reasonably understandable. But it was another thing, and completely uncalled for, to be so annoyed about hearing she had a social life outside the gym.

If anything, this should relieve him. He'd begun to think maybe, despite the age difference, Allison might actually be considering this to be more than the acquaintanceship they had now. Maybe that was why she never spoke of a social life. Of course, Leo refused to ask her about it, so it'd never been discussed. But it made perfect sense she'd have one. As well she should, and this would take the pressure off his constant stressing about whether he should just go with this. Whatever happened, happened. That decision would be out of his hands if she was someone else's chick.

She finished chewing and wiped her mouth. "The dinner was a group thing, I mean. But things between him and me have changed since that evening and . . ."

Of course, the fucking waiter would arrive right at that moment to take their orders. Leo had been so caught up with their conversation he'd hardly looked through the menu. Allison, on the other hand, was ready with her order. "I'll have the chipotle crab cakes," she said, handing the waiter her menu.

Leo skimmed over the menu one more time before just handing it back to the waiter. "I'll take the shrimp cocktail and a couple of ceviche tostadas," he said, going with what he knew was always a safe bet.

"Ooh, ceviche," Allison said then frowned. "I shouldn't though."

"Why not?" Leo asked, annoyed by her constant worry with her weight.

As far as he was concerned, Allison's curves were smoking hot and the reason for too many of his long showers lately. It was absurd to him that she'd think they were anything but cock-hardening and perfect.

"The crab cakes are already fried. Spandex was meant to stretch, but—"

"Bring her a ceviche tostada," Leo said to the waiter before she could finish and give the waiter permission to eye her spandex outfit.

"You got it." The waiter nodded then smiled and walked away.

Leo turned back to Allison. "You were saying?"

She smirked, shaking her head. "I was saying spandex was meant to stretch but not as much as mine do. I need to lay off meals with so many calories."

"News flash." Leo reached for his glass of water. "You look hot as fuck in your workout outfits. Trust me. No one in that gym or anywhere is complaining about how nicely that spandex hugs all those curves."

He brought the glass of water to his mouth when he realized he'd just spewed out a bunch of shit again without even thinking. At least before he was only guilty of admitting he thought his young gym acquaintance was adorable. Now, he'd just admitted he thought her hot and that he'd been enjoying her curves all this time.

No surprise her face reddened in response to his comment. Trying not to panic or bring more attention to his latest fuck-up, he shook his head as he set his glass down. "So, what were you saying about you and Carson?"

Just saying the dude's name already left a bad taste in his mouth. Leo straightened out, needing to get his shit together before she picked up on anything. As good as she was getting at reading him, she didn't even have to try if he was going to be so damn obvious about it.

Allison wasn't the only one good at this reading-people shit. Leo didn't miss the tiny lift of her brow in reaction to his question. Though he wasn't nearly as good as she was in zeroing in on the possible reason. Her face was still pink from his earlier remark, and that lift of her brow he caught wasn't exactly a playful one. So, he was clueless as to what to make of it.

Fidgeting with her napkin, she looked him straight in the eyes. She cleared her throat. It was soft, and Leo suspected she was hoping he wouldn't hear, but he did. At least he already knew what that meant—she was nervous.

"Like I said, he and I butted heads often in the past, but ever since that group night out, things have really changed." She lifted and dropped a delicate little shoulder, and as usual, Leo's eyes followed her every move. "Things have just been noticeably amicable between him and me ever since, and I'm sure it's crossed the minds of some of the others in class that maybe that's why my story made the front page."

Noticeably amicable? What the fuck did that mean? His whole life it'd been impossible to hide any irritation once he'd begun to feel it. Only this was different from any he'd ever felt, and he knew exactly why.

Sucked in.

It was happening faster than he'd dreaded. There was no way to hide it now because he was certain, as good as she was at reading him, she already had. So, he took the only other route he could. "Fuck anyone's assumptions. I read the article. It's front-page worthy, and anyone who reads it wouldn't be able to argue that."

Again, she seemed surprised by his reaction but then smiled. "Well, thank you for that. My sister would agree with you in a heartbeat. Verbatim," she added with a giggle.

A couple of guys he recognized from the gym walked into the restaurant, eyeing him and Allison casually before being seated. Leo knew he should drop it already, talk about anything else. But curiosity got the best of him, damn it. More than anything, he just needed to know. He needed more ammunition as to why he really should cut her off completely. This harmless little just-staying-in-touch bullshit already had him considering doing things he vowed he never would.

"Isn't dating your professor breaking some kind of rule?"

Her eyes went wide, but the waiter with the most fucked timing ever was at the table with their food. He set down their plates and silverware, refilled their waters, and asked if there was anything else he could get them before leaving them the hell alone.

"Carson's not the professor," she explained as she dug into one of her crab cakes with a fork.

Leo waited, still unable to even think about eating because she'd sort of answered the question but not with what he really wanted to know. Was she dating the guy? After a couple of seconds of him still waiting for her to say more, she glanced up at him then at his untouched food. "What's wrong? You don't like the food?"

"Haven't even tasted it yet."

He saw the change in her eyes the moment he said it. He'd been too busy staring at her to bother with his food and she knew it. Gazing into her eyes shouldn't still be so fucking all-consuming.

He shook his head, breaking free of what had begun to feel like another one of their moments. Reaching for his fork, he wrestled with his thoughts. Maybe he really should break free of her before it was too late.

"How's your food?" he asked, spearing one of the shrimp in his cocktail.

"It's delicious," she said, though she didn't sound as convincing as when she usually declared something being delicious. "He's a student editor," she added the clarification without his asking, and Leo couldn't even bring himself to look up from his food at her. "Technically, it wasn't a date, but he mentioned it in class a few times." Now Leo glanced up and their eyes locked. "I just wish the timeline had been a little different. I'm sure it's what at least some in the class must be thinking. That he might be playing favorites with a girl he's gone out with."

"He probably is," Leo said because how the fuck could Allison not be anyone's favorite anything? But then he quickly added because her brow had risen again only not in a playful way, "Not that your article wasn't deserving of the front page. I'm just saying how could he possibly resist not making you his favorite?"

Her expression softened into something so painfully sweet it almost hurt to even think it. But the color in her face once again deepening in response to his continued word vomit had Leo once again contemplating going back to avoiding Allison at all costs. She'd just admitted she gone out with the editor, a college boy likely her age who no doubt was full of goals and aspirations. Someone with a bright future ahead of him and the kind of guy she deserved.

Leo picked up one of his tostadas and took a bite. It was damn good but as usual messy. The damn tostada broke, leaving Leo with a half in each hand and most of the middle part spilled onto his plate.

Allison giggled. "I usually just eat mine with chips. You're gonna end up scooping them up with the pieces of tortilla anyway."

Nodding in agreement, Leo bit one of the broken sides and held the other, but his fingers were full of the stuff. "How's the crab cake?" Leo asked without even looking up.

"Good, you wanna try it?"

When he glanced up at her, she was picking up a piece with her fingers. With both hands still full or messy, she didn't wait for him to clean off his messy hand. "Here," she said, reaching out to feed it to him.

Leo opened up, closing his lips before her finger was all the way out, and she didn't move it. Instead, she let it linger as he licked he crab cake and her finger in the process. As she pulled her finger away, their heavy eye contact remained intact.

"It's good," he finally said, breaking the silence. But he had to straighten up to allow his tightening crotch to adjust. "Very good."

Unable to take his eyes off her for far too long, Leo knew he was in trouble. If he continued to spend time around her, there was no way he'd be able to hold out for much longer. What he'd suspected was clear now. She was feeling more than she should too. But bringing her into his world was still an impossibility. The confirmation that she still had a chance to be with someone safe had already felt like reason enough to step back. But this sealed it. He needed to step back before he was helpless to do so. Already this girl had managed to suck him in deeper than he should've allowed. Just like all the other visuals and thoughts that had tormented him since the day he'd first laid eyes on her, she just added another. There was only so much any man could take, and Leo knew what he had to do before she broke him.

THIRTEEN

Allison

There was no way to explain it, but something in her gut told her today was different. It'd been months since she and Jen had heard about Scar's arrest. Marcelo had even asked them if they had anything to do with the small-time pusher getting busted for selling drugs around campus.

They hadn't even been aware of his arrest, but admittedly it'd been a relief to know the guy was off the streets, since seeing him around always gave her the creeps. He hadn't addressed them again since the day they were making their way to class on campus and he bid them both a good morning using their full names. Then a couple of weeks later he was gone.

Now he was back, apparently done with whatever short stint in jail he'd been given. It'd been a week since they first noticed him lurking around campus again. Each time she'd gotten a *major* case of the creeps, especially because just as

Marcelo had, she and Jen got the feeling Scar might think they had something to do with his arrest. Would he possibly try to retaliate?

This time was worse. Like all the other times she'd gotten the distinct feeling she was being watched, this time there was more to it. Sure enough, she saw him several cars away in the parking lot of her school, eyeing her suspiciously. Then she caught the exchanged glance between him and another thuggish-looking guy on the other side of the parking lot.

Thankfully, Allison was just steps away from her car. She could put to rest the visuals of her frantically trying to fish out her pepper spray from the bottom of her back pack.

"Hey, bitch, you need to stay away from my man."

The girl's voice so near Allison startled her more than it should have. Allison realized how unnerved Scar had made her. She'd been so focused on him she hadn't paid attention to the rest of her surroundings. As close as the girl's voice was, Allison hadn't expected her to be standing right behind her when she spun around.

"Yeah, I'm talking to you, bitch." The ghetto-looking girl who already had a lightly bruised eye got right in her face.

Her equally ghetto-looking friend stood by her, eyeing Allison as well. Allison cocked her head back, confused. "*What?*"

"Leo's my man, bitch. And I'm tired of hearing about your whore ass throwing yourself at him."

Feeling like she'd already been slapped, Allison shook her head. This girl couldn't possibly be talking about the only Leo she knew. Allison hadn't had lunch with him in forever. He'd reverted to his broody tightlipped self over a month ago.

Feeling an unexplainable hurt and anger despite her non-existent relationship with the man, she swallowed it down. "I don't know what you're talking about," she said, turning back to her car.

"Fuck this, Eva," the other girl said. "No guy's worth fighting for."

Allison opened her door and threw her back pack in, ignoring *Eva* as she continued to spew insults at Allison. Feeling her head jerked back and realizing this psycho bitch had just yanked at her hair, had Allison's heart at her throat. She turned around and started swatting the girl's hands away. "Get your hands off me! I don't know who your stupid boyfriend is!"

Eva swatted around Allison's hands, going on about Allison messing with the wrong girl's man and a bunch of other craziness. Then she landed a backhand across Allison's face that had her reeling. For the first time in her life, she understood the fury her sister felt once lit.

All the self-defense tactics she'd learned at 5th Street flew out the door. Allison didn't want to just subdue her attacker so she could free herself to run away. She was suddenly out for blood. Remembering the kick-ass fighting tactics she'd picked up from watching Lila over the years, she reached out for a good grip of Eva's hair, slammed her head against the car, and proceeded to pound her in the face. She went on until Eva broke free from her hold but tried to grab Allison's hair again.

The struggle went on even as bystanders started to gather; though no one even attempted to get involved. To Allison's surprise, though she'd never been in an actual fight, she landed some good ones. At one point, she even headbutted Eva so hard the girl nearly fell, but she recovered and continued to try to swing at Allison.

It wasn't until they heard the sirens that Eva's friend pulled her away and the two ran off. Allison stood there dazed and still unable to believe that just happened when the patrol car pulled up and the cops got out. Some of the people standing by pointed at Allison as if her teary and what was likely swelling and scratched-up face wasn't a dead giveaway about who'd been in the fight.

"Where's the other girl?"

They all looked around, but Eva and her friend were long gone. "They went that way," one guy said, pointing down the street.

"She attacked me," Allison said, her voice finally breaking as the emotion came out of nowhere suddenly. "She attacked me."

Touching her aching forehead with her shaky hand, she immediately regretted it. The fingers she'd used stung like hell, and she realized they might be broken. With the adrenaline settling down, she began to feel the pain everywhere. Her side, her head but mostly her hand—the one she'd done all the punching with—hurt like hell.

Clearly, there was skill involved and something her sister had perfected over the years. Allison's attempt to replicate the fighting moves had been somewhat successful, but apparently her lack of skill had cost her injuries. Despite how hard she'd seen her sister beat on someone, she'd never broken her own bones doing so.

Because of her hand injury, but especially the head injury, the cops and first responders on the scene all agreed she shouldn't drive. If Allison had felt even the slightest bit up to driving, she might've insisted. She knew what a call from the ER letting Lila know she'd been rushed there after being attacked, would do to her sister. But truth was she *did not* feel up to driving at all, and her hand was *killing* her.

Once at the ER, and after calming a bit and being given some pain meds for her hand and side, Allison decided to call Jen first. She knew Lila was going to lose it when she heard the news, and she was most worried about this really being Leo's girlfriend.

Since any of the closeness Allison had begun to feel with Leo had ended over a month ago, she'd never bothered to tell Lila about having kept in touch with him beyond the interview. He'd reverted back to the old him; though he occasionally slipped and she'd see that special something in his eyes she often saw before. But he had put an end to their hanging out outside the gym even for just a bite of something across the street.

Instead, any socializing between them had dwindled down to a few run-ins around the gym, usually at the juice bar or in the break room. While his smiles at times were as genuine as ever, often they seemed strained and his expressions full of panic as they'd often been way back.

That was what worried her now. Admittedly, while she'd tried to hold on to some shred of dignity by respecting his obvious choice to keep their distance, it couldn't be helped. It didn't happen nearly as often as it had in the past, but Allison had been incapable of staying completely away from him. So, all the times they had spoken lately, it had been her doing the approaching. It would stand to reason that a possessive girlfriend of his might see it as Allison pushing herself on him.

But it just couldn't be helped. For as much as Leonardo tried to be indifferent each time they did speak, Allison was certain he had to be feeling the same thing she was. There was no denying it when they'd inevitably have one of their moments again. Except for the way he seemed to panic, his eyes practically spoke to her. He *was* feeling more. Was Eva the reason why he'd been fighting it? If that was the case, then she'd have no choice but to come clean with Lila about just how long she'd continued to stay in touch with Leo even months after her story on the work-release program had been published.

Allison wasn't surprised that her sister hadn't responded to the short text she'd sent to her telling her to call Jen. She'd told her it was too long to explain but assured her she was fine. Though she left out anything about the fight. She'd already been asked to put her phone away a few times, so she snuck a text to Jen giving her Sonny's number so she could text him as well. Somehow, Allison knew they'd be needing Lila's boyfriend—her sister's voice of reason these days—to help calm her.

As she held the icepack up to her bruised head, her stomach roiled. Before today, telling Lila about her continued association with Leo wouldn't have been too big a deal. Maybe it'd be upsetting to her sister, but Allison *was* an adult. For as much as her sister could try and persuade her, who Allison chose to hang out with was ultimately up to her. Had her relationship with Leo gone anywhere, Allison had been ready to argue her case. Leo didn't pose any threat to her in any shape or form. But given the circumstances, that argument wouldn't hold up very well now.

The moment she spotted Jen entering the busy emergency room, Allison felt slightly relieved. She'd been praying Jen would get here first. Even though Allison hadn't told Lila where she was, she'd been worried she'd call Jen and Lila would race down there before Jen could.

"Oh my God, Ali," Jen gasped as she reached Allison's bedside. "Who were you in a fight with?"

"Have you talked to Lila?" Allison asked.

Jen nodded, profusely wide-eyed. "I just got off the phone with her."

"What did you tell her?"

"That you were in the ER and that you were in a fight but that I didn't know more. She's on her way now."

Allison explained quickly about the fight and how she still wasn't sure if it had anything to do with Leo. "That her boyfriend's name is Leo could just be an incredible coincidence. Plus, I haven't even really hung out with him at all in a long time."

Understandably, her best friend seemed lost, and Allison felt a little bad about that. "Leo?"

"The work-release guy I interviewed a while back," Allison reminded her as if it were no big deal.

She'd never really told Jen a whole lot about the time she'd spent with Leo, even after she was done interviewing him. She'd been afraid of sounding delusional. But mostly she had a feeling Jen might agree with her and, in turn, feed her false hope. She'd been glad she hadn't mentioned him when he all but severed any connection they'd begun to make. It saved her the humiliation of having to talk about it.

"So, you think it was mistaken identity?" Jen asked.

"I can't imagine the little contact I've had with the guy since then would be grounds for attacking me. But listen . . ." She glanced around to make sure her sister wasn't charging through the emergency room yet. "You can't mention his name to Lila. We still don't know anything. So, for now, I'm just gonna say I have no idea who this girl could possibly be talking about because I really don't. He'd made his thoughts on relationships very clear on more than one occasion—he didn't do them."

"Maybe this girl is some psycho ex who saw you talking to him?"

"Maybe." Allison went on quickly. "There's more."

She told her about the whole Scar thing before the attack. How she was sure he'd been following her and then his friend being there watching her too.

"Can you text Marcelo and ask if he knows of an Eva who might know Scar or the people he hangs with?"

Jen was immediately on her phone as Allison described Eva to her. "When Lila gets here, you just follow my lead. You know how she gets."

Allison worried that Lila would be adamant about wanting to know *everything*. Jen just might cave to Lila's demands. Not only had Allison kept her continued connection to Leo from Lila; she'd also promised her way back she'd stop chasing trouble with the story about Scar, whose name she didn't even know at the time. If either of her two theories were true, that this happened because she hadn't been forthcoming about either, this could get rough. Allison wasn't worried about her sister being livid more than she was about her being hurt.

Jen glanced down at her phone. "That's Marcelo." She tapped her screen then brought it to her ear, glancing around all sneakily.

Allison listened as Jen told him everything quickly then went quiet listening. "Okay, I can't be talking anyway, but text me anything else you know." She'd already been looking at Allison before she hung up, and the moment she did, she explained. "He said he's heard of her but doesn't know much more. But he doesn't think she'd be Leo's girlfriend anyway because the last he heard she was married with kids and that was a few years back."

As if on cue, Lila burst through the ER room doors, looking just as worried as Allison knew she'd be. Allison lifted the icepack back up to cover the lump on her head, but from the look in her sister's eyes, she'd already seen it. "Okay, so I'll tell her about what happened, but we'll keep our theories to ourselves, okay? No mention of Leo or Scar."

Jen couldn't even muster a convincing expression, so Allison frowned. "Please, Jen, I know she'll push, but if anything, be vague. You don't remember any names. Just say you think I interviewed this guy a while back but you don't remember his name."

The young male ER attendant arrived at her bedside just then with a wheelchair and helped her into it. "You can't walk?" were the first alarmed words out of Lila's mouth.

Allison quickly explained about her bruised rib and how it was standard procedure so she wouldn't be further injured. Immediately, Lila was demanding answers. Allison did her best to explain as vaguely as she could, exchanging glances with a very nervous-looking Jen in the process.

"Do you even know her boyfriend?" Lila asked.

Her sister caught the exchanged glance between her and Jen, and Allison could see how quickly Lila was already losing her patience.

"Hey, you're—" The attendant began to say as he recognized Lila, but Lila brought her finger to her lips and pulled the hoodie over her head.

Lila and Sonny had been *all* over the news lately. Even before Lila had won the title a few weeks prior, the paparazzi had begun to get a little out of control. Sonny had been famous and a household name even before she met him, but now Lila couldn't go anywhere without being recognized.

Thankfully, the distraction was enough that it changed the subject. "Where are you taking her?" Lila asked the attendant.

He explained about the doctor ordering an MRI to rule out a concussion. Then he added that the X-rays would be a while because they'd be taking so many since she was so banged up. "It's just my ribs and hand," Allison said, annoyed that he was making it sound so bad. "Mostly my hand."

"And your head." Lila made sure Allison knew she'd seen the lump on her head, damn it.

Allison gave Jen one last pleading look so her friend would be strong and not cave under questioning, but she wasn't too hopeful. They wheeled her out, and after what felt like an eternity of X-rays and the MRI, she was wheeled back into the emergency room where Lila was now gone and an anxious Jen stood waiting. "She made me tell her," Jen said.

Allison's stomach immediately took a dive. "Tell her what?"

"I was able to bluff about not remembering Leo's name and kept that vague enough, but the moment I mentioned Marcelo knowing who Eva was, she made me call him. Stupid Marcelo told her he might be able to find out how to track Eva down. She asked for my keys so she could get past any paparazzi out by the car that brought her here; then she bolted."

"Oh my God!"

This was a nightmare. Her sister was going to get herself arrested at the height of her career all because of Allison.

"But Sonny called me. He's on his way. He'll calm her, right?"

Like an angel opening the heavens, Lila's boyfriend walked into the ER, turning every head in the room, but he charged through the room on a mission. "You have to find her, Sonny," Allison begged.

"I will, but first I need to know more."

Allison explained as much as she had to Lila. Remembering she'd never referred to Leo by his first name to either Lila or Sonny, she explained about the only Leo she even knew: someone she'd interviewed a while back. She mentioned she was occasionally in touch with him but left out what story she interviewed him for. Also, she made sure to mention there'd never been anything remotely romantic between them. "He said he didn't have time for a social life," Allison said, rolling her eyes. "He called women poison."

"Well, if this is someone he's been involved with," Sonny said, pulling out his phone with a frown, "then I can see why he'd think that."

"Oh, that reminds me . . ." Allison pulled out her own phone now.

She told Sonny about having texted Leo earlier but hadn't checked to see if he'd responded. Scrolling through her texts, she smiled when she saw he'd responded. When he'd gone back to being his broody tightlipped self, he'd also reverted to rarely responding to any of her texts. Not that she texted him much anymore. She hadn't in a while, so she knew this text would catch his attention.

Smiling smugly and feeling almost sneaky, she reread the text she'd sent him first.

Curious. You ever go out with an Eva? She your girlfriend?

She didn't think he'd be able to resist his own curiosity as to why she'd ask something like this so out of the blue. Then her heart thudded, her eyes glued to her text still, because she was suddenly almost afraid to read his response. What if this really was his girlfriend and he knew about the fight now? Maybe he felt obligated to respond to apologize or something.

Glancing a little lower, she held her breath and read his text.

Nope. Never known an Eva. Never done the girlfriend thing. Poison. Remember?

Despite being surprised by the utter relief, she frowned, looking up at Sonny and relaying the response, even the part about women being poison.

"Then who the hell is this Eva chick? You think maybe she mistook you for—"

"She's Scar's girl," Jenny said, looking down at her own phone. "Marcelo just confirmed it with one of his friends."

"Scar's girl?" Sonny asked.

"So, this was retaliation?" Ali's mouth dropped open. "He must really think I had something to do with him getting busted."

Sonny didn't seem convinced, but he was worried because Jen said Marcelo was with Lila now and had told her about Eva being Scar's chick. She was likely thinking the very thing Allison was—that this had been retaliation—and now Lila would likely be looking for some of her own—on Eva.

Jen relayed everything else Marcelo was telling her via text. How he was stalling by taking his time gassing up the car and putting air in the tires.

Good, 'cause something's not right here," Sonny said with a frown. "This doesn't make sense."

"It makes perfect sense," Ali insisted because it did. "Scar sent his girlfriend or maybe he didn't even have to. Maybe she was just waiting to get her hands on me."

"If that's the case, why the lie?" Sonny peered at her. "Why not just say that's what this was? Retaliation?"

They discussed further as Allison pondered that last question, but it could stand to reason and could be as simple as maybe Scar's real name was Leo. She was about to make the argument when Sonny hit her with another good question.

"Why would they just come after you? Why not go after Jenny too? She's the one they saw taking the pictures, right?"

Before Allison could even think on that, he turned back to Jenny, who was busy tapping away at her phone screen. "Who's your brother getting all this info from?"

She glanced up from her phone and shrugged. "He has lots of friends on the street." She frowned before looking back down at her phone again, further explaining about all his illegal connections.

She stopped talking and read something on her phone screen again then looked up at Sonny, eyes wide. "He says he knows exactly where Eva is at right now, where they can find her hanging out, but he hasn't told Lila."

"Tell him not to," Sonny said, tapping at his phone and bringing it to his ear then cursed and hung up when clearly whoever he was calling—likely Lila—didn't answer.

Before they could exchange anything more, he started to walk out, stopping just outside the curtain. "Text me Marcelo's number and tell him to do whatever he has to do to keep Lila put."

As bad as this had the potential to get, Allison felt almost guilty about feeling so relieved. She may have been sitting on pins and needles until she heard back from Sonny or Lila and she knew her sister wasn't sitting in some jail cell arrested for murder, but she at least had this peace of mind. This had nothing to do with Leo.

FOURTEEN

BEAST

It'd been over a week since Allison's too noticeable absence around the gym that Leo paid enough attention to the ongoing tabloid gossip to get a clue. Maybe if he'd paid closer attention, he might've reached out to her sooner to ask how she was doing.

Ever since he got the text over a week ago, he'd wondered if maybe that was why her texts and times she approached him had gone dry. Maybe she didn't believe he hadn't heard about the ongoing gossip about her sister that started around the same time he'd gotten that cryptic text from Allison. Now it seemed all the crap he'd been trying desperately to avoid hearing about on the news and everywhere online may have had something to do with Allison as well.

It was beyond irritating that, of course, the girl he was trying so hard to not think about would have a sister who was a tabloid magnet. As if trying to keep Allison out of his every thought wasn't hard enough. Even before all the crap in the news started, she'd been distant. Aside from a smile from across the gym or a weak little wave, she'd hardly addressed him before she all but stopped showing up. But even then, those few and far between greetings he ever got from her were like goddamn crumbs he'd eat up like a starved man then try desperately not to follow up on them. So, her not showing up for her workouts this past week felt almost like a punishment.

He was done for the day and getting ready to walk out of the gym when he stopped and did a double take at one of the TV screens up on the wall. It was footage of Allison getting out of a car. Her hand was in a brace, and she covered her face with her purse as she rushed into a building surrounded by body guards. The sound was off, but he read the caption:

FIRST PUBLIC SIGHTING SINCE THE ATTACK

"Attack?"

Instantly, Leo's blood began to simmer. The camera was back to the reporter in the studio, who had more to say as the still photo of Allison remained in the background, but he couldn't hear anything. Then they moved onto another story.

"What the fuck?"

His mind raced as the familiar sensation of his blood thrumming at his ears began. Could this possibly be what he'd feared most all this time? Who the hell would want to attack her? Pulling out his phone from his pocket, he scrolled through his texts until he got to the last one between them, the cryptic one where she asked about an Eva. He hit the call button because there was no way he was waiting for her to respond to a text.

It rang several times before it went to voicemail. With a near growl, he stopped to tap furiously at his phone's screen, sending the text saying he needed to talk to her ASAP. Pacing by his motorcycle and taking deep breaths, he refused to get on in case she called while he was driving. He kept checking his phone for anything, even a text response.

After waiting impatiently for several minutes with no response, he hit call again and waited. To his surprise, she answered, "Hey, I was trying to text you back, but I'm a little handicapped right now and—"

"What happened? Who attacked you?"

She was quiet for a moment as he cracked his knuckles with the fingers on his free hand. "A girl . . ." Her tone was a strange one, and she paused momentarily. "You didn't know about it? It happened last week. It's been all over the news. Hold on. Thank you, Gio. Yeah, I'm out of here."

Leo's head was still obsessing about her initial two-word answer—*a girl*—when he heard that last part and spun around. "Are you here at the gym?"

"Yes, I'm just leaving actually."

He searched the exit and parking lot frantically as he started back to the front door. "Where are you? I need to talk to you."

His heart pounded just from the thought that he'd be seeing her again, and here it'd only been a little over a week since he'd last seen her.

"I've been using the VIP entrance in the back to avoid the paparazzi."

"VIP entrance?" he asked, slowing down, then stopped and started toward the back of the gym in an almost sprint. "Wait for me, please. I'll be there in a sec."

He didn't even know they had a VIP entrance, but he supposed it made sense with all the celebrity athletes that visited the gym. As he turned the corner, his heart began to calm a bit and thudded now at the sight of her standing near a town car, facing the other way. But she looked like she was looking for someone—looking for him.

"Allison," he called out, and just like that, the sight of her had him nearly smiling again until she turned to face him.

Feeling the air sucked out of him, he nearly choked at the sight. The attack was more than what he'd begun to imagine. Her face looked like she'd been beaten. The bruises appeared to be fading, but Leo was no stranger to healing bruises. It'd been over a week, and they were still significant. Suddenly, the inferno inside him was blazing again.

The closer he got, the more he thought he might lose his shit. The moment he was close enough, he searched her eyes, taking in all the damage. "Who the fuck did this to you?"

She shook her head, her brows furrowing as if she didn't understand his anger, but then, how could she? "I told you some girl on campus."

"*Why?*" he demanded, bringing his fist to his mouth because he could hardly stand it. The longer he stood there looking at her, the closer he felt to blowing up.

This close he could see the scratches and just how bruised she really was. Girl or not, he felt ready to fucking *kill* someone because his gut was screaming there was more to this than just some cat fight. More than anything, seeing sweet Allison like this was something he'd *never* anticipated.

She started to tell him about the girl who'd approached her in the school parking lot, saying something about her boyfriend.

"Ms. Allison." The driver apologized for interrupting them but then reminded her about a plane she had to catch.

"I'll have to tell you the rest later. Or Google it. It's everywhere."

"No wait," he said, feeling every hair in his body stand at attention when she turned to the driver and he saw the bruised bump on her delicate temple.

"I gotta go."

"*Fuck!*"

She jerked her head back in response to his outburst. Seeing the shock on her face had Leo spinning around, and he stalked off, not stopping even when she called out for him. He had to. He needed to get away from her before he blew.

The whole way he raced home on his bike he cussed under his breath and banged at his handlebars in a fiery rage. He knew it was irrational to think this might have anything to do with him, but instinct told him it had *everything* to do with him. Something told him sweet little Allison's attack wasn't just some random thing as she seemed to think.

By the time he got off his bike in his garage, he felt out of control. He'd always known his demons had only been dormant. That they'd be ready to blow the moment they were triggered and this was proof.

Pacing furiously back and forth, it was all he could do to keep from roaring at the top of his lungs. "Motherfucker!" He lifted a box of tools and smashed it against the wall.

Tool after tool, box after box that crashed loudly where he smashed them only fueled the firestorm inside him, not relieved it like he hoped it might. Visuals of Allison's sweet face all bruised and scratched as she held her hand to her side cautiously only assaulted him, making him growl louder and smash things with even more fury.

He didn't even notice Nine and O in the garage, yelling for him to calm down until O jumped in front of him. "What the fuck, man?"

Leo flung the wrench in his hand at the window in the back of the garage with one final growl, not even flinching at the loud crashing sound. Nine and O stared at him wide-eyed, but neither said anything as he stood there, breathing hard and trying desperately to calm himself.

They hadn't seen him like this in years but knew better than to ask for any explanations. Not at that moment anyway. Leo glanced around the trashed garage, surprised by the amount of damage he'd done in what felt like such a short time.

No one said anything for too long, but Nine began walking around assessing the damage. With his breathing still labored, Leo somehow managed to speak calmly. "I'll clean this shit up after I shower." Before O could say anything, he added, "I'll pay to have the window fixed. But I'll board it up in the meantime."

Without another word, he stalked out of there, leaving his stunned roommates standing there, speechless. There was no time to explain now. His mind was already racing with how to fix this because more than anything his gut was sure now. Allison had been attacked because of him. He didn't know why, but he'd be getting to the bottom of it. Probation or not, Leo had to make sure this didn't turn into another nightmare.

FIFTEEN

Allison

"Yeah, that works," Allison said as she walked out of the ladies' locker room. "It sounds like fun, actually. I've heard good things about that restaurant. Friday night, right?"

She walked out so absentmindedly she nearly collided with someone. It wasn't until she looked up and saw who that someone was that she was reminded how effortlessly Leonardo's intense eyes could turn her into a puddle.

"Ali? You still there?"

Carson's voice snapped her out of the instant trance getting lost in Leonardo's eyes had sucked her into. She shook her head. "Yes, I'm sorry, Carson. I am, but listen. I'm on my way out now from the gym, but I need to do a few things before I leave. I'll call you back when I'm in the car."

To her surprise, Leonardo hadn't budged. Instead, he appeared to be waiting for her to be free to talk. She finished up with Carson then peered at him curiously, feeling a bit breathless, and it annoyed her. Leonardo had made it abundantly clear how *not* interested he was in so much as a friendship with her. Then he'd stormed off so rudely the night he'd questioned her about her attack. He didn't deserve to have this big an effect on her still. She was over the silly crush she'd developed on him—moved on.

"You have a minute?" he asked, glancing around as if already looking for a place to discuss whatever was on his mind.

For a millisecond, she considered saying no, but who was she kidding? Already her stupid heart was thundering away, and she was more than curious about what he might need to talk to her about.

"Yeah." She shrugged, moving aside from the middle of the path on the way to the door outside.

He started to say something but then stopped and glanced around again. "Is it okay if we talk outside?"

Now she was *really* curious. Thankfully, he seemed much calmer this time. His anger last time had confused the hell out of her; though she *thought* she might know the reason. But even that didn't make much sense. Starting to walk was enough answer to his question, but she turned to him as they strolled to the door together. "Something wrong?"

"I don't think so."

They couldn't get outside soon enough now. As soon as they were outside and far enough away from anyone, she stopped and turned to him. But before she could ask, he began.

"Your text. The one about Eva. Where did that come from?"

Allison thought about it for a second then lifted a brow. She'd wondered if he'd care once it inevitably got back to him about the coincidence. But why now? Why hadn't he asked then?

"I don't know. It just seemed the first logical thing that made any sense. I just had to ask to rule it out."

He seemed to ponder that for a moment. "What about Carson?"

"What about him?" she asked, feeling flushed that he'd even remember him; though he'd just heard her get off the phone with him.

"You seeing him now?"

That instantly had the flush heating even further. *Stop it! Stop blushing and don't you dare clear your damn throat.*

Lifting her chin a bit, she looked him straight in the eyes. "Something like that."

"Were you seeing him then?" he asked without a flinch. "When you and I were . . .?"

Allison lifted a brow again when he didn't finish, trying to ignore her pounding heart. Could he possibly be saying he, too, thought there was more to them and now he was questioning whether she was seeing someone else at the same time? Is that why she'd been given the sudden cold shoulder and been shut out for weeks? Then he had a hissy fit when she mentioned the attack had something to do with a boyfriend. Was that what this was about?

"When we were *what?*"

"Still hanging out."

Hanging out? Really? So what? Her seeing someone else while they'd *hung out* really constituted an explanation? "Does it matter?"

"Yeah, it matters."

"Why?" She raised her voice because the fucking balls of steel on this guy!

"Because if you were seeing him, why would you think that Eva chick was referring to me? Or was he questioned too?"

Allison shook her head, thoroughly confused now. "Questioned? What are you talking about? Why would I question *him?*"

"Why *wouldn't* you? If you were seeing him back then, then maybe she was referring to him not me." He brought his hand to his head, looking very exasperated. "Look. Unlike the rest of the world, I just watched that video of your sister confronting that Eva chick in its entirety *today*. It just had me wondering a few things, so I needed to get it straight."

"Get *what* straight?" she asked, feeling as exasperated as he sounded.

"Why you'd ask me if she was my girl?"

Again, she shook her head in utter confusion. "We just went over this. Why wouldn't I?"

"But you wouldn't question Carson?"

"Oh my God." She brought her hand over her chest. "Again. *Why* would I question him?"

"Then why question *me*?" he asked, just as flustered. Here Allison thought she'd seen all his broody sides. That vein on his forehead was already protruding again the way it had the night he'd questioned her about the attack. "You never threw yourself at me or did anything inappropriate. Trust me. I'd remember that. Why would you automatically assume she was referring to me?"

Like a shot out of the sky, Allison finally saw a little clarity. It wasn't until today that he'd seen the entire video, a video that had instantly gone viral and she was *so* sick of. He must not have read all the other articles and seen the endless videos, including the interviews Eva had given since.

"She wasn't vague about who her man was," she explained a little more calmly. "She used the name Leo. Naturally, I had to ask. Even as farfetched as it seemed at the time, you're the only Leo I know, and despite us having stopped . . ." Allison cursed herself for having to pause to clear her throat, but it couldn't be helped. "*Hanging out*, of course I had to at least ask."

"She used *my* name?"

His expression went so severe it had her shaking her head in response. "Yeah, but it's over. It was just a crazy coincidence, and you're the only Leo I know. She's since confessed to the whole thing."

"That asshole in the video. Her boyfriend—"

"Scar?"

The flicker in his eyes under even tighter furrowing brows was undeniable. "That's Scar? The one who made her do it?"

"Yes, they were trying to get a reaction out of my sister. It almost worked, but . . ." Allison smiled proudly. "My sister kept her cool and didn't lose it. Well . . ." She smirked. "Not *totally* and immediately anyway."

Despite her attempt to lighten things up, the vein on his forehead was doing far more than protruding now. Allison could practically see it pulsate. "What's wrong? This had nothing to do with you," she reminded him. "It was all an attempt to lure Lila in and then try to sue her for any damage she did. Eva confessed to it all. He won't admit it, but Eva said she doesn't even know a Leo. It's just the name Scar told her to use—"

"Exactly." He glanced around, his right brow arched so high it almost met with that still protruding vein.

"Do you know Scar?" Allison asked with nervous curiosity.

She'd been so relieved when it seemingly turned out to have nothing to do with Leonardo. But now he was making it sound like it might.

"If it's the same one, I know *of* him. Never actually met him."

Allison followed his gaze as he continued to glance around the parking lot. "What are you looking for?"

He shook his head, and finally his eyes were on Allison again, the alarm—or anger—still in his eyes. "Has anything happened since? Anyone else try to harass you or anything?"

Allison had begun shaking her head until that last part. But she hesitated to say anything.

"What?" he asked because, of course, she'd been too damn obvious.

"Nothing." She shook her head again.

Like earlier, he looked anything but convinced. "Someone harassing you, Allison?"

"No." She shook her head adamantly, feeling silly. "I'm sure it's just me being paranoid. Before the attack, I'd begun to feel like I was being followed. I told you I was nervous Scar might've thought I had something to do with his being busted, so knowing he was out of jail had me on edge."

She explained quickly about how she and Jen had been nervous when Scar had been busted. Like Marcelo, they wondered if Scar thought they'd had something to do with him getting arrested.

"So, when I started seeing him eye me strangely, it gave me the creeps. It started feeling like I needed to be looking over my shoulder all the time." She lifted and dropped a shoulder just as quickly. "I know he's in jail now and all, and because of the unrelenting paparazzi, the security at our place is over-the-top, so I'm never paranoid there. But I can't help continuing to look over my shoulder when I'm at school or even here sometimes."

"Like someone's watching you even here?"

"Yes, but remember the paparazzi are everywhere now. Ever since that video went viral, it's been crazy. It could be them I've felt following me. But not a thing has happened since."

"Listen," he said as two thuggish-looking guys passing by eyed them on their way into the gym.

Leonardo literally stopped talking and stared them down with a purpose. "Do you know them?" Allison asked nervously because he looked ready to say something to them.

The guys continued walking. If they picked up on Leo's glare, they wisely didn't do or say anything about it.

"No," was his only response to her question as he turned back to her. "This Eva chick. Is she in jail too?"

"No." Allison shook her head.

"Why *not?*"

Allison explained how Eva had been given immunity for testifying against Scar, not just about his doing drugs and drinking while he was on probation, but a whole bunch of other things: the conspiracy to extort money from Lila and his affiliations and interactions with the bigger dealers.

"But even if they hadn't given it to her, I'd already agreed to drop the charges."

"What? *Why?*"

He was even more annoyed this time. Already, he seemed disgusted that Eva hadn't had to do any time. "She's a victim too. He made her do it—"

"So, she's out? Any idea where she's staying?"

Shaking her head, Allison tried to make sense of his interest in all this. She understood that, from an outside perspective, it seemed unfair that Eva got off. Their using his name was a little too coincidental, but it was still possible. The fact that he'd care so much touched Allison, but she didn't quite get why he was so convinced it couldn't just be that—a crazy coincidence.

"She's gone," Allison explained. "Her testimony incriminated lots of people. It even helped reopen a murder case gone cold from a few years ago that Scar may've had some involvement in. If they can find their main suspect, they'll need her to testify in that case as well. So, she'll be in the witness-protection program until then. Maybe even after."

"No one knows where she's at?"

Allison peered at him, still not quite sure why this was such a big deal to him. But clearly it was. For over a month, he'd all but severed any association with her, and now here he was because of *this?*

He opened his mouth as if to say or ask something else then seemed to change his mind and shook his head. "Promise me that you'll text me or even call me if anything suspicious happens." Allison started to shake her head in protest because she was sure he was overreacting. "It might be nothing," he added quickly as his expression softened a bit, but it wasn't quite a smile. "Like you said, it could just be one incredible coincidence. Just promise me *if* anything even the slightest bit questionable happens you'll let me know ASAP."

Now he smiled big, and Jesus, with a nod, she instantly conceded. She should have been embarrassed. *Did he know she'd be this easy?* That all it'd take was one of those breathtaking smiles to get her to agree to *anything*?

"I don't think I'll have to." Allison did her best not to look up at him too wistfully. "But if anything comes up, you'll hear from me. I promise," she added with a smile of her own, and there it was.

She'd begun to wonder if it'd still happen. Would the unexplained emotion still be there, or like the connection they'd begun to have, was it gone too? But like all the other times in the past, she was lost in his eyes again, and there was no denying that he was lost too.

After what felt like their longest moment yet, he shook his head and glanced away, muttering something she couldn't quite make out under his breath.

"What was that?" she asked, even as her heart rate spiked because she knew it had everything to do with their moment.

"Nothing." He glanced back at her with that annoyed expression again. "I'm just running late. But I'm glad I got a chance to talk to you. I gotta go." He started backing up toward the gym's entrance again. "Remember you promised." The smile wasn't quite as big as his earlier one, but it still held the power to leave her breathless. "Anything your gut tells you might not be right, you call or text me."

"I will." She smiled back.

He turned and walked back into the gym without another word. "Really?" she whispered to herself as she started to her car. "That's all it took?"

One quick encounter with the man she insisted she was long over—someone whom there was nothing to get over about—and her heart was already hammering away. Just like that, her insides were complete mush, and she was once again convinced there was more to the way he looked at her. Only next time she wouldn't give him such an easy out.

Right then and there she decided. The very next time they fell into one of their moments, she was calling him on it.

SIXTEEN

BEAST

As a felon and still technically on work release, not just probation, Leo had to get special permission to visit his brother Felipe in jail. He was only grateful now that his brother was doing time in LA county; otherwise, with his travel restrictions, he never would've been able to do this. But he couldn't just call and make an appointment, twenty-four hours in advance, like all the other inmate's visitors. So, it'd been over a week since he'd found out about Scar telling his girl to use Leo's name when she confronted Allison.

Of course, he'd be the first Allison would think of.

Of course, Scar expected her to ask Leo about it.

The asshole was counting on it. Only thing he *hadn't* counted on was that while he may've thought Allison was Leo's girl, she wasn't. Obviously, Leo's attempts to keep her at arm's length—make sure no one mistook her as someone he cared for—had been all for naught. Even in the short time he'd stupidly allowed himself to indulge in the danger of being around her, he'd been too damn obvious. She *wasn't* someone he was involved with and cared about. But apparently, it wasn't the vibe he'd given out. It was why he'd forced himself to stay away.

Then talking to her again was proof of what he'd feared for good reason. Being that close to her again was a reminder of how much he did *feel* for her. Not *cared* about her, damn it. Those were too completely different things. He hardly knew her.

At least Allison had kept her promise. Just like few people knew Felipe was his brother to begin with, even fewer knew the power his brother possessed behind bars. He was in for murdering someone with his own hands, but the conviction was reckless manslaughter. The guy he'd killed had been in the underground ring willingly. Felipe liked it this way.

He still held the power in the cartel, but most assumed that like Leo, who disappeared from that life years ago, Felipe had too. He was in jail for something totally unrelated and was thought by many to have cut his ties with the cartel. Yet a couple of orders from him could start a war nobody wanted. It was why Leo was here today to see Felipe.

Leo glanced down at the text he'd gotten just days after he'd spoken to Ali at the gym. He read the short exchange because he'd needed to talk to her and stopped texting to call her. Still, the first text was the most significant.

> You said if my gut questioned *anything* to share. So I'm sharing. Two guys lurking outside the gates of Sonny's property were arrested earlier. You might've heard about it already. It's not unheard of for overzealous fans to hang out outside or lurk in their cars, trying to get a photo. and it's what these guys claimed they were doing. Except they both had warrants and it's why they were arrested. But no harm no foul. They're behind bars now and all is well. Just thought

> I'd mention it because I figured you might hear about it anyway.

Leo shook his head. He had no doubt this had everything to do with him or his brother. Someone had sent them, trying to bait Leo. Just like Scar using his name wasn't sheer coincidence. He read his only response and then hers to his before he'd called her that night.

> Do you have names? Descriptions? Warrants for what?

He remembered feeling like she'd taken forever to respond, and then she finally did and he had to call her.

> No names but I could probably get them. Young Hispanics in their early twenties, I think. And I have no idea what the warrants were for. But don't worry. It's over. =)

This wasn't over by a long shot, and Leo's gut told him this would only get worse before it got better. He hadn't talked to his brother in too long, and now he needed to ASAP. He needed confirmation of what his gut was telling him. Most importantly, he needed to know how to make it stop.

After calling her that night and then talking to her a few more times during the week, Leo had done enough homework on this. What he knew now was even more alarming than he'd thought. He put his phone away and locked it up in the storage compartment of his bike. They'd opened the gate for the eight o'clock visits.

Ten minutes later he was past the metal detectors and the guard who had to double check his special clearance. He sat there in the small room of windows with phones for his brother to be brought out. His brother would not be happy about Leo coming here. For years and for Leo's own protection, Felipe had denied any relation to *La Fiera*. So for just as long, Leo had respected Felipe's wish that Leo not visit him or tie himself in any way to Felipe. But this couldn't wait.

The familiar sound of the heavy gate opening and closing from his own days behind bars had Leo shaking his knee impatiently and craning his neck for a glimpse of his brother. Felipe walked into view, and Leo immediately saw the wrap around his hand. He waited with the phone at his ear as his brother followed prompts on his side, punching in numbers on the keypad. When they were finally given the go-ahead, Leo spoke first. "What happened to your hand?"

"Why the fuck are you here? I told you—"

"I have to talk to you. It's important."

Felipe's brows furrowed. "What's going on? You in trouble again?"

"No, are you?" Leo motioned to his brother's bandaged hand.

Felipe smirked, shaking his head. "You've got perfect timing. I just got out of max a few days ago."

"Why? What happened?"

Felipe gave him a look reminding him he couldn't possibly give him all the details over these monitored phones. "Scuffle. No biggie." He lifted his bandaged hand to show Leo. "May have gotten a tad carried away. The guy's still in the infirmary, but he'll live."

"So, did they add more time to your—?"

"Self-defense," his brother said, shaking his head before Leo could finish. "You know how that works. He either drops any charges or we both get more time. He dropped them in a heartbeat. So why you here?"

If they had more time, Leo would've pressed for more about the *scuffle,* but he knew they only had so much time before they were cut off, and he needed answers. "Any beef going on between you and Chente?"

Felipe tilted his head. "Why? What have you heard?"

"Nothing, but his younger brother Scar was locked up this year, and as soon as he got out, he set up an attack."

"On you?" His brother's eyes were instantly ablaze.

"No." Leo explained about Allison's fight at the school, Lila's confrontation on the video going viral, and how Scar was back in jail again.

Felipe was staring at him too seriously. "So, this is your chick he attacked?"

"No." Leo shook his head a bit more adamantly this time. "But she is someone I've been seen with at the gym. Went to lunch with a few times."

He explained about the interview and how persuasive this *very* young girl was about interviewing him more than once. He also explained his theory that someone could've gotten the idea that maybe something else was going on between them.

"But there's not?" Felipe asked, peering at him.

"No. Not at all."

"You and her tight?"

"*No.* I just hung out with her the few times, and we've gone back and forth, mostly about the interview texts and shit, but no, I hardly know her. She's way too fucking young. But—"

"How young?" Felipe asked then mouthed the word "Legal?"

"Yeah, she's legal," Leo said, feeling the frustration mount. "She's nineteen. Still, that's too young, and I think she has a boyfriend." He added the latter for good measure because, even after all this time of not seeing his brother, he already recognized the stupid twinkle in Felipe's eyes, and the guy didn't know the half of it. "But she's a . . . sweet girl, you know. She's already been in the ER for something I think has to do with me."

He explained quickly about her sister and the whole extortion story. "But I'm not buying that shit. I mean maybe he decided to try and make a little money while he was at it, but that's not all that attack was. And now there's guys lurking around her place. Two guys were arrested this past week, and I looked into it, and they're thugs, Flip. Drug-dealing thugs like Scar and Chente. I just need to know if she's in any danger." He glanced down at his fisting hand. "Is this some kind of message?"

His brother's eyes were on Leo's fist as well, and then their eyes met. He nodded, alarming Leo to no end but didn't elaborate. Leo knew he couldn't.

"You have to call them off," Leo said, lowering his voice. "Whatever's happening, she has *nothing* to do with it. Have those fuckers come after me if they want. I'll deal with them, but if they touch her again . . ." Leo glanced away.

"You sure nothing's going on between you and this . . . young girl, *Fiera*?"

"Yeah, I'm sure." Leo looked Felipe square in the eyes because he knew what his brother was already implying by using that name. That if there was, this could be unleashing Leo's past.

Felipe glanced down at Leo's fisting hand again and then up into Leo's eyes. "You got special permission to come here tonight to see me, even when you know this could out you, just so you can *demand* I help you with this. For a girl you have no feelings for and she's *just* a friend?"

"She's not even that," Leo said through his teeth. "Allison's just an innocent girl who doesn't need to be involved in any of this shit. She's not like any of the women in our world. And worst of all, she has no idea she's even in danger. She really believes that whole Scar thing had everything to do with her sister and nothing to do with me. I just don't want another Kit on my conscience."

His brother's expression went hard. "That was different and you know it. No one went after her. It was just bad luck. It wasn't your fault, damn it."

"I'm not here to talk about that, Flip. Just answer me this. Is Allison in danger?"

"I don't know, but I'll find out. I will say this though. I haven't seen you in years. You've been here all of ten minutes, and already I know you're full of shit about not having feelings for this girl." Felipe shook his head with a frown. "I see it every time you say her name. That fucking vein on your head getting ready to bust over the *possibility* that she's in danger scares the hell out of me. If you're this transparent in here, no wonder they're assuming there's more going on, and if there is, be careful. We knew the possibility of who you are to me would get out eventually. If that's the case, if that's what's happening and they're trying to flush you out, you need to be *real* fucking careful. Think of your future, Leo. No girl is worth your going backwards now. You're doing so good. Promise me you'll keep your cool."

"Just do whatever you have to get them called off," Leo said because he wasn't about to make any promises he *knew* he couldn't keep.

If after only a few minutes his brother already knew what Leo wouldn't even admit to himself yet, he knew it was futile to try and argue that part. So, he didn't address any of the rest of his brother's rant. Getting confirmation that his gut feeling had been spot on only pissed him off further.

"Done," Felipe said. "But it may take a few days, so until then, you just need to warn her to be on high alert. That whole fight thing with Scar's girl was creative, and you could be right—the greedy fuck might've just been trying to make an extra buck while he was at it—but you know how this works, Leo. He didn't need to do all that, not when all he was probably asked to do was send a message, which I'm sure now that's all this is. Anyone who knows anything about you, knows how little it'll take to make you blow. They're looking to hurt me, not her." Felipe pointed at himself, leaning in closer to the window between them. "You remember that. They hurt me by getting to you, and if they do something that'll get your ass thrown back in jail, then they win. So even if someone just spooks her from now until I can call them off, you keep your fucking cool, you hear me?"

Leo nodded, knowing the gesture would be far from convincing. Felipe sat back in his seat in defeat because he knew Leo all too well. "Just try, okay?"

"I'll try."

It was all Leo could give him. If anyone knew Leo, it was Felipe. He and his brother were one and the same when it came to their irrepressible fury. All Leo could promise was to try. But both knew how *impossible* it'd be to keep that promise if he ever witnessed Allison being hurt, or even spooked.

"I'll try," he said again after they were interrupted with the two-minute warning.

Leo warned Felipe he'd be back in a week to talk to him again if he didn't call before then to update him on this. He needed to make sure his brother had been able to call this shit off.

The first thing he did once he got back to his phone was call Allison. Fuck the texting. He needed to warn her she might be in danger, and she needed to hear him say it so she'd know how serious this was.

"Leonardo?" she said after only one ring, and if he wasn't mistaken, she sounded anxious.

"Yeah, what's wrong?" he asked, already mounting his bike in anticipation.

"Nothing." She sounded a bit breathless. "It's just ironic that you'd call right now. I just pulled into a police station parking lot here in Boyle Heights."

"Why?" Every muscle in his body went taut. "What happened?"

"I could be wrong, but I got the feeling someone was following me. They didn't follow me in here, but I'd just parked and was trying to decide what to do." She paused, laughing nervously. "I think I'm being paranoid. I'm just gonna keep going."

"No, no, no," he said quickly. "Wait for me. Which station is it?"

It took some persuading, but he was finally able to convince her to stay put until he got there. After getting the information, he put his helmet on, gripping the handlebars, and reminded himself not to speed. The last thing he needed was to get pulled over, but it was a damn challenge.

If they do something that'll get your ass thrown back in jail, then they win.

Leo replayed his brother's words over and over in his head to try and calm the adrenaline already pumping through his heating veins.

SEVENTEEN

Allison

Her heart hadn't stopped pounding from the moment Allison decided to pull into the parking lot of the police station. She knew it could very well just be another unrelenting photographer following her. The paparazzi had really gotten out of hand lately. But it'd been impossible to get Leonardo out of her mind this entire past week. So, the seed he'd planted in her head, that maybe there was more to the thugs lurking outside her place, was hard to ignore. What if someone really was looking to hurt her?

Now she just felt silly. Her heart beat erratically for an altogether different reason now. She checked her face for the millionth time as the lights that flooded the parking lot weren't him again. She'd just finished applying lip balm to her lips when she heard the roar of Leo's motorcycle engine, and her insides did all kinds of flips. He hadn't even pulled around to park next to her yet, and she was already smiling so big she was sure she looked psychotic.

The moment he killed the engine, he was off his bike and took his helmet off. Allison rolled the passenger side window down for him, trying to calm her crazy insides. "I feel stupid now."

"Don't." To her surprise, he got into the passenger side and dropped his helmet at his feet. Just like the only other time he'd been in her car, his presence in it was enormous. "Was it a black pickup truck that was following you?"

"Yes," she said, feeling her eyes widen. "You saw it?"

I saw it cruising by when I first drove by," he explained. "So, I kept going then turned around, and sure enough it was cruising by again."

"Did he have a camera?" Allison asked, trying not to jump to scarier conclusions.

"No, babe." He glanced around the parking lot. "No camera."

"Oh my God, so what do you think he wants? Should we notify the police? Walk in there and tell them?"

"No. If what I think is going on, really is, just like the other two who were arrested last week, this guy will only be replaced if we get him arrested too. I need to make sure this ends now."

Allison stared at him, knowing she should be feeling more alarmed, but somehow his calm demeanor calmed her too. The fact that he'd referred to her as babe only made her insides crazier when she knew she should be feeling alarmed. "What do you think's going on?"

"It's a long story, and we don't have time right now."

He pulled his seat back as far as it would go and lay back all the way. Taking him in from top to bottom, Allison chided herself for her inability to focus completely on what should be a very disquieting situation. But seeing this man sprawled out in her car was incredibly distracting.

"Right now," Leonardo went on. "What I need you to do is drive. Go out just like you came in and drive up Soto and make a left on one of those small industrial streets like Folsom or District."

Allison started driving, despite her apprehension. Again, just like earlier, something about having Leonardo in her car with her made her feel safe. Lila would be livid should something happen tonight and would question why Allison hadn't just walked into the police station.

Just ten minutes into her drive onto Soto, she spotted the truck tailing her, and now her heart was hammering for the right reasons. "He's following me again," she said, glancing up at her rearview mirror.

"Good," Leo said. "Pull into one of those streets I mentioned."

"What are you gonna do?"

"See if he wants to talk—explain why the fuck he's following you."

The truck stayed at least a half a block behind her. She turned onto one of the streets Leo had mentioned. "What street are we on now?"

"Folsom," she said, her eyes on the rearview mirror again.

The street was a quiet one and, at this hour of the late evening, abandoned. Most of these businesses—auto and recycling shops—had likely been closed for hours. Allison gasped when she saw the lights of the truck turn into the street behind her.

"What?" Leonardo asked anxiously.

"It's him. He turned onto the street."

"That's perfect," Leonardo said an in assuring voice. "It's what we want. Now slow down."

With her heart at her throat, Allison did as she was told, wondering if she'd lost her mind. If the guy following them was armed, he could kill them both in the alley-like street, and no one would find them until morning.

The lights behind them closed in on them as Allison slowed even more. "Is he still following?"

"Yes."

"Okay, so stop the car, but stay closer to the left of the street."

"Why?"

"So it'll encourage him to approach you from the passenger side if he gets out."

Allison stopped the car. Leo there or not, she was terrified now. Why hadn't she thought in terms of weapons sooner? As big and menacing as Leo was, he couldn't beat a bullet. "What if he doesn't get out?"

"Then I will."

"*What?*" Allison's heart threatened to beat right through her chest now. *What in the world had she gotten herself involved in?* "What if he's armed?"

"He probably is."

Her stomach took a diving drop. *How could he be so calm about this?* "Then you can't get out. You *shouldn't.* Oh shit," she gasped again.

"What?"

"He got out."

"Perfect. Now lean over this side and roll down the window. Maybe that'll get him to come this way."

Once again, Allison did as she was told, her heart beat speeding up when her breasts inevitably pressed his hard body as she leaned over him. Trying not to react too prissily about her body lying over him, she concentrated on rolling the window down.

"Okay, now get up and see where he's at."

"It worked," she said, not sure it was a good thing. The guy was walking slowly, cautiously, toward her passenger door.

Her eyes were momentarily distracted by Leonardo's flexing hands as if he were readying himself to give this guy a beating. It was an instant reminder of him telling her about ripping someone's jaw off and his nickname—Beast.

"What if he really is just paparazzi?" she asked anxiously.

"He's not."

"But if he is?" she whispered loudly because the guy was at the back end of her car now.

"Then we're good," Leonardo whispered back. "Tell me when he gets to the back door."

Breathing hard, Allison nodded, watching the guy closely. "He's there," she whispered, and she knew Leonardo could hear him.

The second the guy reached the open window, Leonardo sat up and reached out the window. Within seconds, he had the guy by the throat, pulling him in through the window. "Who the fuck are you?"

The guy gasped as something clunked, hitting her car just outside the passenger side. Leonardo opened the door, pushing it open, even as he held on tight to the guy's throat. The guy's arms flailed about then tried in vain to loosen Leonardo's hold on him.

As soon as he was all the way out, Leonardo had the guy pinned to the hood of the car, face down. "Leave your headlights on and come grab his gun." Leonardo leaned into the window then picked up and slammed the guy's face against the car. "Who the fuck are you?" he demanded into the guy's ear. "And why you following her?"

Allison scurried out of the car and around the front, still unable to believe this was happening. Feeling like an utter klutz when not once but twice she tripped over something, she rushed to where Leonardo said he'd kicked the gun. This man who was following her had a *gun*! Dear God, had he really planned on using it on her? She picked up the heavier-than-expected gun with her shaky hands.

"That thing loaded," she heard Leonardo ask the guy.

Allison looked up just in time to see the guy nod. "You know how to unload that?" Leonardo asked.

"No!"

"Okay, then just put it in the car." Leonardo turned back to the guy still gasping for air and shook him "Talk, motherfucker, before I use that gun on you."

"I-I was just s-supposed to scare her."

"With a loaded gun! Bring me that shit, babe." Leonardo slammed the guy against the hood again. "Who sent you?" When the guy didn't immediately respond, Leo punched his side making the guy groan loudly. "Who, fucker?"

Allison walked up next to Leonardo, almost afraid to hand him the gun, but she did, and he took it, immediately pressing it against the guy's temple. "Leo, no!"

"Get in the car!"

As terrified as she was, she refused to continue to follow his every order anymore. Like a flash in her muddled head, it was suddenly clear as day. After tonight, Allison's life may never be the same again.

"No!" Leonardo's head jerked back to her. "You can't kill him, Leo—"

"Get in the fucking car!" She began to protest, and he turned the gun on her. "Get in the car, bitch. *Now!*"

With her heart at her throat, Allison fumbled around the car and then with the door latch and got in. She brought her shaky hands to her face as soon as she was behind the wheel.

"I'm just gonna *scare* him, babe."

Leonardo's sweet voice had her looking up at the passenger-side window where he was leaning in. "This is almost over." His voice was as calm as he'd been speaking to her when this all started. "Just get ready to drive when I tell you to."

He went back to slamming the guy's face against the hood again. Just like he'd gone from calling her a bitch to speaking to her so sweetly, he was back to yelling at the side of the guy's face in a voice so full of fury even Allison was tempted to just hit the gas and get the hell out of there.

But she didn't.

She sat there and listened to the muffled exchange between the two men. Then she covered her face while Leonardo proceeded to beat the guy with his own gun. It went on forever, and after a certain point, Allison was sure the guy was lifeless. "*Stop!*" she screamed. "Please stop!"

The beating slowed, but she still heard a few more poundings before it finally ended. With the two men off to the side of the lights, not in front, Allison could only make out shadows and a fast-moving silhouette where she knew Leonardo was with her predator. There was a loud thud, and Allison knew it was the guy's battered body landing on the ground. She saw nothing and heard nothing for a few long moments, and then Leonardo was in the car again. "Drive."

She gasped when she turned to him and saw the amount of blood on his hands and splattered all over his face and shirt. "Did you kill him?" Allison asked, crying as she put the car in drive.

"No. I need him to live so he can relay my message."

With a trembling breath, Allison could barely speak because of the huge knot at her throat. "Message?"

"What's up?"

The question had Allison turning to Leonardo, only to see he was on the phone.

"What the fuck does that mean?"

Allison got to the end of the dark street, not sure which way to turn. Leonardo motioned for her to turn left, and once again, she obliged. "Where am I supposed to go, O? I can't be anywhere in public right now. I need to go home and change."

Her heart was still beating a mile a minute as she listened to Leonardo explain to whoever was on the phone what just happened. Allison knew Lila was probably already wondering where she was. In the midst of the chaos, Allison had heard her phone making noises but had no choice to ignore it.

When they reached a railroad crossing with a long train passing, she took advantage of the moment to check her phone, since Leonardo continued to argue on the phone. Not surprising, she had texts from Lila, but she also had some from Jen, Carson, and Drew.

She read Lila's first as Leonardo continued to argue. "I'm a bloody fucking mess, O. I have to get cleaned up. Even a hotel's gonna ask questions."

The phone ringing in Allison's hand nearly made her drop it. Seeing it was Carson, she decided not to answer.

Leonardo's voice lowered noticeably, but the car was too damn small for her not to hear what he was saying. ". . . she lives with her sister and her sister's boyfriend. Her place is swarming with security and even cops. I can't—"

"You need a place to stay tonight?" she asked.

Leonardo glanced at her but kept talking without responding to her. Allison glanced down at her phone again, in no hurry to read Lila's texts after all. They'd only stress her out further, so she clicked on Jen's text instead.

Where are you? There are SO many hot guys here, and it's not nearly as ghetto as we thought it might be. Are you still coming?

Allison had completely forgotten about the party she was supposed to meet Jen and Drew at. Of course, Drew's message was similar. She felt bad, but at least they had each other. They weren't there alone. Allison had introduced them a few months ago, and they'd all agreed to meet tonight at this party Marcelo's DJ friend was throwing.

"It's a long story, O, one I can't get into right now. I just need a place to lie low."

Allison's phone rang again, and this time she did answer it because she suddenly had an idea. "Hey Jen," she said, frowning when the damn train slowed to a stop.

"Where are you?" Jen asked loudly because the background noise was so loud.

"I'm not gonna make it. Sorry, something came up."

"Carson?"

"No. I'll tell you later. Drew's there with you, right?"

"Yeah, but we probably won't hang out too long."

Allison half listened as Jen told her about a fight that broke out and how half the hot guys left. As soon as she was done, Allison hit her with her question about Marcelo's ex-roommate. "Is he still looking for a roommate?"

"I guess," Jen said. "Last I heard he was still pissed at Marcelo for leaving him hanging the way he did. I guess, even with Marcelo's half, he was barely making the rent."

Jen gave her Ron's number and promised to cover for her if Lila should call. "Don't answer. Just text her back saying it's too loud to hear her but that I am with you and you'll tell me to check my phone."

Allison quickly texted Lila to let her know she hadn't heard her phone since the party was so loud but she was fine and not to wait up. Within minutes, she had Ron on the phone while Leonardo seemed to switch callers as well. She'd heard him say he had to take the other call coming in and he was talking to a *Flip* now.

They got off the phone almost at the same time as Allison jumped on the highway. "Where you going?" Leonardo asked.

"Just one exit over to China Town."

"China Town?" Leonardo asked.

"You need a place to stay tonight, right?"

Allison wasn't sure why she was still trying to help this asshole after he'd spoken to her the way he had, but the fact that he'd beaten a guy to a pulp on her account sort of obligated her. Also, he might be the one covered in blood, but her hands were just as dirty. Not only had she driven the getaway car, she still had a million questions for him.

"I know someone who'll put you up for the night, maybe longer if need be, and won't ask any questions."

She turned to Leonardo as they reached the stop at the end of the highway's exit. "Carson?"

That almost made her laugh, even at a time like this. She shook her head. "No. This is a friend of Lila's ex. Don't worry. My sister doesn't talk to her ex anymore, but he happens to be my best friend's brother."

They drove down the backside of China Town until her phone's navigation let her know they arrived at their destination. Both she and Leonardo glanced out at the rundown apartment. It was perfect, nicely hidden in a dark street no bigger than an alley. Even the street light in front of Ron's building was out. It wasn't even until she got out of the car that she realized how weak her legs were, a reminder of the crazy night she'd had so far. Little did she know, it was only getting started.

EIGHTEEN

BEAST

"Why can't you go home?" Allison asked as she took her sweet-ass time parallel parking in front of the sketchy-looking apartment building.

"Another long story." No way was he getting into the fact that there might already be a price on his head. He'd wait until he heard back from O to explain. "You sure about this guy?" Leo asked, looking up at the building.

"Trust me. This guy probably has about as much to hide as you do." Allison glanced at him as she finally put the car in park. "Yeah, he's shady, but if my best friend says he can be trusted, I believe her. I just caught him too, so he's waiting for us because he said he was on his way out. But he's in a rush, so he asked me to hurry."

They got out of the car, and Leo took off the shirt he'd worn over his wife beater and tried to clean his hands and arms a little. The blood had seeped onto the white shirt underneath, but at least it wasn't as bad as the top layer. Flinging the bloodier shirt over his shoulder, he followed Allison. "I think it's this one," she said as they neared one of the doors on the lower level.

"You *think*?"

"Well, I've never been here. I just know this guy's in desperate need of a roommate, so I figured he'd agree to putting you up for the night if we offered some cash."

Leo pressed his lips together, glad now he'd pulled out more cash than he needed tonight when he'd put money on his brother's books. Allison hadn't even knocked on the door when it flew open. Instantly, they were assaulted with the overwhelming smell of weed and smoke that spilled out of the open door. Two guys walked out. The first one took Allison in and nodded in a silent greeting. The other one, who was fiddling with some keys, did a double take when he looked up at Allison.

"Holy shit." The guy's eyes went wide. "*Little* Ali?"

He made a show of looking her up and down slowly, shamelessly, as Leo stood there behind her, gulping hard, and didn't even attempt to hide his glare. Allison nodded. "Hey, Ron. Yep, it's me. Been a while, right?"

"A *long* while, I guess," he said, smiling big. "Damn girl, you grew up good."

You grew up good? What the fuck did that even mean? This was the idiot he was going to be staying with? Leo's head was already working on who else's place he could crash at for a few days because *Ron* was already getting on his nerves and he hadn't even met the guy.

Allison introduced them, and, as promised, without asking a single question about their situation, Ron handed Allison a key. "Just make sure you lock it up if you guys leave."

Leo pulled out a fifty and handed it to him. Ron glanced at the bill. "How long you staying?"

"Hopefully, just the night."

Ron laughed. "Dude, look around. This ain't the Four Seasons. This oughtta cover you at least for the week."

He didn't give Leo a chance to respond because he turned to Allison, blatantly taking her in from top to bottom again. "Aiight, mama. I'd stay and catch up with your grownup hot self, but I gots to be gone. You can have some of my pizza; just leave me some. Pizza man don't deliver round these parts, so I had to go pick that shit up myself."

"We're good," Allison said as Ron and his friend began walking off. "Thanks again."

"No, thank *you*." He turned around and walked backwards, holding up the fifty with a big smile. "I'm about to have me a *real* good time."

Leo followed Allison into the small apartment. "Okay." She glanced around, and Leo closed the door behind him. "Let's take a quick tour. This is the front room, I guess." They walked through it in less than two seconds since it was so small, and Allison walked into the small kitchen, turning on the light. "And this is—oh my God!" she screeched, spinning around and running right into Leo's chest.

Pulling her behind him, Leo caught the tail end of the rodent she was screeching about scurrying under the fridge. Relieved that it wasn't anything else, like someone else in the apartment Ron might've failed to mention, Leo turned back to look at her. "A mouse?" Allison was still holding two fists at her mouth, looking very disgusted. "That's what you're screaming about?"

He chuckled and shook his head, walking through the kitchen to the door at the end of it that led into a short hallway. "Oh, wait. You probably don't know what that was." He turned on the light to another room that turned out to be the bathroom. "That was a little bitty mouse, who I can guarantee is more afraid of you. Some people just have to share their home with them."

"I know what a mouse is," she said, stepping into the small space between them in the bathroom, still looking skittish. "I just don't like them, okay?"

"They're harmless." Leo glanced up from the sink where he was washing his hands.

"They *are* not. They're disgusting and carry all kinds of diseases."

He was about to address that when she flinched, making another yelping noise. They both looked down at whatever made her jump even closer to him and saw the culprit. She'd stepped on Ron's rolled up dirty drawers on the floor.

Allison lowered her foot back on the ground, glancing back at Leo sheepishly. "Ron's *chonies.*"

Her statement and her face instantly reddening would've had Leo laughing in any other instance, but right then, she was too close. So close he could smell the delicate feminine scent that was *all* Allison. A sweet scent he'd picked up from day one and would not be forgetting anytime soon. A smile couldn't be helped though. She was just too damn adorable.

He knew this was dangerous. Judging by how closely behind she followed him down that hall and into the bathroom, she wouldn't be far enough away from him to resist any sudden urges while she was in this shit hole with him.

He turned back to the sink, shaking his head. "Look. I know this isn't what you're used to—"

"How do you know what I'm used to?"

Leo dried his hands on the questionable-looking towel hanging from the towel rack and turned back to her. "I'm just saying I know this is no mansion in Los Feliz. You don't have to hang around anymore. I got it from here."

Her uncomfortable expression went a little blank, and he knew she was wondering how he knew where she lived. But if she really thought about it, that was public knowledge these days. Though Leo had done a little of his homework since the day he found out about Scar using his name. The blank expression morphed into a somewhat annoyed one. "You think I've always lived in a mansion?"

"No, but you're obviously not comfortable in a place like this."

"I just don't like disgusting mice and rats and creepy crawlies. It has nothing to do with what I'm used to. I could live in a rat-infested place my whole life, and I'd never get used to them."

He was done washing up, and she still hadn't budged from where she was standing. Clearly, she wasn't looking to make a move anywhere else in that place unless he was with her. Despite how pleasant the thought of having her stay that close to him was, he needed to get her out of there as soon as possible.

"Can I get by here?" he asked, and not surprising, she moved aside, letting him by first rather than walking out before him.

Leo shook his head again, unable to refrain from smirking. "You really should get going. It's late, and this is no area for a girl like you to be alone at night."

"A girl like me?" she asked, and for all the protesting she seemed to be doing about his comments, he'd been right.

She'd stayed so close behind him the moment he slowed she ran into him from behind. For the second time tonight, he'd gotten to feel the warm softness of her breasts pressed against him. "Sorry," she said, pulling her body away from his back. "I was looking the other . . ."

"A nice girl is all I meant," he said before she could embarrass herself again and start the exasperatingly sweet blushing again.

He walked into the small front room again. Just as he turned, something rattled in the kitchen behind Allison, and she took two quick steps toward Leo.

"Look," he said, feeling the frustration mount because being all alone in this place with her was a big enough risk.

Her continually flocking to him in a way that screamed *hold me, I'm scared*, was just too damn tempting. "You've been through a lot tonight." He looked over in the direction of the kitchen, which she kept glancing at apprehensively. "You still are. I appreciate you getting me a place to crash tonight, but I'm good now. You should go."

"But you can't leave." She looked genuinely concerned. "What about your motorcycle?"

"I already have someone picking it up."

"Are they bringing it to you?"

"Hell no," he scoffed. "I'm not parking my bike in this neighborhood overnight. You should get your car out of here too before you walk out there and it's on cinder blocks. I'm telling you the neighborhoods in this area—"

"I know plenty about." She lifted that stubborn little chin. "For the first six years of my life, I lived just a few blocks from here. After that, I stayed in and around this area, a few years here and a few years there. It wasn't even until a few months ago that Lila and I moved out of the projects and moved in with Sonny. And for your information, most of those places I lived in *were* infested with mice, roaches, and in one case"—she cringed, making a face— "big ole nasty rats."

Leo tried not to smirk. "Okay, so you're used to living with vermin. But they're the least of your worries in this area. It's a good thing you had a sister like Lila looking after you because out there alone you don't stand a chance."

Her brows suddenly pinched, as if that last comment had touched a nerve. He was watching her so closely he caught the barely there shake of her head. Then her hand was on her waist and that chin went up again. "You called me a bitch tonight and pointed that loaded gun at me. I almost forgot about that."

"I had to," he said, frowning when he remembered how hurt she'd looked.

"What do you mean you *had* to?"

"I told you it's a long story."

"I have time." She cautiously took a seat on the chair next to her and crossed her arms in front of her defiantly. "In this case, I think I deserve an explanation. But if my getting attacked and having this guy with a gun following me does have to do with you, then I think you *need* to explain all of this to me. Long story or not."

Leo took a deep breath. *Well fuck.* Obviously, she wasn't going anywhere until she got answers. Not that he blamed her, but he really wasn't in the mood to get into this, and he had phone calls to make, damn it.

"I'll give you the short version."

"I want all of it."

"You'll get all of it. I'll just spare you some of the details."

"Okay, start with why you called me a bitch and why the hell you pointed that gun at me."

Of course, this is where she'd want him to start: the part he wanted to explain the least. He wouldn't remind her of how he slipped and called her babe twice tonight too. He had no idea where that'd come from. but it'd just come so naturally. He was certain she hadn't missed it, but unless she asked, he sure as hell wasn't addressing it.

"This guy was sent to scare you just like Scar telling his chick to use my name was all to send a message. It's this long complicated shit that goes way back to my brother and his ties with the Mexican cartel. He's doing hard time in prison, has been for years. This is how they settle things and keep their power on the inside. For a very long time, we've managed to keep the fact that I'm his brother under wraps so they couldn't use me or his fear of them sending someone to hurt me as leverage or power over him. Tonight was the first time I've seen my brother in years because he's never even wanted me to visit him. Even that can out me as his brother and make me a target. But Scar's stupid message was loud and clear. I was already outed. I just needed confirmation.

This was the first time I've talked to my brother in months. He doesn't call often, and I had no idea when I'd hear from him again, so I just took the chance to go see him. Our conversations in the prison visiting area, just like when he calls, are all monitored. So, he couldn't tell me what's going on with him and his enemies, but he was able to confirm Scar's thing and those thugs getting arrested outside your place were likely because of him. Someone's obviously seen us hanging out. They think you're important to me, so they figured fucking with you would get a response from me. I called you a bitch so maybe that asshole tonight will mention that and the fact that I was willing to point a gun at you to whoever he'll be reporting back to. I knew what I was about to do . . ."

Leo paused, pissed that he'd said so much. What the hell happened to the short version?

"What?"

Shaking his head, he glanced around the room, unwilling to look her in the eyes anymore. "I just thought it best not to be too nice to you in front of him."

He made the mistake of glancing up at her. Seeing the strange almost endearing way she was staring at him had him glancing away fast. "What were you going to say?" she asked.

"About what?" He read the text from Orlando to keep his eyes off her.

"About you knowing what you were about to do. But you didn't finish."

He always thought it annoying as fuck when someone was messing with his phone when he was trying to talk to him. But now, he was desperate, so he started to respond to Orlando even as he shrugged. "I dunno."

"Yes, you do."

Fuck.

With no other choice, he looked up at her. She seemed . . . *amused?* "I just," he started to say as he rubbed the stubble

on his chin. "I knew what I was about to do to him would completely contradict what I was trying to make him think by speaking to you that way. It's why I had to point the gun at you too."
 She seemed to ponder that for a moment. "Do to him? You mean nearly kill him?"
 Leo nodded again, trying his best to keep his eyes on his phone, hoping she'd let it go. He responded to Orlando again.
 "And what were you trying to make him *think*?"
 God damn it, this girl. Was there anything she ever let go? With a deep breath, he looked her in the eyes and just said it. "That they're targeting you for no reason because you're not anyone I care about."
 It sounded harsher than he intended, but this was frustrating as shit. For a moment, she seemed hurt, but then she smirked. "So, you're saying you beating him the way you did completely contradicts that statement?" What had begun to resemble a wicked smirk turned into curious peering. "Have you ever murdered anyone, Leonardo?"
 Leo pressed his lips together. There may have been a lot of things in his past he was ashamed of, but as bad as the answer to this one was, it certainly wasn't one of them. Leo had always known, if he had to do over again, he would in a heartbeat.
 "What do you think, *Jelly*?"

NINETEEN

Allison

Swallowing thickly, Allison reminded herself where she was: in a seedy neighborhood, harboring a convicted felon who still wore blood stains of the man he'd nearly killed. The challenging expression that teetered from a glare to a gaze, had her breathing in deep.

"Jelly?" she asked, lifting her brow before addressing his question.

"Yeah, we've been over this," he said, tightening that jaw.

Refraining from rolling her eyes, she didn't ask the obvious, why he didn't like being addressed as Leonardo. She'd save that for another time. Right now, there was something more pressing she needed to address first because she had an inkling of what he might be trying to do.

"Okay, *Beast.*" She lifted her chin a bit. "I think if you ever murdered anyone you'd still be sitting in jail."

She kept to herself what Gio had told her about doing their own extensive backgrounds on the guys and his no-exception rule to accepting anyone with violent pasts.

Leonardo smirked, shaking his head. "Because everyone who's ever murdered someone is locked up?"

Allison thought about that. "Well, I suppose there are exceptions. Many have killed during wars or out of self-defense. Cops have killed in the line of duty, but then those aren't considered murderers. And I'm not talking about manslaughter either, like accidentally killing someone, so yeah, I think if you were a cold-blooded murderer, you'd be in jail still."

"Well, then, if that's the rule, I guess I haven't."

Allison shook her head. Was he trying to say something more? But her eyes focused on something more curious now. She'd seen it before on his arm but wasn't sure what it was because the tattoo over the skin did such a good job of camouflaging it. "Is that a scar on your arm?"

Leonardo glanced down at it and shrugged. "I have lots of scars."

"I've noticed. Can I ask why?"

He did that thing again where his expression and body language said one thing but his mouth was saying another. He'd begun to shake his head but then answered instead. "Rough upbringing. Rough life." He chuckled dryly, shaking his head again as he threw the bloody shirt from his shoulder onto the sofa. "Guess things never change."

"Is that a burn?" Allison reached out to point at the scar on his arm and he nodded. "May I?"

Ever since the first day she'd seen all the scars on him, something about them drew her to them. She wanted to touch them—touch him. He didn't say anything, so she took it as a yes and touched the scar on his big arm gently. It wasn't exactly random, and touching it, she could see there was a shape to it.

Glancing up quickly, she caught his eyes closed, as if her touch did something to him. "What kind of burn is this?"

His eyes flew open, and like all the other times, they were locked into each other's gaze. Though his was a bit harder than usual. "The worst kind." He paused, still staring into her eyes but went on before she could ask him to elaborate. "Not just because it was inflicted when I was a child, but the malice with which it was done. But seriously, Allison, it's late and you should—"

Her touching the side of his face froze him midsentence. Allison was determined to call him out on this. She wouldn't leave here tonight without getting to the bottom of what it was they were both feeling. Any other girl with half a brain would've already run out of there the moment she'd been given the chance. Here Allison couldn't tear herself away. "Were you an abused child, Beast?" She touched the scars around his forehead and smiled when he closed his eyes and leaned into her hand.

"Something like that," he whispered as he let his eyes flutter open slowly and gazed at her again.

"What is it about you?" she asked softly—gently. "What is it about this?"

She placed her hand over his incredible chest so he couldn't even try to deny he was feeling the insanity too. Unable to help it, she smiled when she felt how undeniably hard his heart pummeled against her palm.

"Tell me. What are you feeling right this moment?" She stared into his eyes as her own heart threatened to burst right through her chest.

He placed his own palm over hers. "You don't need to know."

"Yes, I do," she insisted, her insides already going crazy.

"Something I shouldn't."

"Why not?"

Now he scoffed as dryly as he had earlier, shaking his head, but he didn't move away the way she was afraid he might. "*Why?*" He glanced around, motioning with his hand at their surroundings. "Look at where you are." He sounded a little agitated now. "In this rat-infested hellhole in a neighborhood you shouldn't be in. Because of me. A felon with blood on his hands—"

"We're not that different."

That had him scoffing even louder, and this time he did move away. "When I say I have blood on my hands, I'm not talking about just tonight. To be clear about my earlier answer to your question, yes, I have murdered someone—in cold blood—and I fucking loved every minute of it. I have no business feeling what I'm feeling for someone like you. Nothing good could ever come of it."

"Because I'm a nice girl?"

She crossed her arms in front of her, not entirely sure she should still be arguing about this. The man had just admitted not only to having murdered someone but to enjoying it. Of course, he could be lying—trying to shock her. What he'd just admitted confirmed that inkling she'd had earlier. That this was just another tactic to push her away. Scare her. Remembering Gio's assurance that the work-release guys were thoroughly screened relieved the alarm she'd begun to feel over what he'd just admitted.

"You're a good guy, Beast. Just because you have a past, doesn't mean you're not deserving of a better future."

"There's no way . . ." he began to say, but he stopped to stare at her, and she could see it in his eyes: he yearned for this as much as she did.

Once again lost in his gaze, she walked up to him and took his hand, placing it on her chest. "I'm feeling it too. There are no rules when it comes to this stuff. It just happens."

"You're eleven years younger than I am, and for me, eleven years is a long fucking time, considering all the things I've seen and experienced in life. Stick with *Carson.* He sounds like the kind of guy your heart should be pounding for. But you should—" He paused but didn't remove his hand from her chest. "You *need* to stay away from me."

"What if I don't want to?" She slipped a hand into his. That alone was enough to make her tremble, and she felt him go even more taut. But she refused to stop, and he didn't pull away. He was feeling this as much as she was. There was no fighting it now. Tilting her face against his hand, she gazed deep into those intense eyes then kissed the side of his hand. "What if I just can't stay away?"

Without another word or protest, Leo cradled her face and kissed her as she'd *never* been kissed before—deeply, skillfully, possessively—like he never wanted to stop, and she prayed he didn't. Allison ran her hands down his arms the way she'd fantasized doing so many times. They were as hard and perfectly sculpted as they looked. As feverishly as he kissed her, every curve of his arm muscles felt flexed to the max. Allison wasn't sure that was a good or a bad thing.

Concentrating on keeping up with his delicious tongue, Allison *could not* get enough. His kisses were beyond even what she'd been imagining. Her lady parts were on *fire,* and already her head was wondering how far this would go.

With a groan, he brought one of his hands down and pulled her to him, holding his hand tightly around her waist. There was no mistaking the enormous erection pressed against her now. It was all Allison could do to keep her legs from giving out on her.

Loud voices and something crashing just outside the apartment had Leonardo pulling away and jumping in front of her. "Get down," he whispered loudly.

Allison did as her heart walloped with a new reason now. She heard arguing outside then what sounded like various voices yelling and cussing all at once. Leonardo crept over to the window to investigate as the voices got louder and along with more banging and sounds of things breaking.

Allison watched, practically holding her breath as Leonardo shook his head. A few minutes later, the voices finally calmed and then they were gone altogether. Leonardo turned to Allison from the window. "Bunch of junkies going at each other. Probably fighting over drugs. You shouldn't be here. You need to go. I'm in enough trouble as it is. The last thing I need is for your sister to start a witch hunt if she gets wind that you're with me tonight."

She ignored his comments about Lila because, as much as she hated to admit it, telling Lila about this was *not* happening—not yet anyway—at least until she knew she had good reason to even argue that she believed in her heart of hearts she could trust Leonardo. After that kiss, there was no turning back no matter what he said now. There was no way he could deny feeling everything she'd felt from him just from that one kiss. But there were things she'd meant to ask earlier.

"What about food? Or clean clothes? Is someone bringing that to you?"

Leonardo nodded, opening the front door and looking out as if to check if the coast was clear. "It's all taken care of and your part in this is done." He turned to her as she reached him, flinching when he realized just how close she was again. "Thank you for everything," he said, staring down into her eyes. "I do appreciate it, but I mean it, Allison." His eyes dropped down to her lips. "I may've given into that just now because there was just no way of fighting it, but it can't happen again. You *need* to stay away from here. From me. You hear me?"

Allison caressed his face because once again his actions spoke louder than his words. He was this close to kissing her again, and she wanted him to. *So* bad.

"Allison, please." He closed his eyes in an almost pained way. "You have no idea what you do to me. But this can't be. Trust me." He covered her hand on his face. "You don't want any part of my life."

"You can't know what I want."

His eyes darkened, going hard on her suddenly. "But I know what you don't *need* in your life, and that's me screwing it all up. Nothing's happened yet, and already you've been attacked and stalked by a guy with a fucking loaded gun. This isn't happening, Ali. You need to stay away from me."

As happy as Allison was about finally getting the truth out of him, and as badly as her body would yearn even more for his touch now, she drew the line at begging. The knot in her throat thickened, only there was one thing she needed him to know.

"Carson's not my type."

It was a ridiculous statement at a moment like this, and she knew it, but it needed to be said. She'd never had a type in her life only now she knew with every fiber of her being that Leonardo was all she wanted. Something in that gaze touched her deep in her soul. There was so much more to him she wasn't done learning about, but mostly there was this tender vulnerability she saw beneath the angry glares. The way he'd been so quick to jump to her defense—to risk so much for her—when he hardly even knew her. She knew so little about him still, yet in the short time she'd known him, those moments they'd shared made her feel like she knew him better than *most*.

Leonardo's eyes went from hers to her lips then back to her eyes again. "Maybe you should give Carson more of a chance. He sounds like the kind of guy who should be your type. Because I sure as shit shouldn't be."

Opening the screen door for her to walk out, she did, glad to be in front of him this time so she could swat the tear that escaped the corner of her eye. "You don't have to walk me to my car."

His only response was to keep walking alongside her, looking out in every direction, guardedly. He walked her all the way to her car and waited for her to drive away before she saw him walk back inside.

Even as she drove away, her entire body tingled still from having been touched by him. But the knot at her throat threatened to suffocate her when she remembered how he'd begged her to stay away. How could she feel so heartbroken over this man? She'd only begun to peel away the tons of complicated layers she knew there were yet to be removed. But even more pressing, how in the world was she supposed to stay away from him now?

TWENTY

BEAST

"I thought you said he'd been guaranteed they'd be called off?" Leo squeezed the phone as he paced Ron's small front room.

"He was, but you know he can't explain a whole lot on those phones," Orlando reminded him. "All he said was you shouldn't have to worry about the girl's safety anymore, but he'd just gotten word about Friday night, and he wanted you to lie low until he heard more."

"I have to show up at the gym tomorrow, O. As long as I know she's good, then I'll take my chances on anyone coming after me."

"He's calling back tonight, man. Stay put until at least then. Worst case scenario, if he still insists you stay put, at least wait until morning. Even if you don't have the go-ahead, I'll bring you a change of clothes and drop you off at the gym. This way you're not all alone."

"Trust me. I'm not worried about that."

"I know you're not, ass. But that guy Friday did have a gun. Who's to say they don't send someone packing again—after *you* this time. I'm assuming the only reason he's not in the hospital is he must have warrants or be on probation or something, but from what I'm hearing, you fucked him up *bad*."

That made Leo smile. *The asshole had been sent to scare little Ali and he packs a loaded gun?* In Leonardo's experience, the only time cowards used a gun on a girl was when they were using it to force them to keep their mouths shut so they could do more than just scare them. The very thought made him cringe as he felt his nostrils flare involuntarily. "Yeah, well, he deserved it."

Leonardo decided to take Orlando's advice and wait until Felipe called again later that evening. But he was also taking Orlando up on his offer to bring him a change of clothes in the morning. His ass would be at the gym tomorrow and on time no matter what his brother had to say about it. Orlando reminded him to keep his phone off for now.

"Pretty sure this guy's taking off for the day," Leo warned Orlando.

"Felipe said the latest he'd call would be nine, so don't turn yours on until then, and I'll call you around that time."

Grudgingly agreeing, Leo tossed the phone at Ron when he was done. "Thanks."

Turned out Ron wasn't an annoying asshole after all. Leo could only assume his behavior Friday night had been because he was high. But the next morning, Leo had awoken to the smell of bacon and coffee. Ron had fixed them breakfast. Not once did he bring up Allison, and as promised, he asked nothing about Leo's situation.

The whole day yesterday Ron had kept to himself in his room, but he did hook up the Netflix so Leo could watch something while he went out again since Ron didn't have cable.

Sunday morning, Ron suggested they either get rid of Leo's clothes or, at the very least, throw them in the wash, to which Leo agreed, so his shirts were now blood free. Only thing he was still waiting on were his heavy jeans to dry because Leo had asked him not to put those in the dryer. On top of it all, because Leo knew the drill, he'd turned his phone off Friday night after getting the final word from Orlando. The only thing he'd turned it on for since was to get the numbers he needed because Ron said he was free to use his phone anytime he was home. He'd been communicating with Orlando and his probation officer using Ron's phone ever since. He'd told his probation officer he'd be borrowing phones to check in until he either found his or got another.

Luckily, this time around, Leo lucked out with the PO he'd been assigned. If he'd had the same one he'd had before, the guy would've threatened if not pulled him from the work-release program for not having the proper equipment required to be eligible for it. Even if it was only for a few days like Leo told his PO it would be. Even the bad guys did their homework when it came to technology. There were just too many ways to track him down using his phone these days.

"So, you're good?" Ron asked. "You staying a couple more nights?"

"Probably just one more," Leo said with a frown. "I have to get back to work tomorrow. So, no matter what, I'm out in the morning. But I'll let you know if I need to come back."

"Sure thing. I told you that extra bedroom's a fucking hole in my pocket. Speaking of"—Ron glanced down at his phone— "I gotta get to work myself." He grabbed his keys from the counter and turned to Leo with a smile. "Places to be, people to see. But that Netflix box is still hooked up, so have at it. Oh, and you can bring that fan in my room out here. I won't be back tonight." He smirked, bouncing his brows. "But it's supposed to stay hot through the night, so that ceiling fan may not cut it for you."

Leo thanked him again then plopped down on the dusty sofa for another night of this shit. As usual, once alone with his thoughts, *she* was the first thing that came to mind. Leo could only assume now that a sober Ron realized Leo could be Allison's man. Leo may have been eleven years older than she was, but he knew he didn't look it.

When he'd hit the big three-O in jail earlier that year, many of the guys in there didn't believe he was thirty. So, while he did think he was decades ahead of Allison when it came to life experience, it was hardly the biggest issue keeping him from giving into what he could only ever fantasize about.

This whole weekend was proof of what she'd be dealing with if he allowed himself to pollute her life with his. Yeah, he was doing his best to stay on the straight side this time. But again, here he had proof of how easily he could get sucked back in.

Poison.

Maybe not all women but the ones who mattered had the power to affect Leo the way Allison did. Already his reaction to her was like none he'd ever had for any woman in years. But he was beginning to wonder if maybe this was different even from those he'd been comparing her to. What he felt for her Friday night when he'd been reduced to begging, was like nothing he'd ever experienced before.

A noise at the door had him sitting up slowly. Waiting to see if he'd hear more, he sat silently and began to think maybe he'd just thought he'd heard it. Then there it was: a soft knock on the door. It was dark out, and Ron had shared a few stories about some of the shit he'd had to deal with since moving into this place. Tweakers desperate for money trying to break into his place to steal anything they could sell so they could get their fix. Like when Leo and Orlando had rented the shop in the slums, Ron said females also came looking to suck dick for cash. But the possibility still existed that someone might be there looking specifically for him, so he made his way to the front door, very quietly.

It was almost inaudible, but he was certain he'd heard right, someone calling out for him—*Beast*. Moving the curtain on the side window, with one peek, he confirmed what his heart was already racing about. He muttered under his breath as he opened the door quickly.

Those damn eyes going so wide instantly as she took him in from top to bottom weakened his resolve. But he forced himself to at least *try* and be harsh. Pulling Allison in by the arm before she could even explain herself, he pushed the door shut then spun her around, pinning her against the wall. "What the hell part of 'you need to stay away from me' do you not understand, *Jel*?"

There'd been no time to get clothes on, and it'd been hot as fuck, so he wore only his briefs and nothing else. Feeling the swell of her ass up against his body would have him rock hard in just seconds if he didn't pull away. So he did, spinning her around to face him.

He hated that she seemed frightened, but then it was necessary. If he had any chance of getting through this without taking her mouth in his, he could only hope she was as terrified as he was feeling. "You have to get out of here," she finally sputtered out the words. "Ron's been arrested for dealing, and Marcelo thinks they might come searching his place for more drugs. I'm here to help get you moved somewhere else."

Leo stared at her, breathing heavily. One glance down and she'd see what she'd done to him from just one graze of her ass against his cock. She'd just told him the cops might be on the way, and all he could think of was spinning her around again, ripping those fucking shorts off, and burying himself in her.

Flinching suddenly when he felt her hand touch his forehead, he was surprised she didn't pull it away. He'd been so fixated on his thoughts and once again lost in those eyes, he hadn't even noticed her move her hand. She touched what he knew was the very telling vein on the side of his forehead. She stared at it now too. "You're so on edge," she whispered, her brows knotting up as their eyes met again. "Did something happen?"

He managed a very tight—very strained—shake of his head but said nothing. Then she did the worst thing she could do at that very moment. She licked her lips.

With a groan, his mouth was on hers, and everything he'd been holding in since the day he first saw her sucking that godforsaken donut drained out into that hysterical kiss. A part of him feared she'd push him away while the other hoped—*prayed*—that she might. No part of him expected her to accept his tongue in her mouth the way she had and respond with just as much urgency.

They leaned against that wall, bodies pressed against each other, and Leo knew the moment she felt his throbbing erection against her because she gasped. He nearly pulled away, but once again, she surprised him when she pulled him back and moaned in his mouth.

Leo tried in vain to just enjoy the moment. As much as he knew he'd live to regret this, even if he did make sure this never happened again, he wanted to at least try and enjoy this—for now. But he couldn't. Well, not completely. Not how he knew he could be. He'd lived through so many heart-stopping experiences, and yet this, by far, felt like the most terrifying *ever*.

Not since the day he'd listened to his mother being raped and beaten had Leo ever felt so helpless. Every taste and suckle of that sweet mouth—every touch of his hands and body all over hers—rendered him that much more powerless to stop this.

As he kissed his way down her chin, Allison dropped her head back, allowing him full access to her beautiful neck. He kissed, licked, then finally sucked her warm flesh, feeling her tremble against him. "Jesus," he gasped against her neck, kissing and sucking a little harder, even as the frantic thoughts continued to plague his mind.

"Allison" he said, kissing her neck softly again.

"Please don't stop," she panted, making him realize something even more alarming.

This alone might be taking Allison somewhere he'd all but forbid himself to ever go with her. With her body still trembling, the very thought of hearing her and *feeling* her come undone had him doing just the opposite of what he should be doing. He dove into her neck, sucking in a way that was already making her squirm and moan. "Are you a virgin?" The words flew out of his lips as he nipped at the warm flesh on her neck.

"No," she said breathlessly.

Leo slowed because that surprised him; then he remembered and his head shot up. "Carson."

He wasn't asking her. He was stating the fact that it'd just dawned on him. She was shaking her head, but that wasn't what he wanted to know. Leo started to pull away, but she held his arm.

"I haven't done anything with Carson."

"You said you were with him now."

The haze of red that nearly blinded him from that statement alone was just another reminder of what a mistake this was.

She shook her head again, always looking him straight in the eyes. "We've been talking more. Been out alone, not just in groups a few times, but I'm not *with* him." Her brows pinched suddenly, and her expression went a little hard. "Despite what my actions right now may be saying, I am a respectable girl. I wouldn't be doing this if I had a boyfriend."

"I know you are, and I know you wouldn't. I just . . ."

He didn't want to say it because he was still grasping on to the hope that he could win this battle. Leo searched her eyes in panic as the voice screamed in his head that her *being* with anyone shouldn't matter. He'd fucked plenty of girls who were in relationships or even married. If they were willing, why the hell not? It'd never bothered him then, and it shouldn't now. But God damn it if he didn't need to be clear about this.

He'd done enough lying to himself already when it came to Allison. Like when he'd sworn he could resist her no matter what. When she'd driven away Friday after practically saying she wanted him as bad as he wanted her, he'd assured his freaked-out heart that he could stay away from her. But this wasn't about sex, and Leo knew it. All he'd done so far was kiss her, and already he knew he was in deep, *deep* shit.

"He's actually turned out to be nicer than my initial impression of him," she whispered as her eyes looked deep into Leo's but would drop occasionally back to his lips.

Leo, on the other hand, searched her eyes with every word she spoke. He could tell himself it didn't matter until he was blue in the face. But once again, he was incapable of altering the direction his weak heart had taken. He was glued to her every word about this now. His heart was already *demanding* answers about her relationship with Carson.

"He kissed me once just a couple nights before Friday's incident," she whispered again.

Leo knew with all certainty there was no hiding the scorching jealousy in his eyes that threatened to burn a hole through her now. Lifting a hand to his face, she touched him, softly caressing his cheek as he took a deep breath, closing his eyes in the process.

"The subject of exclusivity has come up, but no promises have been made," she continued even as Leo breathed in even deeper. "But if I had a choice, if you gave me one . . ." Leo opened his eyes when she paused. With an apprehensive smile, she shrugged. "I'd choose you, hands down."

Unable to hold back because his exploding heart was pleading that he do it, he leaned in and kissed her again, softly this time, nowhere near as frenzied as he'd kissed her earlier.

His head argued some nonsense about him encouraging her to be with Carson. That *he* was hands down the better safer guy for her. That they should end this now and get the hell out of there before the damn cops showed up. But his heart, burning body, and soul were not having it. At least not the part about Carson.

Letting a few more kisses linger, because he didn't want this to end just yet, he finally pulled away. "I need to call my friend to come get me."

"What?" she asked, shaking her head as his statement pulled her out of the dreamy state his kisses had left her in. "You don't have time for that. The cops could be on their way now."

"My neighborhood isn't the greatest either, and I'm a little farther out. I don't want you driving out of there by yourself."

She frowned but didn't argue; instead, as usual, she surprised him with another suggestion. "Trust me. I know my way around these parts. I'm in a car not on foot. I'll be fine and I insist. We need to get you out of here now.

Dragging himself away from her, Leo walked back to where his clothes were, sporting the mother of all boners. Within minutes. he had his clothes on. Without saying much else, they were out of there.

With every minute that passed and neither discussed what happened at Ron's, the weight of it only got heavier. They weren't even to his place yet, and already Leo was regretting this. He'd never noticed it until tonight, but it seemed every other corner in his neighborhood was occupied by a drug-dealing thug, a streetwalker, or a gang member up to no good.

Even as they drove into his driveway, he eyed the guys standing around his neighbor's front yard. Mr. Garcia was quiet and kept to himself, but his son Jesse was a whole other story. He was a pusher, and these guys standing around waiting for him weren't just friends. Every last one of them looked shady as fuck. Leo should know. He was no better than them once upon a time.

Jesse knew better than to mess with Leo and his roommates or any of their guests. But these new faces standing around he wasn't sure about. Already he'd seen more than one of them eye Allison curiously as they drove up. Leo would be following Allison out to the freeway entrance, no matter what she said.

Of course, Orlando's truck was nowhere to be seen. Leo could only pray Nine's bike was in the garage where he assumed his was too. Having Allison all alone in his place was a risk. But the bigger danger was leaving her out here to wait for him to find his keys. After tonight, hell even before, he wouldn't have thought it a good idea to risk walking back out to see one of the thugs sniffing around her.

"Come inside with me," he said, eyeing the group on the other side of the chain link fence as he got out of the car. "I need to get the keys to the garage."

"Keys?" she asked but was already getting out.

Glancing next door, she seemed to understand and didn't say more. Leo explained as they walked to his front door that he'd be driving her back out to the freeway entrance but just needed to grab the garage keys first. As luck would have it, Nine wasn't home either.

Despite the neighborhood he lived in, his place was nothing like Ron's. It was clean with newer furniture and no clutter anywhere. He could see the surprise in Allison's eyes as they walked into the front room. She knew he lived with two other guys, so he was sure this wasn't what she'd expected to see. His place was also bigger: a home with three bedrooms, not a tiny apartment like Ron's, and a much bigger kitchen too.

The tension of being alone with her again in the privacy of his home now grew with every step he took around his place. Like at Ron's, Allison stayed close behind as he searched the drawers in the kitchen. He offered her a seat in the front room while he searched for the key, but she said she was fine. With no other choice since the key was in none of the usual places, he walked into his bedroom to search there and prayed she wouldn't follow.

At first, she didn't, and he searched quickly in hopes of getting out of there without incident. The very thought of having her in his bedroom had his crotch swelling already.

"Did you draw all these?"

Her voice at his door startled him slightly as he turned to see her standing there staring at his wall. Gulping hard as she took a few more steps further into the room, he nodded, and she turned back to the drawings. "I didn't realize you're an artist."

"I'm not. But like reading, there's not a whole lot more to do when you're locked up. So, I did some drawing while in there, but I never drew before that."

"These are good." She walked in even further to look at the rest.

Leo watched her cautiously, but inevitably his eyes traveled down her back to her voluptuous ass. This close to her he knew he didn't stand a chance to resist touching her again if she got any closer. He glanced around for the damn keys, feeling panicked.

"Is that what you're looking for?"

He turned to see her pointing at a drawing on the wall. It'd been Leo's attempt at a tasteful drawing of a naked woman lying on a cloud. The moment he saw the key chain with the spare to his bike and the garage door, he knew who'd been in his room—Nine.

There was a tack right on the nipple of the drawing, and the keys hung on it. Smirking, he walked toward it. "My roommate's a real comedian," he explained. "But yeah, that's it."

The relief that they'd soon be out of there was short-lived. His fingers grazed hers just as he walked by her, and that was all it took. Their eyes met, and instantly, his hand was in hers pulling her to him. Once again there was zero resistance on her part, and he was helpless to fight what his body begged for.

Her mouth tasted so damn good. He felt almost feral devouring it and running his hands all over her. "Allison," he said between frantic kisses. "This can't happen."

"It's already happening," she said breathlessly.

Unable to resist, he slipped his hands into her shorts from behind and squeezed her glorious ass cheeks. Swaying his hips against her middle, he pressed against her, envisioning what he could only fantasize about doing to her.

This time her hands did some roaming too. She ran her hands over his shoulders and arms then down his back. As innocent as Leo had Ali pegged, she sure as hell seemed to know what she was doing, and she held nothing back.

No sooner had the thought entered his mind when her hand slid down to his cock over his pants. Groaning, he knew if her hand slipped into his pants, he'd be a goner. Hell, he felt like one already.

"We need to slow down."

It felt stupid to even say it because the moment the words were out of his mouth he was devouring her mouth again, cradling her face in his hands like he never wanted to stop—never wanted to let go.

Letting one hand slide down over that ass he'd been dreaming about for months now, he slid his hand into her shorts again. Just as he'd imagined, her flesh was heavenly.

What she considered too much was perfect as far as Leo was concerned, and he molded her ass, moaning with bliss.

In an instant quid pro quo, Ali flicked the button of his pants open and slid her hand in too. Only she went for the goods. Something had her slowing and pulling away to look at him curiously. "You have a piercing?"

Leo licked his lips, nodding. He'd begun to consider removing the piercing after Friday night when she made it clear she was feeling the same thing he was. As much as he'd told himself he needed to stay away from her, after just one touch from her that night, he knew he wouldn't stand a chance if she persisted. Until she confirmed otherwise today, he'd been sure she was a virgin.

Her finger traced over and below his shaft where the piercing entered and exited making Leo's head fall back in reaction to her touch.

"I wanna see it," she whispered.

As he lifted his head to look at her again, she stared into his eyes very seriously and lifted a challenging brow. Never in his life had Leo felt so conflicted. A part of him wanted to just take her already. He knew showing her his cock would inevitably end that way.

"Allison," he attempted to protest, breathing even harder.

His breath caught when he felt her hand wrapped firmly around his ready-to-explode erection. Those sweet innocent eyes smoldered when she realized her delicate little hand wasn't going to get all the way around. Smiling a little bigger, she pulled his pants and briefs lower.

"Are you really gonna say no to me?"

"Jesus." He panted as if he hadn't had the pleasure of being stroked a million times.

Allison glanced down when he was fully out of his pants but said nothing at first. Then she touched the barbell gently and glanced up. "Is it for your added pleasure"—her face tinged just slightly, but she smiled— "or mine?"

Groaning, Leo took her face in his hands again and kissed her as frantically as he had the very first time. He *could not* get enough of her mouth. Fully exposed now, he rubbed himself against her, and once again she blew his mind when she followed his rhythm. As if reading his already blown mind, she went one step further.

"Do it," she whispered against his lips then sucked his tongue as she continued to stroke him a little harder.

"Baby," he gasped when he could pull himself away from her mouth. "You have no idea how badly I want to, but—"

"Then do it." She lifted a leg around him.

As he'd always known from the moment he first laid eyes on her, there was no way he could refrain once given the chance. As much as he knew he may just live to regret this, there was no way he could fight this anymore. He'd never get any sleep now if he didn't. It'd be one torturous night after another, wondering what being inside her would've felt like.

With a few swift moves, he had her shorts off, closed his bedroom door, and pinned her up against it. Allison moved just enough to pull his pants down his thighs.

Lifting her so she'd wrap her legs around him before she changed her mind, he brought his fingers around the front to make sure she was ready. He felt too close to bursting already. As much as he'd like to take this slow, he knew he'd be a goner too soon if he didn't hurry.

Despite being so wet, her pussy wrapped *tightly* around the finger he slipped into her, and she moaned in reaction. Leo slowed momentarily, as his heart thudded unbelievably faster than it'd already been going. *Could he have misheard her when she said she wasn't a virgin?* Impossible. Why would she be so eager especially after seeing the piercing?

Spreading her legs wider for him, he managed to slip another finger in her, but she was so damn tight it still made him wonder. The arousal beat out the concern that she might be a virgin, and he could hardly wait to be inside her. He brought his finger to his face, smiling at her glistening juices that dripped down them. Licking one clean nearly had him coming.

He spread the juices on the other finger along her lips then devoured her mouth before teasing her wet entrance with the tip of his piercing. Hearing her moan again had him pushing in, but again she was so damn tight he couldn't bury himself in her like he'd planned on doing.

Allison cried out in response to his entering her, and he slowed again. "No, don't stop."

"You okay?"

"More than okay." She gasped as he began pushing in again slowly. "You're just so big."

"You're so fucking tight," he grunted as he pushed his way further in slowly, but *God damn* it felt good.

"It hurts so good." She gasped, holding onto his shoulders for dear life.

It took a while, but once all the way in, Leo let his head fall back in ecstasy, afraid to move because he might just explode right then. Instead of sliding out, he kissed her deeply, savoring the feeling of being so deep inside her for a bit longer. Slowly, he began sliding in and out. As tight as she was, she was so wet it got easier fast.

They moaned in unison as he began fucking her faster— harder. Allison's panting got louder as their bodies banged against the door, making Leo grateful that his roommates weren't home. The feeling was unreal. As many times as he'd done this before, and no matter how many he ever did it again with anyone else, Leo was certain he'd never felt what he was feeling now. Nor would he ever feel it again.

As she dug her fingers into his shoulders, her entire body began to tremble against his, and he knew she was close. A few more deep thrusts and she was crying out in pleasure. That coupled with feeling her pulsating pussy come all over his dick had him burying himself deep inside with a roaring grunt. He came so hard he thought he might pass out.

They stood there for a while breathing hard and holding onto each other like they never wanted to let go. Leo didn't, that was for damn sure. But he felt it in the way she held onto him. The way she'd kissed him. Mostly the way she gazed into his eyes as he leaned his forehead against hers and allowed himself to get lost in those beautiful eyes. Finally, after all the times he'd fought getting too sucked into these moments, he didn't care. There was no denying it now, and if he didn't know better, she'd been well aware of it for some time. He had it *bad* for this girl.

"You're so beautiful," he said, feeling a strange mixture of awe, relief, and terror all at once.

There was no going back now, and as much as he told himself he'd been with plenty of women he never spoke with again or walked away from easily, he knew this was different. There'd be nothing easy about walking away from Allison now. He'd known it even before this weekend, but there was no denying it now.

Slowly, he let her down as her legs slid down his, and he slid out of her. It'd been fast and dirty, but it still felt so much deeper than any other time he'd been with a girl. Her feet were both on the floor now, and he was still pondering what his heart was feeling over this—for her—when he saw it.

Blood on his half-limp cock then between her legs.

The words caught in his throat, and once again, he thought he might pass out. Jerking his head up at her, he was at a loss for words suddenly until he just said it. "You said you weren't a virgin."

TWENTY-ONE

Allison

Of the many sides she'd seen of Leonardo, Allison didn't think she'd ever see a terrified one. While she hadn't considered herself a virgin or innocent for *years*, it wasn't until she felt how huge he was and then the piercing that she considered the real possibility of this happening. But she'd been too far gone at that moment to stop and give him a heads-up.

As big as Leo was, she was willing to bet he'd made even someone having sex on a regular basis bleed. She didn't understand why he looked so horrified.

"I'm not." She shook her head, bending down to pick up her shorts but didn't put them on. Of course, she would be wearing white shorts today. "I mean I wasn't even before today. I need to clean up."

He instantly pointed to the door to the bathroom in his room. Obviously, he didn't understand, and how could she expect him to? She'd explain soon enough, but first things first. Once in the bathroom, she cleaned up quickly, layering the crotch of her panties with toilet paper before putting the shorts back on.

When she walked out, Leonardo was sitting on his bed now. The horrific expression he'd worn earlier was gone, but he still appeared stunned. "Maybe I should've been clearer, but everything happened so fast. Before I could give it more thought, it was already happening."

"If you weren't a virgin, then why . . .?"

"I haven't considered myself innocent or a virgin for a very long time."

He stared at her, understandably confused. So, she took a deep breath as her mind raced to try and explain this. In spite of this entire weekend being so unexpected, the very last thing she thought she'd be telling him about was this. But she knew she had no choice now.

"Growing up in foster care wasn't easy. There was a lot my sister and I had to deal with. She got in trouble a lot for protecting me—her way. I was always scared she was going to be arrested and I'd be all alone. So, I kept some things from her, things I knew she'd be incapable of dealing with without violence. There was a boy . . ."

She paused when she felt her throat swell. She'd never been emotional about this even back then, so why the hell was she getting so now? This was something she hadn't even thought about in so many years, something she'd tried to erase from her memory, and now here she was talking about it to the only man in her life she'd felt so much for.

"Were you raped?" he asked as a more familiar expression replaced the stunned one from earlier.

Reminiscent of her sister and likely how she'd react if Allison were to ever tell her, Leonardo looked ready to kill.

"No." She shook her head then sat down next to him.

His hand was immediately in hers as he searched her eyes. "So, what did you keep from your sister?"

"Let's just say growing up in foster care I had some horrible foster dads . . . I did what I had to do. It was a boy my age. I did what I had to do to keep my foster father away."

Leonardo squeezed her hand, as the unmistakable vehemence in his eyes went more severe. Allison touched his face and smiled, trying to lighten things up a bit. "Alan, another foster kid who lived with us, noticed my stepfather's lustful leering and suggestiveness. He asked why I didn't tell Lila, but in hindsight, I know now he already knew why. That man wouldn't dare even look at my sister the wrong way, much less touch her, but he knew he'd get away with it with me. Like Alan, he also knew I'd keep it to myself for the sake of not getting her in trouble."

Allison explained how Alan offered to help her. He'd stay close by whenever Lila wasn't around so Mr. Castro wouldn't be so open to paw her because it was the only time he ever dared to.

"Alan was sixteen. I was twelve and naïve. I believed he was just looking out for me, until it too escalated. He'd insinuate that maybe he should talk to Lila about my foster dad's behavior anytime I hesitated to let him do more. It went as far as him . . . using his fingers, oral . . . and it went on for *months*. Only reason it stopped was because we were moved to another foster home when Lila got expelled from that school district and it was too inconvenient for the Castro family to drive her clear across town to her new school. Thankfully, CPS did everything they could to keep siblings together, so I moved with her to a new foster home. Otherwise, I'd already decided that if sleeping with Alan would keep Lila from killing Mr. Castro I'd do it."

"So, this was your first time?" Leonardo asked, once again looking horrified; though Allison could tell he was trying to tone it down now.

"Doing this, yes, but . . ."

She shook her head because she hated to have to say it, especially to him, but she needed him to understand. The last thing she wanted was for him to beat himself up over this. Already, he'd pushed her away all this time because he thought her too young and innocent to be part of his life. So, she was putting it out there. All of it.

"By the time I was thirteen, I'd done lots of other things with him most girls even older than I hadn't done. I figured it out fairly quickly. He didn't care about me. He was just using me and my situation to get what he wanted, and I willingly went along. Most girls in my situation fell into a deep depression, and trust me having gone through foster care, I'd heard a lot of stories: girls who needed heavy therapy and some trying to commit suicide over stuff like this. Not me. I was more worried about what Lila would do if she found out."

She shook her head, but even now, she didn't feel as disgusted with herself as she knew most would. To this day, she knew if she had to do it over again she would. She knew her sister too well, and turning to her for help, especially at that age when her anger issues were at their worst, would've been disastrous. But right now, what she really needed to do was convince Leonardo, who was still looking at her so stunned, that he *hadn't* taken her innocence. Not by a long shot.

"You didn't deflower some innocent little virgin, if that's what you're worried about. And . . ." She squeezed his hand again, looking him straight in his eyes. "In case you forgot, I wanted it just as much as you did."

Leonardo stared at her for a moment without saying anything then finally exhaled loudly and pulled her to him. "Just cause some asshole took advantage of you and you handled it as best you could, doesn't mean you weren't innocent. So, don't even compare yourself to the girls that did that stuff for money or drugs. You are better than them."

He kissed the top of her head, holding her tightly as Allison let what he just said sink in. Being held by him like that overwhelmed her with emotion. She'd never felt so safe in her life.

"And I'm not worried about having *deflowered* you," he added with a chuckle. "But you *were* a virgin, baby. I just wish I'd known. I would've been a lot gentler and would've preferred your first time to be more special than me banging you up against my bedroom door."

Incredibly, despite the heaviness of this conversation, Allison giggled, pulling away to look at him. "I liked you banging me against your bedroom door." She leaned in, kissing him softly. "As incredibly exciting and big a turn-on, it was also *very* special to me." Chewing the corner of her lip as they gazed at each other for a few silent moments, she finally added the last and most terrifying part to her statement. "I just hope it's not a one-time thing."

She held her breath because he closed his eyes and didn't immediately respond. "I don't want it to be, Ali. But I don't see how the hell this could ever work. Our worlds are so different, and you deserve better—"

"Better than what?" Allison felt her heart speed up because she didn't like where this seemed to be going. "Better than being with someone who makes me feel things I never have in my life? Better than being happy?"

"There's a lot you don't know about me, babe." He shook his head. "I've done some bad shit in my life. Been involved with some really disgusting people."

"And I haven't? I just told you about two of them. We all have a past. I'd love to hear your story because I'm so intrigued by you and I want to know everything about you. But I'm not looking to be a part of your past. All I'm asking is for the chance to be a part of your future."

Finally, he cracked a smile and then kissed her softly, tenderly, with a gentleness that made her sigh. "You might want a future with me. Even I've begun to dream of one with you, but other people might not be as thrilled about the prospect as we are."

"Other people?" she asked, pulling back. "What other people?"

"Your sister. You can't tell me she's gonna be happy about this."

"You let me worry about my sister. Despite what you might think, she *can* be reasonable." Even Allison wasn't entirely sure if she believed that, so she added. "Besides, I am an adult. Regardless of her opinion, one thing I know about Lila is she'll respect my wishes. What she's mostly ever been worried about when it comes to her *baby* sister is my safety. I won't be forgetting what you did for me Friday night any time soon. I'm pretty sure at this point you'd stop at nothing to keep me safe."

His expression went a bit hard suddenly. "That's what worries me most. My past may be in my past, but I already know for damn sure nothing in this new future of mine will stop the old me—the *real* me—from resurfacing in a heartbeat when it comes to you. That guy's just been dormant for a while, but you have no idea what he's capable of."

"Well, as long as he's on my side, I'm not gonna worry about it."

Allison thought she'd heard the motor of a car or two outside earlier, but now she heard voices in the house and doors opening and closing. Then there was a knock at the bedroom door. "You here, Beast?"

"Yeah," Leonardo called out. "I'll be out in a sec."

"You stubborn fuck."

The voice trailed off a bit as Allison listened to him cuss some more then someone else say something about how Leonardo's obstinate ass just couldn't wait until tomorrow. Allison turned to Leonardo quizzically.

"My roommates." He smirked. "They're real charmers. Feel like meeting them?"

"Sure." She shrugged, laughing nervously.

They stood up, and Leonardo took her hand in his as they walked out of the bedroom. Her hand felt tiny in his. It was just one of the many things she loved about him already. How despite feeling too big for her own skin her entire life, next to him she felt tiny and dainty.

There was only one guy in the kitchen when they walked into it. He was facing the sink where the water was running. From behind, Allison could see he was a big guy. Almost as big as Leonardo. Only unlike Leonardo he was nowhere near being bald. The sides of his head were shaved close, but the dark hair on the top of his head was much longer. While he wore a black T-shirt and jeans that covered most of him, she saw he had something else in common with Leonardo. Every inch of the visible part of his arms was inked.

"Where's O?" Leonardo asked.

The guy turned slightly then did a double take when he realized Leonardo wasn't alone. There was an instant curious smirk on his clean-cut face. With the strangest combination of a clean-cut face and his chiseled features, he was almost pretty, but then even his hands and fingers were inked. From behind, she hadn't seen it, but the hair on top was slicked back, and Allison could see it was all one length and probably fell over the side of his head when not slicked. Like Leonardo, as menacing as his size made him look, his entire demeanor brightened in a very sexy way from just the smirk.

"In the garage," the guy said, openly taking Allison in from top to bottom.

"This is Allison," Leonardo said, leaning against the center island and pulling her to him. "Allison, this is one of my roommates, Nine."

"Allison?" Nine said, lifting his chin and smiling even bigger as she smiled back in response. "So, this why your door was closed?"

He spoke to Leonardo, but his wickedly playful eyes never left Allison. They were this light shade of golden hazel. As usual, she felt her face warm at the implication.

"She's why I was holed up this weekend," Leonardo explained, ignoring the question.

Another guy walked in from a door Allison could only assume went into the garage. He was a hair shorter than Leonardo and Nine but equally big in the arms and chest, and while not as heavily tatted as Nine or even Leonardo, he did have his share of tattoos. He wasn't bald either, nor did he have the long hair on top that fell over the side like Nine's, but it was on the longish side, far unrulier than Nine's. He, too, was instantly smirking when he saw Allison leaning up against Leonardo.

"This must be Allison," he said with a twinkle in his eye.

"Yeah, it is," Leonardo confirmed then turned to Allison. "This is O, my other roommate."

"O, Nine, and Beast." Allison finally spoke up. "All your friends have nicknames? Or is Nine your real name?"

"Name's Rudy," Nine said.

"Rodolfo," O clarified, making sure he rolled the R and heavily enunciated every one of the syllables. "But he's been this close to being killed so many times, we started calling him Nine for his nine lives."

"More like twenty," Leonardo added with a chuckle. "We'll get him eventually."

"Not a chance," Nine said, turning to Allison. "And no one calls me Rodolfo. I only answer to Rudy or Nine."

Allison nodded, making note of that. "Is O just a nickname too?" she asked, turning to him.

"Orlando," he explained. "But most call me O. I'm good with either."

She nodded again. Good to know. Because like with Leonardo, now that things had changed between them, she preferred using the longer, sexier names.

"So, what the hell, man?" Orlando asked, turning to Leonardo. "Your stubborn ass couldn't wait one more night?"

"Nah." Leonardo explained about Ron being arrested and his needing to get out of his apartment ASAP. How Allison was the one that got the call about it and why she was here with him now.

"So, what's the deal with Flip?" Leonardo asked Orlando. "You talk to him again?"

"Yeah, you're good, I guess. You know he can't say a whole lot on those calls, but he did say you didn't have to worry about the girl being harassed anymore." Orlando turned to Allison. "But I am curious now. The whole world's seen and heard how hot your sister can get. What's she have to say about all this?"

Gulping, Allison exchanged a glance with Leonardo then turned back to Orlando. "She doesn't know. I was waiting to get more information because I know she'll want to know everything. But now that I have more, I'll tell her about it as soon as I get the chance."

Leonardo gave her a look that said he wasn't buying her nonchalance. His holding her hand and pulling her to him so openly in front of his two good friends could only mean one thing. He'd given into this being more than just a sexual thing. After today, Allison wouldn't be working up the nerve to explain to Lila about her still staying in touch with this man. She'd be telling her about her relationship with him.

It'd been less than an hour, and already she could tell he knew her well enough to know she was full of it. Telling Lila about this wasn't going to be nearly as simple as she was trying to make it sound. But she kept up the act because she did have every intention of telling her sister *everything*.

Nine let out a slow whistle then laughed. "Any chance you can get that conversation on video? Bet that one would go viral just as fast as the other one."

Orlando laughed with him, and Allison tried laughing too as if the very thought didn't unnerve her to no end.

Lila, Beast is my boyfriend now. By the way, I was almost attacked by a guy with a loaded gun the other night.

You see Leo's brother, a formal cartel member, is doing hard time in jail for murder. His enemies come after his loved ones whenever there's a beef among them. But don't worry. My boyfriend nearly killed the guy then turned the gun on me and called me a bitch. But, but, but! Before you lose your shit, he had good reason!

Dear God, this was not going to go over well at all. Snapping out of her thoughts, Allison smiled sweetly at Leonardo when she caught him still looking at her. The guys spoke a little more about Friday's incident and then a little about a job Orlando was waiting to hear about before Orlando excused himself to get in the shower and Nine plopped down on the sofa to watch some TV.

Leonardo and Allison headed out front after she said goodbye to his roommates. "I'll just follow you in O's truck," Leonardo said as they walked out. "I have to pull it out anyway to let you out."

He walked her to her car then kissed her against it when they reached the driver-side door. "There's still time to back out," he said, leaning his forehead against hers.

"Back out of this?" she asked, rubbing his deliciously muscled back. "No way. I stuck it out too long waiting for this to happen. I think we can both admit now we were hoping and knew long before tonight something might happen."

He smiled that smile she was already in love with and nodded. "I saw you thinking in there. Telling your sister about this is not gonna be that easy, is it?"

Allison tilted her head, trying not to smirk. "It'll be a *different* conversation for us," she admitted. "But then this whole situation is different. Don't worry. I got this. Not sure if you've noticed something about me." He peered at her curiously. "Just like when it comes to getting a breaking story, I stop at nothing until I get what I want, and I want this." She hugged him a little tighter. "So as long as you want this too, nothing and no one is going to stop this from happening."

"That reminds me." His expression went all serious again. "Things happened so fast today, and then they showed up." He motioned toward the house. "I didn't get a chance to address this further."

"What?"

"Carson." He lifted a menacing brow. "I know he's your editor and you do things with him that involve school and shit, but you said he kissed you. I already hate him. I hope you're not planning on still doing stuff with him outside that class. After today, I can't be held responsible for what I'd do to that little fucker if I found out you did."

Allison couldn't help laughing. "Way ahead of you. After Friday night, despite you suggesting that I give him another shot, I knew there was no way I'd be able to feel anything for him or *anyone* now that I knew how you felt. I was supposed to have gone out with him last night, but I cancelled. Told him I'd explain on Monday. Ironically, because of that one kiss we shared, I'm sure telling him I'm in a relationship will make any kind of getting together out of school too awkward now."

"He better not go back to being a dick with you either."

Shaking her head, Allison touched that protruding vein on his forehead. "He was very touchy when I mentioned being nervous about people thinking maybe he was giving me special treatment because we'd gone out a few times. He insisted he's a professional who would never do something like that. I don't think he'll go back to burying my stories just because we're not going out anymore and prove my theory correct."

Leonardo lowered his hand over her ass and squeezed. "But you'll tell me if he does, right?"

"Yes, I will." She smiled, hoping he wouldn't remember her admitting to keeping things from Lila so she wouldn't get her in trouble.

No way would she be doing anything of the sort and risk her boyfriend, who was still on probation, getting thrown back in jail. There was still so much about him she didn't even know. But no matter how far he'd come, he'd admitted it himself and she'd seen bloody proof already. That side of him was alive and well.

Just as her heart began to race at the very thought of just what she was in for, he planted a knee-weakening kiss on her before opening the door for her. "You had your chance to back out," he teased, leaning into her window after closing the door.

"You're not getting rid of me that easy."

"You sure?" He smiled though it faded quickly. "You still don't know my whole *story*. And trust me it's not pretty. Gets pretty fucking gruesome. You sure you can handle it?"

She gulped, trying not to show how nervous his warnings made her. "As long as it's in the past."

He stared at her for a moment with an unsure expression then leaned in and kissed her one last time. "I'll be up for a while. Call me and we'll talk."

She watched through her rearview mirror at the massiveness of the man she could now call hers. Her insides roiled, wondering how bad his past could really be. He'd warned her enough about it. Could she really handle it?

He turned back to her when he reached the truck that was parked at an angle. One smile from him and she was certain of one thing. She'd never felt so much for any guy—ever. After just one day of being indulged with his kisses, his body, and those smiles, she knew one thing she couldn't handle: not having him in her life now. As long as it was in his past, she could handle anything.

"My brother wasn't the only one involved with the Mexican cartel. We were born into it, only we got out when we got the opportunity. Then later, when my brother was given ten to life for killing someone, he made me promise that I'd leave the life of crime we were still living and make a real effort to live on the right side of the law for once."

Allison sat, gripping her phone, and listened intently to all of it. Leonardo said he'd be honest, no matter how brutal and gruesome, because he wanted her to know all of it. He even assured her he'd understand if she changed her mind about him after finding out the whole truth about him.

He wasn't lying either when he promised not to sugarcoat anything. She sat speechless for the most part as he told her everything. At times, she got the feeling he was hoping she'd want out because he spared her no details, regardless how gruesome.

"My mother attempted to hide me, keep me from the life she knew my father would want to drag me into. She could for a long time. But he found us when I was twelve."

He told her about the beating he endured at the hands of his father, how he branded him with the cartel's emblem like an animal then how his father proceeded to rape his mother while Leonardo listened helplessly in the other room.

"When it was all over, I either joined the cartel and represent the family name like my older brother from another woman or he threatened to torment my mother until I did. He mentioned ways he'd do it: have other cartel members gang-rape her while I watched, then torture her. My mom begged me not to. She said she'd hidden us for twelve years and she could do it again, but after hearing her get beaten and raped once already, I wasn't about to chance it happening again. So, I was in."

For the next hour, maybe more, Allison listened to the horror of Leonardo's life. He hadn't been exaggerating about the disgusting people he'd lived his life alongside. He said on the outside he was loyal to his father because he had to be.

Cartel members were merciless. He needed them to think he had his father's back and his father had his. But a cartel member became dangerous when he had nothing to lose. So, when his mother had gone missing when he was just fourteen, he assumed the worst. She'd been killed. Still, a part of him held out hope even to this day. With his mom gone, the only other person the cartel assumed he cared about was his father. A few years later, he and his brother united. Both wanted out of the cartel.

The only thing keeping them as an asset to the cartel was that they were still working with their father, whom everyone assumed they'd be willing to put their lives on the line for. The cartel also assumed you'd be more likely to stay loyal if the threat of that person being hurt existed.

"So, when we decided we were turning our backs on the cartel—moving to the states for good—I murdered my dad, and I enjoyed every fucking moment of it. Beat him to death the way I'd watched him beat my mother and as mercilessly as he'd beaten me."

He paused for a moment as if to take a breath, and Allison had a feeling why. She'd heard the gradual change in his voice as he'd told the story. He still had a lot of deep-seated anger that no doubt talking about this after all these years had brought out. Now she understood where it all stemmed.

"It was as bloody and gruesome a murder as they get, and I became *La Fiera*. All the anger I'd held in for years because of what he did to my mother, what he did to my life, unleashed. Never in my life had I felt such satisfaction. I wanted nothing more than to see him suffer. The few who witnessed it didn't waste time spreading the word. And La Fiera was the name I went by and was very proud of for many years, even after I left the cartel. Even had it tattooed on me as a reminder of one of the most satisfying days of my life."

He explained it'd been easy to disappear since everyone in the cartel thought he and his brother had taken his dad's last name, Valdez. They answered to it, even if on paper each had their mothers' last names.

"I didn't know it, but my brother, who's older, kept some ties with the cartel as a safeguard, in case we ever needed them. Since the house was in my mother's name still, I left it as is, so in case she ever came back, she'd find it just the way she left it."

He paused for a moment, clearing his throat, but before Allison could comment, he went on. "At first, we went our separate ways. I moved around Arizona while he came here. But even then, Ali, we didn't go clean. I was dealing drugs, stealing cars. I'd done a few stints in jail. So had my brother, so it was hard to get decent jobs. Then my brother got involved in underground fighting here. It was lucrative because he was so damn good at it and knew I would be too. I moved out here, and after that fight I told you about with the dirty fighter, I became Beast. It was also where I met Nine and O. It took a stroke of bad luck to have me seriously thinking about turning my life around."

He explained about all the other times he'd been hauled in for underground fighting, which didn't carry too heavy a penalty since both fighters were willing participants. But the guy his brother killed just so happened to be a relative of some legislator. The black sheep of their family. Still the relative made some noise, and the judge decided to make an example of Felipe, and since he was already on probation to begin with, she threw the book at him.

Allison sat there, stunned in silence, listening to all the details as he put them out there, slowly, cautiously, pausing at times to wait for a reaction. Though she'd managed to not react in a way that might come across negative. He'd warned her, and she'd tried to prepare herself for this. She was determined not to judge.

Even when he'd first told her he'd murdered someone and enjoyed it, Allison had assumed he was either lying or it'd been someone he'd killed in self-defense. But she quickly put herself or even Lila in his place. Allison hadn't been exaggerating when she admitted to why she'd done the shameful things in her past. Just like Leonardo, Lila would've snuffed the life out of anyone who'd done what his father had done to his mother, had Allison been the victim. So even this Lila would have to understand, but Allison still didn't understand something. Gio's words were back in her head again. The extensive background checks they did on these guys. How was this missed?

"Did you do time for murdering your dad?"

"Nah. That happened in Mexico. Things over there are nothing like they are here. We dumped the body where we knew it'd be years before anyone found it. There's no CSI over there, babe." He laughed humorlessly. "My dad's was the first murder I did all on my own, but I'd been involved in plenty of others, not actually pulling the trigger or landing the fatal blow, but dumping bodies, being the lookout, driving the getaway car, etc. It comes with the territory when you're in the cartel, and homicide investigations over there are a joke. The entire time I was involved, only time I heard of anyone paying for killing someone else was with their own lives from retaliation. Never by the law."

Allison wasn't naïve. Yes, Leonardo had a dangerous past. Yes, his life's story was heartbreaking. He'd never found his mother and still lived with the torment that she just might be out there being tortured.

In many ways, he and Allison were alike. Everything he told her about his past before his dad came into it, was normal. Just like Allison's had been for the most part until her mother's passing, they both had a loving mother who taught them how to love. He was a good man with a good heart who'd been dragged into the underworld.

Leonardo told her about his brother nearly reaching the ten-year mark of his sentence and of his possible parole if he'd kept his end of it up by doing his best to stay out of trouble in prison. So, he might be let out at the ten-year mark. They had plans, goals, and aspirations, and neither wanted any part of the violent life their monster dad inflicted on them. But he had a good and vulnerable heart she'd witnessed and felt. What more could she ask for?

"I know everything about my past sucks." His voice lowered to a near whisper, and Allison hated the unmistakable shame in the tone. "I know I'm the one that keeps saying you and I are too different. That I'm no good for you. It's why I wanted you to know everything. Because after tonight, after feeling everything I felt this entire weekend, there's still more I need you to know. But I want that to be in person. You gonna be at the gym tomorrow?"

Allison felt her insides tighten. "Yes."

There was more? What could possibly be worse than what he'd already shared that he'd feel it necessary to tell her in person?

"Good, I'll see you then. It's late. I'll let you go now so you can get some rest. Sleep tight, baby."

For a long while after they'd hung up, Allison lay there on her bed, staring at the ceiling. She didn't want to regret anything, but as she replayed everything that happened this weekend, the reality sunk in of who she was now seriously involved with. What in the world had she gotten herself into?

BEAST

The mixture of nervous anxiousness and impatient excitement was as foreign to Leo as the scathing jealousy he'd felt when Allison mentioned that fucking editor kissing her. Since Leo's dad had come into his life right around the time Leo had begun to notice girls but had yet to give much thought to them, Leo had skipped all this. A few days after his thirteenth birthday, his dad showed up at Leo's mom's new home in Yuma, Arizona and announced that was the day Leo would become a man. He drove him over the border to Mexico, and Leo got his first taste of the cartel's whores.

It was only now—until Allison—that he realized he'd been robbed of something huge. In spite of all the things he'd experienced, never in his life had someone made such an impression on him. But there was more to it. Never had any girl made such an impact on him.

Only one other time had he ever felt anything *close* to what Allison made him feel. Now he could say without a doubt he'd been grasping. He'd been hoping it was what he'd missed out on. But the feelings of euphoria he'd felt now just thinking of Allison were like *none* he'd ever felt. Now he knew why those guys in high school came across as goof balls because Leo had never felt goofier than when he was smiling about *anything* Allison.

Case in point, despite how nervous he was about talking to her today, the smile plastered on his face when he'd seen her walk into the gym today was instant. A smile of any depth up until he'd met and begun to get to know Allison had been rare enough for Leo. But the smiles he'd been exhibiting lately for her were ridiculous. He now felt like he owed those goofballs in school a *my bad, I had no idea*.

Concentrating on his training before she'd walked in had been a challenge already, but once he'd laid eyes on *his* beautiful Ali, his training had been all but shot. Now he waited anxiously just outside the front door of the gym where they'd agreed to meet.

She still hadn't told her sister about them because she said Lila had been asleep when she got home last night and then Allison had left before she'd woken this morning. Allison said this wasn't something she wanted to discuss via text or even over a phone call. Leo didn't tell her, but he'd been relieved. He wasn't looking forward to hearing Lila's reaction to her precious little sister's new boyfriend.

"Hey."

Leo turned to face the beautiful sight of Allison and took a deep breath. He knew Lila wouldn't be at the gym today, but he still didn't want to chance hugging her there. He knew the moment he felt her in his arms it'd be impossible to hold back doing more.

Last night she'd told him he wouldn't be seeing her today until the evening when they were both done for the day. So, he planned ahead. Several nights out of the week both his roommates worked late. Today was one of them.

"Feel like barbeque?" he asked, refraining from pulling her to him, but it was a challenge. "I make some killer turkey burgers."

As expected, she smiled big. "That sounds perfect. I haven't had a regular burger in forever, and I'm trying to keep it that way."

"Follow me then. I have my place to myself tonight. I'll make you dinner while we talk." He lowered his voice a little as they started toward her car. "I'll need something to keep my hands off you while I tell you the rest of what I need you to know."

He walked her to her car then took off to his bike, incredibly still not having laid a hand or even his lips on her. But the moment she got out of the car at his place, he was all over her. Never mind the assholes next door watching the show.

Once inside his place, it was a challenge, but he finally pulled himself away long enough to start the unpleasant conversation. They started in his kitchen, where he put together the burger patties. Even with his hands full putting together the food, he still managed to continually sneak in kiss after kiss. But ironically, he was counting on the heaviness of this conversation to keep him from getting too out of control before he could finish.

Bringing her up-to-date again about having finished his youth without a mom and the most fucked dad on the planet, he continued as they moved things out to the back deck. He began telling her about dropping out of school at seventeen. How bitter he'd still been about losing his mom. He'd always suspected his father was responsible for his mother's disappearance. The police investigated him, but he'd been part of the cartel too long. If he'd really had anything to do with her disappearance, his mother would never be found.

"After years with zero leads, I pretty much accepted she was gone. My dad lived in Mexico, and there was no way I was moving there with him. I could hardly stand to look at him after my mom went missing, even though he insisted if he'd done something to her he'd admit it.

"But he didn't want to be bothered with me unless he needed me, so he paid off the little house we lived in with his drug money. I was on my own when it came to everything else. I may've lived a life of crime and was way ahead of most kids my age, but my mom . . ."

He stopped to clear his throat because, no matter how much time passed, the pain would always be there. "She tried her damnedest to make my life as normal as possible in spite of everything. So up until the moment she disappeared, she did everything a regular mom would do for her kid, everything she'd been doing until that man disrupted our lives: cooked, cleaned, bought groceries, paid all the bills, etc. I was fucking lost without her. All I knew how to do around the house was take the trash out among other insignificant chores like emptying the dishwasher and shit. The yard and cars were mine to deal with, but I had no idea how much she did until I had to do it on my own. Fortunately, I had Mrs. Calderon."

He told her about the older widowed neighbor who'd become a surrogate grandma to him. So, when his mom went missing and she found out his dad had pretty much washed his hands of him, the old woman took him under her wing, from teaching him how to get all his bills in order, how to shop for groceries, to reminding him to water his plants and lawn so the place wouldn't look abandoned. "She even supervised and walked me through making a turkey dinner one Thanksgiving when my dumb ass decided to host a small get together."

Leo leaned in and kissed Allison. She was sitting on the deck's ledge, listening intently, and now he wondered if maybe he should've told her everything he had last night in person too. Admittedly, he'd been afraid to see the expressions on her face when he shared all the ugliness of his past. But as usual, he couldn't get enough of seeing every different and new one she indulged him with now.

"Long story even longer," he said, flipping over the burgers on the grill. "When I first moved here years ago, I met Kit, a young girl I'd seen every morning waiting for the bus to school, as I drove by. I'd run into her a few times at the convenience store and whatnot. Saw her buying milk and eggs and shit and counting pennies to get it. I knew most people around here that were low on funds were on food stamps, so I wondered why she wasn't, but didn't think much of it. Fast forward to a few months later. I saw some assholes giving her a hard time at the bus station one morning, so I pulled over and told her to get in. She did. I didn't get her whole story right away, but I started dropping her off at school almost daily. Eventually, she opened up and told me about her life. Her mom was an addict who sold their food stamps and worked tricks to pay for her drugs. She'd never met her dad, but like I was once upon a time, she was basically on her own. What really got me was that *unlike* me, even though by all accounts she should've been a thug, she wasn't. Her grandma had done a good job of raising her, so she was a good kid, made good grades, and was even a star athlete who played on the soccer team and had a real good chance of getting a scholarship. In fact, she was counting on it to get away from her mom. Her grandma had set her up for it. Kit's mom was a lost cause, and Kit's grandma was way older. She knew Kit would be on her own too early in life and she'd been right. Her grandma died when Kit was just a freshman in high school."

Leo took a swig of his beer, needing a break from this, since just like when Kit had told him about her grandmother, it brought back the painful memories of when Mrs. Calderon passed away. He shook his head but went on.

"I went to see her play one time and was hooked. I thought it was a damn shame that she was pretty much the badass of the team and the only one who never had any family there to watch her play. Ali, she was fucking amazing, and I've never even liked watching soccer."

Leo paused as he flipped over the green onions and corn he also had grilling. When he glanced up at Allison, her expression had gone a little tense. "What's wrong?"

She shook her head, but so did he. In the short time he'd known her, he'd stared at her long and hard enough to already notice the change in her moods. "What is it?"

And there it was: the unmistakable clearing of her throat followed by a swig from her water bottle. "You're making me nervous."

"Why?"

"You could tell me about murdering your dad and all the illegal stuff you did over the phone, but this was something you *needed* to tell me in person? I can see how hard just talking about this is for you. My head is racing now about where this is going? Do you have a baby out there? *Babies*? Since she was still in high school and you were an adult, were you arrested for statutory rape?"

Leaning in to kiss her again, Leo knew he should probably be insulted. But given all the other shit he'd laid on her last night about what else he was capable of, he couldn't even blame her for going there.

"Nothing like that. On top of all the shit her mother had put her through, Kit was gay. Just another reason why life was even harder on her than most. But I did become her Mrs. Calderon, as much as I could anyway. Only I wasn't safe for her like Mrs. Calderon was for me. I knew this." He ground his teeth as he moved the burger patties away from the flames and slid the corn cobs over them instead. "I just wanted to help. She told me about some of the johns and other men her mom brought over trying to mess with her. I wanted to be there for her, so I made her call me when she didn't feel safe and got her out of the apartment at least until she thought she was good to go back. I was almost done with the underground fighting."

He stopped to take another swig of his beer because he could feel himself getting worked up again over this—just like he did every *fucking* time he let himself think about it. "It was my last fight and a big one. Good pay out and I was gonna need the money. This was just after my brother was sentenced and I promised him I'd leave the life and try and straighten out, but I knew it was gonna take some time before I could land a decent job with my record. I never even told her about my fighting, but she found out on her own. She wanted to see me, but I forbade it. Those fights were dangerous. I warned her *never* to go there."

He slammed the lid of the grill down and walked away, taking in deep breaths and willing the damn knot in his throat away. Allison waited silently the minutes it took him to pace the emotion away.

"What happened to her?" she asked as he opened the lid to the grill again.

"There was a fight in the crowd, which was the norm. Only this time more than fists and knives were thrown. Bullets flew and everyone scrambled. I didn't even know she was there until I got the call from O. I'd gotten my ass out of there the second I heard the shots because I knew it'd get cops called. O saw her go down and stopped to help her, thinking maybe she'd just been knocked over. That's when he saw the blood. He said it was soaking up the front of her blouse fast. We'd both seen enough people shot to know she wouldn't even make it until the paramedics arrived. But he said what she was most worried about was me being mad." He chuckled as the pain inundated him. "She was fucking dying, and all she wanted was to make sure he told me she just wanted to see me fight one time."

Allison hopped off the ledge and wrapped her arms around his neck. Leo hugged her tightly, willing the infuriating tears away. Swallowing hard, he pulled away when he was finally able to talk again and swatted angry tears away.

"Poison," he said as her brows pinched in confusion. "I know you think I meant women are poison because they're evil or maybe I've been burned. That's not it, babe. "He shook his head, taking her face and cradling it. "It's just that, for me, any woman I've allowed myself to care about has always turned out to be the biggest heartache in my life. It's like a curse. The only times I've allowed myself to get close and care about one, ended in heartache. *Every* time. It's why I'd decided a long time ago I'd never allow another one in. Not another Mrs. Calderon, not another Kit, not even anything romantic. With you . . ." He stopped to take a deep breath. "That first day I laid eyes on you, I saw you from behind and worked my way slowly up. I was lusting over your body the way I would any girl with a body like yours: taking every inch of your beautiful curves in and imagining what I'd do with you not *if* but *when* I ever got my hands on you. It's what a smug asshole I've always been! I was so fixated on your mouth devouring that damn donut, I stopped there."

He closed his eyes as the visual assaulted him for the millionth time, his cock already at attention even at a moment like this.

"Then my eyes finally made it the rest of the way up your face, and you looked *so* young all I could think of was Kit. I was so fucking disgusted with myself. Every time I saw you after that, it was a reminder of how some of her mom's johns could even consider doing something to such a young and innocent girl. Then came the day of the interview and you looked so different: so much more seductive and womanly than you had that first day. On top of that, there was something about the mixture of innocence and spunk I wasn't expecting. The excitement and aspirations for your future were things I'd been deprived of at your age, and I felt almost envious, but most of all, unworthy of someone like you in my life. Your eyes. Jesus Christ, your eyes. Even now they do something to me I can't even explain. So, when it became clear you weren't a high-school kid—you were an adult—you became a poison I knew I had to stay away from, especially once I found out about you and Carson. I figured I'd leave well enough alone and let you be with someone who wasn't gonna come into your life and fuck it all up like I did Kit's. If she'd never met me—"

"That wasn't your fault."

"Yes, it was."

"No, it wasn't." This time she brought her hands up to cradle his face. "You probably helped her in more ways than you'll ever know, and she was just a young girl intrigued by you and—"

"Like you."

He saw Allison take a deep breath and the look in her eyes go even more severe than it already had. "Yes, I'm absolutely intrigued by you, but that's not all it is. There's so much more to you, and I think I knew it the day I finally got to talk to you too. I've been saying since I first found out about the work-release program, everyone deserves a second chance. Kit was in high school, younger than I and why she took such a risk. I promise you, and I owe it to my sister. As much as I'm drawn to you, I won't be taking any risks. If I didn't believe that everything you've told me about isn't really all in your past, then I'd walk. It is, right?"

"Yes, but my life is still a danger to you."

"Why?"

"Because there are still times I'm inevitably around people who for me pose no threat, but I wouldn't want them around you. And this neighborhood . . . it's not for you."

"I lived just a few blocks from here not long ago. You can't hold where I live now against me."

"I'm not. It's just that where you live now is where you should be in the evenings, not coming out here to visit your boyfriend—"

To his surprise, she laughed. "I'm more at home here than I am in Los Feliz, and the only time I'll ever be here is when you are. Do you really think I'll be in danger then?"

Leo wrapped his arms around her again as possessively as he'd ever felt. Fuck no, she'd never be in danger when she was with him. But that wasn't entirely why he told her this. After yesterday, he could never suggest they shouldn't be together. His heart would protest violently. But the one mention that she'd been kissed recently by a guy, likely as goofy as the ones back when he was in high school, made him nervous.

Kit, Mrs. Cardenas, and his own mother weren't the only women he'd cared about who brought heartache in his life. There were a couple of others he'd spare her the stupid details about. But he couldn't imagine things not ending disastrously if he was ever witness to other guys around Allison now. Maybe a *normal* boyfriend would be able to handle other guys in her life, but Leo had been stripped of any normality many years ago.

This was a different kind of poison altogether. He'd felt it that first time he'd been alone with her in that boardroom where all she did was interview him. She'd had that same innocent awestruck look in her eyes Kit always did. Except with Kit, he'd just yearned to help her. With Allison, he'd wanted so much more.

Allison brought her arms down and around his waist, leaning her head against his chest. Wrapping his arms around her now too, he kissed the top of her head. Just like yesterday, he was feeling it again: this all-consuming emotion he'd never felt in his life. He still felt so undeserving of this. After all the evil he'd ever been a part of, how in the world did he deserve this? How could he have possibly earned the right to feel entitled to having someone as special as Allison exclusively to himself? Then he remembered the other more terrifying thing he needed to say to her in person.

"So far, nothing I've confessed to you seems to scare you, babe. I pray what I say next won't either because it scares the hell out of me."

She pulled away, looking up at him, the apprehension in her eyes like it was earlier when she admitted to being nervous.

"This might sound crazy to you, but I've been trying to figure this out for weeks, and after this weekend, I've come to one conclusion."

He swallowed hard but continued to gaze in her eyes because he needed to see what she *felt* when he said this. "I've fallen in love with you." Her mouth fell open, but he went on quickly before she could interrupt. "It didn't happen overnight. I've been fighting it for a while. For most, that would be a good thing, baby, but I'm not sure it is in my case. I've cared about people before, but *never* like this. I'm not sure I'd handle the downs like a normal person would, and I'm telling you this now while you still have a chance to run."

She shook her head and touched his face. "You are normal, Leonardo, and you'll handle the downs the way everybody else does. You'll—"

"No." He shook his head, wishing he could just agree with her, but he couldn't. Not about this. "There's a reason for the nicknames, babe. Both *La Feria* and Beast. It's no coincidence that they mean the same thing, and neither were names I chose. Anyone who's been witness to it came to the same conclusion. It's like there's this switch in my head, and once it's hit, that side of me is unleashed. I can control him for the most part but not when it comes to certain things, and I already know I won't be able to when it comes to you. I felt it Friday."

"Okay," she said calmly and nodded. "I witnessed it too, but you handled it just fine. The guy had a gun. He posed a real danger to us both—"

"To you," he said with conviction. "It's a hundred percent what my reaction to him was about. It was *all* about you, and I'm telling you I know that's how it'll always be when it comes to you." To his surprise, she smirked. *Smirked.* At a moment like this. "I'm serious, Ali—"

"I know you are," she said, smiling even bigger. "They said the threat is over, right? And I don't foresee anything of that nature happening at all anymore. So, note taken, but I'm not worried." She ran her finger down his arm and licked her lips. "I've fallen in love with you too, Leonardo. Maybe we should focus on the romantic side of this predicament instead of the unnecessary worrying. Let's talk about the positive side of this *beast*. I enjoyed unleashing him yesterday. I can hardly wait to unleash him again."

Hearing her say she was in love too then her following it up with this was too much. With a groan, he picked her up, making her squeal. "The burgers!" she said as he began toward the door.

With a swift turn of his hips, he spun around halfway to turn off the burner on the grill. "We'll come back for them. But you just hit that switch."

Allison giggled in his arms as he raced into the house. If he could be sure when his roommates would be home or that his neighbors might not be watching, he would've bent her over right there on the deck. Instead, he'd be unleashing it in his bed this time, and he'd take it *much* slower than yesterday.

"FYI," Bravo said as he walked into the training area where Leo was working on his bicep curls. "We'll be having some company walk through here today. VIP's, so look alive. A few of the Dodgers and even a few San Diego Padres along with some other associates are coming by to take a tour and just check things out. They'll be walking through here. No need to go out of your way to say anything to them. Just do your thing. No biggie, but I thought I'd give you guys a heads-up in case you're wondering what they're doing in here."

Leo nodded along with the others and carried on with his workout. Halfway through his time on the speed bag, the group of men walked in. A couple of the older ones wore shirts and ties; though, instead of professional like he was sure they were trying to look, their choice of tie colors and patent leather shoes didn't say sophisticated. More like gaudy. One of them even wore white shoes. They reminded Leo more of the grease-ball mobsters he dealt with once upon a time. The younger guys were all dressed down in jeans and even basketball shorts.

Seeing Sabian, Lila's superstar fiancé, walk in instantly had Leo on edge. Allison assured Leo more than once now she'd deal with her sister. She'd reminded Leo that she was an adult capable of deciding what was best for her and that her sister would respect that.

You're what's good for me.

As with all his reactions to anything Allison, he didn't even realize he was smiling until the loud laughter snapped him out of it. A few of the guys in the group continued to laugh as they glanced around. Most looked familiar, and Leo was sure it was because they were all players. He wasn't the biggest baseball fan, but Nine was, especially of the Dodgers, so the games were constantly on at their place.

Then he did a double take. One of the guys still smiling big looked familiar, only not like the other guys, not like Leo might've seen him on television maybe even a commercial here and there. There was a different familiarity about him, except Leo couldn't quite place the face.

For most people, this wouldn't be a big deal, but with Leo's past, he had to watch his back. He had to make sure he didn't inadvertently come face-to-face with a past adversary, someone who might make trouble for him.

The group moved along the far side of the room and Leo let it go. If the guy had really been anyone that important, Leo was certain he would've been able to place him. He concentrated on his training again. As he moved on to his speed-bag training, the group of men made it around the room and began passing by where Leo stood.

Leo glanced up and saw them take him in curiously as they had everyone else who was training in the room. The guy he thought he'd recognized was busy talking to one of the bigger guys in the group, someone who Leo recognized, the superstar catcher of the Padres. Much like with Sabian and some of the other big name professional athletes, you didn't even have to be a baseball fan to know this guy—*Rage* Romero. The guy had major celebrity status.

Never one to gawk at even as big a star as Rage was, Leo began to glance away, until he saw the guy with him do a double take when he saw Leo. For a moment, they were locked into a stare down, and despite the guy's big smile slowly waning, Leo still wasn't sure what to make of it.

Thankfully, the guy looked away soon enough, as if he realized he'd been too obvious. But this weirded the fuck out of Leo. Clearly, he did know the guy from somewhere. But no matter how hard he tried, he couldn't remember from where.

Glancing up a few more times as they finished making their way through the training room, Leo thought he saw the guy looking his way casually each time. When the group of men reached the training room double doors, Leo glanced up to see the guy leaning in to ask Bravo something then motion his head in Leo's direction. Bravo didn't turn in Leo's direction, and Leo might've thought he was imagining things if it hadn't been for the heavier of the two older guys with them who jerked his head around to look at Leo.

If Leo wasn't mistaken, the guy he still couldn't place snapped at the older guy, who immediately made a show of looking all around the room. The mystery guy pushed one of the doors open and walked out. Bravo held the door for the older guys who followed and some of the other guys in the group.

Then there it was. Much more casually than the older guy, Bravo glanced in a few different directions of the room, said something to the guys walking out, but didn't walk out before looking at Leo. He smiled, giving him a quick goodbye salute as the last guy in the group walked out and Bravo followed. "The fuck was that about?" Leo muttered under his breath.

He sat there for a few moments, wondering if he should even worry about it. Then he decided it'd be stupid to worry. He'd likely never see the guy again, and for all he knew, the guy could just be someone insignificant from way back. Only like Leo, maybe it was driving the guy crazy too if he was also trying to figure out where he recognized Leo from.

When he was done with his training and sparring sessions, Leo rushed through the motions of showering and changing. It'd only been a week since he'd given in to his carnal desires for Allison, but most importantly, his heart and already his life felt different. He was trying not to panic, but he still couldn't decide if thinking of her every waking moment and then dreaming of her most nights was a good or bad thing.

The terrifying dreams had magically ceased since he'd opened up to her about his past and confessed to being in love with her. Now most his dreams consisted of him being with Allison. He'd gone from waking in terror, to waking up in complete bliss with a much larger-than-usual morning wood every day.

Their agreement to keep things casual and on the down low for now had gone right out the window. They hadn't done anything stupid like make out openly in front of others, but with her sister being away from the gym most of the last week, Allison had been there almost every day.

With Nine and Orlando gone this past weekend, Allison had spent the weekend with Leo at his place. And to his surprise, it hadn't been nonstop sex. They'd spent equal amounts of time talking and getting to know each other. Even more surprising was, not just that so far he hadn't had issues telling her about his past but, how accepting she was of all his past mistakes.

Your past mistakes are meant to guide you, not define you.

Allison had said Sabian had told her sister that when she'd admitted to being ashamed of some of the things she'd done in her past. Once again, Leo walked out of the locker room, unaware he was smiling until he saw her and smiled even bigger.

"Hey," she said as he walked up to her where she was *casually* waiting for him.

"Hey," he said, struggling to refrain from touching her, but he had to be mindful that Sabian could still be in the gym.

"Feel like Barros?"

Leo thought about it for a moment. "Pizza?"

"Yeah." She smirked. "They have very private booths."

"Hell, yeah," he said as she giggled.

Minutes after they'd ordered, they were sitting in a booth at Barros *way* in the back. Allison had just begun to slide in next to Leo, when he pulled her to him, glancing around quickly before devouring her mouth. "Jesus Christ," he said between kisses even as his heart thundered in a mixture of bliss and absolute terror. "I had you all weekend, and I can't get enough of you."

"I promise you." She caressed his face as she kissed him back, just as eagerly. "I feel the same way."

As usual, their conversation carried on as effortlessly as always. Leo loved watching her explain things and get excited. Like when the subject of life goals and dreams came up. She mentioned she had two big dreams in life. The first she spoke of eagerly. She wanted to break into journalism in a big way. "With the Internet nowadays, it's not like before where you *had* to land a job in one of the big networks or CNN or something. Now you can pave your own way. I've started doing podcasts and even have a few sponsors."

She went on and on about it, but when he asked about the second dream, she got a little tight-lipped.

"What is it?" Leo asked curiously.

"I suppose it's every girl's dream—well, most I know." She shrugged. "But sitting here telling my *boyfriend* about it might sound like I'm hinting. And I'm not," she added quickly. "I wanna focus on my career first. But my other dream . . ."

She paused, smiling sweetly as the color in her face deepened, and she took a very telling sip of her water. Leo peered at her as she cleared her throat, and for a moment, he considered glancing away since she seemed so uncomfortable suddenly. But there was no way he was tearing his eyes away from her now.

"I guess once or twice in my life I've visualized what my life might be like around say thirty or so. I'm a successful journalist with a wonderful husband and a house full of kids."

She chewed her bottom lip, pausing as if waiting for a reaction. Leo stared at her, smiling as he too visualized his future with her. "How many kids you want?"

"At least three," she said, smiling big. "And I'll be totally hands-on: class mom, little league coach, the whole nine yards."

Leo laughed, feeling a warmth inside he'd never felt. His whole life not once had he ever thought of his future in terms of marriage and a family. But suddenly, he couldn't think of anything that sounded better.

"What about you?" she asked, squeezing his hand. "You have dreams?"

"I do," he admitted; though for now he'd only tell her about one. "Me and the guys had an auto shop once. Fixing them not selling. Cars and bikes. Me and O did the fixing. So did Nine, but he's a bit of an artist, so he specializes mainly in making them look good: rebuilding them, painting them, that kind of stuff."

"Restoring old cars and bikes?"

"Exactly." Leo smiled, loving the genuine excitement in her eyes. "But it didn't work out. The shop we had was in a real shitty neighborhood. Kept getting broken into, and the landlord was a real piece of work. Everything was broken down, and it was like pulling teeth to get him to fix them, so we closed, but we've all been saving in the hopes of buying our own shop. No more renting. We keep hitting roadblocks, but we'll get there again someday."

She already knew both Nine and Orlando were working for mechanic shops now, and as soon as Leo was done with work-release, he'd do the same.

"I believe you'll get there someday," she said, hugging him tight. "And I'm excited for you. For us."

"For us." Leo smiled, staring down into her eyes. "I like that."

He kissed her softly at first, but just as he'd been every time they'd had one of their moments before that day, Leo lost himself in their kisses. He knew he should be more careful. They shouldn't be so damn blatant in a public place so close to the gym, but he was powerless to fight it. It was insanity. Less than two weeks ago, he'd begged her to stay away from him, and now he felt ready to kill anyone who might try to keep her from him.

Taking a deep breath, he focused on enjoying her instead of getting worked up over something that might never happen.

"You're so beautiful," he said, stopping for a moment to look in her eyes.

She smiled, and as usual, despite her unease about the compliment, she didn't look away. "Thank you."

He kissed her again, softer this time. Sweeter, less hungry.

"I'm telling Lila today."

That made Leo freeze, but he managed to recover fast enough, and he pulled back to look at her. "I thought you said you were gonna wait?"

"I know, but except for when I kept things from her for her own good—so she wouldn't end up in jail—I've never kept anything else from her. It doesn't feel right."

"But what if—?"

She kissed him before he could finish. "Nothing and no one can possibly keep me from you now." She smirked, tilting her head. "Heck, for as much as you tried, even you couldn't."

"That was only because—"

She kissed him again, giggling against his lips. "I understand why you did it. And Lila's just going to have to understand why that's not going to be possible anymore."

Leo stared at her, feeling a terror that only confirmed why he knew he'd never feel for anyone what he felt for Allison. What would Lila think of him sleeping with her *baby* sister? He couldn't even blame her for feeling protective of Allison. She should. He was glad for it, except not when it came to her possibly interfering and cutting him out of Allison's life. He wasn't even sure where this was headed—what he'd possibly ever have to offer Allison—yet the thought of losing her after having her for less than two weeks was a paralyzing one.

Trying not to sound as alarmed as this made him feel, he swallowed hard, searching her eyes. "What are you gonna tell her?"

"Well, she won't be home until tonight because she said she and Sonny were going out." It surprised him that she was still smirking silly, even when his heart was pounding away in his chest. "They're having a romantic dinner on account of how they haven't seen each other in almost two *whole* days."

This made her giggle, and that alone at least had Leo smiling again. She caressed the side of his face as if she knew, even with him trying to hide it, how uncomfortable the idea of her telling her sister about them made him.

"Lila can be a hothead, but, believe it or not, her relationship with Sonny has really changed her for the better. Not that I thought there was anything wrong with her before. She had come a long way from her days of biting heads off."

Leo gave her a look to remind her that Lila hadn't come *that* far. Just a few months ago, he'd seen firsthand how far she *hadn't* come yet. This made Allison laugh, and thankfully, as her smile and laugh usually did, coupled with her touch, they helped assuage the unease he'd been feeling. "Okay, maybe she still needs to work on not reacting so compulsively to defending those near and dear to her," she said, motioning to herself with her thumb. "But this is why I want to tell her about this sooner than later. I know my sister. She's never been violent or ever threatened me in any way. But she would be incredibly hurt if she heard about us from a third party, rather than directly from me. With this . . ." She paused to lift their entangled fingers, and Leo kissed her hand, making her smile so sweetly he breathed in deep. "I've been seriously thinking about telling her for days, but after today I know I better. I mean here I know both she and Sonny are in town and . . ." She leaned in and licked his bottom lip then pulled away and smiled. "Modesty be damned. I can't keep this a secret much longer. So, I need to make sure I'm the one she hears it from, not anyone else."

Their food came, and Allison told him more of what she planned to tell her sister as they ate. Basically, she'd be using her sister's own whirlwind romance with the ball player she was so hopelessly in love with now. She thought it'd help Lila understand why Allison was so sure she, too, needed to follow her heart.

Hearing Allison speak of how sure she was about this relationship, helped ease the disquiet he still felt about having let this happen in the first place. His gut still had its reservations, but nothing could beat out what his heart wanted now. It was insanity and he knew it. She'd technically been *his* for less than two weeks, but already he felt like he'd stop at nothing to keep her happy. If that meant going along with her telling Lila about this and Leo having to face her overprotective sister with any questions or demands she might have for him, then so be it.

If it weren't for the fact that she had class to get to, he would've risked getting home past his probationary curfew just to hang out with her longer. Already, he was doing other things he said he never would. Like asking her to come by his place after class so they could hang out, even though he didn't like her driving around his neighborhood alone.

He followed her out on his bike to the freeway entrance every time. Whatever it took. As long as he got more time alone with her, it was worth chancing getting caught out after curfew.

Yeah, it was happening already, but he was done fighting it. Every taste of her mouth, every touch of her flesh, and, more alarming than anything, every moment just being with her, kissing that sweet smile were hands-down worth the risk.

TWENTY-THREE

Allison

Checking one last time in the rearview mirror, Allison made sure it wasn't so damn obvious what she'd just done—or rather what had just been done to her—over and over. Parts of her body were still tingly, and she was certain, just like her lips, other more private parts were still swollen as well. Already, Lila had said she'd noticed a change in her. Of course, her sister was under the impression that she was still seeing Carson. Since even Carson had been a first for Allison, as far as Lila knew, Allison knew her sister was thinking he had everything to do with the *change* she'd noticed.

She got out of the car, took a deep breath, and headed in the house, determined to get this over with. Allison would stop short of telling Lila she was in love with Leonardo because she knew just telling her she'd been seeing him and planned to keep doing so would freak her out enough.

Admitting she'd fallen that hard for him this quickly even to herself had been hard enough to do. But every time she was with him, she felt it deep in her heart. She'd read about guys being pussy whipped, and since, technically, he was the first to make love to her, she questioned if what she was feeling wasn't the female equivalent.

Except deep in her heart she knew there was so much more to this. She'd known it before he'd even so much as kissed her. There was something about him, and she knew now it was the combination of his hardened and daunting exterior coupled with his vulnerable side that he'd so quickly opened up to her that had her falling hard for him.

So, there were no if, ands, or buts about it. She was doing this tonight, and she was sticking to her guns. Opening the garage door, she walked into the hallway that led into the kitchen. Her heart thudded as she heard voices. Both Sonny and Lila were home now, yet she only heard Lila's voice coming from the kitchen. "She's here. I just heard the garage door," Lila said to whomever she was on the phone with. "Yeah, I'll call you back, if not tonight, tomorrow and give you the rest of the details."

The moment she walked into the kitchen, Lila smiled big and goofily. "Guess what?"

"What?" Allison asked, genuinely curious as she put her backpack down on the kitchen counter.

It wasn't often she saw her sister this giddy. "We have a date."

Allison thought about that for a moment; then it hit her and she smiled. "For the wedding?"

"Yes," Lila practically squealed. "And it'll be a lot sooner than we were planning!"

This was not the Lila she knew, but it made Allison giggle because she loved seeing her sister this happy.

"How much sooner?"

"In two weeks!" Lila brought her hands to her mouth, only this time Allison caught the slight apprehension, and she couldn't blame her.

This was a total shock. "Two weeks?"

"Yes." Lila nodded, the smile waning ever so slightly. "If Sonny had it his way, we'd run out and do it now, but I know his mom would be so hurt, so I convinced him to give it at least that long."

"Convinced him? Why the sudden rush?"

Lila smiled big, bringing her hand to her mouth again but didn't say anything. Allison waited confused, but her sister only smiled, her eyes welling with tears. Then her other hand slowly moved over her belly.

Allison's jaw dropped as the instant knot in her own throat threatened to suffocate her. The hot tears blurred her vision, and she blinked, willing the tears away. "You're pregnant?"

The words came out as squeaks, and as soon as Lila nodded, her face contorting as she broke down, Allison rushed to her and hugged her. Lila hugged her so hard it scared Allison. After a few moments, she pulled away and looked into her sister's tearful eyes, wiping both her own and Lila's tears away. Then she lowered her voice. "But you're happy, right, Sissy?"

Lila nodded adamantly, hugging Allison again, then whispered in her ear. "I'm as happy as I am terrified." Allison pulled away to look at her as Lila glanced away toward the front room then back at Allison and added in a still lowered voice, "What the hell do I know about being a mom?"

Allison laughed even through her own tears. "Are you kidding me?" This only choked her up more. "I couldn't have asked for a better person to take over when Mom died, Lila. Oh my God, you're gonna be an awesome mom."

That made Lila cry more, and Allison had to finally ask after holding her sister tightly for a few moments. "How far along are you?"

"I'm not sure," Lila said, pulling away, and reached for a paper towel from the holder on the counter.

She ripped one off and handed one to Allison. They stood there wiping away tears and blowing their noses as Lila explained why she wasn't sure. "My period's never been regular, so when I missed it last month, it didn't even faze me. But then my boobs got real sore this month. Way sorer than they ever get when I know I'm just PMS-ing. That's when I realized I didn't get it this month either. I was still thinking there was no way, but then I started feeling a little nauseated and going to the bathroom like a kid with the bladder the size of a dime, and I couldn't ignore it anymore. So, this weekend I took a home pregnancy test. Then another." She laughed, still sniffling a little. "And another."

"And now you're crying like I've never seen you cry before," Allison said, shaking her head.

"Yeah, that too." Lila rolled her eyes, just as Sonny walked into the kitchen, smiling big.

"Well, my mom—" He stopped when he got a better look at their faces. "She has you crying now too?" he asked as he pulled Lila into a hug. "So, I take it she told you?"

"Yes. Congratulations, you guys." Allison moved in for a group hug.

"I could hardly wait to get home because I wanted to tell you guys in person," Lila said as they broke the group hug and Sonny wiped the corners of Lila's eyes. "I especially wanted to see your first reaction."

Sonny kissed Lila's lips sweetly then her nose, and Allison sighed at the reminder of Leonardo's tender kisses. "Did you honestly expect anything less than me being over the moon? Speaking of," he said before Lila could respond. "My mom is going nuts. That crazy lady is cancelling all her plans for the next two weeks to prepare for this"—he held up finger quotes— "most epic event of her life."

They all laughed as he went on. They sat around in the kitchen as Lila babied a cup of ramen noodles and Allison made herself a sandwich. After Allison's epic time with Leonardo today, she was ravenous. Sonny made a list of things he'd be sending his assistant out to get for Lila from the market so she wouldn't have to live off ramen noodles. Surprisingly, Lila explained she wasn't eating the ramen because it was the only thing she could keep down. Her morning sickness was minimal, but strangely, she was craving the ramen like crazy. Still, Sonny insisted she needed to eat healthier.

They discussed the wedding, which was less than two weeks away, the Friday after this week's. Even more surprising, they'd already arranged for it to take place at the beach home of one of Sonny's best friends in San Diego.

Allison would've thought they'd just have it there in Sonny's obscenely huge mansion. But he was quick to point out what a nightmare it'd be, not if but, when the paparazzi got wind of it. They weren't making any public announcements about the pregnancy either until after the wedding because that'd only put the paparazzi on high alert. Sonny explained that Lila had given him the good news that morning, and they'd instantly agreed on setting a much sooner date for their wedding. It just so happened that his friend was in town today, so he'd hit him up, and his friend was all for it.

Allison decided to give it a few days before mentioning her new boyfriend to Lila. They were in such high spirits she didn't want to ruin it. As much as Allison would like to think and insist that her sister would be open-minded, she knew this would be a tough topic. As uncharacteristically emotional as Lila had been tonight, Allison cringed to think what that conversation might turn into. Nope. She'd be giving it a few days so at least the newness of this very epic event in her sister's life could simmer a bit.

The less than two weeks between finding out Lila was pregnant and the wedding flew by before Allison knew it. After several failed attempts of trying to bring up Leonardo, only to be interrupted by something pregnancy or wedding-related, Allison decided to just be real with herself. As much as she'd like to think her sister would be open-minded, she knew it was going to take some time to convince Lila she had nothing to worry about. So, she didn't want to sour up a time in Lila's life that she should be walking on air about by tainting it with memories of arguing about this.

So far, the only people who knew about her and Leonardo, besides Nine and O, were Jen and Drew. As inconspicuous as Leo and Ali tried to be, they were going to have to try harder. No one had actually told Drew about them. Drew had told Allison. Apparently, the way they gazed at each other when they thought no one was paying attention was so "disgustingly cute."

Allison had tried to deny it, but just saying his name had Drew pointing at her and smiling smugly "You can't even say his name without getting all dreamy-eyed."

Deciding she was better off just admitting it so she could beg Drew not to tell a soul, not even her like-a-sister best friend Charlee, Allison had come clean. At first, she'd been worried that Drew might not be able to keep it from Charlee, but now she was happy about it. Since Jen's own relationship with Jaxson had heated up, Allison barely saw the girl anymore. Between Allison sneaking every free moment with Leonardo and Jen spending all her time with Jaxson, the only time they'd gotten to chat in the past several weeks was in class. And that usually pertained to their assignments.

So, having Drew there as a much-needed sounding board couldn't have come at a better time. Best thing about it, since she'd decided to wait until Lila got back from her honeymoon to tell her about Leonardo and because there was no way she was springing this on Lila at her wedding, Allison would be dateless for the wedding. With the wedding being so last-minute, Jen had prior commitments and couldn't make the wedding either, and there was no way in hell Allison was inviting Carson as Lila had suggested. So, Drew was Allison's only guest at this very exclusive and intimate wedding.

Even better, Drew was seeing someone now too, but unlike Allison and Jen, Allison got the feeling Drew wasn't nearly as into him as Jen and Allison were into their guys. So, she hadn't even flinched when Allison told her she probably couldn't bring him. In fact, she seemed grateful.

The ceremony on the beach had been tearfully beautiful as the two sisters walked down the aisle hand in hand and Allison gave her sister away to her adoring fiancé. The reception, so far, was just as emotional. Allison had even nailed her maid-of-honor speech, and they were now eating one of the best Mexican dinners she'd ever had.

A couple approached the wedding table to ask what they thought of the dinner. Lila introduced Angel and Sarah Moreno to Allison. They were the owners of the restaurant who catered the wedding and were friends of Sonny's best man, AJ "Rage" Romero. They were something straight out of a magazine: her with her beautiful light green eyes despite her dark hair and lashes and him with that smile, holy shit, and those dimples that looked almost fake.

Neither Allison nor Lila could say enough about the delicious entrees they'd been indulging in. Allison was still watching them walk away as she sipped her drink when Lila leaned into her and whispered, "Remind me to tell you about her and that Beast guy from the gym."

The comment was so unexpected Allison spit out half her drink, reaching quickly for her napkin to clean her mess. Lila tapped her back. "Are you okay?'

Attempting to recover, Allison nodded, still trying to catch her breath through coughing. What the fuck?

"I'm good. Just"—she cleared her throat— "went down the wrong pipe."

After a few moments of recovering and glancing across the room at that gorgeous woman with those to-die-for eyes and her hot-ass husband, Allison had to ask. She took advantage of Sonny being busy talking to his baseball buds. "What about her and, uh . . . that Beast guy?"

"I don't know all the exact details," Lila said softly, holding her champagne flute in front of her lips and glancing around casually. "But I guess years back when Sarah and Angel were still in college, this guy hit her up online and almost had her believing he was related to her. Said he was her long-lost brother or something like that. He even had the balls to show up and visit her, knowing she was already in a relationship with her now husband, and it turned out it was all this bullshit con to try to get with her." Lila lowered her voice even more. "I'm not supposed to be bringing this up because from what Sonny was told, even though she and Angel had been in a relationship for years, according to AJ's cousin, she almost went for it. Can you imagine? That she could be tempted by the likes of that Beast thug, when she had that."

Lila paused for a moment when the waiter stopped to refill their water glasses. Allison took advantage of the much-needed moment to exhale. Of course, Allison could imagine it. Sarah's husband was very handsome, but Leonardo had that bad-boy danger factor that she knew Lila would be furious about if she knew just how much it turned Allison on.

Only right now, all Allison could think of was there was no way Leonardo was a con. He fought getting close to Allison. He said he'd vowed not to allow himself to get close to any girl for years. Why would he trick a girl just to get with her?

As if reading her mind, Lila went on as soon as the waiter was gone to answer the burning question on the tip of Allison's tongue. How did Lila know this to be fact? "A few weeks ago, when some of Sonny's new and ex-teammates had a walk-through at the gym, AJ brought along his cousin and uncles. AJ's cousin recognized Beast and asked Sonny about him. Sonny explained how he was part of the work-release program and the cousin said he wasn't surprised the guy had done time then told him the story. Isn't that crazy? Small world, huh?"

Before Allison could ask any more or even respond about this being absolutely crazy, Lila was whisked away by the handsome groom to go walk the reception and mingle with the guests. Allison stood to help her with her dress then watched as Lila walked away with her husband. Smiling despite the unease she was now feeling, she was still beyond grateful her sister found someone who made her so happy. Lila and Sonny looked so blissfully in love there was no way Allison was ruining this for them, not any time soon anyway, and especially not until she got to the bottom of this newfound information.

There had to be a reasonable explanation. Leonardo's violent upbringing didn't excuse his violent and criminal past, but it, at least, made his explosive temper understandable. Most importantly, he was trying to change that. What he'd done to the guy who'd been following her, while excessive, was also understandable. The guy did have a loaded gun.

Allison sat back down, glancing over at Sarah, who was now seated at one of the larger tables with a bunch of other couples. Her stomach was already knotting up. As if convincing Lila that Leonardo wasn't such a bad guy wouldn't already be hard enough, this just made things worse. There was no denying the disgust in Lila's voice when she'd told Allison about the bullshit con.

"Not even a golf ball has as many dimples as I've seen in this backyard today." Allison turned to Drew, who took the empty seat next to her. "I knew there'd be a lot of beautiful people here considering Lila and Sonny's celebrity status, but this is ridiculous. I give up trying to make any heads turn in this tough crowd."

"You look spectacular, Drew," Allison said, sounding so reminiscent of Lila's scolding tone whenever Allison put herself down.

"Thanks, but spectacular's not gonna get this white girl far in this crowd of Latino hotness."

Allison laughed, glad for the distraction. "Who said Latino guys aren't into white girls? Hector's a perfect example. They don't get any whiter than Charlee, and he's pretty much the epitome of Latino hotness. But aren't you spoken for, missy?"

Drew smirked. "No crime against looking and maybe doing a little drooling." When Allison raised her brows in surprise, Drew laughed. "Nothing wrong with fantasizing either. Brad is great and all, but sometimes it's fun to just, you know . . . daydream."

They chatted a little more about Drew's boyfriend Brad. Drew told her more about him: how he was the first guy he'd ever brought around her daughter Chelsea and she'd dated plenty before him. "Even her snobby dad approves of him. Gads," she added, shaking her head. "How I ever got involved with someone wound up so tight is beyond me."

"And he likes Brad?"

Allison thought of the conversation she'd had with Leonardo about the beast in him. She couldn't imagine having his kid, breaking up, and then bringing another man around their child. The very thought made her cringe.

"What's that about?" Drew asked with a laugh. "I said he's wound tight, but he means well. He just wants what's best for her. He likes what he's heard about him so far, but I'm sure he'll approve." Drew rolled her eyes, shaking her head. "Brad's a publicist. It's in his blood to schmooze. He'd charm the pants off anyone."

Instantly, Allison's mind was back on Leonardo. "I don't know about anyone."

She glanced over to where Sarah was now laughing with the other women at her table. Lila and Sonny were at that table along with AJ and Felix, who were engrossed in conversation as their wives chatted as well. Charlee and Hector walked over, splitting up when Hector joined the guys and Charlee stayed by the women. Within minutes, the ladies took a seat at the table where AJ's wife had been sitting near Sarah. That gave Allison an idea.

"Besides Charlee and the other wives of Hector's friends, do you know any of those other women?"

Drew glanced over curiously. "Not really. Some look familiar. Why?"

Hesitating at first, Allison decided to change the subject and tell Drew what Lila had informed her of. Then she added what she'd been thinking the whole time Lila had told her and still was. Allison admitted she'd been doing the math. Assuming Sarah was Leonardo's age if this went down in their last years of college and assuming they did four years, this still would've happened at least eight years ago. If this happened in their early years of college, then even longer.

"What are the odds that AJ's cousin still remembered the story correctly after all this time?" Allison asked. "Or that Leonardo is even the same guy? One thing Lila did say was that the Moreno's restaurant chain is a family business that their parents first started. All their restaurants were in the San Diego area, which means they were all born and raised here. Leonardo's never mentioned living in this area, only Mexico, Arizona, and then Los Angeles."

Drew glanced over to Sarah several times as Allison told her the story. Charlee was sitting even closer to her now. "Maybe we could ask her about it?"

"No!" Allison said quickly, adding the part she'd left out. "According to this guy who told Sonny about it, he said Sarah nearly went for it." Drew's eyes opened wide, so Allison went on rolling her eyes. "This guy wasn't even in the equation. How would he know if she almost went for it? That's not something a guy would want to admit to friends, right? That his girl had nearly cheated on him. This guy obviously made assumptions, but still Lila said she wasn't even supposed to be mentioning it to me. Not here anyway in front of them. So, no, you can't just go ask her about it."

"Then I won't ask." Drew stood up. "She'll tell me on her own."

"What?" Allison asked, standing up too and feeling a little panicked. "How are you going to do that without asking?"

She'd only hoped to pick Drew's brain a little about Sarah if she knew her, not have Drew go snooping around for answers. Drew tsked, shaking her head. "Ali, you of all people know there's an art to getting people to open up. I may've majored in documentary filmmaking, but I was required to take a few interviewing courses in the process. Don't worry. Whatever information I get out of her, she'll volunteer herself and never even know I was digging for it." Drew motioned for Allison to follow her. "This will be fun."

Allison gulped nervously. Even if it turned out to be true and Drew did manage to get Sarah to talk about Leonardo, she wasn't sure how much fun it'd be hearing about it.

TWENTY-FOUR

BEAST

The feel of the texts and the lapse in time between responses had been Leo's first clue. He understood Allison was playing a big role in this wedding. Regardless of how short the notice was, this guy her sister was marrying was loaded and able to put something huge together in no time. Not only would being part of a wedding of this magnitude keep anyone busy, Ali had all her maid-of-honor duties to tend to during the wedding. Her responding with short texts to his and the long response times in between were to be expected. But he was certain she'd had a few moments throughout the entire day when she could've snuck in a call, or at the very least longer responses.

She'd told him earlier the festivities were scheduled to end about eight in the evening. But she'd also said they weren't throwing anyone out and Sonny had a lot of close friends who'd likely stick around a lot longer. Even if Lila did call it a night, given her condition and how tired she'd probably be by that time, this meant, if the party continued past the scheduled end, more than anything, it would be mostly guys—maybe couples.

Allison mentioned who'd likely be keeping her company most of the day and night: her friend Drew, who was happily leaving her boyfriend behind for the weekend. Glancing at the time on the top corner of his phone, he replayed that conversation in his head. She'd been at his place again, and she'd just told him about the wedding and who she'd be taking.

"Drew seemed more excited about all the possible single ballplayers who'd be showing up than disappointed she couldn't bring her boyfriend."

It'd lit a small fire in the pit of Leo's stomach, and he'd pulled Allison to him. "Are you?"

The expression on her face had made him smile then, in spite of the heat he was feeling, and it nearly made him smile now. "Am I what?"

"Excited about the single ballplayers?"

She'd laughed at him and called him hilarious, another first for Leo. He'd been called a lot of things, but hilarious was right up there with the list of other adjectives like sweet and special that he'd *never* been called until Allison.

Thinking about that was the only thing that calmed him now because it was almost ten and she still hadn't called him to tell him how everything went, even as nervous as she'd been about her speech. But he knew there was no possibility that she might've already gone to bed, spent, and that's why she hadn't responded. About a half hour earlier, she'd finally responded to a text he sent her hours ago asking her how it'd gone. It consisted of a few pictures and a five-word response. *It went beautiful. Still going.*

He stood on the back deck of his place, looking at the photos she'd sent. There was one of the bride and groom looking like a million bucks. A breathtaking one of Ali in her body-hugging very elegant gown. Another selfie of her and Drew, smiling a little too big, which explained why she might be avoiding calling him if she didn't want him to hear her a little tipsy. Then another of the two of them taken by someone else because it was a full-length photo of them posing with the sunset behind them.

"Who's that?" O asked as he and Nine walked out the back door and onto the deck with him.

"Ali."

"That's Ali?" O reached for his phone, and Leo gave it to him.

"Yeah, I told you she's in San Diego this weekend for her sister's wedding."

"That's right," O said, staring at the photo. "Damn, she looks . . ."

Leo glared at his good friend and roommate like he better watch the next words that came out of that mouth of his. O laughed. "Beautiful. *Older*. Who's that with her?"

"Her friend, Drew."

"She's fucking hot," O said then added quickly. "Her friend, ass. Don't look at me like that."

"For a white girl," Nine said, scrutinizing the photo over O's shoulder. "Eh, she's okay. They all look alike."

"This guy." O shook his head as he handed the phone back to Leo then turned back to Nine, who was sitting on the deck's ledge now, a cigarette in one hand and a bottle of Jack in the other. "You always say that. Like you wouldn't do this girl if you got the chance."

"Oh, I'd fuck her faster than I can snap my fingers," he said, taking a swig of whiskey straight from the bottle then handing it to O. "I'm no fag. But I'd send her packing as soon as I was done. White girls just don't do it for me. Why do you think they call them crackers?"

O took a swig from the bottle then frowned. "Really? Because back in the slave days they cracked that whip?"

"Nah, man, that's why black people call them that," Nine said, shaking his head. "Hispanics call them that because they're so bland, not like our hot and spicy chicks. They're what my mom calls *desabridas*." He motioned to Leo as he took a drag of his smoke then let it out slowly. "Beast has the idea with that hot little Mexican girl he's bagging. That's what I'm talkin' about. Long dark-haired beauty with the poppin' curves—"

"Speaking of," O said, interrupting before Leo could threaten Nine about what would happen if he didn't keep his fucking eyes off Ali's curves. "So, how'd the top-secret wedding go? The paparazzi ever catch wind of it? I haven't heard anything about it yet."

Leo finally took his glaring eyes off Nine, who was chuckling and shaking his head. "I don't know." He hated the reminder of this. "I haven't talked to her all day. Last I heard when she texted me was it was *beautiful*. So, I guess they haven't had any interruptions."

"Well, that was a smart move not to have it in Los Angeles then," O said, nodding in approval. "So, Ali's gone all weekend?"

Nodding, Leo did what he normally wouldn't have, but at the moment he needed to; he took the bottle O was offering and downed a good long swig.

Nine hopped off the deck's ledge. "So, what are we doing standing around here? It's Friday night. Let's go get some pussy." He swayed his hips slowly like an idiot. "Just thinking of those poppin curves got my dick—"

Leo grabbed Nine by the shirt and pulled him to him. "You must have a fucking death wish, asshole—"

"Whoa, whoa, whoa," O said, trying to get in between them. "Nine, you stupid shit, you're just dying to cash in that ninth life, aren't you?"

"Ha!" Nine laughed, surprising Leo; though he *was not* feeling the humor. "You were right," Nine said, jerking away from Leo, and Leo let him go. "I thought I hit a nerve earlier but still wasn't buying that this little girl has you so seriously pussy-whipped, dude."

"Shut the fuck up—"

That only made Nine laugh more, but Leo's phone ringing had him forgetting his roommate's stupid remarks and glancing down instead. Without explaining who it was or that he was going to take the call, he walked off the deck toward the driveway that led to the front yard. He could still hear Nine cackling, as Leo brought the phone to his ear when he was far enough away from them.

"Hey." His anxious heart was already speeding up, and he hadn't even heard her voice yet.

"Hey," Ali said, and he could almost hear the smile in her voice. "Finally, I was able to get away long enough to talk to you."

"Away from *who*?"

Leo could still hear music and voices in the background. Loud voices that sounded like mostly guys.

"From the party. As expected, Sonny had a lot of catching up to do with his friends and ex-teammates. Surprisingly, even Lila is still out here. But I think they're getting ready to wrap it up. Lila and Sonny, that is. They have that long flight to Venice, Italy tomorrow. But Sonny's insisting the party go on. The bartender, DJ, and a couple of waiters are getting paid until whatever time the last stragglers leave."

Reminding himself not to be immature about this, that he had no reason to think she might be doing anything that would make him *insane*, he took a deep breath. "So, it was nice then? No incidents with the paparazzi?"

"None," she said, and again he could hear the smile in her sweet voice. "Not a peep until maybe an hour ago."

She told him about the news van outside the property that someone noticed, but they weren't worried about the word getting out. With all the cars, caterers, and DJ setup, it was obvious AJ was hosting some kind of event, but there was no way the paparazzi would know what for. All the guests were close friends and knew the drill, so there'd be no leaks. She said AJ had also explained this wasn't unheard of. One or several cars out there with cameras when he was having any kind of event at his home was normal.

She was interrupted a couple of times. Each time Leo could hear it was a guy, and both times Allison's giggling had the hair on the back of his neck standing and him gripping the phone a little tighter, but he let it go. Leo had never actually been in a *real* relationship, and he'd never thought he'd be one of *those* guys, the ones that lose their shit over something petty like this. But it was becoming increasingly annoying to know this had obviously been what'd kept her too busy to call him until now. She'd mentioned she invited Drew because she wouldn't know anyone else there aside from Lila and Sonny and the owners of 5th street and their wives, but she hadn't wanted to be a third wheel all night. Now these guys, whom he could only assume she didn't know before tonight, had her giggling like a school girl?

"So, Drew's kept you company all night?"

"Hmm, yeah, among some of the other guests."

"Like who?" Leo asked, feeling his insides balling up.

"Just friends of Sonny. He's got a lot of friends—"

"Guys?"

"Yes, but—"

"Drew meeting lots of single ballplayers, Allison?"

"She's met a few."

"Have you?"

"Well . . . yeah—"

"Is that right? Is that what kept you so busy you couldn't call until now?"

Calm your shit.

"*No,*" she said, finally sounding a little irritated with his dumb ass. "You really think *they're* what's kept me busy all day? I've been running around like crazy, but I've thought of you the whole time."

Leo bit his tongue and kept back the words that threatened to fly out his mouth. *Even when you were giggling with all the ballplayers?* But he had to or he'd blow it before he ever got a fighting chance at anything solid with Allison. It still didn't feel real—he still didn't feel worthy of a girl like her—and this was exactly why. He'd just begun to convince himself not to fuck this up, and then she went on.

"I didn't even get a chance to really relax and just mingle until about an hour ago."

"Yeah?" He squeezed the bridge of his nose, pacing in front of the garage, trying desperately to hold it together and not blow this. She was at her sister's wedding for fuck's sake. "So, who've you been mingling with for the past hour?"

He squeezed his eyes shut, bracing himself for her answer. How the *fuck* was he going to handle this shit? He was nowhere near the calmer levelheaded guy he thought he'd become. His response to the guy trying to spook her was a perfect example of that and now this. And this was *nothing* but her possibly having gotten a bit distracted by some single *professional* baseball players. Only he knew that was it. Given a choice, anyone in her life who cared about her would *rightfully* try and convince her who was better for her. Hell, even Carson was a safer, smarter choice, and Leo couldn't even argue that.

"Everyone," she said, but there was something in her tone that made him nervous.

There was something telling about the way she'd lost the conviction he'd heard in her voice earlier when she was being defensive "Everyone?"

"Yeah, I told you Sonny's friend AJ has this huge family, not to mention extended family by way of the family who catered the party. They're like a second family to one of his cousins and now good friends of AJ and his family by default."

She paused for an unnerving moment, and Leo waited because it felt like she had more to say. Like she was setting up for something bigger to say—announce. "I've had some very engrossing conversations with a few."

"Have you?" Leo asked, grinding his teeth. "So, you've met some interesting people. I'll let you go if I'm keeping you from anyone."

"No," she said, back to sounding frustrated, but Leo was beyond frustrated himself now too.

If she had something she wanted to say—let him know about why or *who* she hadn't been able to tear herself away from to call him until now—she should just spit it out already.

"I'm just saying," he said, desperately trying to keep his cool. "It sounds like maybe you'd like to get back to these *engrossing* people. Don't let me stop you."

"Maybe I do. But I'll get back to them soon enough."

For a moment, he was staggered until he recovered. Only now he was on fire, and there was no holding back. "Get back to them now. Why the fuck are you calling me if—?"

"Tell me about Sarah, Leonardo, the girl you conned into thinking you were her brother way back. I met her tonight."

Stunned silent, the inferno that'd ignited inside Leo, oddly petered out, despite the unexpected and rattling topic. While troubling that he'd have to discuss a subject he never thought he'd have to again—least of all with Allison—it sure as fuck beat what he'd begun to think she'd been implying.

TWENTY-FIVE

Allison

There was still no proof Leonardo was the same guy in Sarah's past. Allison continued to remind herself of this even in the wake of Leonardo's sudden silence.

"What do you wanna know?"

His stony tone only knotted Allison's insides up further. Sarah had been understandably vague. But the few facts that did match when Sara's sisters-in-law were far more willing to revisit what Sarah had referred to as a "lost memory" until now, did point at Leonardo. And now here he was not exactly confirming it but definitely not denying it.

"Can you start by telling me why you did it?"

He was silent again for a moment, unnerving Allison to no end, before responding. "I was perfectly upfront with you about having done some bad shit in my past. I'm not gonna sugarcoat anything for you, babe. I was an asshole back then.

Everything I did then was for selfish reasons. There was money in it for me, so I agreed to do it."

"I know it's all in the past, and I'm not holding any of it against you, but I'm curious about something else. She said you did it because you claimed to have feelings for her. Was that a lie too?"

It was the part that made the least sense to Allison. If he was interested in more with Sarah, why have her believe she was a long-lost brother? She knew it shouldn't matter, but for whatever reason, it did. It made her nervous because all his other offenses he'd been forced into. Of the long list of things he'd admitted to being part of, while wrong, most were in self-defense, retaliation, or straight out ordered by the cartel. This seemed more personal. She doubted the cartel had much to do with how he went about deceiving an innocent young girl. And so far, Leonardo had made it a point that he wasn't about that.

"Look, baby. I told you all the need-to-know stuff. The heavier stuff in my past. But there's a lot of the pettier shit I spared you."

"Pettier? You tried to con her. You followed her to Havasu."

She heard him exhale loudly. "Okay, I'm gonna be honest about this one. It's something that never should have turned into what it did. But I never expected it to go more than a few emails."

He explained the convoluted story about being approached by a man who had a job for him. When someone had a job for him back in those days, it never involved anything legal or moral. He was supposed to get close to her by lying and saying he was her long-lost brother so he could get some info about some lost jewels the man was after.

"At first, I didn't even want to do it. I'd gone through all her social media. He'd given it to me to do my homework on her. But when I told him I wasn't doing it, he mentioned who he could get to do it instead: some asshole I knew would take one look at her and do a lot more than just get the info from her if he ever got her alone."

"So, you did it to be noble?" Allison did her best not to sound as sarcastic as she felt.

"No," he retorted immediately. "No. I was still gonna get paid. I went into it with every intention of lying and scheming to get him what he needed and be done with the job. Obviously, in two weeks, there was no way I could catch you up with every fucked thing I did in my past, but I refuse to lie about anything that comes up. I'll admit I did begin to think I felt something for her. At that point in my life, no decent girl in her right mind would give me the time of day, and I didn't expect them too. So, I'd never even tried. She was the first girl I'd gotten close to, fake or not, who was a nice girl. A good girl. But there's something else I hadn't planned on sharing this soon, only I have to now for you to completely understand about this."

Once again, Allison sat and listened to another hair-raising story about her boyfriend's past. This time she sat on the beach as she stared out at the beautiful moon. She'd walked out there and away from the still ongoing party after the second interruption and Leonardo's near outburst.

Leonardo explained about the first time he became a man. "I was thirteen. I'd never even kissed a girl. I was living with my mom in Yuma, Arizona by then, and my dad drove me over the border a few days after my thirteenth birthday, where I got my first taste of the cartel whores. Ali, I'd never even held a girl's hand. I'd only begun experimenting with taking care of myself that past year. Suddenly, I'm thrust into manhood just like that."

He paused when this time he was interrupted by someone saying something to him in the background. "Hold on," he said as he proceeded to yell back that he was good.

Allison gulped hard as what he'd just told her sunk in. For as much as he'd been through in life, with all the experience he had over her, had they been the same age, at twelve-years-old she'd have been the one far more experienced than him. At least when it came to sex. Somehow, that revelation was oddly mollifying. It calmed the worrisome thoughts that had begun to fester today that maybe they were too different as he'd insisted at first. As different as they may seem, their pasts were sadly a lot alike. Leonardo apologized about the interruption then went back to telling her about the night he lost his innocence. "In one night, I experienced more than some grown men ever experience in their lives. I'll spare you the details, but use your imagination. Just about everything we've done and then some I experienced in one night."

Despite his saying that, at the time, it was the best damn birthday gift he'd ever gotten, the rest of the story was told with an air of resentment. He said one of the few requests his father had granted his mother was to let Leonardo continue school like all the regular kids.

"It wasn't even until I was in high school and I listened to the goofball guys my age talk about getting to second base and feeling up a girl they were into, that I realized I skipped over all that stuff. At the time, I thought it was funny. I thought them all fucking lame. Who the hell gets so worked up over making out or feeling someone up? But later, when I was older, going on nineteen and getting laid way more than most guys my age, it felt like something was missing. It's, uh . . . the real reason for my piercing. For a few years after getting it, I honestly thought it'd been the answer I was looking for."

He paused for such a long moment Allison had to ask if he was still there. "Yeah. I am." But he went quiet again. "Allison, I'd never share this kind of shit with you because God knows I wouldn't want to hear about your sexual experiences, but I'm only telling you this because I need you to understand this. That piercing is as pleasurable for you as it is for me. Back then, the added pleasure of seeing these chicks' eyes light up with a mix of curiosity, dread, and excitement was hot as fuck. Feeling what it added to their orgasms was what I thought I'd been missing until I met Sarah, and I never even kissed her. I'd never been inclined to get that close to a regular girl: a sweet innocent girl with a normal life—normal family. I could excite her with the simplest things, like talking about our fake dad and relatives she'd never met. It was so fucked up because, apparently, she'd never had any family but her mom. So, seeing her eyes light up over something so trivial like the possibility of meeting her brother—me—for the first time in person, did something to me. It was refreshing to talk to a girl about regular things, not drugs, or pushing tricks, or discussing jobs and shit. For the first time in my life, the thought of kissing a girl excited me. It was when I realized I didn't just skip over that exciting but gradual change from innocent kid to manhood; I was robbed of it.

"So, instead of dropping the act when it was clear she didn't have the answers the guy who hired me needed, I kept it going. I knew before I met her in person that it was pointless to continue with the sham. If I worried about it now with you and all that illegal shit is behind me, it was even worse then, when I was at the height of that lifestyle. There was no room for a girl like that in my life. But I thought if I met her just once I could get her out of my system."

He explained about Havasu. He lived there, he didn't follow her there, and when he found out she'd be there, he hadn't been able to resist finding her and hanging out for the day. "But nothing ever happened between us, and when I realized nothing ever would, I tried to make a clean break. Only I hadn't counted on her being so hurt when she found out the truth. So, I made one last ditch effort to explain. And, yes, I did tell her I had feelings for her, because I thought I did, but I know now they weren't what I thought they were. They weren't what I yearned to feel and thought I never would. I know this because what I felt then doesn't even begin to compare to what I'm feeling now with you. With her, it was just the idea of it that excited me. With you, it's the real deal."

"How did you just do that?" Allison whispered.

"Do what?"

Allison gulped, willing the fear and doubt away. So, he'd nearly conned another girl into believing he was really her brother who was just as excited to meet her as she was him. Leonardo had been nothing if not honest with Allison thus far. Vanquishing her qualms, she decided to be just as honest as he'd been so far and say it. "I went from dreading asking you about Sarah, to falling in love with you all over again."

She heard him chuckle under his breath. "Well, that's good to know. Very good to know because it happens every time I hear your voice and see your face, Ali. It scares the hell outta me."

"Sup! Sup! Super Sonic!"

Allison turned to her gracelessly dancing very white friend with a laugh and asked Leonardo to give her a sec. "Are you drunk?"

Drew held a shoe in each hand and shook her hips, missing every beat so bad it almost looked like she was doing it on purpose. "No, but I love this song!" Drew proceeded with her awkward moves, and to Allison's surprise, continued to follow the rap song playing word for word. *". . . yeah, it's finally my turn to rock the mic. Because my devastating beats I know you will like."*

Allison laughed even louder this time. "How in the world do you know the words to this ancient song? It's gotta be as old as you are."

"Older," Drew clarified. "But my mom and grandma used to clean the house, listening to the eighties and nineties music."

That only made Allison laugh even more. She could just picture Drew's lily-white mom and granny dancing around the house and rapping to this song. "Come dance with me!" Drew insisted.

"I'm on the phone."

Paying Allison no mind, Drew was back to rapping along loudly with the song word for word. This time even Leonardo was laughing. "Go dance with her, babe," he said then added, "*Her*, not any of the single ballplayers."

While Allison was sure he was serious about it, his tone was far more playful than it'd been earlier when they'd touched on that subject.

"Got it." She smiled big. "No single ballplayers for me. I'll call you tomorrow when I'm on my way home."

"I can hardly wait to see you again," he said, making Allison take a big relieved deep breath.

She'd begun to think this night might end badly. Instead, she was walking on air again. "Me too. I love you."

"I love you, too, baby."

With Drew still dancing so close by, their goodbye was cut short. As soon as Ali hung up, Drew was pulling her back to the party with her. They waddled through the sand until they were back on the cement. The song Drew had been singing was over, but the next one had everyone jumping, so Allison and Drew didn't bother putting their shoes back on. Instead, they proceeded to the dance floor and began to jump. Clearly, someone was requesting music in Drew's mom and grandma's era because Allison knew this one was an old one too.

As expected, Drew knew the words to this one too. *"Pack it up, pack it in, let me begin . . ."*

Laughing again because she would've never thought Drew would be into this music, Allison didn't even care that they were quickly joined by several guys. The song was not the least bit romantic or even sexy. It was fun, and she decided after the stressful night she'd had listening to Sarah and her sisters-in-law's account of Leonardo's con, she was just going to enjoy herself now.

"Jump up, jump up, and get down!"

Allison turned to see AJ's uncles dancing and singing even louder than Drew. That explained who might've requested this music. The guy dancing across from Allison smiled at her with a little too much smolder. Allison smiled back politely then turned to Drew as the only part she knew came up and they both chanted it together, jumping even higher with each word. *"Jump! Jump! Jump..."*

It went on forever it seemed because Allison was a sweaty breathless mess by the time the DJ slowed it down. The same guy who'd smiled at her earlier approached her as bodies started coming together on the dance floor to the slow song playing. He touched her elbow gently. "Dance with me?"

That close, Allison could see just how good-looking he was. She smiled, feeling bad because she was sure a guy like him wasn't used to being turned down. She knew it would be awkward, but there was no way. "I'm sorry, but my boyfriend wouldn't like that."

The smile waned ever so slightly, but he nodded and walked away. She turned to walk off and came face-to-face with a curiously smiling Lila. "Your boyfriend?"

BEAST

"Only because you're asking," Allison said as Leo wrapped his arms around her waist from behind. "I don't want you to think I'm *that* kind of girlfriend, the kind that *tries* to make her man jealous."

"Trust me. You don't have to try."

That made her giggle, but she went on. "But I'm also telling you because I have to share with you about it anyway."

Leo listened, trying not to go too stiff as Allison told her about one of the guys who'd joined her and Drew among a few other girls on the dance floor to dance upbeat songs that didn't involve any touching.

"So, the DJ finally slows it down to this romantic slow song and not a moment too soon; I was so tired." She went on as she rinsed grapes in Leo's kitchen sink. "This guy asks me to dance. Of course I said no," she added with a laugh as

Leo squeezed her playfully—or not. "I even explained why. I said my boyfriend wouldn't like it."

"You're damn right," he said gruffly against her ear then kissed her nape.

She giggled, putting the grapes down onto the counter and turned around to face him. Leo's hand's never left her waist, and now he rubbed his ready-to-go cock against her. Allison's eyes widened in reaction, but then she shook her head. "Here's the kicker. Lila had been standing behind me and heard the whole thing."

Like he had earlier when she mentioned the guy asking her to dance a slow song, Leo's muscles went taut again. "Did she say anything?"

"Yes!" Allison said, popping a grape in her mouth. "She asked about my boyfriend."

"So, she knows?"

To his utter relief, Allison shook her head immediately. "No," she said a bit too cautiously. "She's going away for two weeks on her very romantic honeymoon. I'm not ruining that for—" Obviously catching herself, she shook her head and touched his face. "I didn't mean—"

"I get it babe," Leo said before she could start kicking herself about it. "Trust me. I'm in no hurry for you to tell her. I don't care how reasonable you say she is; this isn't going to go over well and I totally understand why. If you were my sister, I'd be worried too. Hell, I'm still worried this might be a mistake—not us," he added quickly because of her instant flinch to that last comment. "I'll always worry that something might happen to you because of me—my life. I worry about having given into this," he reiterated. "Not regret." He kissed her tenderly then spoke against her soft lips. "It's hard not to think maybe I should do something preemptively, but at this point, there's no way I could walk away, even if your sister demanded I do."

Allison pulled her head back. "She'd have no right—"

"I know, but you know what I mean. Even if you asked me—"

"That would never happen."

Leo let his head fall back and laughed. "Thank God you're so damn stubborn."

This time he flinched when he felt her hand slide over his crotch. He glanced down at her, surprised to see her smiling. He was beginning to think he might've upset her. "She asked if I was talking about Carson."

Leo closed his eyes, concentrating on what she was doing instead of what she'd just said. "Don't ruin this moment."

"I'm not," she said, continuing to run her hand over his throbbing erection. "I'm just explaining how I got out of answering. I neither confirmed nor denied about Carson, and I'd just started to say something about feeling too sweaty and icky for a slow dance, when she was quickly whisked away by her groom—"

Leonardo had heard enough. His roommates would be home in a couple of hours. She could tell him the rest then. He devoured her mouth now as ravenously as he'd felt all day yesterday knowing she was at a party without him but more than anything missing her like crazy.

It was insanity. It'd only been a month since he'd made her his, and already he didn't want to think of another day like yesterday when he wouldn't be seeing her the whole day. Now he understood why her sister and her husband made up for being away from each other for two whole days. Already, he had plans for the next two weeks when she'd be free of trying to hide anything from her sister. But he'd run them by her later. Right now, he had other things in mind.

He'd begun to unzip his own pants while she'd explained what she'd told her sister. She'd since pulled him out of his pants and wrapped her hand around him. No time to talk now. Before he could lean over and pick her up, she slid her back down the counter of his sink until she was on her knees in front of him.

"I've been doing my homework," she said, playing with the barbells on his piercing with her tongue.

"Oh fuck." He reached for the counter for support in case his legs gave out on him.

Allison continued to play with the bells, going back and forth from them to his shaft and balls, as Leo held her hair for her around her neck so he could watch. He pushed the thoughts away, as she pleasured him so magically, of her admitting to having gotten good at this at a very young age. He wanted to think Allison doing this to him was what made this so damn good. Just like everything else they'd done, which he'd experienced many times before, never had any of those things felt the way they did when he did them with and to Allison.

They'd since talked more in depth about her other experiences, and since her time with Alan, she'd had very little practice. She knew what he might be thinking because he couldn't help but groan at the feel of her warm tongue working its magic, so she glanced up at him and pulled away. "Just like riding a bike. Haven't done this in over six years and certainly not to anyone with a piercing, but it's all coming back to me now." She licked the dripping opening of his tip, licked her lips, then swallowed and smiled. "Only now I finally get to enjoy it too."

⋈

The first several days of Lila's honeymoon Leo and Ali spent every evening of the week together. After she hung out at Leo's place for a few hours, he'd follow Allison out to the freeway entrance, and she'd go home for the night. But by Friday night, since Allison had mentioned she had no weekend plans other than doing what they'd done all week, Leo brought up the suggestion he'd wanted to since day one.

"What's the point of going back and forth all weekend? Why don't you stay the night and tomorrow you go home and pick up a bag so you can stay the whole weekend?"

"But Nine and O will be here this time," Allison said, looking a little surprised by his suggestion.

The only other time she'd spent the night was the weekend his roommates had been away. But they'd been here all week when she was over in the evenings, and no one seemed to mind. In fact, after she'd put together a few home-cooked meals three nights in a row and made enough for his roommates, Nine had already asked that morning what was for dinner tonight. So, despite her cooking mostly *healthy shit*, Allison had already worked her way in with Leo's roommates' good graces via their stomachs.

Tonight, they'd stopped at the dollar store on their way to his place. Last night, she'd asked if he had chicken in the fridge. They had lots in the freezer. Most of the times they were supposed to be cooking they opted for takeout or threw together a sandwich or something. Since he'd taken it out that morning for her to put something together tonight, she wanted to stop and get some key ingredients.

"This is a marinade I've been perfecting for a few years now," she'd said when she first pulled the bottles out of the bag in his kitchen. "As you can imagine, Lila and I did a lot of shopping at the dollar store when we were on a budget, but I still love shopping there." She'd showed him the bottles of olive oil, apple cider vinegar, and rice vinegar she'd be using for their chicken tonight. "Three bucks and you'll have a lot left for future dishes."

Leo had sat on the counter, sipping on his beer while she put it together. She insisted she didn't need help, so he sat and enjoyed the view as she talked him through it instead. After she put the key ingredients together, Leo took advantage of the time they had to wait for the chicken to marinate and the time they had before O and Nine got home, by taking her into his bedroom.

Now they stood out on the back deck, grilling the chicken, along with a few other interesting things Leo had never thought to grill, but Allison assured him he'd like them. Now, his only concern was if she'd agree to stay the weekend. He still couldn't get over how good it'd felt to sleep with her in his arms all night and then wake to her beautiful sleeping face the next morning.

"If you don't think Nine and O would mind . . ."

"Why would they mind?" Leo turned away from the grill to look at her. "You're not like the typical girls any of us have ever brought around. No one has to worry about anything going missing or things getting ugly. They like you, baby."

"I think they like my cooking," she said with a smirk.

"Yeah, that too." He leaned over and kissed her. "Even if Nine complains about the healthy stuff, he still eats it."

"Aside from grilling, do you guys really never cook?"

"Breakfast." Leo shrugged. "Omelets are hard to mess up, and we throw whatever's in the fridge in them" That reminded him of something that made him laugh. "Nine threw pizza in his one morning."

Allison laughed. "No way."

"Yeah," Leo said, flipping over a piece of chicken. "Said it was good too."

"Something smells good," Nine said as he and O walked out to the deck.

"Yeah, it does," O added. "You better be making enough for all of us."

"We made plenty." Allison smiled proudly.

"The fuck's that?" Nine said, staring down at the grill.

Leo smirked because he'd known it the moment he saw Allison slicing the zucchini and eggplant and then brought the asparagus out to the grill. Nine would be the first to protest their side dish.

"It's parmesan garlic grilled veggies," Allison responded as if she thought it might excite Pizza Omelet Man.

"I ain't eating that," Nine retorted, staring at the vegetables in that same disgusted way as when he first spotted them.

"They're really good," Allison insisted. "You can't have any chicken if you don't at least try them."

"Nah, fuck that," Leo said, matching Nine's disgust. "You don't have to convince him, babe. He can heat up a cup of noodles for dinner and be done with it."

"Easy with the cup of noodles," Nine said, hopping onto the deck's ledge. "Not with all that chicken on the grill. I'll try some of that rabbit food if I have to."

Orlando was busy changing the channels on the small TV on the deck's corner table. "Ooh, College World Series." He set the remote down.

"Those are chicks," Nine said, once again his face all screwed up.

"Yeah, even better," Orlando said, taking a swig of his beer. "It's hot."

"No, it's not," Nine argued as Leo pulled Allison in front of him, bringing his arm around her neck while they both listened to his roommates' debate. "Softball chicks are thick as shit."

"Not all of them." Orlando pointed at the girl on the mound talking to the catcher with her mitt over her face. "She's cute. So's the catcher."

They all watched as the ump approached the mound. Leo closed his eyes for a moment, taking a deep breath because the ump was as butch as they got and he already knew what was coming.

"See that's another thing." Nine pointed at the screen, right on cue. "I'm not into butch chicks. Look at that shit. How do you even address that thing? What's up, *dude*?"

Thankfully, Allison giggled and wasn't offended by his roommate's embarrassingly offensive attitude. But Leo readied himself to tell him to shut up if he had to. Allison's curves were very feminine, not *thick* the way he knew Nine meant. Most of the girls on TV were full of muscle and not like Lila either. They weren't nearly as defined, therefore *did* look on the heavy side, and yeah, a bit manly. Allison wasn't anything like that, but he knew Allison considered herself heavy.

Fortunately, they dropped the subject when the game went to commercial. Highlights of the news after the game had their attention instead when there was mention of a high-speed chase in the area. Then the broadcaster mentioned the other local story: a woman in Burbank paid over a thousand bucks to have a tumor removed from her beloved goldfish.

"Get the fuck out!" Nine said with what Allison probably now thought was his only expression—disgust. He shook his head. "Swear to God, white people. A goldfish?"

"Jesus," Leo muttered under his breath as Allison walked away to move the vegetables on the grill.

Nine was still staring at the TV, looking all irritated. "This is why I'll never get white people." Thankfully, his rant was interrupted by a honk out front. Orlando turned to them from the TV. "You expecting someone else?"

"I am," Nine said, jumping off the deck rail. "That's gotta be Mariana." He bounced his brows. "Now *this* shit's what I'm into!"

Great.

Leo could only hope Mariana wasn't spending the night tonight too. For all the shushing Allison did when she and Leo were messing around in his room and his best friends were home, Mariana was just the opposite. It's like the bitch wanted everyone else in the house to hear her coming. She was loud as fuck.

This was the kind of stuff that worried Leo most about this relationship. Allison lived in a luxurious mansion with housekeepers and drivers who were likely always on their best behavior and never said the kind of shit his roommates did. From what she'd told him about the place, it was so big they used an intercom or texted each other sometimes to say goodnight or announce they were leaving. Now here she was in this dump, and if Mariana spent the night, they'd have a play-by-play of what Nine would be doing to her all night.

As if this shit wasn't bad enough, Nine didn't walk back out to the deck with just Mariana. She'd brought her friends Blanca and Carla with her. All three were dressed in their "eat your hearts out, boys" attire, the kind that made it hard to tell if they were street walkers or just regular girls out for a night on the prowl. The smell of their food grilling was temporarily trounced by the stench of their overpowering perfume as all three stepped onto the deck.

Instantly, Leo was working his jaw. Even as Blanca went directly to Orlando's side and Carla stood there taking in Leo from top to bottom, Allison seemed oblivious as to what Mariana might've had in mind tonight. Before meeting Allison, Leo would've been all for it. Except now this was awkward as shit.

"Allison, this is Mariana," Nine said then motioned to the other two respectively. "And these two are Blanca and Carla. Allison here is Leo's new girl."

Of course, Carla would be the first to address Allison. "*Really?*" She smiled sweetly enough at Allison; though the surprise in her tone was a little too fucking over-the-top. "Nice to meet you, Allison. Isn't this a surprise? How long?"

"Few weeks," Allison said as Leo pulled her back against him.

He hugged her from behind, leaning against the deck's railing. He kissed Allison's temple, and his eyes met Carla's with a telling glare. She knew him well enough now. As many times as he'd fucked Carla, he'd never once been this openly affectionate in front of others with her or anyone else for that matter. He hoped she was smart enough to know Allison was different from any of the other girls Carla might've seen around him in the past. This was not a competition or even an invitation to join them. Like Nine, Carla had an unpredictable mouth, one he never minded before, given who they were around. But the way Leo felt about Allison now, girl or not, things would get ugly if Carla even thought about getting catty with Ali.

Ironically, Nine's stupid comments about the softball game on TV took center stage again. The girls all turned to the small television as his commentary continued with each girl that got up to bat.

"I played all the way up into high school," Blanca informed him. "Then I discovered boys, ditching, and weed. Forget about it. My days on the mound were over."

"What's wrong?" Allison asked in a lowered voice, turning around slightly to look up at him. Leo shook his head, but her brow went up. "You think I didn't notice how tense you got when they all walked in?"

Leo stared at her but refused to discuss this now, especially with Carla standing just a few feet away. Allison turned all the way to face him, bringing her arms around his waist. "I know you had a life before me, Leonardo." Thankfully, her voice was a near whisper, and she didn't seem upset in the least. "It's inevitable that we may run into people from our pasts."

"Oh, you don't want me running into anyone from your past."

"Really? That's how it's gonna be?" She smirked, still looking up at him. "Should I get ready to start swinging?"

"No." He chuckled, holding her a little tighter, then whispered in her ear. "You're not me. Remember that."

To Leo's relief, after about a half hour of awkwardness, his roommates left with the girls to a party. The food turned out to be a hit. Aside from Allison, none of the girls ate and still every bit of it went. Even Nine had no choice but to concede, "These veggies are pretty fucking good."

Allison insisted on cleaning up before they headed for his room. Leo explained about Carla as they cleaned up. She was just another body whom he took care of business with.

"But now that things have changed with me, I'll be letting Nine know I don't want her around."

"If it bothers you that much," Allison said as she rinsed dishes, "so be it, but don't on my account. As long as she's as respectful as she was tonight, I'm not opposed to her being around."

"Nope," Leo shot back immediately, "because I'm *absolutely* opposed to being around you and anyone from your past. So, fair is fair. Fuck that. I don't like the awkwardness of it anyway. There's no reason for her to come around here anymore."

Discussing Carla was nowhere near as uncomfortable as Leo had anticipated it being. They finished cleaning up the kitchen then sat and watched TV. It was supposed to be only for a few minutes, but they got caught up in a movie that had just started and ended up watching the whole damn thing.

The evening came to an end with a long lustful shower that moved on into the bedroom. Leo had just slid into Allison when they heard the front door open loudly then giggling. There was no mistaking Nine's voice as they trudged through the house, stopping every now and again. There were moments of silence followed by groaning and moaning as they moved it along until Leo heard Nine's bedroom door close. But the moaning didn't stop. It only got louder.

Leo had all but stopped, and he could see through the moonlight that came in from the window that Allison was smirking. "I guess she's not as shy as I am about being loud."

"You don't know the half of it, sweetheart," he warned with a nervous smirk.

The headboard banging against the wall started up, and Mariana's moans along with Nine's grunts continued. Instead of protesting or being appalled, Allison covered her mouth to muffle her giggling.

"Harder!" Mariana called out as Leo pulled himself off Allison and lay down next to her.

Another reason Nine had blown through so many of his lives, was his competitive streak. They'd learned over the years to never challenge him to *anything:* street races, downing the most shots the fastest, playing chicken on the highway. You name it. But even something like this broad yelling out for him to go harder he'd consider a challenge. Taking a deep breath, Leo decided now wasn't the time to share this fun fact with Allison. But no way was he continuing with that noise going on.

Allison only laughed more as they got louder. Leo banged the wall so his friend could have a little consideration, but in the past, this never worked. It seemed once Nine was into whatever he was doing, especially if he was drunk, which knowing Nine he probably was, he wasn't hearing shit.

There was more indiscernible talking going on. Maybe Mariana had heard the knock, and she was telling Nine about it. Leo could only hope. The headboard banging and moaning continued with Leo taking solace in Allison's now nearly uncontrollable laughter. She laughed into her pillow as an apparently just as drunk Mariana continued to demand Nine fuck her harder. There was some other muffled exchange between the two as Leo kissed the side of Allison's head playfully, since the rest of her face was buried in her pillow where she continued to laugh.

"I'm sorry," Leo whispered in her ear. Allison shook her head but wouldn't lift her face. "I am. He's an inconsiderate asshole when he's drunk."

And when he's not, but Leo would keep that to himself. His friend was a good guy with a heart of gold that would stop short of murdering someone for Leo. Even then, Leo wasn't so sure Nine wouldn't snuff someone out for Leo if he had to. He was as loyal a friend as they came. But still he could be such a shit-for-brains when it came to some stuff.

"You asshole!" Mariana yelled out.

Leo stopped nibbling Allison's ear as something crashed loudly in the other room. "What the fuck?" Nine yelled back.

Mariana yelled something else as the footsteps stomped around Nine's room. Allison's head was now popped up from the pillow as she stared at Leo wide-eyed. The bedroom door next door slammed open, and the noise was in the hallway now. "You told me to slap you!" Nine protested loudly.

"Not that hard, you fucking asshole."

There was more stomping and yelling through the house as Leo got up and put his pants on. "Fuck!"

"Where you going?"

"To make sure his ass doesn't go out there and make a scene and the cops get called."

To Leo's relief, Nine stood at the front door in nothing more than his underpants, listening—quiet for once—as Mariana continued to rant all the way to her car. He turned to Leo when he heard the footsteps. "These crazy bitches," he said, shaking his head. "Probably for the best anyway." He closed the door and started back to his room as the car outside skidded away. "I didn't see myself finishing anytime soon. I'm all fucked up. Sorry if I woke you."

"Woke us?" Leo asked incredulously. "You two probably woke the whole damn neighborhood. Do you have to be so fucking loud? Allison's here, remember?"

"Oh shit." Nine laughed as he reached the fridge and pulled out the milk gallon. "I forgot about that." He chugged the milk straight from the gallon then wiped his mouth with the back of his arm and continued to laugh. "Sorry, Ali, baby!" he yelled out obnoxiously. "Hope I didn't traumatize you."

Before Leo could strangle him, Allison responded. "No worries. I'm fine."

Turning back to a glaring Leo, Nine put the milk back in the fridge, making a show of how scared he was, and scurried away. He hit his toe on something and cursed the rest of the way, limping.

Leo hung his head as he took the walk of shame back into his bedroom. What the hell had possessed him into thinking having her here all weekend with his two roommates home was a good idea? Allison was sitting on the bed, sheet up to her chest, smiling big. "Never a dull moment?"

Leo groaned, slipping into the bed next to her. "I should've known better." Allison laughed, which only made him appreciate her sweet sense of humor even more. He buried his face in her neck. "I'll talk to him when he's sober. I promise."

"Don't worry about that." She giggled. "Just fuck me." Leo's body froze, but his face jerked up to her. It was only then that he realized she was only half serious because she seemed to be stifling a laugh. "Fuck me so hard I wake your neighbors. Just don't slap me."

She burst into laughter, and Leo groaned, burying his face in her neck again.

The knock against the wall had him lifting his head again. "Keep it down in there!" Nine yelled out. "Some of us are trying to sleep." That only made Allison laugh more. "Ali, baby, don't let 'em slap you!"

Leo started to sit up. "I'm gonna kick that guy's ass."

Allison pulled him back down, still laughing her head off. This time even Leo laughed, despite his annoyance with Nine. "I love you," she said, wrapping her arms around his neck.

Leo had questioned more than once now if maybe his feelings for Allison weren't just a fluke as they had been with Sarah. Maybe he'd just convinced himself of it, but there wasn't a shred of doubt now. For once in his life, he knew what everyone meant when they talked about this shit.

Allison owned his heart and soul now. "I love you more, baby. So much more."

TWENTY-SEVEN

Allison

"That party Martinez said he'd let me know about is happening this weekend," Orlando said as he walked into the kitchen from the back door. "More proof that this shit is lucrative, it's taking place on the rooftop of his fancy-ass apartment building in downtown Los Angeles."

"No shit," Nine said as he walked in the room from the other direction. "They still looking to recruit?"

"Yeah, but only people they trust. So, don't tell anyone else. They asked specifically for *Beast.*"

"Recruit?" Allison asked, not understanding but had a bad feeling. "What are they looking to recruit you for?"

Leonardo, who sat across from her at the small kitchen table, frowned. "A job."

"Finally," Nine said as he opened the pantry and pulled out a box of cereal. "I'm sick of these piddly checks we've been making. I need some real cash already."

"What kind of job?" Allison asked cautiously.

"The kind no one talks about." Nine laughed as he poured his cereal in a bowl.

Leonardo's eyes locked on Allison's. "I'll tell you about it later."

"No, tell me about it now." Allison was already feeling a sort of betrayal she thought she never would from him. "Is it illegal?"

"Sort of."

"What do you mean sort of?" Allison's heart rate spiked as she stared him down for a *real* answer. "Either it is or it isn't."

"It's complicated."

"It's a yes or no question, Leonardo. Are you really gonna get involved in something illegal when you're not even off probation?"

"No. This won't start until I'm done with probation. Few months from now at the soonest."

Allison's jaw dropped, and it took a minute for her to catch her breath. "So, it does involve illegal stuff?"

Leonardo shook his head, glaring at Nine, who was now sitting on the kitchen counter with his bowl of cereal, chuckling. "Just tell 'er, man."

Allison could hardly pull her eyes away from Leonardo, who was working his jaw now. But she did. She turned to Nine, since clearly Leonardo didn't seem in any hurry to explain. "What is it?"

Unlike Leonardo, Nine was more than willing to oblige. "It's the stuff of super heroes."

"Shut up, Nine."

"Your man's gonna be saving lives and bringing families back together or die trying."

"Shut the fuck up, Nine!"

Allison shook her head, even more alarmed. "You'll be risking your life?"

Leonardo shot to his feet so fast it startled her. "Let's go outside."

Instantly on her feet as well, Allison rushed around the kitchen table, dreading that her heart could be breaking in any second. The exchanged glance between Leonardo and a very repentant-looking Orlando wasn't missed.

"My bad, man, I didn't know—"

"Don't worry about it," Leonardo said, interrupting Orlando before he could finish.

Orlando's near apology was proof enough of what Allison could only assume now: Leonardo was keeping something big from her, something even his friend didn't realize he was doing.

The moment they were out on the porch, Allison spun around to face him, pissed that the tears were already blurring her eyes. "Okay, so tell me."

"Baby, don't cry."

Leonardo reached out to her, but she flinched, pulling her arm away. Not since the moment he realized he'd technically "deflowered" Allison, had she seen him look so terrified, but she didn't care. This terrified her too.

"Just tell me." She swatted angry tears away. "Are you seriously gonna get involved in something dangerous? Something illegal?"

"No." He shook his head. "Listen to me. I was going to tell you. I'd just forgotten all about it."

He explained quickly about being approached by an old acquaintance about this "job" just before he got arrested the last time. "It's not a job like what you're thinking, but it can be dangerous, only he'd explained there were some jobs that were less dangerous. At the time, I was all for any level of danger because it didn't matter to me. Even when I was in the can, he contacted me to feel me out, see if I was still interested, and I told him I was. I told him when I'd be done with probation and for him to contact me then. But now the only jobs I'd even consider are the ones that are less risky."

Allison still didn't get it, and she refused to let him touch her until she knew just what these *jobs* consisted of. "So, what'll you be doing? Why would you risk anything?"

"It's something I have to do, babe. You remember what I told you about my mom. She got involved in my dad's life before she realized just what she was getting into. There were many others just like her. They also had family try to get them out, but the only ones that ever stood a chance of making it out alive and staying out, were the ones who were saved."

He paused as if letting what he'd just said sink in. Allison shook her head. "Saved? So, you'll be going back into that world to save people?"

"Not *that* world. Like I said when he first approached me, I was willing to, but not anymore. I won't get involved in anything that might put you in danger. Only he also explained it's not just the cartel; his clients come from all walks of life. They have family members who've gotten caught up in cults and abusive marriages they feel trapped in or can't leave because they fear losing their children. Others are stuck in bitter custody battles, or their kids have been taken away because of some legal loophole, and now those kids are being abused, but again, the fucked system is too damn slow. You hear about it all the time: kids who die at the hands of their abusers, and it's later disclosed that child protective services were aware of the abuse allegations, but their hands were tied to do anything about it. It's bullshit." He took a deep breath then exhaled loudly. "Remember we talked about our dreams? I told you about one of mine, but this is the other. It's something I feel obligated to do. Me and Flip didn't just walk away from the cartel. We were helped. I'd probably be dead right now if it hadn't been for them. I need to pay it forward, even if it's not someone in the cartel. Just someone in trouble. Get someone's kid back."

Allison wasn't sure if her heart should be breaking or bursting. This scared her, but at the same time, she was once again in awe of this man. Leonardo was willing to risk it all to save lives.

"What about the shop?"

"That's the best part. I need to keep that going. I won't be doing this other stuff full-time. It'll be on a case-by-case basis, especially since I'll be telling him I'm out of any of the stuff that has to do with the cartel. Right now, most of his cases involve it. But from what he told me, it's good money. These clients are willing to pay big bucks to get their family members—kids—back."

She was almost afraid to ask. "How illegal is it?"

"I don't know for sure yet. He never has formal meetings with anyone. Everything he does is on the down low. Never discusses business on the phone either. It's why he said he'd send word when we could set up an unplanned *run-in*, where we could just chat casually. There's no danger or risk to meeting with him. I'm not committing to anything yet. It's a party where I'll be casually running into him, and we'll discuss details."

"I wanna be there."

"No," he said immediately.

"Why not? You said there's no danger or risk involved."

"Because."

"Because *what?*" she asked again. "Unless you're lying to me—"

"I'm not. I just don't want you involved in any way."

"It's a party, baby." She smiled when the term of endearment just slipped out as it so often did when he addressed her. "You said it's meant to be casual and on the down low. I'd just be a guest." He continued to shake his head. "I could bring awareness to this. Write a story about why there's a need for these kinds of vigilante groups." She reached out for his hand and squeezed it when he began to protest. "I wouldn't give any specifics—no names, nothing like that—just write about how broken the system is and why the courts should show some leniency toward anyone ever in trouble for trying to save someone." The more she thought about it, the more it excited her. "I could research and give hard facts about the real victims, innocent children who could've been saved but instead lost their lives. I know firsthand what it's like to be an abused child. My own sister would've taken matters in her own hands had she known, but because of my fear of her going to prison for the rest of her life, I never told her. Had there been someone or a group out there like this one, maybe I and so many others who were in similar situations could've been spared what we were forced to live through. I won't ask any questions, just observe, and you can tell me what you're allowed to. I'd never give up my sources, but most of all . . ." She squeezed his hand. "I need to see for myself just what this is all about. I trust you, but I know what it's like to tone things down and keep things from someone for the sake of them not worrying or protecting them. I don't want you sugar-coating anything. I understand why you'd feel the need to be part of this—"

"I'm not even sure I'll be doing it yet. It's why I want to talk to him. Before you, I would've been all in too, just like O and Nine. They're still saying they'll take whatever jobs he might give them. But everything has changed for me now. I need to see what's involved in these so-called less riskier jobs."

"So, we'll find out together." She slipped her other hand into his and pressed her body against his. "I'll be there with you."

Leonardo pulled his hands out of hers and brought them around her instead. Yelping when he picked her up suddenly, Allison wrapped her arms around his neck, feeling slightly relieved. Leonardo set her down on the porch rail and leaned his forehead against hers. "Have you always been this damn obstinate?"

"Yes," she said proudly. "Yes, I have. Don't get Lila started on that, but you better get used to it."

He wrapped his big arms around her and squeezed her with a groan. "Alright, you can come with me, damn it." He spoke against the side of her head then kissed it. "But I have strict rules."

One of Leonardo's stipulations for this party was that at no time would Allison be left alone. If he had to step aside to speak privately to Martinez, she was to stay by Nine's or Orlando's side at all times. Problem was he was worried Martinez might just want to have the casual meeting with all three at once, which would mean leaving Allison alone.

Before he could change his mind, she offered to bring Drew along. "This way, in case the three of you get called away, this little *damsel in distress* won't be left all alone. Don't worry. Drew's gotta killer left hook. I've seen her train on the punching bag."

Of course, Leonardo wasn't a hundred percent content with this. But as she'd warned him, she was going to be there one way or another. So, having Drew along to keep her company, if need be, seemed better than nothing.

They met at the party where she had strict orders to wait in her car until Leonardo and the guys arrived in Orlando's truck. "Seriously? We can't even go inside and get a drink or something?" Drew asked.

"That's them." Allison waved at the truck that pulled into the paid parking lot; then she opened her door.

Drew got out of her side, and Allison walked around to meet with her as they started toward where Orlando was parking his truck. His truck was a four door. Good thing too. Allison couldn't imagine those three guys fitting up front.

Nine jumped out of the backseat. Allison heard Drew gasp under her breath at the sight. Understandably, she was reacting to Nine. In all the times Allison had been around him, he was either in worn jeans, T-shirts, or wife beaters. She'd even been privy to seeing both Leonardo's roommates shirtless, since it seemed they often walked around that way at home.

He almost didn't look like the same guy. None of them did, not in the buttoned shirts they all wore with the sleeves folded up just below their elbows. Orlando wore a print one with dark jeans and looked very handsome. Nine wore a solid black one over distressed but stylish looking jeans. The top of his hair was slicked back, and he'd gotten a haircut so the sides of his head were shaved real close, giving him an even more clean-cut pretty-boy look. Leonardo looked especially yummy in his white shirt and black jeans. Allison couldn't breathe in deeply enough.

"Holy shit," Drew said under her breath.

Allison giggled as the guys approached. Leonardo reached out for her hand the moment he was close enough. "You look good," he whispered against her lips before kissing her. "Too good," he added before she could thank him.

Allison glanced down at her snug little red dress and matching strappy heels, not sure if she should be flattered or feel a little self-conscious. "Thank you?"

Leonardo smiled and kissed her again. "You and that smokin' dress better just stay near me tonight."

Even as the butterflies fluttered in her belly because it was still too surreal to think this guy was *her* man, Allison did her best to compose herself and regain the strength in her legs. "This smoking hot dress and my shoes are all I'm wearing tonight." She chewed her bottom lip, feeling shamelessly sinful. Leo's eyes widened as he glanced down and then up at her again. "Never been to a rooftop party before," she explained, still whispering. "But I had a few ideas and figured easy access might come in handy."

His jaw falling open made her giggle, but she turned to Drew, feeling bad suddenly that she hadn't introduced her.

Turning back to Leonardo, she motioned to Drew. "You've heard enough about her, but now you can officially meet Drew. Drew, this is Leonardo and his roommates, Nine and O."

Despite Drew's equally eye-catching dress, which proudly showed off what she called her new and improved *tight* curves, Orlando was the only one whose polite smile seemed to appreciate any of it. Nine barely acknowledged her with a slight lift of his chin.

"Are you kidding me with this shit?" Nine asked, looking up at the soaring and luxurious building they'd be walking into shortly. "Does he live in this place?"

"Not sure," Orlando responded as they all looked up now too.

"Well, shit, if he is, I'm all in." Nine laughed. "This guy must be making bank."

"It's way the fuck up there?" Leonardo asked, looking up as well.

"He said rooftop." Orlando shrugged. "So, I guess."

The building must've been minimum fifty stories high. It was *ginormous*, bigger than any Allison had been in anyway and far more luxurious. They walked into the lavish lobby. An enormous crystal chandelier took center stage in the middle of the huge room. The ceilings were so high the lobby alone took up at least three of those first few stories. At least.

"Holy shit," Nine said what Allison knew they were all thinking as they all glanced around.

"I've only ever seen casinos this fancy," Drew said.

They made their way to the elevator. Even that was beyond fancier than any Allison had ever been in. It had glass walls with views of the entire city as it went up the side of the building. The long ride all the way up to the roof was understandably a quiet one as they all took in the spectacular views.

Allison did a double take when she glanced up at Leonardo and saw he was the only one looking straight ahead at the doors of the elevator and not out the glass windows. "Did you see the view?" she asked in a lowered voice.

He nodded but didn't turn his eye from the doors of the elevator. As odd as that seemed, with others in the elevator aside from their party of five, Allison didn't ask more. For a moment, she thought of how much he'd lived through being part of such a violent mob. How paranoid he was about something happening to her had to go hand in hand with what he'd seen happen firsthand. Maybe he was watching the doors so he'd be the first to see if anyone dangerous was outside them?

They finally reached the top and exited the elevators. The roof was even more spectacular than she expected. But if she had to be honest, she hadn't been sure *what* to expect.

Two long pools took up almost the length of the entire roof. Alongside and in between, there were tables and elegant but comfortable sofa sitting areas with fire pits. From the angle they walked into the crowded party, Allison could see at least two full bars manned by a minimum of three fast-working bartenders each on either side of the roof. Thankfully, while some guests were dressed in almost black-tie attire—tuxedos and full flowing gowns—others were as laid back as Leonardo and his friends. There were plenty in dressy jeans and buttoned-up shirts as well as cocktail dresses like Allison's and Drew's.

Waiters and waitresses walked all around with trays of drinks. One approached them; the tray he held offered several different kinds of drinks—champagne, wine, and martinis. Allison glanced up at Leonardo for guidance. Did she dare try one or would security be escorting her out the moment she reached for one. Leonardo nodded subtly with a smile as he reached for a martini. Drew took a martini as well, but that looked way too potent. So, Allison reached for the champagne flute instead. As thin as the flute it came in was and it only being half full, it seemed the safest route.

"You got any beer, chief?" Nine asked, eyeing the tray.

"The bars are fully stocked with everything, but if you'd like me to bring you one, I'd be happy to," the young waiter said with a big smile. "What kind would you like?"

Both Nine and Orlando put in their orders as Allison sipped her champagne, trying to look old enough to be drinking it.

"No one's gonna card you here, babe," Leonardo assured her as the waiter walked away. "But you sure you're gonna be okay drinking that? They have non-alcoholic drinks you can order."

Allison smiled, feeling silly about the visuals she had of being escorted out by the elbow immediately. "I'll be fine."

She wasn't so sure about that. As different as Leonardo had pegged them to be from the get-go, and remembering how he'd first referred to her as kid, she kept to herself that this was her first alcoholic drink *ever*. She'd be babying it; that was for sure. She *did not* want another repeat of what happened with the energy drink.

A couple of men in bigwig suits walked by, and then another couple in their near black-tie apparel strolled by as well. Admittedly, she'd been worried before tonight that this place would be full of lowlife thugs and Leonardo had tried to sugarcoat the whole situation. Allison leaned into Leonardo. "I didn't realize this was going to be so fancy. These must be real highbrow peeps. I can't believe you were worried about leaving me alone at a party like this."

"Trust me. I found out real fast the fancier dressed they are, the more you need to worry."

That made sense in a cartel setting maybe, but here? "Yeah, but this is different from the parties you were used to."

He shook his head as they started toward the building's edge where Drew said she wanted to check out the view. "I've already explained to you this job doesn't come without risks. Most who are willing are not doing it for the reasons I feel compelled to. Most of the people he's looking to recruit, ones who are willing to take the risk, are people with criminal and violent pasts. But unlike me and these two and Martinez, a lot of guys are never really reformed. They just look the part on the outside." He stopped just before they reached the side of the rooftop and looked her square in the eyes. "Trust no one, okay?"

Allison still thought he was being paranoid but agreed with a nod. She started toward Drew and the guys, who were looking over the ledge and out at the gorgeous view. Leonardo dropped her hand, making Allison turn to him. "What's wrong?"

"Nothing." He sipped his martini then motioned with his head for her to keep going. "Go ahead."

"Aren't you coming?"

He shook his head, glancing around. Allison remembered how he kept his eyes on the elevator door and away from the windows, and it dawned on her. "Are you afraid of heights?"

"No," he retorted but avoided her eyes.

"So why don't you come over here?" Nine asked with a chuckle.

"'Cause I don't feel like it."

Both Orlando and Nine laughed, and Allison regretted pointing it out that loudly now. To her relief, a guy in a suit approached Leonardo just as the waiter brought Nine and Orlando their drinks.

"I'm glad you made it," the stocky man in the suit said, clapping Leonardo on the back.

Orlando and Nine walked over to him to say hello as well. Leonardo looked over at Allison, but she glanced away and went to stand with Drew. She was only a few feet away from him and still in full sight, for crying out loud. She didn't want him feeling like he needed to babysit her all night.

Drew giggled as soon as she reached her. "Is your big scary boyfriend really afraid of heights?"

Allison smirked. "He said he's not."

"Is that why he stayed way over there and refused to look out the window in the elevator?"

This time Allison laughed. "You noticed that too?"

"Yes! Oh my God, that's so funny. Brad's afraid of spiders."

Drew laughed even louder, bringing her hand to her mouth, and Allison had to wonder how strong that martini was. Leonardo being afraid of heights was funny, in a cute way, but not *this* hysterical. Drew's laughter had actually turned a few heads.

Shaking her head, Drew covered her mouth as she continued to laugh. "I'm sorry," she squeaked. "It just reminded me of hearing him scream like a little bitch and nearly jump out of his skin over a little spider."

The explanation and Drew cracking up so much had Allison giggling too. One of the guys whose head Drew had turned, smiled at Allison when their eyes met. He was standing a few feet over, admiring the view as well. Allison smiled back nervously. He was one of the more sharply dressed guys at the party. Full suit and tie. He looked about Leonardo's age, maybe a little older. Allison caught the way he sized Drew up then smiled even bigger when he saw she was still laughing. Interestingly for a guy this good-looking, he was alone. At least right that moment no one was standing with him.

Allison turned her attention back out to the fabulous Los Angeles skyline. "Don't look now," she said in a lowered voice. "But it seems you have an admirer at nine o'clock."

Drew's laughter calmed, and she took a sip of her martini. Allison had since decided Drew's silliness couldn't be blamed on her drink. The girl had drunk as much of her drink as Allison had hers—very little.

Glancing around in the opposite direction of the guy, Drew took another tiny sip of her drink. "Is he cute?" she asked, after taking the sip.

"Very," Allison said, enjoying the girl time.

She so rarely went out and much less to parties like this. She didn't even own party clothes. The dress she was wearing was Lila's. Luckily her sister didn't like wearing clothes that were too skin tight. But that didn't mean it wasn't on Allison. Since Allison's curves were a bit fuller than Lila's, it only meant she could get *into* the dress. But it was far more body-hugging on her than her sister.

Seeing Drew make the move to glance in the guy's direction, Allison glanced the opposite way, feeling silly.

"OMG, he smiled at me," Drew whispered, glancing out at the evening view again. "*Damn,* he is cute. What's he Hispanic? Italian? Oh, what does it matter?" She shook her head. "I have Brad. Be good, Drew. Brad's perfect."

"Except when he's screaming like a *little bitch,*" Allison reminded her with a giggle. "Don't be silly. Nothing wrong with looking."

"Looking at who?"

Leonardo's voice startled Allison, making her flinch when she felt his hand slip into hers and pull her back. She turned to him with a smile as he pulled her farther away from where she'd been leaning over onto the ledge. "Drew's feeling guilty about enjoying some guy giving her goo-goo eyes." She glanced back casually so she could point him out, but with Leo and his friends back, it seemed the guy changed his mind about continuing to flirt with Drew. "He's gone." She fixed the collar on Leonardo's shirt. "I didn't even get the chance to tell you, you look smoking hot tonight too."

Leonardo peered at her playfully. "Thank you."

He pecked her sweetly, surprising her. She was sure he'd have something to say about her "nothing wrong with looking" comment. But he seemed to have something else on his mind. And she was right because he got right to it.

"Listen. This guy's gonna round us up again a little later. I thought he might be talking to us out here. But he's having us meet him down in his apartment. So, I'll be gone for a little bit."

"That's fine." Allison ran her hands over his chest because she could already feel how tense his muscles were.

Orlando walked up to them. "Is that who me and Nine think it is? Behind me?"

Both Leonardo and Allison glanced over Orlando's shoulder casually. There were several guys in the area behind Orlando, a group of guys near the bar and then a whole group of people sitting by a fire pit. Allison glanced up at Leonardo to see him press his lips together.

"Sure as fuck looks like him, but I don't know. It's been so long."

"Who?"

Allison glanced back in that direction but still had no idea whom they were talking about because it could've been anyone in the several groups of people in that area. The only consolation was they were all so well-dressed and not the least bit threatening.

"Look." His troubled eyes met hers. "I wasn't sure what to expect tonight, but seeing faces I hadn't anticipated seeing again—ever—wasn't one of them."

"Like who?" Allison asked, her eyes going wide as she lowered her voice. "Bad people?"

"That depends."

"On what?"

"If everyone here is really reformed like we'd all like to think we are, then we're cool."

His brow went up and he paused. As if their minds were connected, she immediately knew what he was saying. As reformed as he'd like to think himself, Leonardo had almost killed someone with his bare hands just recently.

"That's different. You had good reas—"

"If I'd known these people would be here, I *never* would've brought you."

"Leonardo," she said firmly because he was beginning to sound not just worried but pissed—at himself. "I'm gonna be fine."

She dared not say what she was thinking. That he was overreacting. But so far, this party had been perfectly pleasant and without the slightest bit of drama.

"I'm gonna be fine," she repeated, gently smoothing the vein on his forehead.

Sliding his hand into hers, Leonardo kissed her then exhaled as if he were done with the subject. Allison promised to keep her eyes open and stay near him at all times.

For the next hour or so, the five of them strolled around the roof, munching on fancy appetizers, sipping on their drinks, and checking everything out. There was even a band playing on a small stage in one of the corners they all stopped to watch and listen to.

Several times Allison had made eye contact with that same guy who'd checked out Drew earlier. Each time he'd smiled at her again. He wasn't alone anymore. He was talking to another couple. There was nothing noxious about the way he'd eyed her then smiled. It just seemed odd that he'd keep doing so when she was obviously with someone.

Only a handful of times had Leonardo let go of her hand and stepped away from her, mostly to talk to the guys in a lowered voice in that same uptight manner as earlier. Drew took advantage of one of those times to lean in and say something to Allison in a lowered voice.

"That guy you thought was admiring me . . ."

Allison glanced at Drew when she paused and saw that she was making sure Leonardo wasn't within earshot. He wasn't. He was too engrossed in whatever he was discussing with Nine and Orlando.

"Pretty sure he's into you not me," Drew went on. "He keeps looking at you, and the more he drinks, it seems the more blatant he gets about it."

"You noticed too?" Allison asked, feeling a little uncomfortable about it. "How stupid is that, though. I mean isn't it obvious I'm with Leonardo?"

"Exactly. I don't think he'd be stupid enough to say something to you with those three around. But I just thought I'd give you a heads-up because I saw him doing shots earlier. You know how dangerous that liquid courage can be."

Allison glanced around casually as the guys walked back toward them. This party was full of what she'd considered *grownups*. She knew how naïve she'd sound if she said aloud what she was thinking: that aside from her sister's wedding, this fancy party seemed far safer than any of the other parties she'd ever attended—backyard parties where fights often broke out.

But she'd be mindful of what Leonardo had shared with her. Just because the people here were grown adults, didn't automatically make them mature and trustworthy.

They took a seat at one of the sitting areas with a firepit since the evening breeze was making things chilly. They'd only been there for a few minutes when Leonardo got a text. "Alright guys," he said after reading it. "Let's get this done. They want us down there now."

He turned to Allison with a very serious expression. "Call me if at any moment *anything* makes you uncomfortable. Trust your instincts, babe. No matter how small a gut feeling you get, *don't* blow it off. *Call me*."

He closed his eyes for a moment as if he were rethinking leaving her there. Allison touched his face. Knowing the guys were just a few feet away and waiting for him, she whispered, "I'll be fine. I promise to call or text you if there's even the slightest indication that something's wrong."

He took a breath and exhaled, kissing her softly before getting up and walking away. When he was far enough away, Drew turned to Allison. "He always wound up this tight?"

Aside from sharing with Drew that she was now in a *hush-hush* relationship with the guy, Allison hadn't shared a whole lot of details. Drew knew about some of his past and all, but she didn't know how hesitant Leonardo had been about anything happening between them or why. She explained briefly their history and about why he seemed so uptight tonight.

Drew glanced around. "You really think something would happen here?"

"I don't know." Allison shook her head as Drew checked her phone. "But after what happened with the one guy following me, I think he's a little paranoid."

"Hmm." Drew was still reading whatever was on her phone screen. "I guess I don't blame him." Tapping away at her screen, she finally looked up and shook her head. "I'm sorry, but Phoenix texted me earlier to let me know Chelsea was running a slight fever. I was just checking on her."

"Is she okay?"

"He said she finally knocked out, but he's still monitoring her fever. It's gotta be viral; she wasn't coughing or sneezing, but she did throw up."

"Poor baby."

"She should be fine," Drew said, looking around. "I need to use the ladies' room. Have you seen any?"

"I haven't." Allison pointed at one of the doors leading out of the rooftop. "But I've seen people going in and out of that entrance."

They both stood up and headed that way. A waiter along the way confirmed they were headed in the right direction. Drew groaned when they turned the corner and saw the line.

"Oh my God! Why can't they ever double the ratio of ladies' to men's restrooms at these places. Look at that." Drew motioned toward the wide-open door to the men's room across the hall where men were walking in and out without a care. "That's so unfair."

Two women coming from the other end of the hallway overheard Drew. One of them leaned into them. "If you keep going," she said in a lowered voice, motioning in the direction they'd just come from, "past those double doors, the doors to your right and left are doors to the stairwell. Go one floor down, and they have the exact bathroom set up as on this floor only empty."

"Thank you so much," Drew said, already reaching for Allison's arm.

They hurried past the ridiculously long line to the ladies' room. As promised, the stairwell doors were just after the double doors. When they were finally in the bathrooms downstairs, Allison realized why the line upstairs was so long. There were only three stalls. One of the ones in this bathroom was out of order, but the other two were working. Only one of them was in use. Since Drew seemed to be in a bigger hurry, Allison let her go first.

Allison studied herself in the mirror for a moment, smiling when she remembered Leonardo's remark about her smoking hot dress. Okay, for once, she'd finally admit it. She did look pretty hot tonight.

Drew was out of the stall before the other person in the other one. Allison had just locked the door when she heard Drew curse under her breath. "Ali, I gotta call Phoenix. He just texted me he might be taking Chelsea to urgent care. Her fever's up. I'll be outside."

"Go ahead," Allison said, feeling a little alarmed for Drew. "If you have to go, I can take you. I'll just text Leonardo."

"I'll let you know."

Allison heard the door open and close then the other person in the other stall washing her hands. Taking a deep breath, she wasn't even disappointed. Leonardo would likely be relieved if she had to suddenly leave this place.

By the time she was done, whoever had been in the other stall was long gone. Allison washed her hands and air-dried them under the machine then walked out. Drew wasn't out in the hallway. Allison glanced around the empty hallway then down at her phone to see if maybe she'd texted her. She hoped it wasn't that urgent that Drew left without waiting for her.

She had no texts, so she walked toward the stairwell door. Maybe she took the call in there. There was no one in the stairwell either, but the door at the top either opened or closed. "Drew?" Allison called out. "Is that you?"

Footsteps started down the stairs as Allison started up. Almost at the halfway point of the stairway where it turned to the second half of the flight, she saw him come into view, the guy who'd been eyeing her most of the night. "Hey," he said with a big smile.

"Hey." She smiled nervously, not sure how else to respond.

"How we doin, beautiful?" he asked, and that's when she realized it. It wasn't just the very heavy and distinct accent; he was drunk. "I was hoping to get a moment alone with you."

The overly stretched-out smile was creepy enough, but the idea that maybe this guy had followed her here was even more alarming. Was he just some drunk guy trying to hit on her or was there more to him?

If I'd known these people were gonna be here, I never would've brought you.

She stood frozen on the step she was on, not sure whether she should keep going or let him by. "Um, I'm doing fine."

She almost didn't, but the way the guy leered at her, had her rethinking whether she should panic and dial Leonardo or just relax and get past the guy.

Trust your instincts, babe.

Glancing down at the phone still in her hand, she used her thumb to tap on the icon she'd set as the speed dial for Leonardo. She prayed this guy wouldn't hear it ringing or Leonardo's voice if he answered. Deciding to keep going since he all but stopped, she took a few more steps until she was at the middle point with him that turned onto the next flight. He took a step in front of her, not letting her by. "What's the hurry? I just wanna a moment with you."

Feeling her heart spike, Allison tried in vain to get around him because he blocked her again. "My hurry is my boyfriend is waiting for me up there."

"No, he's not." He stepped in front of her again, making her flinch and squeeze her phone even tighter. His big body seemed to expand, making it even harder for her to go around him. "I saw him leave."

"No, he didn't." Allison contemplated running back down the stairs. "He's coming back, and he'll be looking for me."

Her phone rang, but before she could bring it to her ear, the guy grabbed it, smiling when he hit something on the screen that made it stop ringing. Leaning into her, he stuck it in her cleavage, his fingers caressing the top of her breasts.

"Maybe he is looking for you. Better make this fast." The guy stepped closer to her, inhaling deeply, and Allison took a step back. "You smell that?"

He kept taking steps closer even as he continued to inhale deeply through his nose. Allison stupidly stepped backwards until she realized he'd cornered her into the wall. That's when she finally snapped out of her terror-induced trance and tried to push him away, but he was too big—too strong. He continued to do the exaggerated inhaling thing. "That's the smell of another man's pussy." He lifted his hand against the wall next to Allison's face. "And you're the most satisfying kind. My favorite."

"Fuck you!" she finally said, trying to slap him, but he grabbed her wrist so hard she thought it might snap.

"Oh, no." He pressed his heavy body against hers. "I think I'll fuck *you*."

She started to cry out in pain because he squeezed her wrist even harder, but he grabbed a fistful of her hair and yanked hard. "Shut your fucking mouth," he said through his teeth as he spread her legs with his knee.

The door at the top opened, making him freeze for a second, but he recovered quickly. He kept his body over hers and kissed her, rendering her voiceless. His disgusting rancid tongue violated every corner of her mouth. Whoever had opened the door must've changed his mind about coming down when he saw the two *love birds* going at it in the stairwell. "Guess fucking you right here might be too *risqué*." He dropped her wrist only to wrap that hand around her neck instead, making her gasp. "Move or make a sound and I'll snuff the life out of you right here." An evil smile lifted the corners of his mouth when her eyes nearly popped out in horror. "Wouldn't be the first time I had to do that."

Like in one of the nightmares she used to have as a child where she couldn't move or make a sound, she stood frozen and mute as his hand continued squeezing her windpipe. She felt completely helpless.

He pulled her dress up, smiling big when he realized she wore no panties, then squeezed her neck a little tighter when she began to cry.

"Please don't!"

"Shut the fuck up," he hissed, spreading her legs, then closed his eyes as his fingers grazed her slit. "Fuck yeah," he said, dipping a finger into her.

Allison cried at the horrendous sensation of another man touching her. "Stop!" she sobbed, but he only squeezed her neck more, and Allison only prayed she'd pass out now before he could do more. She'd rather die a million times than experience the rest of what he seemed to have in mind.

Twenty-Eight

BEAST

Not all were there. Of the faces Leonardo had told Allison about, the ones he'd thought and hoped he'd never see again, only a few were in the apartment with the others Martinez would be briefing. Which meant there were still some up there—with Allison.

Pacing as they all waited for Martinez to get there, Leonardo debated whether he should just head back and have the guys fill him in on what he missed later. His phone ringing made him flinch. Seeing Allison's name on his screen already had him heading to the door.

"Where you going?" Orlando asked, but Leonardo just held up a hand as he brought the phone to his ear.

"What's wrong?"

It was muffled, and for a moment, Leonardo actually felt relieved and slowed. He could hear footsteps echoing loudly. It calmed the alarm that Allison would only call if something were wrong. This sounded like she'd dialed him accidently. Then he heard it.

"What's the hurry? I just wanna a moment with you."

Leonardo froze in place at the sound of the man's voice. It took a second, but he recognized that unmistakable smug accent of that fucking douche he thought he'd *never* see again. Hearing Allison's response only made the heat rip through Leonardo's body even faster.

"My hurry is my boyfriend is waiting for me up there."

"No, he's not."

The line clicked, and Leonardo nearly roared. Martinez and his entourage walked in the door just as Leonardo rushed to it. "You leaving?"

"Yeah, I gotta go."

There was no time for explanations. He tore by him headed to the elevator as he dialed Allison back. After the second ring, the call was sent to voicemail, which only alarmed him further. He hit the up button for the elevator, looking up to see what floor the elevators were on, cursing under his breath. All three were near the bottom floors. Martinez's luxury apartment was just three floors down from the roof. Fuck it. He'd take the stairs. Nine and Orlando walked out into the hallway.

"What's going on?" Orlando asked as Leonardo rushed to the stairwell door.

"Allison," he said as he reached the door. "That piece of shit DeMoss is with her."

"Who?"

"The fucker who ran the *Coyotaje* rings down in Yuma." Leonardo pushed the door to the stairwell open. "Flip nearly killed his ass when he caught him messing with one of the little girls he was supposed to be smuggling."

Leonardo started up the stairs, not sure who he was more pissed at: that fucker for approaching her at all or himself for getting Allison involved in his shit to begin with. The blinding rage only intensified with every step he took.

He cleared the first floor up easily then turned the corner to the next, nearly colliding with Drew. She was on her phone—alone—which only confirmed that wherever Allison was with that prick she was alone too.

"Where's Allison?"

Drew pointed up. "The restroom," she mouthed then covered her phone with her hand. "My daughter's in urgent care," she explained. "I had to take the call in here so I could hear better."

Leonardo tore up the rest of the stairs, skidding when he heard Drew clarify that Allison was on the floor before the roof. Not *on* the roof.

Opening the door to the last floor before the roof, he rushed into the empty hallway. There was no time for etiquette. He rushed right into the ladies' room. "Allison!" he called out leaning over to see under the stalls.

He didn't see any feet, but he knew better, so he kicked them open, ready to kill if anyone was holding her in there. When it was clear she wasn't in any, he rushed out into the hallway again. Nine was just walking out of the stairwell behind Orlando. There was another door across the hall from that stairwell with a window just like it. Leonardo hurried toward it, looking in the window. Another stairwell.

The movement on the upper part of that stairwell caught his eye, and in the next instant, everything but a loud buzzing noise in his ears went silent. He didn't remember smashing the door open or tearing up the stairs to pull the fucking animal off her. He was so blinded by the rage he didn't even stop to check if Allison was okay. All he knew was he'd forever have the image of that fucking bastard holding her neck with one hand and his other hand between her legs. Worst of all, the image of her horrified crying face.

DeMoss was on the floor, and Leonardo had no recollection of how he got there. But the asshole's face was already a bloody mess, so Leonardo could only assume he pummeled him the moment he was close enough.

"Look at me, you piece of shit." He lifted the guy by the shirt. "I'm the guy who's gonna end your fucking life."

Leonardo spit in his face. Then just like when he'd done this to his own dad, he knew the moment he started bashing DeMoss's face he wouldn't stop until the guy stopped breathing. It didn't take long. What took longer was convincing Leonardo that he was dead.

The moments after they were finally able to pull him off DeMoss's lifeless body were a blur. Somehow Allison got whisked away; though Orlando had to shake Leo to get him to calm the fuck down and listen to what he was saying.

"She's fine, damn it! Nine's with her now. He took her to Drew and will make sure they get home okay."

He didn't even remember taking his shirt off or who took it off him, but he assumed it was Orlando since he was now wearing Orlando's shirt to cover his bloodied wife beater. He and Orlando were rushing down the stairwell with Orlando reminding him every few minutes under his breath, "Keep your fucking head down. Do not look up. There's cameras everywhere."

When they'd gone down a few flights, Orlando finally walked out into the hallway as Leonardo followed, his adrenaline still pumping through him like water through a fire hose. Next thing Leonardo knew they were in a restroom with Orlando ordering him to wash his hands.

His friend moved quickly, drenching paper towels and roughly cleaning off the splattered blood all over Leonardo's face. As soon as Orlando deemed the cleanup good enough, they grabbed the elevator the rest of the way down.

The moment they were in the elevator, Leonardo realized it all happened so fast it suddenly dawned on him that he didn't even know for sure. "Did he rape her?"

Orlando stared at him with a blank expression. "Dude, you killed the guy. What does it—?"

Leonardo grabbed him by the shirt. "Did he fucking rape her?"

"I don't know. I don't think so. But he sure as fuck was going to."

Leonardo let go of Orlando and brought his hands to his face instead. "*Fuck!*"

An endless trail of expletives followed as he banged the walls of the elevator. Leonardo could kick his own ass for having brought her into this life. He'd known it was dangerous. He'd known he'd ruin anything he touched. His phone rang just as they exited the elevator.

"Are you okay?" was the first thing he said after hitting the answer button.

"I'm fine. How are you?" Allison may have sounded well enough, but there was a slight trembling in her words.

"Baby, I'm so sorry." Feeling his own words tremble and then the huge boulder in his throat nearly suffocating him, he kept walking farther into a corner of the parking lot instead of toward Orlando's truck. "I'm *so* sorry," he whispered even as Allison insisted it wasn't his fault.

Of course she would. She had no idea who that bastard was or why he'd target her. Swatting the tears in anger, he took a deep breath.

". . . didn't do anything but touch me."

Even hearing the tail end of what she was saying so frantically made him want to kill the guy all over again. When he was finally able to breathe a little calmer, he took one big deep breath. "I don't know what's gonna happen, baby, but whatever does, just remember I love you."

"What do you mean?" She sounded even more frantic now. "You were defending me, Leonardo, stopping a potential rape. You did what you had to. Just turn yourself in and tell them that. I'll testify on your behalf. But don't run."

There were sirens in the distance followed by more and more. "Dude, we gotta go," Orlando called out from inside his truck already. "We need to get you out of here."

Leonardo thought of what Allison had just said, but he knew he couldn't chance it. "I gotta go, babe. I'll get in touch when I can. I love you."

He hung up before she could say anything more, before she could try to convince him to turn himself in. Maybe someone with a clean past would get off. Not Leonardo. Not a former cartel member.

He got in the truck. "Where should we head to?" Orlando asked. "I gotta hide you out somewhere then wait for Nine to call in case he needs a ride home from the hospital."

"Hospital?" Leonardo turned to him in a panic. "But Allison said—"

"Not Allison," Orlando clarified. "Drew's kid, remember? Since Allison's feeling okay and Drew was worried, they decided to go straight to the hospital first. Nine said he'll let me know if it's gonna be long or if Allison can just drop Drew off and bring him home. But I can't take *you* home. That's the first place they'll come looking as soon as they get wind it was you who killed that guy."

Leonardo let his head fall back on the seat. He was so fucked now. On the run again, he had two choices. He could get on his bike and head back to where he said he never return. It'd be assurance of two things. He'd never be caught by the cops, and he'd never see Allison again, so he wouldn't have to worry about dragging her into his shit again.

His second choice would be calling his probation officer and explaining what happened. Lawyer up and pray for a miracle. If he beat the charges, he'd still have a chance to stay in Allison's life. Be happy, but the risk of his past possibly catching up to him—yet again—and putting her in danger would still be there.

"Just get me to my bike. I know what I gotta do."

TWENTY-NINE

Allison

The good and sad thing about a big city like Los Angeles is even big stories are yesterday's news as soon as a bigger story hits the headlines. Allison had numbly watched the footage on the news of the videotape showing both the censored part where the man began to attack her and the part where the other man ran in and saved her, killing her assailant in the process. An assailant who was a registered sex offender. Needless to say, there was little to no sympathy for the deceased.

The first few days they'd aired it time and time again. Thankfully, none of the footage had a clear shot of any of the *heroes'* faces. Just as she'd thought when she'd first seen all three guys that evening, with their attire and the way they'd cleaned up, they looked so different from their norm she could only hope it was why they'd yet to have anyone identify them. At least nothing was reported about it.

They'd also blurred out Allison's face, who they believed hadn't come forward for fear of her life. Allison assumed that was because evidence of the rapist's past ties with organized crime had also surfaced. Despite all that, the broadcasts still urged her to do so. Little did they know, she had. Thankfully, with her gym bag she kept in the car, she'd been able to change into her gym clothes at the hospital when they arrived. She had to. Her dress was ripped, and she needed to get any smell of that filthy rapist off her.

So, when she'd finally gone into shock and was forced to be looked at by the medical staff, she wasn't in that same little red dress seen around the world in the footage. She admitted to being attacked. Only she claimed it happened while she was running by a total stranger and that she'd been able to get away before he'd actually raped her.

They'd administered a rape-kit exam. There was obviously no semen since he hadn't gotten that far, but there was evidence of injuries to her privates since he'd been so rough. Not that any of that mattered since the guy was dead, but she hoped the report might at least come in handy should she be able to convince Leonardo to turn himself in.

But it'd been three and a half days now, and she still hadn't heard back from Leonardo. She'd had enough of waiting on pins and needles. She needed answers. She needed to know what he planned on doing? He couldn't just run for the rest of his life. What about her? What about them? Did he really expect her to just forget about him so easily?

Wiping away tears, she drove into his driveway. Only Orlando's truck was in it. He walked out onto the porch before she even got out of her car. Allison tried to make out his deadpan expression.

"How are you?" he asked as soon as she was out of her car. "I heard you went into shock."

"Where is he?" she asked, still wiping away at the corners of her eyes.

Orlando shook his head. "I don't know."

"Don't lie to me." She rushed toward him. "Of course you know."

"I don't. I really don't. He left that night, and all he told me to tell you was that he loved you but he had to go. He won't be back."

Allison felt her brows pinch at the same time she felt something stab her heart. "What do you mean he won't be back?"

"How can he?" Orlando asked. "They'll lock him up for good."

Shaking her head adamantly, Allison spoke; though she knew she'd barely be able to without turning into a blubbering mess. "No, they won't. He was defending me. Everyone who's seen the video agrees that monster deserved it. It wasn't the first time he'd assaulted someone, and it wouldn't have been his last. The world is better off without him. Even a judge would agree to that."

"He didn't want to take that chance, not with his record."

"So that's it?" she squeaked out the words. "He's just gone and he's never coming back? But he said he'd call me."

Orlando shook his head sympathetically. "He can't, sweetheart. He left his phone here. Too easy to track him down that way. But trust me; no one's gonna find him now."

Feeling completely sick to her stomach, Allison sat down on the porch steps, defeated, and cried. Orlando sat down next to her and hugged her. She cried against his shoulder for what felt like forever until she was finally able to get herself together and left.

It was easy to claim a stomach virus as Allison's reason for barely leaving her room the week that followed her visit with Orlando. Allison blamed her time around Chelsea that horrid night at the hospital, since it turned out to be what landed the little girl in urgent care. But it was really beginning to feel like a phantom virus. Since she hadn't had much of an appetite and hardly ate, the dizzy spells and headache were inevitable, so she felt like crap.

But there was more to it. She was downright miserable, both emotionally and physically, so much Allison had looked it up, and she'd been right. Broken Heart Syndrome was a real fucking suck-ass thing, and Allison had a major case of it. She'd done so much crying the last several days her nose was raw and her eyes were a puffy mess. She hadn't even been able to wear her contacts for days, since all the crying irritated her eyes when she wore them. So, she'd been back to her bookworm-looking days, only this bookworm's eyes were permanently bloodshot, which matched her bright red nose.

Drew stopped by late that week, feeling guilty that maybe her daughter had really been the reason for Allison being so sick. She came bearing homemade chicken soup; though she admitted she hadn't actually made it.

"I might've already been responsible for your getting sick. I refuse to add the nail to your coffin with my cooking," she explained as Allison and Leticia, Sonny's housekeeper, walked around the kitchen, getting bowls and spoons together. "When I lived with Charlee, she refused to let me handle poultry after I made us both violently ill one time from salmonella. But this place by my townhouse has some really good comfort food, and their chicken soup is one of the best I ever had. Made fresh."

Lila walked into the kitchen. "Something smells good." She did a double take when she glanced at Allison. "Ali, you look awful." Switching gears, she hurried to Allison instead of toward the soup where she was first headed. "Do you have a fever?"

"No," Allison said, touching her own forehead, then took a deep breath.

For a moment, she considered the idea of just coming clean about why she felt like staying in bed forever. But Drew spoke up before Allison could.

"If it's the virus Chelsea had, it's pretty nasty. It landed my baby in the urgent care, but Allison should be okay," Drew explained. "The doctor said little ones and elderly are the ones who get hit the hardest with it."

"Well, looks like it's hitting you pretty bad," Lila said with a frown. "Maybe I could stay home this week and fly out and meet Sonny next week when you're feeling better."

"No." Allison shook her head. "I'll be fine. I just need to rest. I won't have you sitting around staring at me. There's nothing you can do for me anyway. It just needs to run its course."

The last thing Allison needed was for Lila to hover over her all week. When would Allison get a moment alone to sob? The mood struck so often and unpredictably, Lila would eventually figure out there was more to this. Her going on the road with Sonny was something Allison had been counting on. She'd use the time to cry until she just couldn't anymore and then dust herself off and get over it. As if that could ever happen. But she'd do her best to try and snap out of it.

Drew explained about the soup and more about her daughter's virus; though she already knew to leave out the part about having to leave a party to get to her. Allison had yet to even mention the party to Lila. The entire situation was still too painful to talk about, and she figured why bother now? If she hadn't wanted to share with Lila before, telling her about the harrowing incident now in Lila's fragile state was out of the question.

Surprisingly, Lila was able to enjoy a bowl of what really was good soup. Not so surprising, she said it made her sleepy. It seemed everything made her tired these days, and just seeing her yawn with such content had Allison yawning too. "Stop that," Allison said, covering her mouth.

"That was really good," Lila said, thanking Drew, then excused herself finally so she could take another marathon nap.

While Allison found it too painful to tell Lila about Leonardo because she'd have to tell her everything—how she'd fallen in love, all the things she loved about Leonardo, and why she missed him terribly—she did need to vent to someone. So, she was happy for Drew's unexpected visit. Allison had been so deep in despair the past week she hadn't even bothered returning calls or texts to anyone, so even Jen didn't know about what happened. But now she was ready to talk about it.

"Leonardo's gone."

Allison immediately regretted not having waited until she was in the privacy of her own room because she was instantly choked up.

"What do you mean gone?" Drew asked just as Leticia came back into the kitchen.

"I'll clean up, mijita," Leticia said, already opening the dishwasher. "You should go lie down. You really don't look well."

Swallowing back the tears, she nodded, thanking Leticia before motioning to Drew to follow her, and rushed out of the kitchen.

"He's gone," Allison said as soon as her bedroom door was closed and she gave into the tears. "O said Leonardo didn't think he could beat the charges and would end up locked up for good. So he left. He's gone into hiding and he's never coming back."

Drew hugged her then pulled away to look at her. "But the video is proof he was just defending you. Albeit," she added, opening her eyes wide, "some might argue he went way overboard. Still, who's to say how they'd react if they saw their loved one being attacked, especially a boyfriend or husband seeing their girl sexually assaulted. I think any man would agree they'd be out for blood. In fact, I've read the comments online. The majority are hailing him a hero."

"But they don't know he's also a convict," Allison argued what she knew Leonardo was thinking. "That he did this while on probation. The moment they find all that out they'll want him hung."

"That's not true. He wasn't on probation for anything violent. 5th street would be the first to attest to that. In fact, it's killing me that I can't tell Charlee because she said everyone down there's been so concerned about why Leonardo disappeared. She said all the owners would believe foul play before they'd believe he'd willfully not show up. It's why Gio hasn't called the work-release place. He said he's waiting for them to contact him in case it's something totally explainable and just out of Leonardo's hands. He doesn't want to get him in trouble. None of them do."

Allison shook her head. This was such a nightmare. On top of her heartache, not only was she keeping something so huge from everyone, she also had the enormous burden of knowing she was forcing Drew to do the same.

Feeling the familiar dizziness she'd felt all week, only a bit more severe, she lay back on her bed, staring at the ceiling, feeling like all was lost. She'd never be the same person she was before she met Leonardo. She'd never feel for another man the enormity of what she felt for him. The last thing she remembered was Drew asking her something and Allison answered absentmindedly before closing her eyes.

When she woke, she was surprised to see it was morning. Drew was obviously gone and Allison felt bad. Here Drew had gone out of her way to bring her soup, and Allison had fallen asleep on the girl.

She picked up her phone so she could call or at least text her to apologize but read the several texts she had. First Lila's:

> I waited, hoping you'd wake before I had to leave for the airport, but you never did. After the last few miserable days you've had, I didn't have the heart to wake you. Call me later today and let me know how you're feeling. Kiss, kiss, I love my sis!

Allison smiled, standing up but immediately sitting back down when the entire room spun. "Oh my God," she gasped, grabbing on to the mattress with both hands for support, dropping her phone on the floor in the process.

She sat there for a moment, closing her eyes. Even with her eyes closed, it still felt as if she were spinning. It felt like forever, but it finally subsided, only she was afraid to even move to reach for her phone, much less stand up. "What the hell?"

Her mind raced to think of what medications she might've neglected to take during the past week. Who was she kidding? Everything she'd done this past week was a no-no for her. From depriving herself of enough fluids after losing an ocean in tears when she knew how bad her body reacted to dehydration, to barely eating. More than once she'd remembered she hadn't taken her thyroid meds and didn't even care, she was so damn depressed. Of course, it'd all caught up with her.

She began to reach for her phone and so far, no spinning. "Okay," she said, trying to pep herself out of the scare. "You just stood up too fast. Not the first time that's happened, right?"

No, but it was the first time it was that bad. Glancing down at the phone, she saw it was already past eight. Despite the stupid dizzy spell, she was determined to get out of the house today. She had plenty of errands to run and things to catch up with. No more excuses. She needed to get out there.

Standing very slowly, she held onto her nightstand for support. The room didn't spin, but she felt lightheaded as all hell. God, she felt stupid. On top of everything else she'd gone through this past week, she did this to herself as well?

Shaking it off, she stood up straight. "It's okay. I'll just get some breakfast and some orange juice, and I'll be fine."

She started to the door, and midway there, it started again. She slowed, holding onto the wall, taking deep breaths, and trying to remain calm even as her heart beat wildly. Since this wasn't as bad as the first time, it passed quickly.

Feeling a little better, Allison attempted to walk again. While she was still shaky, she made it to the front room where Leticia was already busy folding a pile of clothes. Wednesday, laundry day, was like clockwork. She'd have it all done, including every sheet and pillow case in the house done before noon.

"*Mijita*," Leticia said as she picked up a towel she began to fold. "Is there anything in your hamper? I didn't want to wake you so—" She stopped when she looked up and saw how slowly Allison was walking. "*Que te pasa?*"

"I'm fine. Just a little dizzy," Allison continued to the kitchen. "I just need to eat something."

Leticia popped out of the chair she'd been sitting in and was immediately by Allison's side. "Let me help you. Why don't you sit down and I'll make you something, yes? You still don't look too good."

With another dizzy spell coming on, Allison didn't argue. She sat down on one of the plush sofas and requested something very light. "My stomach hasn't been the greatest. My doctor takes walk-ins. I think I'll go in today."

"Yes, yes, you should," Leticia said, speaking loudly from the kitchen. "I will call Mrs. Lila and—"

"No, no, don't do that." Allison stood up, surprised that the room didn't spin, but she took it as a good sign. "I'm feeling better actually," she explained, which was half true. She did feel better than she had when she first stood up from her bed. "I don't want to worry her. I've been bad about taking all my meds this week, and it's made me sluggish and dizzy, but I'll be fine."

"You should go back to the sofa, Ms. Ali," Leticia insisted as Allison walked into the kitchen. "I'll bring you some *cafe con leche* and some *chorizo* I had left over from this morning. I always make too much."

Allison smiled. Typical Leticia. Even when Allison reminded her she was trying to watch her weight, the woman would cook what she insisted made real women curves.

"My stomach's not feeling up to chorizo, Leticia. I'll just take some tea and a boiled egg."

Leticia stopped her fast movement around the kitchen to look at Allison. "That's all?"

"Yes." Allison nodded. "When I get back from the doctor, I'll have some of the leftover soup my friend brought me yesterday."

Pouring herself a small glass of juice so she could take the last of her meds, she explained she was going to shower and then eat. Getting back to her room wasn't nearly as bad, and by the time she was out of the shower, she felt refreshed. But just like in the shower, she knew the waves of sobs would continue to come at any moment, so she skipped the contacts and slipped her bottle-cap glasses on instead. The dizziness was almost completely gone except for a few instances where she just slowed and it went away.

Once at the doctor's, he confirmed her blood pressure was way low and she was very dehydrated. He ran a few more tests and said he'd call her with the results in a few days then refilled her prescription. After chugging an entire bottle of Gatorade all the way there and having taken her meds for the first time that week, she was feeling much better by the time she left the clinic.

When she got to her car, she saw she had a missed call from Drew. Feeling bad, she hit the call button and waited to hear Drew's voice through her speakers. "Hey, how you feeling? You poor thing. You looked so beat last night."

Allison explained about not taking her meds and then about the dizzy spells that morning but that she'd just left the doctor and was on her way to fill her prescription now. "I'm sorry I fell asleep on you last night. That was so rude."

"No worries, girl. I know what you've been through this week, and I didn't buy for a second that you picked up Chelsea's virus. You were around her all of two minutes."

"You didn't?" Allison asked, surprised. "But the soup?"

"Eh," Drew said with a chuckle. "I just wanted an excuse to see you."

"Like you need one. You know you can always . . ." Allison paused when she saw the van in her rearview mirror.

"Ali?"

"Yeah," she said, still staring in her rearview mirror.

The van was one she'd seen earlier when she pulled into the clinic. Ever since the first time she'd been followed, she'd been paranoid about it happening again. So, she paid close attention to any suspicious cars possibly tailing her.

"Something wrong?" Drew asked.

"I don't know," Allison answered absently.

She turned left onto the bigger street where the drug store was. The van turned left as well but stayed several cars behind her.

"What is it?" Drew asked.

When Allison turned into the parking lot of the big drug store, the van kept going straight, and she exhaled. "I'm just being paranoid again. I thought this van might be following me, but I turned and it kept going."

She'd since told Drew about the first guy Leonardo had beaten for her. So, Drew wasn't dismissive about it all, even commended her for continuing to stay vigilant. Allison ended her call with Drew and was beyond grateful that she was feeling so much better.

By the time she walked out after dropping off her prescription, she even had a little pep in her step. Despite her heart still being so heavy, she managed to respond to a silly text Lila had sent with one just as silly so it'd at least appear that she was in better spirits.

Dumping her purse and phone on the passenger seat, she put her seatbelt and started the car. "Jesus Christ!" she gasped, clutching her chest when she saw the pair of eyes from her backseat in her rearview mirror.

THIRTY

BEAST

The house was exactly as he'd left it: all the old furniture from his days of youth and the appliances his mother used in the kitchen and small laundry room. The gardeners still tended the landscape on a weekly basis, so the flowers and shrubs Leo's mother had planted so long ago still adorned the entrance in hopes that one day she'd return.

But she never had.

While his heart wanted to believe she was still out there, Leo had reluctantly accepted years ago that she was gone, and there was still no sign that she'd ever returned. Leo knew his days here were numbered. It'd be just a matter of time before he was tracked down. Even if the house had and always would remain in his mother's name, he was linked to it. But for days now, he'd been there mourning the loss of yet another loved one, another woman his heart would never forget. Only this time it was so much more torturous than any he'd lost before.

If Leo had known it was going to be like this, he might've given turning himself in more consideration. He figured he'd seen and experienced things no man ever should. He could deal with a little heartache. But the torment he was living now was like nothing he'd ever imagined.

Thoughts of Allison plagued him day and night. Was she hurting as much as he was? Had that bastard injured her and she'd kept it from him? Was his girl crying? Was she suffering from post-traumatic stress syndrome?

He'd stopped calling Orlando days ago. There was never anything new to report. Leo wasn't going back, as much as he yearned to see her again. Seeing those videos of what that piece of shit had done to her before Leo got there that night, he didn't regret for a second having killed him. His only regret was having been so enraged he beat the life out of him too damn fast. If he had to do it again, the only thing he'd do different is slow it down. Take his time and prolong the guy's pain.

He'd gone back to doing what he'd been forced to do when he first met Allison, back when his delusional ass believed he could do the impossible—not be brought to his knees by her—he stopped watching the news altogether. The risk was too high and it was too torturous. From the videos of the near rape to the endless stories of the media's favorite sports royal couple—Lila and Sonny—all were constant and painful reminders of the dream future he'd been so close to having with the love of his life. He didn't even turn on the television anymore, and he steered clear of the Internet unless he needed it.

His roommates were divided on their thoughts of his running. At first, they'd both agreed he should run. He'd never beat the charges, and he'd be doomed to a life behind bars. But Orlando had since changed his mind. "I think you have a good chance of beating this, man, especially now that they have footage. That shit's gone viral, and everyone seems to feel strongly that what you did was justified."

Nine still thought he should lie low, at least until things died down and they were certain that there'd be no retaliation from those who recognized Leo on that video. They couldn't come forward because of their own connections with organized crime but would still want Leo to pay for taking out a made man—someone who should've never been at the party in the first place. At least not if Martinez had had his way.

They now knew that DeMoss being there was coincidental. This was proof that some of those out of the life still stayed in contact with those still in it. DeMoss was there working on an entirely different deal with someone else. Martinez hadn't even been aware of his attendance.

Leo could only assume DeMoss had seen Allison with him and decided it'd be good retribution for what Felipe had done to him years ago. Only he fucked with the wrong guy's girl.

Nine's idea wasn't such a bad one. Leo wasn't actually due to check in with his PO for another few weeks. They'd kept his phone on so, in case the PO called, they could give Leo a heads-up that the clock had officially started ticking. But so far, his PO hadn't.

If no one ever came forward to identify him as the guy on the video, technically, Leo could sneak back into his life and possibly not have to answer to any of that. But when they got word that DeMoss was now a made man, that halted everything. Orlando and Nine had already seen what they thought looked like suspicious cars drive by, even guys sitting in their cars up the street who just didn't seem to fit in. The cops may not be looking for Leo yet, but someone was.

Leo mixed the olive oil with the vinegars he'd picked up from the dollar store. He knew he was just torturing himself, but his soul felt so empty he hadn't been able to help himself. He'd made a U-turn when he passed the store after he'd been assaulted by the memories of that smile as they'd done something so simple.

Now he stood there dipping a pitiful chicken breast into the marinade she'd schooled him on. He'd forgo the barbeque for one measly breast. Instead, he'd be cooking it on his stovetop.

His burner phone dinging in the front room caught his attention. Only Orlando and Nine had the number, and neither had called or texted in days, not since he'd let them know he'd only be checking in every few weeks from then on. Orlando had promised to only call or text if he had any pertinent news.

Leo covered the container with the marinating chicken and stuck it in the fridge. His phone dinged again before he reached it. Even more curious now, he picked it up. The texts were from Nine.

> Hey, man, how goes it?

"The hell?"

Two things were instantly in Leo's cynical head. Either Nine's phone had been compromised, and this was someone else using his phone to get to Leo. Or this was his anything-but-subtle friend's way of feeling him out before dropping something big on him. He scrolled down and read the second text.

> You still in Yuma, right?

Leo's heart sped up. His gut said this was Nine trying to feel him out, but he wouldn't chance it. He sent off a text with two words:

> Call me.

No way was he giving out any info unless he knew for sure he was talking to Nine. To his relief, the phone rang, but he still answered cautiously. "Nine?"

"Yeah, who else would it be?"

"Why you being so fucking weird?" Leo asked as he walked back into the kitchen.

"Weird? I asked two questions. You're still there, right?"

Instantly, Leo was feeling irritable, but he'd since accepted he'd likely be irritable for the rest of his life. "Yeah, who wants to know?"

"I was just wondering."

Stopping in the middle of the kitchen, it dawned on Leo. His second thought. "Why? Did something happen?" Nine did something he rarely did—went quiet. "What the fuck? What's going on?"

"He doesn't know," Leo heard Nine's voice trail off. "You tell him."

"Tell me what?" Instinct had Leo heading for his bedroom where his shoes, wallet, and bag were.

"Hey, man."

Orlando was on the phone now, which only panicked Leo further. What was it Nine didn't want to tell him? He stopped in front of his bed, swallowing hard. "What's going on?"

"She's missing."

Feeling his heart nearly stop, Leo knew exactly who the only person they'd be calling him about was, but still, his hopeful insides had to ask. "Who?"

"Allison."

The rest of the conversation was a frantic string of questions and answers as Leo threw things in his bag then ran around, turning shit off and locking things up. Orlando knew as much as the news was saying.

"Two days ago, Allison left her home in the morning to see the doctor because she wasn't feeling well. According to her sister and the housekeeper who'd seen her last, she hadn't been feeling well all week. Her doctor confirmed she'd been there, had a check-up and some blood work, and left his office. They've since released footage of her from the drug store where she dropped off her prescription. It shows her arriving, shopping around, leaving her prescription at the pharmacy, and walking out—alone. It was the last time anyone saw or heard from her.

"Then they found her car yesterday morning in an apartment building parking lot just a few blocks away. There were no signs of blood or struggle, but there was one witness who remembers seeing a young couple walking hand in hand in the parking lot on the same floor her car was found.

"What no one knows is about her involvement with you. If they do, you'll be the first they come looking for. You're her boyfriend and haven't shown up to your work-release program in over a week. So, you're really there in Yuma and haven't been back at all?"

"Yeah. What the fuck?" Leo asked, pacing in his backyard now that he'd locked everything up and packed up his bike. "You really think I wouldn't tell you if she was with me? I'm about to lose my shit here, O."

"Alright, alright, I was just trying to rule out that maybe you were down here keeping an eye on her and she didn't know it."

"No, why—?"

"Drew tracked Nine down. It's why he called you. She said she spoke with Allison last, just before she got to the drug store where she was last seen. She said Allison mentioned feeling like she was being followed."

"*What?*"

"Yeah, Drew said she talked to Lila and told her about the call because she figured as soon as they pulled Allison's phone records, they'd see the last calls she made."

Orlando said Drew told Lila about Allison saying she thought someone might be following her. But she figured Lila would assume it was the paparazzi, and she'd been right.

"It's the first thing she said, especially when Drew told her Allison said it was a van."

"A van?" Leo stopped his pacing.

Visuals of what they could've—might've—done to her the moment they got her in it had Leo pacing again, fisting his hand.

"Can you think of anyone she might've known well enough to be holding hands with?"

Leo stopped again, feeling his insides heat. "No, no, I can't, O. Why the fuck would you even consider that couple had anything to do with her? You know the drill. They'll probably get a hundred bullshit leads, a thousand useless eye witnesses before they get a single helpful one and—"

"The lady described her before they released the footage. She said the one thing she remembered with all certainty was the girl's thick eyeglasses . . ."

Orlando paused for a moment as the memory of the first time Leo had laid eyes on Allison torpedoed at him. He'd almost forgotten about her glasses.

"She was wearing them in the footage, and Lila and Drew said she hadn't worn her contacts all week. The housekeeper confirmed she wasn't wearing them that morning when she left either. The clothes the witness said the girl was wearing were also pretty accurate to what she was last seen in. She also described the guy as big and tall, much taller than her, but just as young as her. Maybe someone from her school?"

Carson.

As nauseating a thought as that may have been, it beat the alternative. "There was a guy named Carson she told me about, the editor from her school paper. Ask Drew or her other friend Jen about him. She was seeing him just before she and I got together. He's the only other guy I can possibly think of that she might be holding hands with. She never mentioned he might be a threat, but she'd also never just disappear without telling anyone. She wouldn't do that to her sister, so he needs to at least be questioned."

That they were holding hands held little significance to Leo. She might've been forced to hold his hand to give the appearance of a happy couple, not someone being taken away against her will.

"I made an appointment to go see Felipe tomorrow morning," Orlando informed him. "I know he won't be able to tell me much, but I figure it's worth a shot. He might know something."

"Thanks, man," Leo said, hopping on his bike. "I'll be there before morning."

For the first time in so many years, Leo prayed. He prayed he was right about Carson: that this had something to do with him and not anything else related to Leo. But his gut said otherwise. Suddenly, his being found didn't matter in the least. If something had happened to Allison, it didn't matter if his enemies found him or if they'd lock him up for good. If this was what he thought it might be, and he was too late to save her this time, his life was over too.

※

The sound of the car door opening woke Leo, and he immediately sat up. He'd gotten back just after seven that morning. After nearly dozing off the second time last night, he figured he'd be more help to Allison alive than splattered all over the highway. He forced himself to get a room where he slept for a few hours before getting up and driving the rest of the way.

Nine and Orlando had done well so far. They'd been all over it, doing exactly what Leo planned on doing once he arrived. They'd contacted everyone they knew who might know about a bounty out for Allison and had gotten their hacker contact, Voodoo, involved. They'd had several bites from insiders who said they'd heard about a bounty on a girl from the Los Angeles area but didn't have all the facts. They were still waiting on the call back. But they'd also gotten even more confusing info. They said there'd initially been a bounty out for Leo, but it'd been called off days ago.

Despite his exhaustion, Leo had insisted on accompanying Orlando on his visit with Felipe. He couldn't go in since he wasn't on the list to see him today, but he wanted to hear any info his brother might have, the moment Orlando was done.

"So, what'd he say?" Leo asked anxiously as Orlando got in the car.

"He heard about DeMoss. And he knew there'd automatically be a bounty out for whoever killed him, but he had no idea it was you. He just about lost his fucking mind! I had to tell him to sit down and calm the hell down before they cut our meeting short." He chuckled, shaking his head as he started the car. "You two are one and the same, man."

"What else did he say?" Leo asked, losing his patience.

"He said the same thing that guy told us. That he'd heard the bounty had been called off. I guess DeMoss was that big of a fucking douche. Even his own people changed their mind about avenging his ass."

That made no sense. If they'd called the bounty off on Leo, why would there still be one out for Allison?

"Flip's all fired up," Orlando continued. "He said he's nipping this shit in the ass ASAP, and we'd hear from him as soon as he did. I don't know why he was so pissed, but I guess he said that piece of shit DeMoss is not worth a war and everyone knows it. But if they ask for it, that's what they'll get."

"Fuck," Leo muttered, glancing out the window.

As promised, not even halfway home, Felipe called. Orlando handed the phone to Leo almost as soon as he was done accepting the charges. "There shouldn't be any more trouble, and I have people trying to get the word on where your girl might be. So far, no one knows anything. It's the damnedest thing. Usually someone knows something, but this time they're all stumped. In the meantime, I need you to stay out of trouble, you hear me? I know, if you find her, whoever she's with will have hell to pay, but whatever you do, *do not* do what you did to the other guy."

"How can you be sure there won't be any more trouble?"

"Because I'm done with this shit." Orlando had been right; Felipe did sound fired up as fuck. "I'm up for parole in a few months, and I'm going clean, but they don't know this. As far as anyone's concerned, I'm still running the show. If these assholes insist on starting a war over DeMoss, I just made it clear that's exactly what they're in for. An all-out fucking war. Everyone's seen what that piece of shit did. They know what you did was personal, not business. Word's out unless they wanna be watching their backs and their families from now until I'm satisfied, this ends now."

Nine called just minutes after Leo got off the phone with his brother. "Just got off the phone with Drew. Carson's clean. The guy wasn't even in town the day Ali disappeared. He has a solid alibi and is cooperating with authorities. Even agreed to a poly if need be."

"What do you mean if need be?"

"He's got no motive and a solid alibi. He doesn't have to."

"He's her scorned ex who got dumped for someone else. Of course there's a motive."

"Dude." Nine chuckled. "He's clean, man. Drew said she talked to him herself, and she believes him. Called him a dweeb." He laughed again. "She said he's just not the type, and her other friend confirmed he is an anal dweeb who'd never get involved in anything illegal."

As if that weren't exasperating enough, Orlando got another call just a few minutes later. There had been a bounty out for Allison as well. Had been. That one, too, had been called off before she'd gone missing.

"What the hell?" Leo asked, bringing both hands to his head.

He wanted to be relieved, but fact was she was still missing. Nine said Drew told him Lila was beside herself and Drew was so close to telling her about Leo since she was certain this had everything to do with him. But Nine had been able to talk her into giving them at least another day. He'd assured her Leo was just as lost and going crazy about this as they were.

"So, let me ask you something, but don't get all crazy."

Leo turned to Orlando without comment and waited for his question. Orlando stared straight ahead but seemed to be stalling. Leo's patience was done. He didn't have time for this shit.

"Just ask already."

Orlando glanced at him but turned back to the road. "Any chance Allison might've moved on this quickly? Maybe had someone on the side? She might be holed up with this guy somewhere and just been too . . . busy to watch the news or check her phone?"

Grating his teeth, Leo stared out the passenger window without responding but shook his head.

"I'm just saying," Orlando went on. "Couple of the times she stayed over and you two were holed up in your room, she left her phone out in the kitchen or front room, and I know I heard it make noises, but she was too busy—"

"That's not it, okay?" Leo said, gripping the door handle until he thought it might break off. "No matter what, she wouldn't do this to her sister. Lila's over-the-top when it comes to worrying about Allison, and she's pregnant right now to boot. There's no way Allison would do that just to be with some dude."

"She did it for you."

Orlando said the very thing Leo was thinking. Drew had told Nine Lila was supposed to be gone for over a week, like when Allison had stayed for days over at Leo's. If she'd planned a rendezvous with someone else, Lila would've never known. Only difference this time was she apparently hadn't covered her ass with the housekeeper. When the housekeeper got there the next morning and saw that Allison had never made it home all night, she panicked when Allison also didn't return her calls or texts. So, she called Lila, and that's when the shit hit the fan.

"She would've checked in with her sister by now, O. I hear what you're saying. As much as it pisses me off, I can admit that might be a possibility if she didn't care that her sister's a mess right now."

Leo could barely believe that he'd even consider it a possibility, but at this point, he had to be open to all options. No matter how infuriating.

"I'm just throwing it out because we're heading for a dead end pretty fast here." They turned into their driveway. "You think Drew might know more than she's saying?"

Just then Nine flew out the front door, holding his phone, and jumped off the porch. Leo and Orlando got out of Orlando's truck, not sure what to expect.

"She checked in," Nine said with a big smile. "The day she disappeared she checked in on her Facebook that evening that she was at some hotel, but within minutes, the post was gone. But," he added with a bounce of his brows, "just goes to show nothing is ever deleted from the Internet. Good ole Voodoo did it again. He ran all her shit even the deleted stuff and found it."

"Back up," Leo said, holding his hand out. "Did she post a picture or say anything when she checked in?"

His heart had begun to thud again for more than one reason. One: he could have her safe and happy back in his arms as soon as tonight. But two: a hotel? What if they did find her tonight with some dude in a hotel room? What if she was there willingly and, as Orlando suggested, had just been too busy . . .?

Leo didn't even want to think it, but son-of-a-bitch if he didn't instantly feel ready to murder someone a second time for this girl. Nine filled them in on the rest. She hadn't posted anything. It was a generic check-in. Voodoo suggested it was either a post she didn't mean to post so she deleted it or it was her desperate cry for help. Voodoo seemed to believe the latter because it was deleted just minutes afterward. That could mean she'd been caught and they'd made her delete it.

The motel she'd checked in at was just outside Los Angeles, a motel near a truck stop and nothing else, so it was nice and out of the way. "This here"—Nine showed them on his phone screen— "is the list of people who checked into the hotel this past week. Voodoo has broken it down to the dates everyone checked in, but most importantly, which of the tenants who were there the day she checked in and haven't checked out yet."

Leo took the phone and studied the names. None rang a bell, but then Leo would have been surprised if they'd actually used their real names. Only three of the ones who'd checked in around the day of Allison's disappearance were still there. All the names on the list were men with the exception of one woman: Samantha Bozigian.

Leo paused at the name. If that had, in fact, been Allison who the witness saw in that parking lot, Allison was with a guy. There was nobody else with them.

He took in the names of the other two. "Richard Nixon?" he read aloud then looked up at his friends. "That's gotta be fake, right?"

Nine laughed. "That's the first thing I thought when I read it. But I don't know. Both first and last names are pretty common. Maybe his parents had a sense a humor?"

Leo read the last of the three to himself. Jonathan Brown. Nothing jumped out at him with that name either. Well, at least they'd narrowed it down to the three it could possibly be if they were still there. It was still well before check-out time at most hotels. If they were all still there, they still had a chance to catch them before any possibly checked out today.

"I gotta go," Leo said, starting to the garage.

"No way you're going alone," Orlando said. "Jump in my truck."

THIRTY-ONE

It felt like an eternity, but when they finally got there, they circled the one-story motel slowly. Nine had jumped in too, so the three of them sat there, waiting impatiently now. Without going to the doors of the three rooms in question, there was no way of knowing what was behind the closed doors. So, they waited a bit out of sight but close enough they still had a clear view of all three rooms, including the one closest to where a van was parked. Even if they weren't checking out today, there'd have to be some movement soon.

After an agonizing, uneventful twenty minutes, the door closest to the van opened, and all in the truck sat up tensely. Leo exhaled when they saw a woman in dark sunglasses and a sun hat—Samantha Bozigian. She carried what looked like empty bags, the kind you have to take into the supermarkets or pay for your own bags. She hopped in the van but then killed the engine and walked back to the room. She opened the door, stood halfway in with the door open, then closed the door and walked back to the van.

They debated whether they should follow her but decided she was likely coming back. She would've had suitcases or at least filled bags if she were leaving for good. After doing the waiting game again for another agonizing while, they finally had movement again. One of the other doors they'd been watching opened.

Richard Nixon, an older man, and what appeared to be his wife, walked out of the room with their rolling carryon bags. Leo and his friends watched them load the bags in the trunk of their car and drive off. Leo and his roommates exchanged frustrated glances. With two eliminated, Leo was done waiting to see what was behind door number three.

"You guys stay here." He reached for the door handle. "I'll go—"

"Whoa, look," Orlando said, tapping Leo's arm.

Leo turned to see a guy walk out of the room Samantha had walked out of. A tall well-built young guy, he was carrying the room's ice tub. They watched as he started to walk away, but then the door opened, and he turned to it. From the angle they were sitting, they had no visual of whoever was standing at the cracked-open door. The guy, who looked to be in his late teens possibly early twenties, exchanged words with whoever was in the room, and then the door closed.

As his breathing and heart rate sped up, Leo kept his eye on the guy, who stopped right in the middle of the motel where the vending and ice machines were. He filled the bucket then stood in front of the vending machine.

"Check it out," Nine said, pointing at the window of the room the guy had walked out of.

The thick curtains were drawn open. But the sheer curtains were left closed, and it was hard to make out anything more than a figure. Not from as far as they were sitting anyway.

Leo peered harder, trying to make out if it could possibly be Allison in there. Unless there was someone else in there still holding her captive, this would've been a good opportunity for her to run. Yet the door remained closed, and no one came running out. Of course, these could just be Samantha's travel mates, and Allison might not be in any of these rooms. But if Leo had to go with his gut, that wasn't the case.

They all saw it at once. Door number three. A woman carrying a baby and holding another little one's hand walked out of that room, leaving the door open behind her. Then a kid no more than ten years old and a man walked out, pulling rolling suitcases. Seemed Jonathan Brown and his family were on some kind of road trip.

Leo's eyes were instantly back on the guy from the other room, walking back with the ice and drinks he bought from the vending machine. The door opened before he even got there, and whoever was inside reached out to help him with the drinks. The whole thing was a little too fucking friendly for him to stomach if, in fact, that really was Allison in the room with this guy.

Leo waited until Jonathan Brown finished packing up his brood. He didn't want an audience or innocent kids around in case this got ugly. As soon as they drove away, he opened his door.

"Where you going?" Orlando asked.

"To get a closer look. You two stay here."

He got out and walked across the parking lot. His adrenaline was already thundering. A small part of him hoped Allison wasn't in there because, regardless if she was in there willingly or not, shit was about to go down. This time there'd be no justifying what he might do to this guy.

Reaching the room in question, Leo walked over to the car parked in front of the window and pretended to fumble with invisible keys at the door. He glanced up and saw the two figures move about in the room. That was when he got a glimpse of the other person—a much shorter person—who had long hair. There was a light on in the background possibly to the bathroom or hallway just outside the bathroom. The long-haired person's body moved just so it was silhouetted by the light.

If Leo hadn't been so obsessed with that ass and those curves he may not have been so sure it was her. The buzzing in his ears began even as he started toward the door, but only grew louder when both figures moved onto the bed. Fuck knocking. As soon as he was close enough, he kicked the door with the bottom of his foot as hard as he could.

"Allison, you in there?"

Before he could kick it again, Orlando and Nine were already there.

"You saw her?" Orlando asked as Leo kicked the door again, this time making it crack.

"I know you're in there, Allison," Leo yelled, feeling like a madman already. "Open the fucking door!"

Before he could kick it again, the door swung open, and he was face-to-face with his beautiful Allison. Only she didn't look the least bit happy to see him. The buzzing went silent, like a deadly calm before the storm as he took her in from top to bottom. She was half dressed in a tank, short loose-fitting shorts, and no shoes. His heart went from bursting at the sight of her to pounding nearly out of his chest. The guy wasn't in the room anymore. Leo glanced around behind her.

Slamming the door the rest of the way open, in case the little fucker was hiding behind it, Leo felt a fury that came close to what he'd felt the night he saw the other asshole's hands on her. Only this time an agonizing ache in his heart accompanied the all-consuming fury.

The door to the bathroom opened. "Ali, you okay?"

"I'm fine. Stay in there."

Even as the pain of knowing she was protecting this guy suffocated Leo, he focused on the raging inferno instead. "Who the fuck is he?"

THIRTY-TWO

Allison

Leonardo took a step inside the room with conviction, as if Allison might try to stop him. Of course, he seemed surprised when she pulled him all the way in and motioned for his equally stunned friends to come in too.

"You're making a scene!" she hissed.

"What?"

Allison hurried and closed the door after Leonardo and his roommates were all the way in. The relatively small room was very crowded suddenly. She spun around to answer Leonardo's understandably exasperated question. "Do you want someone to call the cops?"

"I don't give a fuck about that right now! Why are you here?" Leonardo turned to the bathroom door like he might start kicking that too. "Who's is this guy?"

Allison rushed to get between him and the door before he could get any ideas. Despite the anger and hurt that he might be thinking what he was clearly not trying to hide, she had to fight the urge to jump into his arms. Being this close to him again was absolute heaven, even if he did look ready to combust.

"Do you know everyone's looking for you?" Leonardo's voice continued to boom. "You know your sister's worried sick, and everyone thinks you've been abducted or have you been too busy to . . .?"

Cutting it short as his already lit eyes seemed to explode with even more anger, he started to the bathroom door.

"No!" Allison said, pressing her open hands against his big chest. "I was abducted, but he's been good to me."

Leonardo's head snapped back as his brows furrowed and the pulsating of the vein on his forehead was the worst she'd ever seen it.

"What the fuck does that mean?"

He banged on the bathroom door behind her head so hard Allison thought he might crack that one too. But something seemed to stop him, and he peered into her eyes. "Did he drug you?"

"No."

She reached to touch his face, but he flinched away with a disgusted expression. "Then explain this! He abducted you, but now you're here willingly because he's been good to you? Who the fuck is this asshole?"

"He's your brother."

They all turned to the opened hotel room door, looking as stunned as Allison felt. They'd managed to convince her they weren't going to hurt her. Allison believed the woman when she'd told her who she was because she'd confirmed stuff only she could know, but even Allison didn't know this. Apparently, they'd been so loud and all so fixated on the argument at the bathroom door, none of them had heard Patricia open the room door. Patricia set her bags down on the table near the door then took off her hat and sunglasses.

"Mom?" Leonardo's eyes were instantly ablaze again, not the reaction Allison was expecting. "What the fuck did you do to her?"

Allison jumped in front of him when he started to charge at his own mother. "Leo! Don't you see? She was protecting me—for you."

Leo looked down at Allison and seemed to search her eyes then glanced back up at his mother.

"It's true, son. I couldn't stand to think of what it would do to you if something happened to her." Her eyes welled up as she took a trembling breath. "It's a long story, but I've been here all this time behind the scenes, and I know what she means to you."

In three long strides, Leonardo was at his mother's side, his big arms swallowing her up in a big bear hug. The sound was so foreign, but at the same time beautiful. Leonardo's muffled crying against his mother's shoulder was as heartbreaking as it was momentous. Even when he'd shared with Allison about the painful memories, she was certain he was holding back the emotion. All Allison could think about now were his tears, his pain; he was finally free.

The sound of the door opening behind Allison had her turning around. Byron walked out slowly, taking in the scene in the room. Looking at him now, Allison couldn't believe she hadn't made the connection before. Because of his size and height, she'd been shocked when she found out his age. At sixteen, he was a younger, far more innocent, and incredibly sweet version of his older brother.

Someone's phone rang, breaking the awkwardness in the room; though Leonardo didn't seem to notice. His mother had since moved him over to the bed where they now sat. While the crying had subsided, his arms remained tightly around her as she caressed his back gently, kissing the side of his head periodically. Whatever she whispered in his ear was meant only for him because it was too low for anyone else to hear.

"No, no, relax. It's okay, "Nine said into his phone. "Not sure what's gonna happen, but I'm pretty sure she'll be home in a few hours. All I can say for certain right now is she's fine. Tell her I'm standing here looking at her. She can talk to her if she wants."

Allison's heart sped up as Nine paused, listening to whatever was being said on the other end. "Drew's freaking out because she broke down and told your sister about you and Beast, and now Lila's out for blood." He went back to listening intently and nodding as if someone was talking to him again. "Yeah, hold on."

Nine's expression said it all. This was going to be bad. She took the phone from him and immediately felt terrible when she heard her sister's broken voice as she spoke to someone else. "Lila—"

"Oh my God, Allison! Where are you?" she cried.

"It's a long story, but I'm fine," she assured her, feeling choked up now after hearing her sister's unabashed emotion. "I'm sorry I couldn't contact you, but it was for my own safety. I'll explain it all when I get home."

"And when's that?"

"Today," she said as she turned to Leonardo and Patricia, who were looking at her now. "In a few hours, I think. By tonight for sure."

"Were you with him all this time?" Lila asked, sounding beyond hurt.

"No." Allison shook her head. "Even he didn't know where I was. He just found me a few minutes ago. I would never do that to you. I promise you everything is explainable and all is well. Okay, sissy?" Allison tried to smile, but the truth was she was wiping tears away now too. "There's a lot I need to explain, but the bottom line is I'm fine and everything's gonna be fine. You stay calm for that baby."

"Allison, how can I be sure you're okay? How do I know there's not a gun being held to your head right now?'

"Because Drew called Nine, remember? Not the other way around. He could've just said he still had no clue where I was. But he didn't because he's here and he knows I'm fine."

It took a while longer to convince Lila that she was fine and wasn't still being held against her will, but she finally did.

The questions started from Leonardo as soon as she was off the phone. How? Why? Where had his mother been all these years? What was she doing here now?

Understandably, Patricia gave short vague answers to the heavier questions. Those were things they'd need to discuss privately, but it seemed to calm his inquiring mind for now. Most of her answers assured him he'd have full answers later, but first things first.

"You need to turn yourself in, Leonardo," Patricia said, changing the subject. "Living on the run is no life. Trust me. I did it for too long."

Nine's phone rang, and he fumbled in his pocket for it. "It's Drew," Nine said to Allison the moment he looked at the screen. "She texted me a few minutes ago that she'd be calling to talk to you. She's not with Lila anymore."

Allison took the phone and answered. "Allison, Thank God, you're okay. Holy cow, it's been such a crazy week!" Drew began without taking a breath. "You've heard of Felix's wife's sister-in-law Sonia, right? She was raped years ago and was the reason why Ella started the whole self-defense class at 5th Street?"

Drew explained the whole thing in what seemed like one breath. By the time she was done, it really felt like there might be some light at the end of this nightmare tunnel. When she hung up, all eyes were on her. Allison reiterated what his mother had begun to say earlier. "You need to turn yourself in, Leonardo. The guys from 5th Street already have their attorneys ready and willing to represent you. Your probation officer doesn't even know you haven't shown up for work-release. Gio never called him." Knowing there was so much more she needed to share but this wasn't the time or place, Allison stopped to attempt a shaky smile. "Everything's gonna be fine."

The plan was supposed to be Leonardo would meet with his new attorneys at the home of Felix and his wife, Ella. They'd gather any and all pertinent information from him before accompanying him to turn himself in. Allison had heard Ella's sister-in-law Sonia had suffered some kind of sexual assault years ago. It was part of the spiel Ella and Sonia gave at the start of their self-defense classes.

Apparently, Sonia's situation with her then boyfriend, Memo, was very similar to Allison and Leonardo's, and he'd beaten the charges. Drew said after all the owners of 5th Street found out Leonardo was the hero in the now viral video, they were all certain he'd beat the charges as well. So certain they were willing to put their own money on the line.

While Leonardo agreed to anything asked of him, he insisted on being there when Allison finally spoke with Lila in person. So, instead of heading straight to Felix's home, they went to Sonny and Lila's. Allison wasn't sure what to expect as they drove up the long driveway of the estate.

Lila and Sonny waited on the porch in front of the circular driveway where Allison told Patricia to stop the van. Leonardo got out first then turned to help Allison out. As expected, the reunion was emotional and drawn out as Lila hugged then examined Allison thoroughly as if she didn't trust that Allison was being honest about being perfectly fine. When they were finally done with the hug fest, to everyone's surprise, Lila turned to Leonardo and hugged him too.

"Thank you," she said tearfully. "Thank you for everything you've done to keep her safe."

Allison should've known Lila was not about to wait around for Allison to get home for answers. Lila had thoroughly interrogated Drew, so she knew most of their back story already. Allison introduced Patricia and a very starry-eyed Byron to Lila and Sonny. They went inside and sat in the den as Allison explained the rest of the convoluted story to them.

Allison felt like this was just the beginning of a story that would play out over and over because she'd already heard the next part twice—once, when Byron and Patricia first explained it to her and then again on their way to Lila's when Patricia explained it to Leonardo. Allison gave Lila the condensed version of this part since a lot of it was personal and between Leonardo and his mom.

"Leonardo hasn't seen or known anything about his mother since he was fourteen. For personal reasons, she had to stay away, only she's followed his life all this time. So, she knew Leonardo had left town. When she heard about the bounties put out for us, she wasn't nearly as worried about him as she was about me."

"I knew what it would do to Leonardo if something were to happen to her," Patricia said then turned to Leonardo. "I know about Kit and how you blamed yourself, only I also knew how much worse it would be this time. It's why as dangerous as I knew it'd be to come forward even after all these years, I knew I had to get to Ali before anyone else could." She turned back to Lila. "I'm sorry I had to put you through this, but even if Leonardo hadn't shown up today, I planned on bringing her home tonight. I just wanted to be absolutely sure she was safe to go home."

"We still don't know for sure that she's safe," Lila said, raising a brow.

"She is," Leonardo said, speaking up for the first time in a while. "As long as she's with me—"

He stopped when Lila shook her head adamantly. "Listen. I appreciate what you did for her—more than once now. But you can't be with her twenty-four seven."

"Nobody can," Leonardo responded politely but firmly. "But I can do my best to be around her as much as possible." He turned to Allison. "It's all I thought of on the ride here from Yuma last night. I planned on talking to you about it first chance I got, but . . ." He glanced around at the unforeseen circumstances they were now in.

"Talk about what?" Lila asked, peering at him then at Allison.

"Moving her in with me."

"What?" Allison and Lila asked in unison.

Both their jaws had dropped open, only their expressions were just the opposite. Allison was certain Lila's heart wasn't bursting like hers was. For days, she'd sobbed about how easy it'd been for Leonardo to just walk away. Now he'd soared back into her life with a vengeance and was talking about moving her in with him?

Before Lila could retort, Leonardo went on. "Her safety is only part of the reason why I want her by my side as much as possible. But as far as her being targeted again because of anything that has to do with me, I can assure you that won't be happening anymore."

"How can you be sure?" Sonny asked this time.

"I got word from a very trusted source today that it won't." He turned to Lila, who they all knew would be the hardest to convince. "I'd trust this person with my life. Allison or even me being targeted for that guy that died, it's over."

"But you don't want her out of your sight?" Lila asked, and Allison could hear it in her voice. Her sister was forcing herself to sound as calm as possible. "The first time she was followed had nothing to do with this second incident. How can you be sure she won't be targeted for other reasons?"

Leonardo took a deep breath. "Because that part of my life is officially over. It had been for a while, but my brother still had issues. He took care of things today, and like I said, I trust him with my life. If he says that part of the danger is over, then I believe him."

"But you still feel the need to move her in with you?" Lila asked, glancing back from Leonardo to Allison.

"No." Leonardo shook his head. "I just mean, after getting a taste of what life without her by my side is like, it's a no brainer." He turned to Allison, squeezing her hand. "I didn't plan on having this conversation in front of anyone else, but I don't even care anymore. You're it for me, baby. I just don't see the point of not being able to wake up next to each other every day, starting as soon as possible. I know my place is nowhere as fancy as this, but it's not forever. I promise. I have plans."

Allison brought her hand to her face, unable to hold in the emotion. Her heart swelled, and she was so choked up she couldn't even get the words out.

"Allison, honey," Lila started to say, and she sounded so worried Allison felt for her. "I know Drew said you're in love. I get it, okay? And I know firsthand how fast these things can happen, but don't you think you should think on this a little more?"

Allison shook her head profusely, smiling when Leonardo's apprehensive expression eased up. "My—" she started to say, but her voice betrayed her.

She cleared her throat even as Leonardo rubbed her back and kissed her temple. "I love you," he whispered in her ear, "more than you'll ever know."

Taking a trembling breath as his words sealed it—he officially owned her heart forever—she smiled at the love of her life then turned to her sister. "My place is with Leonardo," she was finally able to say.

"But—"

"I'm pregnant," Allison squeaked, interrupting Lila and silencing the room all at once. "I didn't plan on having this conversation in front of anyone else either, but I just found out yesterday, and I couldn't hold it in anymore."

It was hard to make out their expressions, but ironically, both Leonardo's and Lila's were similar. Their expressions both looked as stunned as they did alarmed.

"Well, fuck," Leonardo said, sounding like he'd just let a breath out he'd been holding in for too long. "You're coming home with me tonight and never leaving my side now."

He bear-hugged Allison the way he had his mother when he'd first seen her. Allison was bombarded with hugs from his mother then Byron and Sonny and finally Lila.

Even as she hugged her sister, Allison understood why she'd still have her reservations about this. It'd all been dumped on her at once. Pulling away to look at Lila's apprehensive face, she wiped her sister's tears. "I know you're going to be super worried at first, and I totally understand, but please trust me when I say I'm gonna be fine. More than fine, I promise."

Lila hugged Allison a bit more gently than she had earlier, then hugged Leonardo again. "I see it in your eyes, big guy," she said as she pulled away from Leonardo. "You love her almost as much as I do."

"More," Leonardo said very seriously.

Staring at him for a moment without saying anything, Lila took a deep breath and seemed to gather herself. Suddenly looking like her usual tough-as-nails self and not the whimpering sister she'd been a moment ago, she finally nodded. "That's a bold statement, but I like it. Just understand this. I don't care how big you are. I will hunt your ass down if you ever break her heart."

"Never happening," Leonardo said with a chuckle. "She's who I'll live for now"—he turned to Allison, reaching out his hand to her and she took it— "and forever. My Allison."

THIRTY-THREE

BEAST

The familiar feel of a holding cell was something Leo hadn't had to endure for more than a few minutes before a judge ordered he be released. The world now knew who the infamous man was on the viral video where DeMoss was pummeled to death. Orlando had been right. Most were hailing him a hero, demanding he not only be exonerated but honored. Of course, there were those who demanded justice and said no man had the right to take another one's life. If Leo had it his way, he'd confront every one of them and ask what they'd do if they walked in on one of their loved ones being raped.

As they waited for the trial, Leo got all the answers he needed from his mother and began getting acquainted with someone he already knew he'd be willing to kill for as well: his kid brother Byron.

The night he'd been released, the guys insisted he stay somewhere safer where he wouldn't be swarmed by paparazzi or possible eager do-gooders. They had just the place. Noah and his wife owned a place in the nicer side of Boyle Heights, a modest home in a quiet neighborhood that stayed mostly vacant except when they allowed someone to stay there. Like Leo's mom's home in Yuma, they kept it up, even though no one lived there. It'd been Noah's wife's childhood home, and she wanted to keep it in the family for as long as she could.

They'd set up round-the-clock security, and now Leo and Allison along with his mother and brother would be staying there until the end of the trial. The night they got there after his bail was paid, Allison was there waiting along with his mother and Byron. His mother sat him down and attempted to explain everything to him. How she'd decided to make a run for it when she found out she was pregnant again with Rogelio's baby. How she'd planned it along with Mrs. Calderon, who agreed to take Leonardo under her wing until his mother could come back for him.

Only she couldn't show her face until she wasn't pregnant anymore. But then it was one thing after another that kept her away. When it wasn't a threat to her, there was the possibility of making Leo a target if word ever got out that she was still alive.

"I kept in touch with Mrs. Calderon up until she was too ill to talk to me," his mom explained with tears in her eyes. "I never lost track of you, even when you moved to California. With Rogelio dead, I took the chance and relocated here. But there was always something. Always one danger or another why we couldn't reunite just yet—"

"Stop," Leo said before she could go on. "You don't have to tell me about the dangers. I'm glad you're here now, but you're right. I probably would've done to you what I tried to do to Allison in the beginning anyway. Pushed you away. After what happened to Kit, I vowed to never let anyone close again. I would've been terrified every day that something might happen to you because of me. It's better this way. You don't need to explain anymore. We're together now, and that's all that matters."

As the weeks went by, Leo got better acquainted with his mom and brother. Unbeknownst to Byron, his mother had enrolled him in martial arts at a very early age for his own safety. At fifteen, he was well on his way to becoming a black belt one day, and Leo was glad his mother had thought ahead. That'd be one less person he'd have to worry about protecting.

Not only was Leo completely exonerated from any wrong doing, in the following weeks as the media covered the story, he'd become somewhat of a celebrity. Because of the changes in his life and the need for the extra money now, he agreed to fighting. His first few amateur fights were sold out with some in attendance having flown in from as far as the Philippines. It was no surprise to anyone that he was soon being challenged and offered to fight professional fighters.

They sold the house in Yuma, and his mother used the money to purchase a modest home in one of the better neighborhoods in Los Angeles so she and Byron could stay close by and be a part of Leo and his new family's life.

Those plans he'd mentioned to Allison would be happening sooner than he thought. Since the professional fights would be paying a lot more than he'd anticipated, buying the building he and the guys had been eyeing to set up their shop was now doable. They'd continue to rent Noah's house for now, but with the offers he'd already seen and sponsors lining up, Leo knew they'd only be there for a little longer before he'd set his soon-to-be expanding new family up in a bigger home.

"What do you think?" Leo asked as he walked his pregnant girlfriend through the empty building. "It's zoned for commercial use, which we'll be using it for, but it's perfect for the guys in the meantime until we get the business off the ground because there's living quarters upstairs. Full kitchen and bathroom with a shower. The rooms are even on either side of the building in case Nine has anymore noisy sleepovers."

Allison laughed as if the memory suddenly hit her. The big back garage door slid open, making them both turn to look. Nine and Orlando walked in with the real estate agent, Jon.

"Check it out," Nine said with a big smile. "That alley back there is big enough for trucks to go through. We got ourselves a delivery entrance."

Jon began naming off more of the amenities, but Leo didn't even have to hear them. He was already sold. "If we're all in agreement," Leo said, still glancing around and barely able to believe this place would be theirs soon. "I say put in an offer ASAP."

"That's what I'm talking about!" Nine said, high-fiving both Leo and Orlando.

Jon had them all sign his tablet so he could get things moving along and assured them he'd have a response from the seller in no later than forty-eight hours.

Leo and Allison stuck around even after the guys had left. They'd all seen the entire place more than once now, but Leo wanted to show her around a bit more. He took her upstairs so she could see the living area Nine and Orlando would be living in. When they got to the kitchen area, he picked her up and set her on the counter, leaning his head against hers.

"I got you something," he whispered with a nervous smile.

Her brows lifted in curiosity. "You did?"

Leo nodded, reaching under the counter, and pulled out the long box. Allison took in the box then Leo with an even more curious smile. "What is it?"

He had a feeling what she must be thinking; though she still smiled genuinely. In their many talks, she'd mentioned not being big on flowers. This box looked big and long enough to hold several dozen long-stemmed roses.

"Open it."

She did eagerly then stopped and gasped when she pulled the lid off. Bringing her hand to her mouth, she looked up at him and laughed.

Leo glanced down proudly at the bouquet of donuts in the box. "They're all filled with raspberry jelly."

Allison lifted the bouquet, which actually held together. She bit into the top one, making that euphoric face that had Leo groaning in response. "Stop that," he said, doing what he remembered wishing he could do that very first day he'd laid eyes on her.

He licked the smidge of jelly off the corner of her lips. "Mmm," he said, licking the rest of her lip then kissing her deeper, but pulled himself away before he could get carried away.

She smiled big, looking down at her gift again. "Best bouquet ever," she said, pecking him again. "Thank you. I love it. But what's the occasion?"

Leo cleared his throat a bit nervously. "Well, I know it's old-fashioned, but I really want this kid's parents to be married when he or she arrives."

Allison's eyes opened wide as he nodded with a smile and pulled the ring out of his pocket. Her hands were over her face immediately, and her eyes flooded with tears.

"You're everything I never knew was missing in my life. I meant what I told your sister, Ali. You and this baby and however more you give me are all I'll be living for from here on, and I can't think of a single thing that would make my life more perfect, except"—he brought the ring up to her face so she could get a better look then lifted her hand— "you saying you'll marry me."

She nodded but was apparently too choked up to respond.

Leo slipped the ring onto her finger with a smile then kissed her softly. "Thank you for being so damn stubborn." Allison laughed at that, still sniffling as he kissed her again and said, "Thank you for refusing to give up on us."

"Thank you," she whispered back, staring deep in his eyes, "for letting me in."

Leo caressed her face gently with the back of his hand as she so often did to him. "You were in the moment I laid eyes on you. I just had no idea how impossible it would be to get you out."

"It'll never happen now." She nudged him in the gut with her hand playfully.

Laughing at that, Leo let his head fall back. "God, I love you."

"I love you too, Beast."

Hearing the name had him lifting a brow and glancing down at her. "Haven't heard you call me that in a while."

She tilted her head with a smirk, still dabbing the corners of her damp eyes. "Maybe you haven't been very beastly lately."

He lifted her off the counter so fast she yelped then laughed. "Where we going?" she asked, holding on for dear life as he cradled her in his arms, already headed for the stairs.

"Home, where I'll have you screaming the name over and over."

Allison laughed, wrapping her arms around his neck. "This pregnancy is adding a lot of padding to these curves, you know." Leo groaned, squeezing her tighter in his arms. "Are you ready for this jelly?"

This time Leo laughed. "Ready for it? I fucking own it."

Wrapping her arms around his neck even tighter, Allison laughed, kissing his cheek. "Yes," she said, smiling big. "Yes, you do. Forever and ever."

THE END

BONUS SNEAK PEEK OF THE NEXT STORY IN THE SERIES

Drew

There was no such thing as love at first sight. It was as illogical as Drew had *always* thought it. But clearly, there was such a thing as *lust* at first sight. The man was beautiful, even if only on the surface. Even Allison had told her enough about him that Drew knew better than to get any ideas about a guy like him. Doing so was a big fat no-no, even if she was single and able to do so.

No matter how fun flirting with the bad boy had been, Drew had put an end to it, and it was the right thing to do. As innocent as it was, she was engaged now, and she'd begun to enjoy it a little too much. But she could do this. She could deal with being around him—a guy she'd begun to daydream about a little too much about—without any dire consequences.

She opened her car door and stepped out in front of the shop, taking a deep breath. "Just walk in and ask for what you need then walk out," she whispered to herself then added, "ASAP!"

Praying he wouldn't be there, she walked into the noisy greasy auto repair shop, looking around. Allison had told her they'd since picked up more employees, and Drew was suddenly full of hope that maybe none of the owners were there this late.

One guy eyed her then smiled. "Can I help you?"

"Yes." Drew took off her sunglasses. "I'm a friend of Allison's, Leonardo's wife. I'm here to pick up her purse. She left it here yesterday."

He looked lost and glanced around at the other two guys washing their hands at a sink. They both shrugged; then one of them made her heart stop when he yelled out, "Nine!" *God no.* "Someone's here for Beast's wife's purse?"

Trying not to look like she might faint, she stood there chin up as she glanced around at the far more fancier shop than she expected. To her horror, the guy she'd been greeted by and the guys washing up at the sink, started getting their things together, turned off the loud music that had been blaring when she walked in, and shut down some lights.

"He should be coming down in a bit," the first guy told her as he wiped his hands off then glanced upstairs. "Nine, we're out!"

Thankfully, Drew's phone dinged, distracting her for a moment. She clicked on the text from Brad and read it.

Meet you tonight for a drink at Moby's? I should be done here in about an hour. You don't have Chelsea tonight, right?

Despite her drumming heart, she smiled and responded.

No, she's with her dad until tomorrow morning. I should be good to meet you in an hour.

She'd barely finished typing up her response when she heard the footsteps coming down the stairs. Hitting send on her phone, she closed her eyes before taking a breath and glancing up at the sight of Nine coming down the stairs in jeans and a wife beater, displaying his heavily tatted muscles with that smirk she was sure she was in love with now.

Lust. Just lust, Drew. Nothing more. You got this.

"I was beginning to wonder if I'd ever hear from you again."

"I, uh . . ." She took a few steps around the motorcycles in the middle of the shop. "Allison asked me if I could stop by and pick up her purse. She left it here last night." Drew shrugged with a smirk. "Wacky pregnant brain and all."

Nine eyed her playfully from top to bottom like he always did: unrestrained, unabashed with that gleam of approval. "Yeah, Beast said someone would come by for it today." He got to the bottom of the stairs and headed away from her to what appeared to be an office. "If I'd known it was you, I could've planned something. We could still go grab a bite or a drink or something. That is, of course, if your boyfriend wouldn't mind."

"My *fiancé*." She wasn't sure what hurt more, correcting him or turning him down, but she had to. "And thanks, but I'm actually meeting him for drinks in a little bit."

He slowed so much she thought he might stop, but then he kept walking, grabbing something just inside the office door. Taking a second to examine the purse, he finally turned around to face her.

"Is that right?" he asked, walking back toward her.

Drew nodded but said nothing more. She couldn't, not when he looked at her in the way he was looking at her now. The smile was gone, but he didn't look upset or angry, and why should he? Drew felt stupid for even making note of it. He was just peering at her with intense curiosity, and that was normal. Well, the curiosity anyway.

"So, you're getting married now?"

"I am." She tried to smile as genuinely as she could.

"Is that why you stopped returning my texts?"

He was close enough to hand her the purse, but he still took a few more steps even closer to her. Drew gulped but had the presence of mind not to flinch and embarrass herself. "I've been really busy." She shrugged, refusing to let him rattle her like he always seemed to do. "So much . . ."

She paused with a gulp when his eyes went straight to her lips, and he licked his. The man had features any woman would envy, from the perfectly shaped and arched brows to the long thick lashes and those naturally full and crimson lips. Yet, everything else about him oozed of carnal masculinity.

"So much going on," she went on even as her voice began to trail.

"I guess congrats are in order."

She nodded, not sure what that meant until his arms were around her and she felt the warmth of his breath at the side of her head. "Congratulations," he whispered without pulling back. "I'm happy for you."

To her surprise, he kissed her cheek, making her freeze even as she'd begun to hug him back. Her hand stopped on his upper arm as he pulled away to look at her. Just touching him was something else. She'd been privy enough times to the sight of his big tatted muscles, but feeling how hard they were and being this close to him had her breath catching.

He was staring at her now as if he knew what that harmless little kiss had done to her. As if he'd known for weeks now what he did to her and now her trembling body was proof he'd been right. He licked his own lips then glanced down at hers again.

NINE

Boyle Heights #3

2018

Add to your TBR shelf on Goodreads.

ACKNOWLEDGMENTS

I can hardly believe this is my TWENTY-SIXTH book out! So, for starters, I'd like to thank all my loyal WONDERFUL readers and all the bloggers who've stuck with me all these years! Without you, this would never have been possible. I started this journey in 2010 and watched many author friends climb to unimaginable success. But sadly, I've also seen many who have left the world of writing after not seeing the success they'd hoped. While my journey has had its ups and downs and this business is VERY different from when I first started, I'm still here because of YOU and plan on staying here for the long haul. So, thank you, thank you, THANK YOU for your continued love and support. As long as you keep reading and reviewing, I'll continue writing!

As always, thank you Mark, my "assistant," my everything, my inspiration for so many of the funnies in my story. LOL Thanks for constantly keeping me giggling, laughing, and even snorting! I love you!

I lost a few beta readers this year because life happens. But I'd like to thank my longtime STILL WITH ME beta readers: Emily Lamphear, Theresa Wegand, Judy DeVries, and, last but CERTAINLY not least, Amanda Clark.

Once again, A VERY special thank you to my "critique partner," JB Salsbury! Your input as usual is invaluable. I love your sincere honestly and awesome suggestions. I'm sure this book is better now because of your input! I know you have so much going on with your own writing and such and still you take the time to do this. I promise you it's VERY MUCH appreciated.

Thank you to [Theresa (Eagle Eyes) Wegand](), my one-stop superhero, beta reader/editor/formatter, listener to all my whiny rants/vents and obsessive worrying. As always, your work is impeccable, and I can't say enough about it. Thank you for sticking with me, too, even with everything that's changed. Here's to many more years of doing this together!

Thank you to Amanda Simpson of [Pixel Mischief Design]() for my cover art. You're an amazing talent and awesome to work with. I love, love, LOVE how all I have to do is tell you what I'm envisioning for the cover and you always deliver. I'm SO excited about the next two covers for *We Were One* and *Nine*. My readers are going to LOVE them!

Shout out to my street team "[Reyes Royals]()" and to my admins, Leslie Cary, Jenn DaSilva, Delashawne Acevedo, Sarah Mannering. Finally, I've met you all in person! Thank you for all your work and continuing to be part of the team. I COULD NOT do it without you, ladies! MUCH LOVE!

Lastly, *gracias a mi "par de consentidas DRAMATICAS"* for making me laugh so much and ALL your love!

ABOUT THE AUTHOR

USA Today Bestselling Author Elizabeth Reyes was born and raised in southern California where she lives with her husband, Mark and their two adult children, Mark & Megan, a Great Dane named Dexter, and one big fat cat named Tyson.

She spends most her time in front of her computer, writing and keeping up with all the social media, and loves it. She says that there is nothing better than doing what you absolutely love for a living, and she eats, sleeps, and breathes these stories, which are constantly begging to be written.

Representation: Jane Dystel of Dystel & Goderich now handles all questions regarding subsidiary rights for any of Ms. Reyes' work.

For more information on her upcoming projects and to connect with her--she loves hearing from you all—here are a few places you can find her:

Website: www.ElizabethReyes.com
Facebook fan page:http://www.facebook.com/pages/Elizabeth-Reyes/278724885527554
Instagram
Twitter: @AuthorElizabeth
Amazon Author page
Email EliReyesbooks@yahoo.com

Follow her on BookBub.

Add her books to your Good Reads shelf.

Join her FB Street Team for exclusive giveaways, excerpts, read-alongs, book chats, and much, much more!

She enjoys hearing your feedback and looks forward to reading your reviews and comments on her website and fan page!

Made in the USA
Middletown, DE
04 June 2020